Lady in White

Denise Domning

QuestMark
**HISTORICAL
ROMANCE**

Questmark, Inc.

Published by the QuestMark Book Group
QuestMark Inc., 15 Paradise Plaza, #351, Sarasota, FL 34242
www.questmarkinc.com

This is a work of fiction. Names, characters, places, and incidents either are the product of the author's imagination or are used fictitiously, and any resemblance to actual persons, living or dead, business establishments, events or locales is entirely coincidental.

LADY IN WHITE

A QuestMark Romance / Published by arrangement with the author.

Copyright © 1999, 2008 by Denise Domning.
www.denisedomning.com

Cover design and interior text design by Jeanie James | Shorebird Media.
Cover photo: © Amy Goodchild | iStockPhoto.com
Back cover photo: Joris Van Ostaeyen | Dreamstime.com

ISBN: 978-0-9798856-3-1

PRINTED IN THE UNITED STATES OF AMERICA.

10 9 8 7 6 5 4 3 2

Dear Reader:

This book was born on my first trip to England, which my husband arranged for me. Our first night in an ancient inn included doorknobs that rattled all night long as something invisible kept trying to get in. We visited eerie Glastonbury Tor and haunted Evesham. On our very last day we stumbled on Clearwell Castle, a picturesque castle converted into a hotel.

We stepped inside the foyer and looked through a pair of closed glass doors into the great hall. Thinking we might stay, I went around the corner to the concierge's desk while Ed waited in the foyer. Above the desk was an old newspaper article, telling how the castle's owner rebuilt the main stairway to stop the ghost from running up and down them. As I was reading that, poor Ed was watching the hall's glass doors open by themselves. When the concierge escorted me back to the foyer to join Ed, the doors slammed shut with such force that everyone jumped.

She followed us out the door and all the way to the castle's gate—and, yes, I am very certain she was a she. I wanted to stay the night, just to see what would happen next. Sensible Ed talked me out of it.

It was this experience I remembered as I spun the haunting tale of Belle, Jamie, Nick and Cecily.

— Denise Domning

Dedication

Over the years friends would ask
why I didn't include psychic elements in my work.
After all, ESP and ghosts are part of my everyday life.
When the chance came to finally write a ghost story,
I jumped for it and *Lady in White* was born.

I am so grateful to Denise Marcil
and Jennifer McCord for reincarnating this book.

Prologue

CECILY RAN, the rhythmic beat of her bare feet and the steady pant of her breath echoing among the darkened trees. Although there was no moon, she'd traveled this path so often in the night she could have raced along it without even starlight to guide her. Beneath her sleeveless bodice her shirt clung to her skin; her single skirt felt leaden around her legs. Past midnight, and still the air was heavy.

As she rounded the massive bole of a tall oak, an owl loosed its mournful cry, then swept into the black sky on silent wings. Startled, she nearly stumbled. Fear washed through her. An owl's call on this night of all others could only be an omen, a warning of death. Still Cecily ran, her heart driving her on even as her head pleaded with her to turn.

The scents of manure and new-mown hay announced the village bounds. Within the embrace of the outlying fields, cottages were strewn helter-skelter. Every roof was gentle thatch, making them look more like haystacks than housing in the dark.

Nearing the first house, she slowed and closed a hand over her mouth to mask her rasping breath. What happened this night was trouble enough; there was no need to invite more by stirring the dogs and geese into sounding an alarm. At the village's end, the church rose up, its square tower cutting through the milky river of stars in the sky behind it. Past the sanctuary she went, drawn to the steady gurgle of tumbling water.

She halted at the river's edge. Stripped of color by the sun's setting, willows trailed their silvered branches against the water's pewter skin. Starlight gray, the reeds along the banks whispered and sighed in the current. Across the water, a massive wall thrust up, framed by two rounded towers. Its surface was blacker than the night, except where glass pierced its stones.

Her gaze flew across it, finding the windows she knew as well as her own. The panes were lifeless, no spark of a candle behind them. If he wasn't in his chamber, then he was still waiting for her.

Fear rose like a wild thing in her throat. What he wanted was lunacy, sure to cost them their lives. But even as she retreated a step, her gaze shifted to the ebony thrust of the footbridge that spanned the water.

He'd already waited hours for her. She knew him. He would wait all the night long, until dawn's pink fingers drove him back into hiding. How could she leave him standing there without an answer, even if that answer were nay?

Madwoman! her mind screamed. It wasn't nay she'd say if she saw him. Once in his presence, she wouldn't have the strength to refuse him.

Glittering starlight poured through an empty arch in the wall's stony blackness. Not only was the postern gate unlocked tonight, it was open. She almost smiled. Just as she knew him, he knew her. The awareness that he stood alone in the night pulled her onto the bridge.

As she stepped onto the grassy bank on the other side, a breath of cold air sighed through the postern gate. It pooled around her, tendrils snaking up her arms, feeling almost like fingers where it touched her flesh. A shiver shot up Cecily's spine. It was as if the air itself were trying to prevent her from entering.

Unnerved, she sprang away from the coldness and dashed through the waiting gate. She flew into the quiet yard, not daring to look behind her, and sprinted across the soft sod. She passed the darkened house with its long gallery, then beneath the great hall's glowering windows. It was the garden she wanted, or rather the square tower on its ancient mound that rose at its center.

Her senses filled with a tangle of perfumes as she neared the garden wall. With no breeze to carry it away, the scent of roses, stocks and pinks clung to the stones. She looked up. A single candle's weak glow showed in one of the old keep's tiny windows.

Just as she knew he would, he stood at the darkened gate. Cecily stopped just out of arm's reach. There wasn't light enough to show her his features, but she knew he wasn't masked. That cumbersome disguise was for those unfamiliar with his scars, never for her.

His white shirt gleamed above his dark breeches. As with her, the night's heavy heat had stripped him of excess clothing, teasing him into leaving off his customary bulky robe and doublet. But without the robe, not even starlight was dim enough to hide how thin he had become.

Cecily stifled her quiet cry. She was losing him. Aye, and if she refused him tonight, she'd lose him even sooner.

He held out his arms in invitation. She fell into his embrace, burying her head against his shoulder. There was only ever joy to be found in his arms. He pulled her closer still, resting his cheek against her uncovered hair. In that instant, with his heart beating against her, she forgot that what he wanted was madness.

"You came," he murmured.

"You knew I would," she returned, just as softly.

"I had only a small hope," he replied. She heard the smile that came to life in his voice. "You called me a mad idiot."

Cecily straightened in his arms until she could press her lips against the column of his neck. He drew a swift breath at her caress. She smiled against his skin. Even after all these years, it still astounded her that her touch could give him such pleasure.

"It is madness," she whispered against his throat, "and I do not like it at all."

Catching her chin in his hand, he raised her head so he could look into her face. She leaned her cheek against his palm, having long since forgotten to feel the rugged scarring that webbed it. If shadows softened his ravaged face, she didn't see it. All she ever saw in his features was his love for her.

"Like it or not, will you stand with me in the chapel of my ancestors and give me your vow?" he asked.

His words reverberated in Cecily, waking both joy and fear. As much as she didn't want to lose him to another, the certainty that they would both die if they did this filled her. Caught in the battle between the two, her tongue wouldn't move.

In the quiet that followed, he released her to brush the

back of his hand down her cheek. Tears started to her eyes with his touch. There wasn't flesh enough left to pad his bones. It was the feel of his hand that tilted her into a decision. If death was coming for him so soon, then he would be hers until the moment she had to bid him farewell.

"I will," she whispered, catching his hand to press a kiss to his knuckles.

His laugh filled the heavy air around them. "One miracle out of two, Lord," he cried quietly to the sky. "Not that I'm content with only this," he warned his heavenly Father. "I want them both."

Reaching out, he caught her by the hand. Together, they strode into the garden, then on toward the old keep tower where his priest waited.

Chapter One

❦

HER HUSBAND WAS DEAD, her half-brother was on the Continent, and her mother was nowhere to be found. Lady Arabella Purfoy wiped damp palms on her black skirt at the thought of facing England's queen without a family member at her side. If only she knew what she'd done to warrant Elizabeth Tudor's attention. And if all that weren't bad enough, a brief spate of illness on the road made her days late for this audience.

Belle's head began to spin, her weak-wittedness all that remained of her ailment. Stopping in the center of Richmond Palace's outer courtyard, she pressed her fingers to her temples and willed the whirling to stop. Instead, the narrow brick and timber residences crammed against the walls around her began to careen in earnest.

"Wait," she called to the page.

Already well ahead of her across the courtyard, the lad, dressed in a gray doublet with a flat red cap upon his head, turned. His eyes narrowed. "Sir William said we weren't to delay," he chided, then turned to continue across the cobbled yard.

Too intimidated to argue, Belle put her head down and followed as fast as she dared, praying she could hold tight to her senses. If only she knew where her mother was! No matter how awful their reunion was bound to be, Lady Elisabetta Montmercy was still one of Elizabeth Tudor's ladies-in-waiting. Surely, Lady Montmercy would offer her only daughter the protection of her powerful position, if for no other reason than to guard her own reputation.

Access to the queen's Privy Garden was but a wee gate caught between Richmond's enclosing wall and one of the houses lining its outer courtyard. Two of Elizabeth's life guard, wearing their scarlet and silver, stood at either side of the gate. Music drifted from inside, its sweet folds carrying the sound of voices, some raised in amusement, others in irritation; most were masculine. The queen and her courtiers. Belle's heart rattled in her chest.

A wave of the page's hand and the guards lifted their pikes. She followed her guide past them, then stopped stock-still and stared. The garden was vast, stretching the whole length of the palace complex. At the far end, running the length of the east and south walls, was a covered wooden walkway. Or rather, it had been a loggia, until someone added an enclosed second story complete with fine windows. However strange-looking this gallery, there was no doubting it was meant to shield gentle strollers from the vagaries of English weather.

Caught between the walk's arms and the onion-domed towers of Richmond's royal residence was a bower meant to please a woman's senses. Edged by walls of cypress, herbs and carefully pruned trees outlined masses of roses mounding over daises. Showy peonies and orange lilies raised their heads above shy violets.

Ah, but nothing of God's making could hold a candle to the dazzling creatures who strolled the pathways or lounged beneath gnarled crabapple trees. Silken doublets and satin bodices shone in the mid-morning sun, their colors as true as the sapphires, rubies and emeralds that studded them. Ribbons, their ends encased in golden tips, glinted from every sleeve, doublet and skirt. Why, even the musicians in the walkway's far corner glimmered.

The page strode ahead, leaving Belle where she stood. Whatever grain of confidence that might yet have lingered within her disintegrated as she looked down at her simple black mourning attire. The queen's secretary had been wrong to think urgency more important than dress in this instance. No matter how fine the brocade or how rich her single golden pin, her clothing wasn't fit for a royal audience. Elizabeth would be enraged when her already tardy subject presented herself in such drab garments.

Again, Belle rubbed her damp palms on her skirts, only to start, then stretch out her hands before her. She stared in horror at her naked fingers. Not only was she underdressed, she'd left her gloves in Sir William's chambers!

That was it. Entering the queen's presence with bare hands was truly unthinkable. Even as she took a backward step to retreat, it was too late. The page had returned with a man dressed in a doublet and breeches of bright blue silk trimmed with silver lace, the long white staff in his hand proclaiming him the queen's usher.

Belle clenched her naked fingers into fists and buried them into the folds of her skirt. As man and boy stopped before her, the usher eyed her from her headdress to her toes. His lips curled.

"What is this?" he hissed. "Cecil knows it isn't Her Majesty's day for public pleas. Begone with you." He gave

Belle a dismissing wave of his hand.

Belle meant to run, but his rudeness pricked what little pride she owned. The words were out before she could stop them. "You mistake me. I am Lady Arabella Purfoy, come at the queen's command."

The usher's jaw dropped. Beside him, the page gawked in surprise. Ancient pain surged through Belle. So it was every time those who knew Lady Montmercy met her; Belle saw it in their faces, each of them wondering how one of England's greatest beauties had managed to produce so plain a daughter.

Collecting himself, the usher bowed to acknowledge Belle, or rather her rank as a knight's widow. "A thousand pardons, Lady Purfoy," he said as he straightened, his tone yet tainted by surprise.

He looked to the page. "Did you tell the guards at the gate?"

The lad blinked and shifted nervously from foot to foot. "Tell them, Master Bowyer?"

Master Bowyer nigh on threw up his hands in frustration. "Has Cecil lost all capacity for thought this morn? Run, lad, and tell Her Grace's guards that Lady Purfoy has just come into the queen's presence. They'll know what to do."

As the page leapt to do his bidding, the usher turned to face the flower of England's gentry gathered in the bower. He slammed the base of his staff against the ground to herald an announcement, even though it made no sound at all as it struck the thick sod.

"Lady Arabella Purfoy," he shouted.

All conversations halted. Fabric rustled, shoes scraped

on gravel as those in the garden turned to stare at Belle. She flinched. Pointed interest marked every face.

The breeze lifted, turning the singing decorative vanes on Richmond's bulbous tower tops. As the quiet garden filled with their hollow, moaning music, the crowd shifted, a corridor of sorts forming between their ranks. At its end stood England's queen.

Beneath her tall yellow hat, Elizabeth Tudor's long face was framed by fiery red curls held in place with jeweled pins. An airy ruff clung to her delicate jawline. So thick was the golden handwork decorating her doublet little could be seen of the garment's white fabric. Strands of pearls, each as big as Belle's little fingernail, looped to well past the royal waistline. Smaller gems picked out a whimsical pattern on the queen's green sleeves and matching outer skirt, while tiny emeralds sparkled on the golden brocade of her underskirt.

For a long moment, the queen eyed the daughter of her lady-in-waiting. No hint of kindness touched her dark eyes, no smile bent her thin lips. Then she turned, retreating to a gilded chair set beneath a crimson awning, her ladies following in a pretty multicolored cloud of silk and satin.

It was yet another moment before Belle realized this was her sign to approach. Heart hammering, senses spinning anew, she started forward, stopping only when her legs gave way and she dropped onto her knees.

Bending her head over folded hands, she opened her mouth to offer the clever speech she'd contrived for this moment. It was gone. All she could think to say was, "Majesty, you called for me and I have come."

"So you have," Elizabeth snapped, "albeit greatly late.

You were commanded into our presence by July's end. If We are not mistaken, this is the fourth day of August."

Belle's shoulders hunched against the sarcastic blow. "I beg pardon, Your Grace, but my daughter grew ill upon the journey," she said, thinking the tale of a sick child had a better chance of softening her female monarch's anger over the delay than any mention of her own illness. Nor was it a lie. Lucy had suffered the same fever alongside her mother. "I sent word to your secretary that we would tarry until she recovered."

"You put a child before your duty to your prince?" Outrage rang in the queen's voice. "It was you We commanded into our presence, not your daughter. You should have left her behind."

Trembling at her error, Belle shifted on her knees and set herself to repairing the damage as best she could. "Majesty, on the very day I received Your Grace's command to come to court, my stepson demanded that I and my daughter vacate my late husband's home. With no time to make my jointure property habitable, I could but bring her with me." Belle wasn't about to tell her monarch she'd rather die than be parted from Lucy.

All her explanation won from Elizabeth was a harsh sound. "Lady Montmercy did not warn you We intended to call you into our presence?"

The words struck Belle like a slap. Not only had her lady mother known the queen's intentions, she'd abandoned her daughter to them without warning. That brief bubble of surprise and pain burst into dull acceptance. Rejection and scorn was all her dam had ever shown her. Why should she expect anything else at this late date?

"Madame," she said, "I've had no communication from my lady mother since my marriage to Sir William Purfoy ten years ago. When I arrived at Richmond this morn, I asked after her of Your Grace's secretary, only to be told she is not presently in residence."

"Then Cecil was right," the queen replied, the steel easing from her voice. "You are as much an innocent as the maid your lady mother meant to abuse."

Startled, Belle peered up at her monarch. "Madame?"

Elizabeth leaned forward in her chair, her pearls rattling softly as the thick strands slid against her doublet's breast. Her perfume, a musky scent, reached out to envelop Belle in a choking cloud. "Your lady mother plotted the rape of one of our maids of honor," she said almost gently. "God be praised the plot was exposed before harm was done. Lady Montmercy is presently residing in the Tower as We ponder her punishment."

Terror roared through Belle, the emotion so intense stars burst to life before her eyes. Here was why her half-brother had so abruptly left England to begin his Grand Tour. He was running from royal wrath! Oh, dear Lord, but the queen meant to wreak her vengeance on all of Lady Montmercy's line for her lady mother's sin. She sagged on her knees.

"As part of her plot," Elizabeth continued, "Lady Montmercy promised your hand in marriage to Squire Nicholas Hollier. Your marriage was planned in trade for the abasement of my maid."

Astonishment wiped out Belle's fear. She forgot herself to stare boldly upon her queen. "She did what?"

Why in heaven's name would her lady mother do such

a thing? As a widow of nine and twenty, Belle was well past the age when a parent might arrange a marriage for her child.

Behind her, whispers hissed among the watching courtiers. The queen lifted her hand to demand quiet, but someone missed the sign. Amplified by a trick of the surrounding walls, a low-voiced comment rang out clearly.

"I hear the squire's a monster, so disfigured he'll not leave his home."

Belle wrenched around on her knees to stare in the direction of the voice. Her mother had promised her to a monster? The truth lay in the malicious smiles that touched some of the faces around her. Indeed she had.

With her spirits now firmly ensconced in her shoes, Belle again shifted to face Elizabeth. The queen watched her, expectancy filling the cock of her faint, fair brows.

Belle could but stare helplessly. What in the world was she supposed to say? She settled on a dodge.

"Madame, I cannot imagine why my lady mother might promise me to the squire. She knows I am too newly widowed to consider remarriage."

Elizabeth's brows flattened over her dark eyes. Disapproval nigh on pulsed from her. Belle's trembling returned full force. Refusal had been the wrong choice. So, the price Belle would pay for the misfortune of being related to a woman England's queen now despised was forced marriage. She turned her attention back to her shaking fingers.

"It's a fit match in rank, age and income." The queen's voice rose. "Despite the squire's infirmities, We are informed that he is yet capable of siring children. Moreover, our wedding gift to you is the restoration of the squire's title as Lord

Graceton, which has been in abeyance since his father's time. Bear him a child and it will be an advance for both you and your line."

It took a moment for Belle to catch the whole of the meaning woven into these bits of information. There was more at stake here than revenge, or even the simple union of man and woman. The queen was playing some greater game, one in which she had need of pawns.

Belle stifled her protest as she saw the trap close around her. If Elizabeth wanted the squire married, then his bride would have to be someone incapable of refusing him, no matter how monstrous he might be. Who better for this purpose than the daughter of an imprisoned woman, one over whose head hung the possibility of joining her dam in that horrid confinement?

It was for Lucy's sake, to keep her precious child out of that awful prison, that Belle gave way. "As it pleases Your Majesty, I will wed the squire. Your Grace is generous indeed to arrange a union on my behalf. You spend more care on this humble subject than I deserve." How hard it was to spew these lies and sound truly grateful.

"Well said," Elizabeth cried with a pleased clap of her hands, although there was no telling whether it was Belle's agreement or her compliment that gratified the queen. "The moment We saw you, We knew you were a reasonable woman, unlike your lady mother."

Reasonable? Belle caught back a bitter laugh. Who wasn't reasonable with a noose around the neck?

Whispers rose from the watching courtiers as they recognized their queen's triumph, then they lost interest in the proceedings. Conversations hissed back to life. The queen's women drifted away from their royal mistress into the garden. The musicians took this as their cue to once more tease a sweet and gentle tune from their instruments.

Praying only that her ordeal might soon be over, Belle waited for her dismissal, her spine feeling like jelly after this royal trampling. But Elizabeth wasn't yet finished.

"By and by," the queen said, happy confidence filling her every syllable, "word of your stepson's treachery has reached us. As Master of the Court of the Wards, our secretary will see to it an inheritance is secured for your daughter."

Astonishment struck Belle a second time, strong enough to make her sit back on her heels and gape at her beaming monarch. Her husband had been barely cold before his son, Philip, long married with a large family of his own to support, had claimed the income his sire intended for Lucy. Nor did Belle's jointure, the wee bit of her husband's property meant to support her in her widowhood, offer enough income to provide for Lucy's marriage. But how did the queen know?

Belle's stomach took a sour turn. Elizabeth knew because she'd made it her business to know. Once the queen found the woman she meant to be the squire's bride, she saw to it no opportunity of escape was left to her victim. Now that Elizabeth had what she wanted, she could afford to be generous.

"I am honored that you should concern yourself on my daughter's behalf, Madame," Belle offered, grateful in spite of the circumstances. "You are indeed a most caring prince."

The pleasure on Elizabeth's face deepened. Shifting in her chair, she beckoned to someone behind Belle. The usher stepped forward and dropped onto one knee, his head bowed before his queen. "Madame?"

"Make certain Lady Purfoy's accommodations in the palace are appropriate to her new status as the future Lady Graceton," Elizabeth commanded, not waiting for a response from the man before her gaze returned to Belle.

"Your betrothal is set for the morrow. Squire Hollier's steward, Master Wyatt, will stand as his master's proxy. This is done so you might travel to Graceton Castle in his company without fear for your repute. Had you arrived in a more timely fashion, We would have witnessed the deed ourselves."

The queen's pause was pregnant with the reminder of how near Belle had come to owning her monarch's enmity instead of her favor. Only when Elizabeth was certain this unspoken message was understood did she continue. "As We and all our court leave for our summer progress upon the dawn, We've named Sir Edward Mallory to serve as our witness for both betrothal and wedding."

She paused again, this time to eye Belle's black garments and her single pin. "Four months is twice the time most widows mourn," she said. "See to it you're dressed more appropriately for the morrow's ceremony."

This time when Belle bowed her head it was to hide the relief rushing through her. God be praised she hadn't listened to her maid and come planning to borrow court attire from her lady mother. If Peg had had her way, Belle's clothing would be with her dowry furniture, in a wagon so heavily laden that heaven only knew how far behind them it was on the road.

"Aye, Madame," Belle replied meekly enough, then

once more awaited the queen's dismissal. A quiet moment passed, then another. Still Elizabeth said nothing.

At last, Belle raised her head. The queen was watching the shadowy walkway. Her expression might have been carved from stone; her eyes had darkened to a stormy black.

Startled, Belle shifted to see who it was that won such a glare. A short, dark-haired man shifted out of the shadows. Beneath the bangs that crossed his broad brow, his brown eyes were caught in lines of worry. His hat was in his hands, his fingers clenched so tightly that he was crushing the velvet.

Although Belle didn't know him, she had no trouble recognizing his nobility. The massive golden chain resting against his green doublet's breast bore the emblem of the garter knights. Diamonds studded his sleeves, while heavy pearl pendants hung from his golden garters.

Elizabeth shot to her feet with a creak of her farthingale. Caught by surprise, those courtiers nearest to her pulled frantically at their hats as they bowed. Their queen paid them no heed as her mouth stretched into what should have been a smile.

"Why, here is our noble cousin Norfolk, just returned into our presence," she called out, a strange note of challenge in her now brittle voice.

Belle glanced in surprise at the nobleman. He seemed too young to be England's highest-ranking peer.

As she watched, the duke paled, although the day's sun was bright and hot. "Madame," was all he said as he dropped to one knee and bowed his head.

"Have you news for us?" Although the queen framed

this as a question, it was a demand. A nervous titter rolled over the watching courtiers. As if at a tennis match, every head turned to witness the duke's response.

"News, Madame?" Norfolk asked in return. Despite his calm voice, his expression was wretched and his face ashen.

"What?" Elizabeth's gaze bored holes into her duke as her faint brows arched high upon her forehead. "You've come from London with no news of a marriage?"

Belle drew a sharp breath. The queen's tone was dangerous indeed. The duke's only response was to blink furiously.

A happy laugh rang out from the back of the garden. Oblivious to what was going forward between queen and nobleman, one of Elizabeth's women danced forward, her steps keeping time to the quiet music rising from the garden's end. Pretty and dark-haired, she held a single rose in her hand.

"Oh, Madame," she cried to her royal mistress as she came to a halt, her pink and green skirts swinging around her, "you must look upon this bloom. I vow it's the most perfect blossom I've ever seen."

Her jaw tense, the queen glanced upon her lady's flower. The very instant he was free of the royal gaze, Norfolk came to his feet and backed into the walkway's shadows. In the space of a breath, he'd disappeared into the garden beyond it. If he thought his departure went unnoticed, he was wrong. From where she knelt, Belle could see Elizabeth watch him go out of the corner of her eye.

Then, as if nothing unusual had occurred, the queen lifted the flower from the noblewoman's hand, turning it this way and that in a pretense of study. "Indeed, Lady Clinton, it is a beauty," she said at last, handing it back to the noble-woman, then threw her arms wide.

"Faugh! We've had enough of gardens and flowers for one day. What say you?" she bellowed. "What say you to an activity more like to stir the blood?"

Caught unprepared by her challenge, her courtiers only stared at her. A touch of a smile bent the queen's lips. She whirled and strode at a smart pace down one leg of the walk toward her palace. Just beyond the loggia's far end was a door. If two guards at either side were any indication, this was access to the royal apartments.

Elizabeth paused before that door to look back upon her startled courtiers. "What? Do all of you plan to stay the day in the garden, leaving us to ride out by ourself?" she called, then ducked inside and was gone.

With her words, the crowd around Belle exploded into frenzied motion. The queen's women sprinted after their mistress with squeaks and quiet shrieks. Noblemen shouted for their attendants as men scattered into the garden, dodging one another as they raced toward the public gate. In no time the bower was empty.

Left alone in that new quiet, reality settled heavily upon Belle's shoulders. Easing herself to the side to sit upon the grass, tears rose, stinging her eyes. She was to marry again, only this time instead of an ancient and uncaring man, her husband would be a monster so scarred he never left his home.

Belle surged to her feet, wanting to run as far and fast as she could from this place. Instantly, spots danced before her eyes. Her senses swam, her legs wobbled. With a groan, she pressed her hands to her head. May the Lord save her, but she was going to swoon in earnest this time. Slowly, carefully, she began to make her way by tiny steps toward the garden's gate.

"Oh, help," she murmured as she went, but there was no one in the world left to help her.

Chapter Two

❧❧❧

"**N**ot once in the month of my attendance upon Her Grace have I been denied access to her royal presence." Master James Wyatt, steward to Squire Nicholas Hollier, glared at the Privy Garden's guards. No matter that both he and the soldiers knew that this inclusion in Elizabeth's court was but a sop, meant to disguise the fact the queen was holding him here against his will.

Elizabeth's men only stared back at him, their faces closed and quiet. "We have our orders, Master Wyatt," said the leftward man, "and they are that you shall not enter."

Jamie snapped his teeth shut on an angry bellow and sent his uncle a pleading glance. Not that he believed any hope of rescue remained.

At only five years older than Jamie's own five and thirty, Percy Neveu was dressed more like a grandfather, what with a long black robe belted atop his doublet and breeches and an unadorned black cap perched atop already graying hair. Percy offered Jamie a brief nod, a promise to do what he could, then turned to face the guards. Thin nose quivering with manufactured indignation, his brows flattened over eyes as blue as Jamie's. With all the authority of his position as the Lord Chamberlain's undersecretary wrapped around his long, lean body, he took a step toward the gate.

"I demand you allow my kinsman entry."

The soldiers' pikes didn't waver where they crossed in the gateway. "If you have complaints, Master Neveu, you may take them to Sir William Cecil." The guard to the right spoke this time.

Whirling, Jamie stormed a few yards from the gate with Percy at his heels. When they were out of earshot, he sent his uncle a seething, aching look. "Death," he snarled, filling the word with all the rancor this stay at court had made in him, "would be easier to tolerate than standing idly by while Elizabeth interviews that Protestant bitch she means to wed to my employer."

So honest an expression of emotion made Percy catch his nephew by the arm and drag him a few feet farther from the garden gate. "Are you mad?" he demanded when they halted. "Spew that sentiment too loudly and you could find yourself imprisoned for impugning Her Grace. If that happens, what sort of help do you think you'll be to your squire in this marriage of his?"

Jamie freed a bitter laugh. "Marriage? This is no marriage. This is blackmail. Unless my employer agrees to wed, all he's worked for these last years trying to reestablish the power and prestige of his family, will come to naught."

Percy's eyes went round as his face paled. He shot a frantic glance around him. Relief gusted from him on a sigh when he saw none of the servants or underlings were near enough to have overheard.

"Mind your tongue," the courtier whispered, despite their distance from any nearby ears, "or it'll be both you and your squire who could pay the price in some prison. Me, as well!"

Although his uncle was named for the Percys of Northumberland, Percy owned none of that family's bluster and bravado. However, what Percy lacked in courage, he made up for in sheer cunning.

Jamie offered his uncle a tense smile. "Your advice is kindly given and well received. Once again, I give thanks for having you at my side. I'd not have survived these past weeks at court without you."

Percy gave a nod. "Jamie, my lad, it's a good thing you chose the bucolic life over that of court. It's just not in your nature to be a reed like me, bending whichever way the wind blows, friend to all, enemy to none. Nay, you're forever ready to defend to the death whatever untenable position you've taken no matter how sensible or profitable retreat might be. Do us both a favor and stay in England's backwaters."

Jamie laughed "Now, you wouldn't be calling me muleheaded, would you?"

Percy winked, "I might just be. I expect you inherited it from that Scots mother of yours, along with her copper hair and fair features. God knows you didn't get it from my brother," he finished, with no idea the pain his comparison woke.

The childish urge to scream that he was nothing like his mother rose in Jamie. His dam had owned a wanton temper and a vicious nature, her battles with his father having more than once driven their youngest son into hiding. Although he'd been but ten when his sire had sent his wife back across England's northern border to Scotland and her own barbarous people, there'd been nothing but relief for Jamie with her departure.

"Bah," he said, to hide his hurt, "I happily leave you to your life here among these gentleman snakes and noble carrion eaters. Give me the quiet countryside, where if one man hates another he commences an open and honest feud."

Then, seeking to divert Percy from a conversation that was rapidly becoming too personal, he turned to look at the garden's gate. "May God take me, why didn't I realize how Elizabeth would twist the squire's offer to resume his title to suit her own purpose?"

Percy peered down his long nose at his kinsman. "I think this marriage a small price considering how both the Hollier and Montmercy families insulted her court. Indeed, the squire should be grateful. Her Grace could have refused his request to restore his title and still demanded he marry Lady Montmercy's daughter."

"True enough," Jamie replied as his head began to pound. "Ach, this is all my fault. If only you'd received word of Lady Purfoy's arrival here sooner, then we might have been already within the garden when she entered. Now I've lost my last chance to outmaneuver the queen and save the squire from this awful union. I intended my introduction to the lady to leave her so terrified she'd refuse to wed the squire, even if it meant joining her scheming dam in the Tower's confinement."

A dry laugh left Percy's thin lips. "As if the lady has any more choice in the matter than the squire," he replied with the lift of a chiding brow.

"Save your defense for a woman who deserves it," Jamie shot back. "You know as well as I that apples never fall far from the tree. Lady Montmercy's daughter will be no different than her dam. Trust me, she'll find the way to manipulate this marriage to her best advantage, even if it means destroying Squire Hollier to do it."

Percy opened his mouth to argue, only to catch back his words as angry shouts and frantic calls exploded from the garden. The commotion grew steadily louder. Startled, both Percy and Jamie stared at the wall as if they could peer through bricks.

"Heavens," the courtier murmured, "if I didn't know better I'd say the whole of Her Majesty's court was running in this direction."

Elizabeth's usher appeared in the gateway. "Stand aside, they come!" he cried to the guards, his eyes wide, only to be shoved out of the garden by the weight of those behind him.

It was the flower of England's manhood that fought its way through the opening. Jamie watched in perverse pleasure as men accustomed to moving no faster than an arrogant strut dashed past him. Ribbons streamed and hats were knocked askew as the courtiers battled their way into the outer courtyard.

"Well, well, it seems my chance to meet the lady is not lost. Watch for her," Jamie warned his uncle. "I warrant you'll know her immediately. She'll be the only woman— nay, the only *person* in all the court you do not recognize."

Percy preened just a bit at this compliment. He prided himself on knowing everyone and everything around Elizabeth. Indeed, it was a source of income for him, what with country gentlemen like Nick paying him a small fee for regular letters updating them on court doings.

They scanned the passing crowd. No woman, be she beauty or crone, appeared, though a popinjay dressed in a yellow satin doublet and ballooning breeches in the fashionable shade of "goose-turd green" broke from the tumble and tear of men. Jamie's stomach soured as Sir Edward Mallory came toward them. Despite his friendship with Kit Hollier, Nick's younger brother, Mallory was no friend to Nick. Not only was the knight a Kentsman and a fervent Protestant, he was the man Elizabeth had named her witness in the matter of this marriage.

Percy leaned his head close to Jamie's. "Look closely at yon knight and you'll see a man who gave free rein to his ambition, only to live to regret it. I fear he'll soon be a reminder to us all of how swiftly a man's career can come and go. Tut, he wears panic like a cloak."

Jamie hid his smile. It was Kit Hollier who'd warned them against Sir Edward. Allied with Norfolk, Sir Edward Mallory found both his financial and political careers were in jeopardy as Norfolk's fortunes sank. And Jamie knew the knight wouldn't hesitate to throw Nick's body in the breach if he thought it would save him.

Both Jamie and his uncle swept their caps from their heads. "Master Neveu," Sir Edward said in abbreviated greeting to Percy. With only a nod for a response, Percy turned his gaze back to the departing courtiers, yet seeking Lady Purfoy.

Shifting his gaze onto Jamie, Sir Edward's mouth thinned to a harsh line. "Why, Master Wyatt, dare I say I'm astonished to find you here?"

"And why would that be?" Jamie asked, his tone innocent as he took care to hide his country burr. It could serve Nick no good to remind the queen's witness that Graceton's steward came from England's Catholic north. There was already a close enough connection between the Holliers and the earl of Northumberland, one of the Catholic plotters.

"I didn't expect to see you until the morrow's betrothal," the knight replied, pressing a graceful hand to his chest as his mouth lifted into a taunting smile, "when the guard drags you into the chapel, forcing you to stand as the squire's proxy."

It was so obvious a goad that Jamie would have laughed, except that it also told him Lady Purfoy had agreed to this wedding.

"How can you think me so poorly mannered, Sir Edward?" he offered in a gentle chide. "You must know I need to introduce myself to Lady Purfoy as soon as possible. To delay, even for a moment, would besmirch the squire's repute and insult his future wife."

Panic darkened Sir Edward's fair complexion. "*You* speak of slurs? How dare you protest the marriage our Gloriana arranges for your squire after she so graciously granted his request for his title's restoration and his brother's wedding?" This goad was even less subtle.

"It wasn't the marriage I protested," Jamie replied, using but half a lie to parry it. He'd taken care to vent his protests out of all hearing. "All I wanted was to contact Squire Hollier before having to answer on his behalf."

"What need was there to ask when the squire could give but one response to his queen?" Sir Edward snapped back, his voice filled with all the venom of a striking adder. "All Her Grace asks is that the squire do as all eldest sons must: wed and breed up heirs."

Here, the knight paused to sneer. "I say any man who won't or can't do so basic a thing isn't worthy of either his estate or his title."

The blow blindsided Jamie. Anger rose like a red haze before his eyes. Bitch's son! How dare he disparage the man who was Jaime's closest friend, especially when Nick was far more frail than he'd have the world believe?

Although Percy's gaze never left those departing the garden, he laid a hand on his nephew's arm. It was enough to give Jamie the edge he needed. Rage receded. Again, he gave silent thanks for his uncle.

"And when I did receive word from Squire Hollier, didn't he agree to the queen's request?" Jamie replied. "He's content with the union."

This was a lie of the highest order. The only woman Nick wished to wed was a barren cottager's daughter who had rightly and repeatedly refused her gentleman lover's offers.

Sir Edward leaned close enough to make his next words a threat. "That I'll believe only when I witness this wedding's consummation. And witness it I will. The squire will do his duty to his queen, or I'll drag him to court so he can explain to Her Grace why he refuses." With that, he turned on his heel and strode for the side gate.

"Stinking codpiece." Jamie threw the insult only after the man was out of earshot.

"That he is," Percy murmured in agreement. "Jamie, the guards are leaving. Lady Purfoy never departed."

"What?" Jamie pivoted to stare at the Privy Garden's gate. The two men who'd earlier blocked his path were shouldering their pikes. Together, they marched across the yard toward Richmond's middle courtyard gate. It meant that all the courtiers had left the garden, and it was again open for public use.

If Percy hadn't seen her, she had to be within those walls. Turning, he stormed toward the gate, thrust himself into the garden beyond it and collided with a small woman dressed all in black.

Their meeting was so forceful Jamie's breath huffed from him. She tumbled backward with a quiet cry. He snatched her by the arms, catching her just before she hit the ground. As he lifted her back onto her feet, she made a tiny sound. All the color drained from her face. Her clear gray eyes lost their focus.

A spark of worry hit Jamie. She was going to swoon. "Nay, now, don't you leave me," he warned her.

Too late! She sagged against him as she took leave of her senses. There was nothing for Jamie to do, save sweep her up into his arms. She radiated a delicate aroma of roses atop the clean scent of soap.

As Percy came to a halt beside him, Jamie turned so his uncle could see her face. "Do you know her?" Hope filled his voice.

"Nay," Percy said after a moment's study, "but this can't be Lady Purfoy. No knight's widow would present herself to the queen bare-handed, with a single brooch to break the sobriety of her dress."

Jamie stared down at the woman in his arms. Percy was right. And the daughter of England's most notorious beauty would hardly own so plain a face set with such unremarkable features.

Frustration gnawed at Jamie's vitals. If this wasn't Lady Purfoy, there was but one place the lady could be. He stared across the garden toward the royal residence. Walls of solid red brick stared back at him.

Once again, he and Elizabeth made their moves in this game of theirs and, once again, he came up wanting. What a fool he was to believe the queen would leave her pawn open and vulnerable to his capture. Exhaustion crept into his very bones. Lord, but he hated feeling trapped and helpless and that was all he'd felt since coming to court.

"The queen keeps her close until the morrow's ceremony," he said.

"My pardon, Jamie," his uncle replied, sounding truly chagrined as he offered a crooked smile. "I should have realized this would be Her Grace's plan." He nodded toward the woman in Jaime's arms. "Set her down and we'll be on our way."

"What, and leave her sprawled upon the grass?" Jamie shot a chiding look at his kinsman. "Nay, we need a decent spot to deposit her, some place she might lay unmolested until she awakens. There," he said, as he saw an L-shaped bench in the corner of the garden's wall. Built of the same rusty red brick as the enclosing wall, it served as both chair and planting bed with low-growing thyme and grass sprouting from its seat. Moss and tiny star-bright daisies covered its sides and back.

As he started toward the bench, the woman's head slid along his shoulder until her brow nestled against his jaw. Warm and even, her breath caressed what little bare skin was exposed above his ruff. Of a sudden, he was aware of her breast where it pressed against his chest. Desire stirred within him, sharp and strong. He slaughtered his reaction. If it wasn't a sin to lust after an unconscious woman, it ought to be.

Setting her in the bench's corner, he took a backward

step. Rather than remain upright, she slumped forward, her head sagging until her chin almost rested on her chest. He eyed her in concern. From this angle it looked as if her ruff and shirt collar were choking her, while the ties of her headdress seemed to be slicing into her flesh. Still, he took another backward step. Either she'd awaken on her own in a few moments or a servant would be along to tend her.

"Come then," Percy said, turning to retreat from the garden. "I've an appointment with a wine seller. Let's go wash away the sting of defeat by tasting his wares."

Bitter amusement lifted Jamie's mouth. "There isn't enough wine in all the world for that."

As he started after his uncle, the nagging of his conscience grew. It was wrong to leave a woman alone when she was so defenseless. Jamie stopped to look back at her. "Percy, go you on ahead. I find I can't leave her."

Halting, his uncle shrugged. "Suit yourself," he said, then wove his way among the trees toward the gate.

Returning to the bench, Jamie crouched before the woman. Loosening her headdress, he slipped it off. Caught in a plait, her golden hair spilled from her veil to trail over the bench's back. He removed her ruff, then lifted her chin and opened the laces on her shirt collar. As they slackened, she drew a deep breath. Pleased, he shifted back onto his heels to study her.

Although no man would ever call her beauty, not with her small nose and full cheeks, there was a sweet delicacy to the way her fair brows lifted over wide-set eyes. Her golden lashes fanned in pretty crescents against smooth, white skin. It was the siren's mouth that transformed her face, her upper lip a provocative bow over a lush lower mate.

Attraction again stirred in Jamie, startling him. Why her? Again, he scanned her features, only to grunt in understanding. It was her very plainness that called to him. In all his life, from his mother to that deadly bitch, Lady Montmercy, no pretty woman had ever done him a favor.

Hoping to rouse her from her unnatural slumber, he caught her hands in his. He moved his thumbs across their backs in a slow and steady caress. Beneath her closed eyelids, her eyes shifted.

He smiled. "There's a good lass. Come now, come back to me."

Chapter Three

⚜

The voice was warm and deep, with just a hint of a north country lilt. Awareness flowed through Belle, bright specks came to life in the blackness enshrouding her. Thyme's peppery scent filled her lungs. A bird chirped, branches rustled.

Something brushed at the backs of her hands. Her fingers curled in instinctive reaction. It was soft leather she felt and, beneath that, strong palms. Her eyes flew open. A man crouched before her, holding her hands.

Belle caught her breath. Nay, not just any man, but a handsome man. Beneath a light brown cap, his hair was a red so deep it was nearly brown. It had been cropped with care to frame his broad brow and high cheekbones. His nose was arrow straight, nostrils slightly flared, while his brows arched sharply over eyes of clear blue. A fine dimple marked the center of his clean-shaven chin.

He smiled. She sighed. There was nary a gap or black spot to mar the beauty of his straight teeth.

"You're back then, are you?" he asked, his thumbs moving absently across her hands.

His touch sent a languid current through Belle. The sensation was just delicious enough to make her fingers tighten on his. He started. Eyes wide, he snatched back his hands and lurched to his feet. Crossing his arms over the breast of his golden-brown doublet, he stared down at her, his expression utterly blank.

Only then did Belle recognize her reaction to him. So dry and dusty had the last years of her marriage been, she'd forgotten what it was to feel desire. Mortification washed over her. Dear Lord, but hand-holding and other such sultry games belonged to courting couples. No wonder he'd stood so swiftly. Handsome men never played those sorts of games with women as plain as she. Belle lowered her gaze to a spot near his feet and prayed he'd leave her alone in her embarrassment.

"You are recovered?" he asked with none of the scorn, contempt or indifference she had expected.

"I am," she managed in a small voice. "It was kind of you to stay with me whilst I was senseless."

As she spoke, Belle glanced to the garden beyond him. A tall young man, golden-haired and handsome to the point of prettiness, stood a few yards distant. The golden chain of knighthood was displayed proudly across the breast of his yellow doublet.

The stranger's gaze caught hers, then slipped downward from her face to her throat. Disapproval twisted his fine mouth. Belle glanced down at herself and gasped. Her headdress and ruff lay in her lap. May God have mercy on her, her shirt collar was open! Snapping upright on the bench, she yanked her shirt closed and fumbled the collar strings into knots.

"Madame?" her rescuer asked, his brows lifting.

She jammed her ruff back atop her collar, not caring that it wasn't straight. "We aren't alone," she whispered and slapped her headdress back upon her head.

He whirled. For the briefest of instants his shoulders stiffened, then he pulled his cap from his head and bowed. "Twice in one day, Sir Edward," he said as he straightened. "I am honored indeed." However respectful his words, there was nothing deferential in his tone.

Even as dislike seethed in the young knight's eyes, he gracefully inclined his head. "The honor is mine, Master Wyatt."

Master Wyatt? Belle stared at her rescuer's back. Could it be this was the same Master Wyatt the queen mentioned, the man who was her intended husband's steward and proxy? Oh, she hoped so. This Master Wyatt had been nothing if not honorable toward her. Squire Hollier could hardly be a monster if he employed so kind a man.

Sir Edward glanced slyly from Master Wyatt to Belle. "Dear me, it seems I've intruded."

A shaft of worry shot through her at the knight's misinterpretation of her disarray. Oh, Lord, what if he repeated what he'd seen to the court and the queen heard of it? It'd be the Tower for her, of that Belle was certain.

Master Wyatt glanced over his shoulder. In his blue eyes was the promise to protect her from slander. She sent him a grateful smile. The corners of his mouth quirked upward in response, then he turned back to face the knight.

"There is nothing upon which to intrude, Sir Edward. The woman swooned and I came to her aid."

"Did you?" Cynicism scorched the knight's words. "Master Wyatt, you simply must make up your mind. First you spurn Lady Purfoy as unfit to be Squire Hollier's wife. Now, here you are, coming to both her aid and her defense."

Master Wyatt whirled on Belle. "*You* are Lady Purfoy?"

Stunned by his rapid change from savior to attacker, Belle shrank back against the seat's warm bricks and gave but the barest of nods. Master Wyatt's lips drew into a snarl. Planting his hands on the bench at either side of her hips, he leaned toward her until they were nigh on nose-to-nose.

"Swooned, did you?" he asked, his whispered words sarcastic. "I think not. How you must curse this interruption. Your wee drama was spoiled before you could find anything in me to exploit."

Although his words made no sense, his threatening tone set Belle's head to spinning anew. "But I did swoon," she protested, her voice barely audible even to her own ears.

"Pray tell me what cause might Sir Edward Mallory," he gave the man's name malicious emphasis, "have to seek you out before the morrow's betrothal?"

Belle dug her fingers into the bench's grassy seat. Sir Edward Mallory was the man Elizabeth named as her proxy and witness. A shake of her head told Master Wyatt she knew neither the man nor why he would wish to find her. Anger only blazed brighter on his face at her denial.

"You err greatly in thinking me so dense I wouldn't know why he comes to you," he snapped, yet keeping his voice low enough that his words stayed private between them. "Be warned! If you care for your health and well-being, you'll reconsider this wedding. Graceton Castle will tolerate no spies within its walls."

Had Belle not been certain it would make matters worse, she'd have laughed. Of all the people in the world, she could think of no one less suited to spying than she.

Straightening, Master Wyatt turned on his heel. As she watched him stride away, his path taking him so near to Sir Edward that their shoulders almost brushed, she sagged back against the bench. If what Sir Edward said was true, that Master Wyatt had protested the marriage, then it was only the queen who wanted this union. At least her first husband had desired the little bit of property her stepfather had made her dowry, if not her. What sort of life would she have if she were shoved into wedlock with a man who didn't even want that much?

❧

Sir Edward Mallory fought to tame his outraged honor as the northerner strode toward him. If ever there was a man who behaved prouder than his station deserved, it was this one. Master James Wyatt was nothing but a country squire's steward, yet this *servant* had dared refuse a knight's challenge, striking back with scorn instead of a sword. That Squire Nicholas Hollier would hire and condone so disrespectful a man made it that much easier for Ned to justify misusing the squire for his own purposes.

Master Wyatt slowed as he neared him. Ned's jaw clenched. The steward shot him a single, sidelong glance, then strode on toward the garden gate.

So, Lady Purfoy was now his only hope of rescue. There had to be a way to twist her into helping him. As he saw it, he had but two options, neither particularly attractive. His first was to convince the lady to not only refuse her marriage, which guaranteed her Elizabeth's rage, but stand firm against royal wrath. That would delay the betrothal for a few weeks, and his departure from court along with it.

And if he failed at that? Ned's stomach writhed. Then he'd have no choice but find a way to force the lady into becoming his ally.

Until this moment, he'd never considered himself a cruel man, but desperation called for extreme measures. Somewhere at Graceton Castle was a bit of information he could use to shield himself from the storm about to break. With his goal firm in his heart, Ned crossed the yard to drop onto one knee before Lady Purfoy.

"Sir Edward Mallory at your service, my lady," he said, catching her hand in his. "As the queen's proxy in the matter of this marriage, I want you to know I'm appalled at Master Wyatt's rude behavior toward you. I intend to see he pays for how he's treated you this day." He let his voice fill with outrage, in case the lady was as dull-witted as she was plain; it was something her lady mother had often suggested. His ploy wouldn't work if she didn't realize the steward had insulted her.

Rather than reward his offer of protection with sighs of gratitude, this country bumpkin caught a sharp breath and snatched her hand from his. Fear came to life in her clear gray eyes. "Master Wyatt did me no wrong, nor will I have you tell anyone at court that he has."

Ned hid his flinch. Careless fool! Meek as she was, of course she'd be more afraid of the queen's reaction than any slight done to her pride.

He used his most charming smile to bandage his error as he tried again. "I see the rumors are true. You are a Christian woman, quick to forgive as your Lord commands."

His false compliment sent hot color creeping up into her cheeks, making her look far younger than her years. "I do my best to keep our Lord's commandments," she said quietly, eyes downcast.

His honor squirmed. What sort of man misused one so innocent? Ned's eyes narrowed in determination. His sort.

"Given your depth of faith, how your heart must wrench over this marriage." He shook his head sadly.

Gentle surprise filled Lady Purfoy's face. "My faith? What has my faith to do with this union?"

Ned let his brow crease. "Ah, I hope I'm not speaking out of turn, but you do know the squire's a Papist?"

Her face paled until he thought she'd swoon again. Reaching out, she caught his hand, holding on as if for her life. "The queen wants me to wed a Catholic? Nay, I won't do it. What if my new husband won't allow me to hold my own church service?" she pleaded, as much to the world as to him.

Ned caught back his crow of triumph. Victory wasn't his yet. She had but a toe upon the path he wanted her to take. Now he needed to lead her gently into the first step. Laying his other hand atop hers, he gave her fingers an encouraging pat.

"Our Gloriana has always appreciated strength of religious conviction, especially in a woman. My lady, if this marriage so frightens you, you need only to speak to Her Majesty. Explain to her the strength of your beliefs. I'm certain your faith will convince her to find the squire another wife."

Triumph slipped from his fingers to shatter on the bricks before him. Resistance drained from Lady Purfoy. She sagged back against the bench.

"I dare not," she breathed. "Nay, I must marry the man

she's chosen or Her Grace will confine me to the Tower with my mother."

"Nay, my lady. Our sweet Elizabeth would never be so harsh." Ned stifled his frustration. May God take the queen and her penchant for bluster! Although he knew Elizabeth meant nothing with her threat, he'd never convince Lady Purfoy of that. It was time to try another tack.

"If you'd rather not face Her Grace yourself, you can make me your advocate. I'm certain I can negotiate some solution that suits you both."

What a fool he'd been not to offer this first! It could take months just to get her an appointment to have a hearing with the queen. A smug smile tugged at his lips as he looked to his victim.

The warmth of achievement turned to ice as Lady Purfoy's eyes narrowed, her jaw tightened. Wary distrust gleamed in her gaze as she came to her feet and crossed her arms over her bodice. "What profit do you intend to extract from this wedding that you should offer to be my advocate?"

Ned quickly rose after her, using the slapping of grass from his knee to hide his reaction. "Profit?" he asked, striving for an innocent tone. "What profit can I have save the desire to help a widow in distress?"

"You don't even know me." There was a steely edge to her words that didn't bode well for his cause.

Ned damned himself for inattention, and for believing anything her lying mother ever said. Shy and plain Lady Purfoy was, but not simple. As he floundered for something to say, the answer came in a flash. If religion wasn't a powerful enough reason to make her resist this marriage, surely the possibility of ruin would do the trick.

"For all these years, Her Majesty has coddled her Papist peers in their heresy, my lady. And do you know how they thank her for her leniency?" Giving a scornful snort, he answered his own question. "They plot, my lady. Squire Hollier, included. They plan to depose our sweet Elizabeth in favor of that whoring, husband-murdering Mary Stuart."

This wasn't untrue, just incomplete. Aye, the northern barons were spoiling for a rebellion, but Elizabeth had spent the summer preparing for it.

"I'd not see you marry the squire, knowing you'll soon be sharing a rebel's exile and impoverishment with him." His false words seemed to echo into the deep silence that enclosed them. Licking his lips, he tried not to squirm as he waited for her to speak. Then, as if she'd read his true intent somewhere in his face, one brow lifted as her eyes hardened to a dark gray. She nodded, the movement of her head slow.

"How considerate of you to concern yourself with me," she said coolly. There was something in her words that reminded Ned of Master Wyatt's scorn. Anger swirled in him, then exploded into rage.

How dare this nothing laugh at Sir Edward Mallory? He would not be mocked! Damn her, she'd do as he needed, even if he had to destroy her.

Ned leaned near to her, letting his lips draw back into a snarl. "Since you're set on wedding one of the barons plotting to raise rebellion, you owe it to those of your own faith to aid me in return. I know the earl of Northumberland has asked the squire for aid." More fool Kit Hollier for sharing this bit of information. "Once we are at Graceton Castle you'll find a way to enter your husband's study. Read his messages, and once you have the proof I seek, you'll bring it to me so I may expose the traitors."

Lady Purfoy rocked back on her heels as if he'd struck her, then caught a handful of his new doublet to hold herself upright. Her grip was so tight he saw the fabric's weave open as the jeweled buttons strained. Fearing for a garment that had cost him almost fifty pounds, he yanked her hand off his doublet.

"He knew," she cried, her fingernails now digging into his hand. "When Master Wyatt saw you, he accused me of being your spy. Oh, may the Lord save me," she moaned. "Master Wyatt will carry the tale of our meeting to the squire and tell him I'm your spy. How could you do this to me? You've destroyed my marriage ere it even begins!"

Desperation flashed in Ned. The rest of his life hung in a balance that for some godforsaken reason this woman held. If he was to reclaim it, she had to be well and truly cornered.

"What does the opinion of an unwanted husband matter when I've just told you the squire plots to force Catholicism back upon England's citizenry? A faithful woman," he gave just enough edge to these words to indicate he thought her no such thing, "would do what she could to preserve her faith. That, madame, is your only purpose in this marriage."

Here, he paused to eye her down the narrow length of his nose, knowing it was his most intimidating expression. "If Master Wyatt already believes you my spy, then it seems you have no choice. As you say, any hope of a true marriage with the squire is dead, killed the fortunate moment I came upon you in his steward's company."

The words should have had her cowering before him. Instead, Lady Purfoy's chin lifted. Her eyes snapped fire.

"You arrogant ass," she said. "You don't care what becomes of me, so long as you achieve your own end. You, sir, are no gentleman."

The insult shot from her lips like an arrow. It pierced Ned to the core, mostly because he knew she was right. What he'd just done to her was beneath a man of honor. But then, he'd already turned his back on honor.

"Slander," he hissed, catching her by the elbow. His grip was so tight he could feel her flesh beneath the layers of her sleeve and shirt.

"It isn't slander when it's true," she retorted, then shot an icy glance from his hand to his face. "Now, release me."

"Or you'll do what?" he mocked.

Pain exploded in his gut as she drove her elbow deep into his midsection. Ned gagged. He bent. Stars swam before his eyes as all the breath left his lungs. Arms crossed over his belly, he gasped like a dying fish and got about as much relief.

With the blow came realization. A calm man would have seen that every woman had limits beyond which she wouldn't be pushed. Now, because of panic, he'd destroyed his only chance for rescue. She'd never pardon him, not unless he admitted why he needed it. And to do that was to commit political suicide.

Chapter Four

❧

Belle staggered back a few steps and watched Sir Edward gasp for breath. Hard, cold satisfaction filled her. His first mistake had been in forgetting she'd been raised in a household of liars and schemers. The only people who'd ever asked her to trust them were those who wanted to use her.

She didn't care how noble his cause or how simple what he wanted might be. Never again would she be used the way her lady mother and the queen had used her this day.

As the man before her ceased to gag and began to straighten, anger died, taking courage with it. Belle's hand flew to her mouth. May the Lord have mercy on her, what had she done? Once he recovered, he'd murder her for certain, if for no other reason than the damage she'd done his pride.

Snatching up her skirts, she whirled and raced through the trees. Through the garden's gate she went, then out into Richmond's outer courtyard. Panting, she dashed to its center, only to stop in confusion. The queen had commanded her party moved and she didn't know where. Belle turned a circle, scanning the square for anyone wearing a courtier's silk.

The yard was even more crowded now than it'd been

when she entered the garden. Serving men, their doublets off and their shirts lying open to the sun, were busy carting their betters' baggage from the palace to the battalion of wagons waiting in the nearby green. Where the queen went, so did her nobles, with all their chairs, chests, tables and carpets.

Belle threw a desperate look over her shoulder. Sir Edward was entering the courtyard. Although he didn't run, his legs stretched into a long stride as he came toward her. With a yelp, she turned a wild pirouette in one last, hopeless attempt to find someone to aid her.

"Lady Purfoy !" Peg Hythereve's gravelly voice boomed down into the yard.

Belle's maid from her earliest years leaned out of a second-story window in one of the residences crowding the courtyard walls. Framed by the fine mullioned glass panels at either side of the opening, the grinning Peg still wore her stained brown traveling garments. "You must come and see the house they've given us," she called with a wave of a hefty arm.

"Open the door," Belle called as she sprinted in the house's direction.

Astonishment splayed across Peg's fleshy features, then she disappeared from the window. By the time Belle reached the door, it stood open but blocked by Peg's bulk.

"Back," Belle cried, giving her maid a goodly shove so she could enter.

"My lady," the woman cried as she staggered back into the room's dimness, then collapsed to sit upon the floor with a gusting thump.

Belle slammed the door. It struck the frame and

bounced open. Heart in her throat, she shoved at it again, then, fingers scrabbling, caught up the bar and tossed it into its brackets.

It settled with a satisfying *thunk*. Sighing, Belle leaned her overheated brow against the door's cool wood. She was safe. Still fighting for breath, she rolled to the side to sag in the wall's corner.

Peg stared up from her seat upon the floor. Beneath her pique over being shoved, worry touched her broad face. "Belle, love, what is it?" she asked, forgetting rank and tradition amidst the panic of the moment.

All Belle could do was shake her head and stare into the quarters the queen thought fit for a lord's bride. It was a narrow chamber with a tile floor. The walls were no different than most houses, being plastered and painted white. Already low, the ceiling seemed even closer to the floor, what with the thick, dark brown beams crossing it.

A steep staircase climbed the leftward wall. It wasn't a clever stairway, not when access to the upper floor was a simple square cut from the upper floorboards. There was a hearth in the room's far wall, barely big enough to warm the room, much less allow for cooking. But then, what need was there for cooking, when all courtiers and their servants were expected to take their meals in Richmond's hall?

Richard Moorward, the young footman whose contract of service had shifted to Belle upon her husband's death, squatted near the hearthstone, his saddle packs beside him. Small and sensible with narrow face and shoulders, Richard claimed to be a simple man, asking no more of life than three meals a day, a new set of clothing at Christmastide and the occasional gratuity to augment his yearly wage. Just now, his tawny brows were lifted high onto his forehead in surprise as he looked between Peg and his mistress.

The metallic sound of the door latch jiggling against the bar exploded into the room's quiet. Belle sprang away from the panel as if pricked. Of a sudden, Richard was at Belle's side, his every muscle tense. Despite his small size, he radiated strength and confidence.

"My lady, what is it?" he whispered.

There was a quiet tap. "Lady Purfoy?" The call came softly through the door. "Please, it's Sir Edward Mallory."

Hearing a gentleman's name, Richard relaxed. Relief whooshed from Peg and she heaved herself to her feet with a groan. Belle caught her maid's hand before the woman could open the door.

"Upstairs, and swiftly," Belle whispered in command, already turning to lead the way, Peg's hand yet in hers.

Richard only stared at her, his face alive in surprise at so strange a command. Servants such as he rarely entered their better's private chambers. Over their weeks of traveling she'd come to value Richard for his calm assessments and quick understanding of situations. It was this she needed from him now and in a place where there was no chance Sir Edward might overhear.

"Come," Belle urged, and Richard followed her up the stairs.

Sir Edward tapped again, this time with more vigor. "Please, my lady," he said, sounding frantic indeed. "If I could only explain."

Ignoring him, Belle stepped into the upper chamber. Brigit Atwater stood near the window. Pretty Brigit, Lucy's reluctant governess, was not yet twenty. Wearing a bodice and skirt of green with a white coif atop her black hair, her face was pinched in worry.

Clutched tightly to her side was Lucy. Belle's precious daughter wore only her shirt, with a wee white coif atop her golden curls in preparation for napping. "Mama," Lucy cried.

Tearing away from her governess, Lucy launched herself into Belle's arms. Belle balanced the lass on one hip. Downstairs, Sir Edward nigh on pounded on the door. The sound filled the upper chamber through its open windows.

"What's happening?" Brigit cried out. "Why doesn't someone answer the door?" Her words died into a gasp as Richard followed Peg into the upper chamber, then she blushed prettily. Despite the difference in their ranks and backgrounds, she and Richard had become friendly during the journey to Richmond.

"Please, my lady." Sir Edward's voice rose in desperation. "A moment is all I ask. Please, open the door."

Richard strode across the room and closed the window. The knocking stopped. A moment passed, then another. All was quiet.

Lucy's grip around Belle's neck loosened. She pressed her lips to her mother's ear. "Why are we afraid?" she whispered loudly, sounding nothing of the sort.

"We aren't afraid," Belle replied, to hide her own cowardice from her bolder daughter.

"We aren't?" Peg cried, now wringing her hands along with Brigit. "Then why are we all up here? What has the knight done that you must run from him?"

Another gentlewoman would have held back, waiting until she had one of her own class in whom to confide. Not

Belle. "He's asked that I should be his spy, prying into the affairs of the new husband Her Majesty has found for me."

"A new husband?" her maid gasped, her eyes round as coins.

"Aye." Belle's lips formed a weak smile. "However, the bridegroom no more wants the bride than she wishes to wed him."

"But not even the queen can force others to wed against their will," Brigit offered stoutly. Then she glanced uncertainly at Richard. "Can she?"

"Only if our good queen Bess has some way of twisting Lady Purfoy and this man into accepting the union," he said, then looked at his lady. "Does she?"

"She does," Belle replied with a sigh. "If I resist Her Grace, I may find myself sharing my lady mother's Tower confinement."

Peg blanched at the mention of that horrid prison. Brigit gasped and eased a half-step closer to Richard. The footman stood as he always did, solid and sober. In that quiet moment, Lucy leaned her cheek against her mother's. Belle's arms tightened around her beautiful child and her heart steadied.

"Why is your lady mother imprisoned?" Peg demanded, trading on nearly thirty years of familiarity to pose so blunt a question.

Belle set Lucy on her feet to give her servants the explanation they deserved. "It seems my lady mother plotted the destruction of another woman at court, one of the queen's maids. Somehow, the promise of my hand in marriage was a part of their plan. Although my dam's plot failed, I think the queen is avenging herself upon her lady-in-waiting by seeing this marriage accomplished. I cannot say what hold Her Majesty has over the man she'd have me wed, but someone mentioned he is disfigured and never leaves his home. Perhaps it's that he's not powerful enough to resist her?"

Peg's brows flattened in consideration. "Never leaves his home, you say? Well now, that's not so bad. If we find he's not to our liking, we can take ourselves out of his reach, then." She nodded to herself. "Aye, chances are our life with him will be much the same as it was with Sir William in his last years, him keeping to his own sphere, while we do as we please in ours."

A great stone dropped from Belle's shoulders. Peg was right. A man who had no interest in her would hardly demand anything from her.

"What's his station?" her maid asked. "He must be your equal. Even I know no nobleman would stand by whilst the queen forced a match that was beneath him."

"He's a squire," Belle said, "but the queen's wedding gift is the restoration of his family's title."

"A lord?" Color blazed on Peg's cheeks. Her smile was so wide, it nearly split her face. Clapping her hands, she did a little jig, heavy breasts bouncing in her bodice as she danced.

"You're marrying into the peerage! God be praised, my lady, at last you'll have the husband you deserve." The move to an aging knight's country manor had been quite the comedown for Peg, who had relished all the pomp and style of Lord Montmercy's household.

Belle was just irritated enough to deliver the rest of her news with nothing to cushion the blow. "I hadn't realized you were so fond of Papists."

"They're *Catholics?*" Peg squeaked.

"He and all his household," Belle replied, her own fear of entering a heretic's household returning.

Brigit moaned. "What if they take our Bibles and prayer books? My lady, I cannot enter the devil's house. I pray you, release me from your service so I might return to my father's house."

Behind Brigit, concern shot across Richard's face at the possibility of Brigit departing from their household. "Nay, Mistress Atwater, you mistake our situation," he said, a new intensity in his voice. "This is an opportunity to show poor, misguided sinners the path to righteousness."

Belle watched as Brigit glanced at Richard, then sighed. Not only did the girl have too much spirit for her quiet household, but no gentlewoman should look so at a footman.

The governess drew a tremulous breath and clasped her hands before her. "Aye, you're right. After all," she continued in a small voice, "we're none of us going to this place alone, are we? I mean, there's all of us."

At her words, Belle's confidence returned. Wherever she went, so did this wee family of hers. With these precious people at her back, there was nothing she couldn't survive.

As her world steadied, her stomach grumbled. "Peg, have we anything to eat?" she asked her maid.

"Nay, naught," the serving woman replied, "but I'll just hie me down to the queen's kitchen to find us something to nibble on. If any dares complain, I'll tell them it'd be no good my lady marrying into the peerage with naught but skin atop her bones." She turned and clattered down the stairs.

Brigit held out a hand to her charge. "Come, Mistress Lucy. You need that hour's sleep if you're ever to regain your health."

"Nay," Lucy squealed, edging around behind the fullness of Belle's skirts.

Drawing Lucy out of hiding, Belle lifted her daughter's chin. It was in Lucy that Lady Montmercy's famed beauty found expression. Although only five, Lucy's face owned a doll-like perfection, every feature finely chiseled and perfectly formed. Her eyes were a blue so deep they seemed the color of sapphires. Just now, the downward pull of her mouth and her tears spoiled her beauty.

"You must nap, poppet," Belle said, smoothing a stray curl. "Sleep will make you feel better."

Lucy's lower lip began to tremble. "But I don't want to sleep on the pallet from our wagon, Mama," she complained. "It's lumpy and it stinks. Can't we go back to that inn where we stayed?"

Belle smiled. It wasn't the inn's bed Lucy wanted, but the innkeeper's daughter. The same age as Lucy, the child had kept her company during her illness.

"Nay, love. We cannot go back, but if you sleep now, you'll be well enough to attend my betrothal ceremony on the morrow."

"What's a 'trothal ceremony?" Lucy asked, testing to see if the sop was worthy of her compliance.

"On the morrow I will give my promise before God to marry my new husband at some later date," Belle replied.

Deep in Lucy's eyes, interest sparked. "My father was

your husband."

"So he was," Belle said, not seeing the trap laid for her, "and my new husband will be your stepfather."

Lucy bounced free of her mother's hold to turn a circle. "My stepfather!" she cried as she whirled, then grabbed one of her mother's hands. "Is he kind? Will he play with me? Can I ride his horse?"

Belle sighed. William Purfoy had filled his youngest child's head with impossible expectations. In his last months he'd even promised her a new stepfather to do all the things he hadn't.

Belle doubted that Sir William, an indolent man by nature, had ever climbed trees with anyone. Aye, lies were all her husband had ever expended on behalf of his youngest child. He'd not even lifted a pen to clarify his will and protect Lucy from her half-brother. As much as Belle wanted to believe the queen could pry a bit of wealth from Philip Purfoy, she doubted it would happen. It was Brigit's fate Lucy faced in the future.

"I cannot speak for a man I don't know, poppet," Belle warned, putting a hand on top of Lucy's head to still the bouncing. She gave her child a gentle push in the direction of her governess. "Now, go take your rest as a good child should."

Although Lucy whimpered in a last protest, she went to Brigit. The governess led her toward the rear chamber. As with the lower level, there wasn't a stick of furniture in evidence. Nor would there be, not for the duration of Belle's short stay. She wouldn't see her belongings—two beds, a very nice writing desk and her collection of silver plates and cups—until they reached her new husband's home.

With Brigit and Lucy gone, Belle was alone with Richard. The footman shifted uneasily. "If I may be so bold, my lady?" Belle's nod gave him leave to speak his mind.

"The man at the door," he said, with a jerk of his head in that general direction, "this Sir Edward Mallory. You said he wished you to spy upon your new husband. May I assume because you refused him entry, you've also refused his request?"

Worry tugged at Belle's stomach until it twisted into a knot. "Not only did I refuse, I fear I knocked him breathless and insulted him whilst I did it," she whispered.

Up until this day, she'd managed to live her life without offending anyone. Now, in less than an hour's time, she'd earned the hatred of two men: Master Wyatt, because he thought her a spy, and, no matter what sweet words he'd uttered at her doorway, Sir Edward, for how she'd abused him.

Her footman's eyes widened. His mouth worked a moment, words seeming to form although he made no sound. At last, he managed a breathless, "You assaulted the queen's proxy?"

A grin followed, flashing across Richard's face to reveal a glimpse of the cheeky boy this somber man had once been. He laughed. It was the first time Belle had ever heard him do so. It sounded much like the purr of a contented cat.

"Well done, my lady, well done indeed! After this, I vow I'll believe anything possible. Now, if you don't mind, I think me I'll make myself useful and find Mistress Lucy a pallet that doesn't reek."

With a daring and impertinent wink, he descended the stairs. Belle watched him go, her heart warm with his praise. If Richard thought she'd done right, then all was not as hopeless as it appeared.

She moved to the window to stare down at the courtyard below her. If only she'd known to attack Sir Edward the moment she'd laid eyes on him, before Master Wyatt had a chance to decide she was the knight's spy.

Richard appeared in the courtyard. There was a jaunty spring to his step. It was as she watched him cross the yard that the answer sparked.

What a fool she was, making such a mountain out of mole's hill! If she wanted to convince Master Wyatt or the squire that she was no spy, all she need do was keep her nose out of what didn't belong to her. Time itself would prove her honorable.

Chapter Five

"**For God's sake and mine,** leave off." Jamie glowered at his manservant as Tom again adjusted a short brown cloak in its fashionable drape over Jamie's shoulder. "It's good enough."

Towheaded, his face touched with the ravages of the pox, Tom ignored his master's complaint. Already dressed in his own finest, Graceton's livery of a maroon doublet atop gray breeches, he stepped back to eye his handiwork. Their chamber was so tiny, Tom nearly backed into the wall.

In their lodgings in one of Richmond's exterior towers it took no more than three long steps to travel from one end to the other. A single beam of light shot through a narrow window and dropped onto the bare wood floor. Save for the straw-stuffed pallets they'd used for bedding, and the saddlebags containing their few belongings, the room was empty. Jamie hadn't come to court expecting to stay, so he'd brought no furnishings with him.

Cocking his head, Tom squinted in study, then glanced at Percy. "What do you think, Master Neveu? Does it hang properly?"

It was to honor the Hollier name and Graceton's house that Percy had thrown aside his somber black for a pair of scarlet ballooning breeches under a bright green doublet.

His gray silk cloak clung precariously to a single shoulder, just as Jamie's now did. A narrow line appeared between Percy's thin brows. "Perhaps a little more to the right?"

Irritation flared in Jamie. "You're both a couple of old women. I say it's good enough."

Percy tsk'ed. "Testy, isn't he," he said to Tom.

"He didn't sleep well last night—tossed and turned," the servant replied in quick defense of his master as he reached out to again adjust Jamie's cloak.

Tom's reminder made Jamie bite back a groan. Even now, Lady Purfoy's innocent touch stirred the most ridiculous desire to enfold her in his arms and protect her from the world. So potent had this need been he'd nigh on made a fool of himself, scrambling back from her to keep it from happening.

Oblivious to his nephew's inner torment, Percy beamed and clapped his hands. "That's it, Tom! Now he looks every bit that knightly ass's equal. It's a miracle worker you are."

Tom grinned, knowing full well it was true. After three weeks of almost constant wear, Jamie's best golden-brown doublet and breeches now were not only clean, their slashes wore new lace, as did his ruff. Much to the detriment of Jamie's purse, golden beads now traced out the fabric's pattern on his doublet and a good-sized garnet was pinned to his cap.

"If you've both looked your fill, we're late," Jamie snapped, lashing out at them from the stew of exhaustion and emotions that seethed in him. "Or would you rather the guard dragged me to this travesty?"

Tom's face fell. Percy straightened upright to his tallest, his brows high upon his forehead in pained surprise. Jamie grimaced.

What sort of cad was he, attacking others because he couldn't control himself? This was all Elizabeth's fault. Three weeks in her court and he hadn't an iota of civility left in him. God be praised he didn't have to stay another week, or he'd soon be no better than the barbarians of his maternal lineage.

"I beg your pardon, Percy. Yours as well, Tom," he said, laying a hand on his man's shoulder. "It's a poor master you've got when he doesn't thank you for your efforts. Percy's right." He shot a brief smile at his uncle. "You're a miracle worker indeed."

Tom accepted the apology and the gratitude with a deep bow. As Jamie was a solitary sort, theirs had ever been a solemn relationship. "As always, it's a pleasure to serve you, Master James."

"So, you're convinced Lady Purfoy will be waiting for you in the chapel?" Percy asked.

"She'll be there," Jamie replied, snatching up his gloves from where they rested on his saddle pack. "With no hope left of rescuing Squire Hollier from this unholy union, all I want now is to close the door on this hidey-hole," the wave of his hand indicated the tiny chamber, "and return to Graceton, where I belong."

"Aye, and me with you, Master James," Tom seconded quietly as he crossed the room to open the door.

Percy glanced between them and shook his head. "Yokels, both of you," he complained. "Lord help me, but I'm surrounded by men with no taste for the high life. It's not the size of the chamber that counts, but the fact that you live on the queen's bounty that signifies. Not everyone can do that." His tone was earnest, as if he sought to sway Jamie's opinion.

Jamie laughed as he went to the spiraling stair and started down with Percy following close on his heels. "Then you should be grateful we're leaving, since it means more bounty for you." His words echoed against the stone walls around them.

"I hadn't considered that," his uncle laughed in reply.

Together, they exited the tower into the brilliance of this August day. There, leaning in what little bit of shade they could find in Richmond's enclosing wall, were the four footmen who'd accompanied Jamie on this misbegotten quest. Like Tom, they were dressed in Graceton's maroon and gray. All four snatched their caps from their heads as the gentlemen passed them, then took up their place at Tom's heel.

Satisfaction filled Jamie. Although it wasn't much of a procession, at least there was some pomp to add to this unfortunate circumstance. No matter how little he might like what was happening to Nick, he meant to see the ceremony did justice to the Hollier name.

As he made his way across the cobbles of the outer court, Jamie glanced around him. It was strange to see the courtyard empty. This morn, everyone who was anyone had departed, the queen and her nobles sailing for Oatlands in a small flotilla of gilded, bannered barges, while their belongings left in hundreds of groaning wagons.

The breeze lifted, turning the vanes atop the royal residence's tower. Their moaning music shattered the silence. Jamie started at the eerie sound, then smiled at his nervous reaction. He was but the bridegroom's proxy and still he suffered from pre-wedding jitters.

Striding through the shaded archway of the middle court's gatehouse, he entered the second of Richmond's three courts. Caught between outer walls of mundane rusty brick and the royal residence with its fanciful domes, the palace's stone hall and chapel looked as solemn as a pair of twin cathedrals. Between them stood a fantastical fountain, with crystal streams of water tumbling out of the mouths of lions and dragons, while even stranger beasts crouched amid ironwork roses. Having seen enough of the things royal to last his lifetime, Jamie passed it without a glance to climb the royal chapel stairs to its raised doorway.

The door was ajar, as if to chide him for being late. Inside, light slanted down through tall windows to pierce the chapel's dimness. Against that hazy illumination, the cloth-of-gold hangings decorating the walls gleamed. Dust motes, stirred to life by his entrance, danced above ranks of empty pews.

He made his way to the central aisle and turned toward the altar. Sir Edward stood at one end of that broad dais. Of a sudden Jamie was grateful for Tom's care. The knight was dressed as befitted a queen's proxy, with pearls and tiny diamonds decorating his green and silver attire. An emerald dangled from his ear, while silver garters were tied at his knees.

Like Jamie, Sir Edward had his supporters. At one side stood six guards in the queen's livery and the knight's prissy little manservant. At his other were several gentlemen of Elizabeth's court.

Jamie scanned the chapel as he strode up the aisle. Not a soul sat in any of the pews. Hope dared to raise its well-beaten head. Was it possible he'd succeeded in his plan to frighten the lady?

Fabric rustled at the altar dais's opposite end, the scrape of leather on stone echoing in the sanctuary. It was Richmond's chaplain. His face as round as his body, the minister stepped forward to stand before the altar table. Caught in a shaft of muted light, his ruff glowed stark white against the black of his long robe.

The churchman turned toward the queen's pew. A roofed box built out from the wall, it sat perpendicular to the other seats filling the chapel. Draperies hung in the open square at its front to conceal its occupants from the room.

"Lady Purfoy," the minister called, his words ringing up into the stone fan-vaults that held up the ceiling. "You may come take your place. Master Wyatt and his party have arrived."

Jamie stepped onto the dais and watched for the bride's entrance.

The first out of the royal closet was a tiny girl, wearing a pale blue bodice and skirt sprinkled with white embroidery, while a pearled cap clung precariously to her mop of golden curls. No more than five, the lass dashed down the steps to stop a yard or so distant from the altar step. Eyes narrowed, she studied him, worrying her lower lip with tiny teeth.

Jamie caught his breath in surprise. This was Lady Purfoy's daughter, there could be no doubt of it. The babe owned her grandam's face in its every fine line and perfect curve.

"Mistress Lucretia!" The whisper sounded as loud as cannon shot in the chapel's stillness.

Young and pretty, a dark-haired woman now stood at

the far end of the forward pew. Although her green attire was fine enough, its lack of decoration named her the lass's caretaker. Whirling, the child retreated to join the woman. As they settled themselves into the forwardmost pew, a single, small man and a hefty woman joined them. Their plain dress named them both servants.

Her head modestly lowered, Lady Purfoy descended the pew stairs to the chapel's floor. Gone were her widow's weeds. In their place she wore a feminine doublet and underskirt of pale pink beneath an overskirt and sleeves of gentle gray. A simple gray cap was her only head covering. Her hair was upswept beneath it, with soft golden wings falling forward to frame her face.

She was a dove caught in a room full of peacocks and it suited her well indeed. The thought slipped past his defenses. He tensed. This softness of his toward her simply had to cease. Jamie reminded himself that Lady Montmercy had seemed no less innocent or fragile and she was now confined in the Tower for plotting another woman's destruction.

Glancing beyond Lady Purfoy, he waited for the remainder of her party to appear. There was no one. In confusion, he looked back at the lady. What sort of gentlewoman brought no one of her own rank to witness the day's event? Then again, what sort of gentlewoman came into the queen's presence bare-handed and dressed as she had?

When she stopped beside him on the altar step, Jamie was surprised to find her head barely reached past his shoulder. The corner of his mouth lifted. Of course, there'd been little time to gauge her height prior to knocking her down.

He breathed and his lungs filled with her perfume. She raised her head to look up at him. The delicate bend of her brows was marred by worry, while her clear gray eyes pleaded for comfort.

The need to enfold her in his arms again surged through him. Appalled, he forced his gaze away from her to stare at the chapel's back wall.

Clearing his throat, the chaplain came to stand before them. "If you will join hands," he commanded.

The memory of what happened the last time their fingers touched scourged Jamie. He glanced at her hands. She wore gloves today, a fine kidskin dyed the same gray as her sleeves. He was safe.

He extended his hands. The frown on her brow deepening, she laid her fingers into his. Jamie waited. No untoward wave of tenderness followed, no burning need to hold her close. He must have grinned in his relief, for the corners of the lady's mouth trembled upward into what was timid mimicry of a smile.

"Gather near, you who will witness," the chaplain called out to the empty chapel. "Standing before you is Master James Wyatt. Is there any among you who have reason to believe he is not the acknowledged proxy for Squire Nicholas Hollier?" Only echoes responded to his question.

"Is there any among you who have reason to object to the betrothal between Lady Arabella Purfoy and Squire Nicholas Hollier?" Again, only echoes answered.

"Aye then," the chaplain said with a brisk nod. "Now, repeat after me, Master Wyatt: 'I, Squire Nicholas Hollier, vow that I shall take thee, Arabella Purfoy—' "

❦

As Master Wyatt repeated the traditional words, Belle stared up into his face. Oh, but he was a handsome man. Her gaze traced the fine line of his nose and the arc of his brows over his blue eyes. But it wasn't his fair features that had her heart hammering today.

Belle could hardly believe he hadn't even frowned at her when she joined him at the step. Indeed, only a moment ago, he'd actually smiled at her. This, when she'd fully expected him to glare. After all, he'd been very angry with her yesterday. Instead, it had been the same kindness she'd seen in his gaze before Sir Edward interrupted them yesterday that flashed through his eyes a moment ago.

If only there were some way to tell him how much she appreciated this. He couldn't know how the fear of being glowered at throughout an already difficult ceremony had plagued her. It had even infested her dreams, until she'd awakened feeling bruised and beaten.

As Master Wyatt finished his part of the vows, Belle looked to the minister. The churchman offered her a smile. She returned it, filling her expression with all the gratitude she could manage. Here was another kind man. He hadn't even asked why she wanted to hide from Sir Edward, only offered her sanctuary in the queen's pew-box.

"Repeat after me, Lady Purfoy," the churchman said.

"I, Arabella Purfoy, shall take thee, Squire Nicholas Hollier, as my wedded husband, to have and to hold," Belle echoed, looking up at Master Wyatt as she spoke. He was watching her, a slight frown touching his fine brow.

" 'At board and at bed,' " the chaplain promoted.

"At board and at bed—"

With the word *bed* something flared in the depths of Master Wyatt's cool eyes. Instantly, the image of him atop her, his mouth touching hers, his hands caressing and stroking, sailed through Belle. She started at so sinful a thought, a blush burning her cheeks. Lowering her head, she stared at the center of his doublet.

"For fairer and fouler," she repeated softly. Surely, a man with so broad and strong a chest only had fair times. Aye, and his arm about her would keep any foul times at bay.

God have mercy on her! This wasn't her husband, this was his proxy, a mere prop taking the squire's place until she could reach Graceton Castle and wed the man himself. Belle closed her eyes, hoping to find safety in her own inner darkness.

"For better, for worse, in sickness and in health, till death us depart, and thereto shall I plight thee my troth."

As she finished, she breathed out a long, slow stream of air. It was done. She and Squire Hollier were betrothed. From this moment forward, any inappropriate images she entertained that included her new husband's steward were sins of thought.

Master Wyatt released her hands and stepped back. Opening her eyes, she looked at him. He stood in a shaft of sunlight, the brightness at his back shadowing his face even while it outlined the breadth of his shoulders and traced the fine line of his long legs. Slow and languid, a wave of desire rolled over her.

Belle turned her gaze to her toes. It'd be best if they arrived at Squire's Hollier's home sooner rather than later. As much as she disliked thinking this about herself, she feared there'd be much sinning in her thoughts between here and there. Thank heavens there was nary a chance of sinful thought becoming adulterous deed. A man as handsome as Master Wyatt would never be interested in a woman as plain as she.

Chapter Six

❧

Spoons scraped on wooden trenchers, while here and there, men sipped ale from their cups. A breeze, born of the sun's setting, blew through the inn's slatted shutters, bringing both flies from the stables and blessed coolness to the stuffy room. Shadows crept into the chamber, throwing their graying cloaks over those traveling to Graceton.

Jamie pushed away his trencher. The stew was bland, and he was just too edgy to eat. Across the table, Tom looked up from his empty trencher. "Are you finished, Master James?"

"Aye," Jamie said, shoving his dish toward his servant. "Take it with my blessings."

"My thanks," his man replied, pulling the wooden platter closer to bend his head over it.

Bracing his shoulders against the stones of the inn's barren hearth, Jamie stretched out his legs beneath the table. With the dimness to disguise his interest, he studied his traveling companions.

Near the midpoint of the inn's second table sat Sir Edward and his escort. His party had diminished to two of the queen's guard and his manservant. Jamie's lip curled. As hard as it was to conceive, the servant was a greater popinjay than his master. At least Sir Edward had sense enough to trade his bright feathers for attire similar to what Jamie wore, a leather jerkin atop a plain doublet and boots gartered above his knees to protect his hose. The knight's servant affected a red riding costume, complete with ribbons and a day's worth of dust.

Jamie's gaze slipped to Sir Edward. The look on the man's face was better suited to a lost lad than one of Elizabeth's courtiers. A tiny flame of satisfaction woke. Twice today, the knight had tried to ride near Lady Purfoy's wagon, only to be rebuffed each time. It seemed he was having difficulties convincing Nick's new wife to aid him in his plot.

Jamie's gaze moved to the end of his own table where the lady and her party sat. That they'd chosen the spot closest to the exit made him wonder if they feared needing to make a swift escape.

Behind him, the kitchen door creaked as it opened. Heralded by the hiss and spit of burning oil, the landlord's youngest daughter carried two torches into the chamber. Caught in a circle of illumination, the child's fine, fair hair glowed where it straggled out from beneath her dirty coif. Trailing writhing tendrils of black smoke behind her, she marched halfway down the room's long wall and wrestled one torch's handle into its basket. Light flowed out over the empty expanse of table between Jamie's and Lady Purfoy's parties. The glowering shadows shattered, bits of darkness flying upward to cling like cobwebs between the thick ceiling beams.

Her second torch went into a sconce near the door. Lady Purfoy's servants appeared out of the dimness. The pretty governess's hair gleamed a true ebony beneath her spotless coif. In contrast, there was Lady Purfoy's maid. Beneath her stained cap the big woman's thin brown hair was plastered to her skin by sweat. Not even the torch's olden light could soften the servant's coarse features. This was hardly the sort of personal servant one expected for a woman as supposedly delicate and timid as Lady Purfoy.

His gaze shifted to the only man in the lady's party. Across from the governess, torchlight gave the footman's hair a reddish-blond hue beneath his brown cap. A day's exposure to the sun had left its brand upon the fair man's face.

What sort of gentlewoman traveled across England's breadth with but a single guard at her side? His eyes narrowed. No woman could be as naïve as Arabella Purfoy was portraying herself, especially one who had sprung from Lady Montmercy's loins. Nay, Lady Purfoy was both reckless and a schemer, willing to jeopardize her child's safety in order to portray herself as guileless. Lifting his chin, he tried to see either the lady or her daughter at the table's end. The servants were clutched too closely around her to allow even a glimpse.

It was with thoughts of yesterday's ceremony filling him that Jamie relaxed back against the fireplace. How strange it'd been, speaking such intimate vows to a woman meant for another man. Indeed, while the lady said her piece, he'd felt almost as if he were standing outside himself, as if some other man were inhabiting his body. In that curious state, images had raced through his mind, some hopelessly lewd, others startlingly homely.

Of them all, the strongest had been a sudden, poignant longing for a family of his own. Jamie freed a scornful breath. Marriage was something he'd never craved, and not just because he was a younger son with only the stipend Nick paid him to recommend him. Nay, it was a lesson learned well and true at his father's knee. Wives brought naught but pain and trouble with them, only to shatter hearts and homes when they left.

The kitchen door again opened, this time admitting the landlord's elder lass. Her arms were filled with empty trenchers. There was a cheery bounce to the girl's step as she started down the table's length. At her heels came her mother, hefting a good-sized pot.

The scent of steaming stew made Tom's head lift. "Is there more, mistress?" he asked, turning on his bench as the landlord's wife passed him.

"There may be," the woman called over her shoulder to him, then jerked her head toward Lady Purfoy's party. "I'll know after I feed them."

The lady and her servants were the last to dine, having lingered in the courtyard for a goodly time before entering the inn. Wondering what kept them, since he'd paid the innkeeper to care for their wagon and the dray horses, Jamie watched as they were served, then waited for the party to bow their heads in prayer. Instead, they simply began to eat. He started in surprise. There wasn't even the pretense of good Protestant holiness.

Across the room, a bench squealed in protest. Sir Edward crossed toward the lady's party. Silence fell as the young knight stopped beside them.

"My lady," Sir Edward said, "will you not give thanks to God before you dine?"

Jamie's brows rose. Never would he have guessed the arrogant bastard capable of so gentle a manner.

It was Lady Purfoy's maidservant who answered. "We did our duty to our heavenly Father before we entered," she said, her voice as coarse as her face.

So, it'd been prayer that kept them in the courtyard. A smile tugged at Jamie's mouth. Witnessing yet another of Sir Edward's blunders was almost compensation for having to travel in his company.

Pride seemed to drain from the young man. He humbly inclined his head. "As a man of faith, I'd happily join you in your prayers, if you'd have me," he said.

Such false meekness! By God, but the bitch's son almost sounded as if he were apologizing for pressing his attentions upon the lady.

There was no response from either the lady or her maid. Sir Edward's shoulders lowered just a mite, then he turned and strode out the inn's door, as if exiting had always been his intent. When the door closed, the governess leaned across the table.

"My lady, should we not include him?" she asked, her voice low as she spoke to her mistress. "If he is a faithful man, it would only be Christian of us."

John, the younger of Jamie's two footmen, had been content to eat, sip his ale and stare at the tabletop. Now, he spat over his shoulder into the rushes. "Heretics, all of them, just like Anne Bullen's bastard who dares sit herself on England's throne," he snarled, his voice not quite held to a whisper.

Bracing his arms upon the table, the footman twisted his face into a scowl as he glanced at his traveling companions. "I tell you, we'll not have any of them at Graceton. See if we don't drive them away before the month's out," he threatened, speaking for Nick's household, which was as insular as its squire.

John's words brought Jamie upright on his bench. For himself, he didn't care if all the Catholics in the world slaughtered all the Protestants, or vice versa; he'd long ago turned his back on either religion, believing nothing save that whatever god there was owned a wide cruel streak. But his loyalty was a different matter, given in its entirety to Nick. Threats and this sort of prejudice spewed so openly by Graceton's servants would hardly win their squire Elizabeth's love, especially when Sir Edward longed to hear even a hint of insult aimed in the direction of his queen.

Laying his hand on John's shoulder, Jamie glanced at Tom and Watt, the other footman, then leaned forward so what he said remained private among them. "Have you already forgotten the words of betrothal I spoke yesterday? Their utterance made Lady Purfoy the squire's wife. Strike at her now and you strike at Squire Nicholas. Are you man enough to attack your master?"

John blanched. Not only was such a thing disloyal, it guaranteed his dismissal, if not his death. "Pardon, Master Steward," he whispered. "I spoke without thinking."

"No harm's done," Jamie assured him with a smile. "Can I count on you to explain this to the others at Graceton, just as I have explained it to you?"

All three men nodded, but Jamie knew the cause was hopeless. Even if they traveled a year, instead of the little more than a week it would take the lady's wagon to reach Graceton, he doubted there'd be time enough to devise a way to ease her party into the household's arms without a battle. Pondering that sour puzzle, he again leaned back on his bench and stretched out his legs. One boot made contact with something soft. Whatever it was brushed over the top of his foot and was gone.

Startled, he yanked back his leg, his bench hopping with his sudden movement. Tom and the two footmen stared at him in surprise. "A rat," he said, drawing his dagger.

Since one less rat in the public room meant one less rodent to plague them in their sleep, he signaled the others to do the same. All four of them leaned down to peer beneath the table. Lady Purfoy's daughter peeked back at them.

The child sat on her knees on the inn's hard earthen floor, her bare hands in the dirty rushes that covered it. A day's travel had pulled thick golden curls from her short braid, leaving them bouncing about her face in winsome disarray. She smiled at them.

Tom grinned back at her. "Why, Master James, this looks to be the prettiest little rat I've ever seen."

"I'm not a rat," the girl replied, wrinkling her nose at such foolishness. "I'm Mistress Lucretia Purfoy."

"Well now, Mistress Purfoy," said Watt, who had two babes of his own, "I think your lady mother wouldn't be much pleased to see you sitting where you are. Come then." Reaching beneath the table, he pulled the child out and set her on her feet.

Like every other female in Lady Purfoy's party, Mistress Lucretia wore a plain brown bodice over a simple skirt of matching fabric. Whatever else, her lady mother was a sensible woman when it came to travel, preferring comfort over fashion. There was no farthingale beneath the child's petticoats or ruff around her neck. Unlike her elders, the girl sported a white apron atop her skirt. Given the dark streaks staining that garment, it was a necessary affectation. Not that it stopped her from rubbing her dirty hands on her skirt.

The lass turned her smile on Jamie. He offered her only the quick lift of his brows in return, then shot a look to the table's end. Her governess was already on her feet. The woman shot out of the room for the darkened courtyard.

"Mistress Lucy!" Her shout was cut off by the slam of the door behind her.

"For shame," Jamie scolded the lass. "Your keeper has had to leave her meal to search for you. I think you'd best go back where you belong, ready to apologize for your misbehavior." Turning the child, he gave her a little push to send her on her way.

Instead, she whirled back on him, her lower lip edging out. Pique darkened her blue eyes. "I don't want to go back," she cried with a stamp of her foot. "I want to ride your horse."

"Ride my horse?" Jamie repeated in surprise. His eyes wide, he glanced at his servants in bemusement. Tom and the footmen were laughing. He looked back at the child.

"Whyever would you want to do such a thing? And why my horse and not his?" he asked, pointing to Tom.

Mistress Lucy's mouth narrowed as she crossed her arms in perfect mimicry of an impatient woman four times her age. "Because you are my stepfather."

Shock drove Jamie back on his bench. "I most certainly am not!"

Even as the words flew from his lips, yesterday's strange longing for home and family returned. An image formed in his mind, a comfortable scene, a man, a woman and a child seated at a table for a meal.

"Lucy!" Lady Purfoy materialized next to Jamie.

The lady looked sweet indeed, with only a simple white coif upon her head. At some point during the day, the wagon's canopy must have been rolled back, for there was a new pink in her cheeks. Lifting her daughter, she balanced the lass on one hip, then frowned at her child.

"Shame on you, sweetling," she chided the girl. "You gave us all a fright. Why, Brigit even went to look for you in the courtyard."

Jamie gaped at the lady. Where were the slaps the child had earned for her misbehavior? Or the pinches that would make certain she'd not repeat her mistake?

However gentle her mother's scold, it was enough to drive Mistress Lucy's cockiness from her. The child's lower lip trembled. Wrapping her arms around her mother's neck, she buried her head into the Lady's shoulder.

"Pardon, Mama," she muttered into the curve of her dam's throat.

Mama? Peasant children used that name but Lady Purfoy's title required the more formal *my lady mother*. Jamie's gaze shifted to the lady, certain that no matter how unconventional she might be in her parenting, she wouldn't tolerate such a slur to her rank. Lady Purfoy didn't seem to notice. Instead, she stroked a hand down her daughter's back as if to soothe, then pressed a kiss to the dirt-streaked curve of her child's neck.

"I am only glad you're safe," she whispered, her face softening with the love she bore for her daughter.

Jamie drew a sharp breath. Never had he seen anything more beautiful. Deep within him, something stirred. This, not beating and pain, or the hatred and rejection he'd known, was the way it should be between mother and child.

Lifting her head, the lady turned her gaze on Jamie. "My apologies, Master Wyatt. She slipped away from us while we were distracted."

Jamie could only stare at her. After spending a month at court to pry the truth out of the sly faces of those around him, it took him a moment to recognize the sincerity that filled her gray eyes. An open and honest woman. Now there was a rarity indeed.

Jamie cleared his throat and managed to say, "My lady, your daughter has mistaken me for her stepfather. You must tell her that I am only Squire Hollier's proxy."

"Ah," the lady breathed, understanding filling her sweet eyes. As she looked at her daughter, her sultry lips parted in an amused smile. "I wondered what set you to wandering up here," she said. "Sweetling, this is Master Wyatt. He is steward to the man I'm to wed. We won't meet your stepfather until we arrive at our new home."

Disappointment clouded the child's pretty eyes. Her mouth twisted downward. "But I wanted to ride my stepfather's horse!" She buried her face into her mother's neck to sob as if her heart was broken.

Lady Purfoy gently rocked the child. "Pardon, my sweet. I thought you understood." With a quick bob to Graceton's party, the lady carried her crying child back down to the table's end. "Peg, call to Brigit and tell her Lucy is well."

As the coarse woman did as she was bid, Jamie watched her mistress. An odd sense of connection woke in him. It was as if there were some invisible silken cord stretching between them. Shock brought him upright on his bench. May God damn him, but she belonged to Nick. Only the basest man, the earth-wallowing, shit-eating sort, would pine for the woman married to his dearest friend.

Then he was a base, earth-wallowing, shit-eating sort of man, because want this woman he did. Anger woke, cleansing in its heat. He wasn't some callow youth to fall prey to wayward emotions, but a full-grown man in control of his heart. He would end this obsession with the lady. Now!

He came to his feet, his hands clenched into fists. With a cry, Tom rose beside him. "Master James, what is it?" he asked, his voice pinched with worry.

Jamie shot a narrow-eyed look at his man. "You take the room. I'll sleep in the stable to guard the horses," he snarled.

Aye, sleeping with beasts was a good place for one as low as he. Without another word, he strode toward the room's exit, passing the lady as he went. She didn't notice, busy as she was settling her daughter on a bench.

Ah, but he noticed her. He noticed the gentle turn of her back and that without her farthingale her skirts clung to the roundness of her hips. He noticed the sweet look upon her face as she stroked her child's cheek.

Throwing open the inn door, he entered the darkened courtyard and followed his nose to the stables. Sir Edward and the governess stood near the wall. The rising moon was just bright enough to show him they were watching him.

A courteous man would have stopped and told the woman her charge had been found. There was the rub. Courtesy belonged to true men, not the sort that pined after their employer's wife. He passed them without a word.

❧

Lady Purfoy's ugly servant had barely called out her warning that the child had been found when the inn's door flew wide, then crashed back into its frame. Although they'd been doing no wrong, Ned took a quick step back from the governess, then laughed at himself. No doubt, it was guilt over his own improper thoughts about the woman beside him that made him do it.

Master Wyatt strode out into the yard. Rather than stop and acknowledge his better, the northerner's gaze barely flickered in their direction as he continued on toward the stable.

Anger lifted in Ned. "That man is insufferable."

"And a Papist," the governess said, a tremble in her voice.

Only as he recognized her fear of Catholics did Ned see the opportunity that stood beside him. Mistress Atwater might well serve where Lady Purfoy refused. His stomach twisted. Honor protested. He ignored them both. This time he'd be very, very careful.

The governess shifted toward him. Although the movement was subtle, Ned recognized it. Despite his depression, desire flared in him. On this night above all others, it was nice to know she found him as attractive as he did her.

She lifted her head, gentle concern marking her face. "I apologize for my lady's brusqueness toward you."

The urge to pretend insult about Lady Purfoy's rejection rose. He bit it back against the possibility that the lady had confided in her employee. "She is justified in her reaction. I was unpardonably rude to her."

As he spoke, she pressed a hand to her bodice. Ned's gaze followed her movement. She wore her shirt open, to signal her unmarried state. Moonlight gleamed on her bared skin. She drew a deep breath. It was a man's appreciation that sparked in him at the way her breasts lifted above her bodice top. The thought of forgetting his troubles by touching his lips to their crests was pleasant indeed.

He killed his lust. Governess though she was, Mistress Atwater was still a gentlewoman, thus undeserving of such base expression. More to the point, there'd be no hope of forgiveness if he used one of the females under Lady Purfoy's protection.

"Peg will come for me if I don't return soon," she said.

"Nay." The denial shot from his mouth, sounding more like a command than a request. "Nay," he repeated more softly this time. "Please stay, Mistress Atwater. It has been a difficult day and I could use a friendly ear."

Her smile gleamed in the night. "What makes you think my ear will be friendly, when my lady has been so harsh toward you?"

It was an innocent tease, as befitted a chaste and unsophisticated woman. Ah, but lurking in its depth was a coquette's taunt. Despite himself, Ned smiled. So, she would try her wiles on him, would she? This was just the sort of sport he needed tonight.

Chapter Seven

Lady Purfoy's cart so slowed their pace it took them a full ten days to reach the edges of Nick's lands. Long before the sun had risen on the eleventh day, Jamie forsook his stable bed and rode the remaining distance to Graceton Castle. It was Nick's paramour, not Nick, he had to see before the lady's arrival, and to meet Cecily Elwyn, he needed to arrive with the sun. Her path to and from Graceton was a constant; she came with night's falling and left with day's dawning.

Now, striding along Graceton's gallery, Jamie stopped before his employer's apartment door. Ten years as Nick's steward meant he didn't pause to consider that he yet wore garments befouled by travel. It also meant he reached for the latch without knocking. But for the first time in his memory, Nick's door was barred.

Approval warmed him as he tapped. Until Sir Edward Mallory departed, Nick would be wise to keep what few secrets he did harbor behind a locked door. Cecily answered his knock.

Narrow of face and plump of figure, Nick's paramour was dressed for departure, wearing her customary plain red bodice, a skirt of chestnut brown and a simple kerchief atop her dark hair. Her eyes widened in surprise as she recognized him. A strange sense of irony crept through Jamie. Save for the unusual yellow color of her irises, Nick's lover was no prettier than the lady his queen was forcing him to wed.

"Jamie!" she cried.

Jamie buried his wince. It was at Nick's behest that he and the cottager spoke to each other as equals. Nick had even teased Jamie into allowing Cecily to use his name's diminutive. To her credit, Jamie suspected Cecily was no more comfortable with this level of intimacy than he.

"Good morrow, Cecily," he said, stepping inside the chamber.

All Graceton's apartments were the same, made up of three chambers. The back two were bedchambers, one large for the occupant, one small for a servant. Fronting the sleeping rooms was an antechamber. What was a sitting room in all the other apartments, Nick used as his closet. His desk stood near the hearth, with two thick tables extending out into the room from either end.

During the nearly six weeks of Jamie's absence, Nick's usual clutter had become an avalanche of debris. On both desk and tabletops, branches of candles rose from a sea of papers, quills and inkpots. Jamie's carefully kept account books were strewn haphazardly on the floor.

Cecily closed and barred the door behind him. "Nick didn't expect you until later in the day."

"It's you I needed to see before they arrive," Jamie said. "So, how is he?" It was always his first question to Cecily when he'd been away from Graceton for any length of time.

"More fragile than I would like," she replied, her voice

low and her expression tight.

"I am not, Jamie." Nick's voice floated out from his bedchamber. "I'm as hale and hearty as ever." A spate of coughing followed, brought on by the strain of raising his voice.

Her hands set on her generous hips, Cecily turned toward the squire's bedchamber. "If that's so, then why are you coughing now?" she called back, sounding every inch the wife she could never be. She started for the bedchamber. "Did I not warn you your lungs would worsen if you kept fretting yourself into knots over your visitors?"

Visitors. Jamie strove to keep any reaction from his face as he stepped into the bedchamber at Cecily's heels. Now there was a euphemistic way to refer to the woman who would marry the man Cecily loved.

Graceton's master stood at the open window beside his hearth, his back to the room. There was enough daylight to make his golden hair gleam, the color as rich as the great silver crucifix that hung on the wall beside him. Since Nick kept no servant, he relied on either Jamie or Cecily to dress him. Thus, although it was early, he already wore a sleeveless green doublet over a pair of brown breeches. The thick floor-length black robe he always wore atop his attire lay waiting for him at the end of his bed.

Jamie frowned. There was something odd about the way Nick's doublet hung on him. As he realized what it was, his feet froze to the floor. He swore that a month ago the doublet had been a snug fit. Now, it hung from Nick's shoulders as if made for a far larger man. With vision sharpened by absence, Jamie saw what he'd never have noticed had he remained at home. The castle's squire was fading away before his eyes.

Premature grief, a harbinger of the ache that was sure to come, washed over Jamie. As if to echo his pain, the mournful low of cattle rose above the steady tumble of the river. A breeze sighed into the room. Too soon, it seemed to say as it stirred the brocade curtains on the massive bed and made the illegal prayer candles on Nick's private altar flicker. Too soon.

Cecily touched his hand. Jamie glanced down at her. Unshed tears glistened in her eyes. Last winter had been the coldest they'd ever known. The severe weather had taken its toll on Nick, eating at lungs weakened by his boyhood spill into a fire. In Cecily's gaze lived the knowledge that if the coming winter was as harsh, Nick wouldn't survive it.

Jamie closed his fingers around hers, ever so briefly, to tell her he shared her fear. At his touch, something flitted over her face, the emotion disappearing too quickly for him to identify. She left him, slipping around the two chairs that sat before the hearth to join Nick at the window.

As she wound her arm around him, Graceton's master turned to look at his steward. Scarring webbed Nick's face from brow to chin, this unnatural layer of skin so stiff it wreaked havoc with his enunciation and made smiling out of the question. His eyelashes and eyebrows had never returned after their scorching. Only patches of fair hair remained at the front of his head to frame his brow and ears.

"Well now," Nick said, as he eyed his prodigal steward, "I send you off to court to do a simple task, one that should've taken no longer than a week, and you're gone for over a month. Sluggard! Any more of that sort of behavior and I'll have to get me another steward." What Nick's mouth couldn't do, his eyes could. His affection for Jamie glowed from his green gaze.

Although Jamie knew Nick meant nothing more than to tease, his words cut sharper than any knife. "Would that I'd never gone," he retorted. "The queen's court is a filthy place, full of self-servers and ambitious parasites. Unfortunately, I'm forced to bring two of those same carrion eaters back with me."

His scars too stiff to allow the expression, a grimace shot through Nick's gaze. "I can't say you didn't warn me against using Graceton's title as a marker in that game of mine. See how I have again tried to play where I shouldn't, only to once more burn my fingers because of it." Alluding to the mock battle with his younger brother that resulted in his fiery tumble, Nick held up the scarred and bony remains of one hand, rendered so by immersion into the hottest of the coals.

"I think you have beautiful hands," Cecily murmured, pressing a quick kiss to his cheek. At her caress, Nick's eyes softened. Reaching up, he stroked the relatively unscarred back of his maligned hand against his lover's cheek.

Feeling like an intruder, Jamie aimed his gaze out the window behind them. To keep from hearing the murmur of Nick's affectionate response, he concentrated on the distant calls of the villagers as they made their way into the fields. So intense was his effort, he almost didn't notice that he'd imagined himself in Nick's place, Lady Purfoy's gray eyes aglow with the same love for him that filled Cecily's for Nick.

The fruit of a week's worth of self-imposed punishment withered on the vine. God save him, but what if Nick looked into his eyes and saw his new wife's reflection there? Even though his logical brain told him such a thing was impossible, Jamie steeled himself and turned. With his traitorous thoughts shielded from his employer, he concentrated all his energy on battering the image out of existence.

"Jamie, what is it?" Nick asked as he placed a hand on his steward's shoulder.

"Nothing," he managed, sidling away to collide with one of the chairs. He let himself drop into its seat as if he'd meant to sit, then crossed his legs and smiled up at Nick. "That is, nothing a week's worth of sleep and the death of the queen's proxy wouldn't cure," he amended. "We need to talk."

Nick sighed and dropped into the other chair. "Aye, I expect we've much to discuss. Will you share a sip with me?" His words were more than an offer for drink, they were Cecily's cue to leave so the two men might speak in private.

"Aye, that I will, but Cecily cannot leave," Jamie replied, catching the healer's gaze as she moved to the bed stand where the wine was kept. "At least not yet."

Her brows lifted in question as she filled two cups with water sweetened with the wine she used for her lover's possets.

"We need to talk about how you'll come and go from now on," Jamie told her.

"Oh, really?" Sharp amusement filled Cecily's gaze as she offered Nick his cup. She waited until he balanced the container between his scarred palms before handing Jamie his, then retreated to stand beside Nick's chair. "I hope you don't expect Mistress Miller to let me use the hall door."

Jamie almost smiled. Despite Nick's command that

his housekeeper accept Cecily, Mistress Miller persisted in myriad subtle and underhanded ways to keep the woman she considered beneath contempt away from her beloved lord's grandson.

"Nay, you'll still be entering through the postern gate and coming up through the corner tower," he replied. "But rather than using Nick's door, you'll come in through my chambers and enter by yon portal." Jamie pointed to the wall on which hung the silver crucifix. The intricately carved paneling hid a door that connected this room to the neighboring apartment. Nick's chambers had once belonged to his lady mother, while the apartment Jamie used was intended for Graceton's lord.

"I knew it!" Nick's laugh was a raspy cough. Amusement glowed in his gaze. He leaned to the side until his head rested against Cecily's hip. "I knew one day jealousy would overcome you, Jamie. Be warned, my love. He plans to steal you from me by waylaying you when you pass through his bedchamber. Although I daresay you'll not want him if he doesn't bathe. Faugh, Jamie, but you stink. It's the first time I've had reason to regret my scarring didn't affect my sense of smell."

Knowing full well that he reeked, Jamie laughed. "My apologies. I didn't realize you were so sensitive."

The teasing in Nick's eyes softened into a gentle smile. "If your intent is to hide my liaison with Cecily, you're a tad too late. After so many years, there's no one in this house or village who doesn't know."

Something more than his thinness was different about Nick. As Jamie again studied his employer, he found it in the new contentment that clung to every line and plane of Nick's scarred face. Contentment, when the thought of meeting strangers usually set Nick to pacing the room? Yet here he was, not anywhere near as nervous as Cecily claimed when he'd not only meet strangers, he'd wed one of them.

Apprehension prickled up Jamie's spine. If Nick wasn't nervous, it was because he didn't believe he had to marry Lady Purfoy. Well, the sooner he disabused his employer of this crack-brained notion, the safer Nick would be.

"It's not our folk from whom I'd shield Cecily, it's the queen's proxy, Sir Edward Mallory," Jamie said.

"Ah, the horse's ass," Nick murmured, sitting forward in his chair as he spoke.

Jamie stared at Graceton's master.

"You mean the man's not an ass?" Nick said in false astonishment. "How could I have been so mistaken?"

Jamie grinned, charmed despite his worry over what his employer might have planned. "Oh, an ass Sir Edward surely is. But how is it you know this about him?"

"What do you think me, some invalid who never leaves his rooms?" Nick sniffed, teasing as his eyes filled with satisfaction at amazing his steward. "Kit wrote to warn me against him, although he was more circumspect in his phrasing than I've been. My brother wrote, asking after the date of my—" Nick's voice broke as he tried to say the word *wedding*.

Behind him, Cecily made a tiny sound, then pressed a hand to her lips. Again, that strange expression flashed across her face. As she realized Jamie watched her, she hied herself to the window to stand with her back to the room.

Pity filled Jamie. It didn't take much to guess what plagued the woman. How difficult it must be for her to watch the man she loved wed another.

He stared at her back, wondering if she now harbored regrets at refusing Nick's many proposals. Not that she could have accepted, given her circumstances. Cecily's mother had been a strange woman, more at home with forest creatures than humankind. Between her mother's oddness and her own unusual eye color, most of the villagers named Cecily the devil's spawn. It was Cecily's fear of being hanged for witchcraft that kept her from wedding the villagers' lord.

Nick cleared his throat and glanced from his paramour to his steward. "If Elizabeth gives him leave, Kit would like to attend the upcoming event," he said, managing to completely skirt the word this time. "My brother also warns that Sir Edward's dislike of Catholics and his ambition may lead him to do something I'll live to regret."

Jamie nodded. "If Kit's said that much, then I owe him a debt. Best you heed your brother."

"Ha! Those are words I never thought to hear from you," Nick laughed, knowing full well how little his steward liked his brother.

All this gentle jibe won from Jamie was a narrow-eyed look. "Aye, well, now that you've heeded Kit, listen to me. Nick, I've come ahead of Lady Purfoy's party to make certain you know you must marry her, doing so as if she were your heart's own true love. Nothing can go amiss, not even something so small as Sir Edward witnessing Cecily coming and going from your bedchamber."

Reaching out, Jamie laid a hand upon Nick's arm, hoping his touch would help drive home his next point. "More than anything, the knight wants to find something to carry back to Elizabeth, something that will convince her of your supposed faults and insults. Nick, his intent is to drive the queen into a rage against you. If he succeeds, you can be sure Elizabeth's anger will be so great she'll order you into her presence, not caring that the journey could mean your death."

At the window, Cecily moaned. She turned, her fingers clasped as if in prayer, her face white. "Oh, Nick," she cried.

So swiftly did Nick set his cup on the wee table between the chairs, it nearly spilled. He leapt to his lover's side. As he pulled her close, she buried her face into his shoulder and sobbed. Pity for her again filled Jamie.

"Nay," Nick murmured as he stroked her back, "I'll not have you crying when there's no need. You must trust me, love. Armed with Jamie's warning, I can chart a course to avoid all the dangers he sees."

Another shiver crawled up Jamie's spine. May God save him, but Nick wasn't listening if he still thought he could slither out of the wedding. Across the room, Nick leaned his forehead against Cecily's. She sniffed and rubbed away her tears, then caught her arms around his neck.

"But you cannot—" she began, only to have Nick place a scarred finger against her lips to silence her.

"Say no more," he said, his voice low. Catching his arm around her, he led her to the hidden door in the wall.

"Go now," Graceton's master told his lover, "but not until you vow to return tonight."

"I can't, they'll be here," she protested.

"Would you abandon me to them?" he pleaded. "Now vow."

Beneath her fear, what looked like frustration dashed

across Cecily's thin face. "You're impossible, Nicholas Hollier. My mother warned me when she strove to heal you two decades ago. She said I'd come to no good if I let myself be charmed by you. See, now, how her words come to pass?"

Nick coughed out another laugh. "Your vow, love. Promise you'll come to me tonight."

Cecily sighed as she relented. "Aye, I'll return. I've brewing to do, so don't look for me until two hours after moonrise."

Jamie hid his flinch as she named the hour. Since he didn't much care to be undressed and abed when she came through his chamber, two hours after the moon's rise meant he wouldn't see his pillow until well after midnight. Ah, well, there was a month's worth of work waiting for him in his office and he could nap in the afternoon, once Graceton's *visitors* were settled.

Nick set his knuckles to a spot on the wall near the end of the crucifix's crosspiece and pushed. The hidden catch snapped as it released. With a well-oiled whisper, the door swung wide. Air drew from one room to the next, making Jamie's blue bed curtains stir.

Jamie eyed the doorway. If Graceton's previous lady had walked this path more than a dozen times before her husband moved to the gatehouse, he'd have been surprised. He, on the other hand, often slept with the door ajar. Nick's ailments were such that he might need aid at any minute.

With a brief kiss to the spot where his jaw met his ear, Cecily stepped out of her lover's embrace. Then, ducking her head to hide her tear-stained face, she slipped from one chamber to the next. Nick waited until he heard Jamie's apartment's outer door open and close before he shut the panel.

Once they were again private, Jamie came to his feet and faced his employer. "Nick," he said, warning deep in his voice, "I heard what you didn't say to Cecily. If you'll not heed me for yourself, then listen because she cares so deeply for you. There's no way to escape this marriage."

Nick's brows rose to the limit of their mobility as his gaze hardened. "But of course there is and you'll help me do it. No one, not even a queen, is going to tell me who I must wed. I've thought it through. We need not defy Her Grace directly, only postpone, delay, and reschedule until she's lost interest in the union."

Frustration rose. Nick had a talent for hearing only what he wanted to hear. "Try it and you'll lose not only your title's restoration, but her approval for your brother's wedding," Jamie warned. "Listen to me again. Sir Edward knows you don't wish to marry Lady Purfoy. He's waiting for you to do something, anything, in order to avoid it. And no matter how innocent the ploy, he'll find a way to use it to twist Elizabeth into raging against you."

"Oh, come now, Jamie." Nick lowered himself back into his chair. "The queen can only be pleased by what's happened. After all, Kit's now my proxy in all matters regarding the title she's to restore on me. This gives her yet another Protestant nobleman in the House of Lords."

Jamie picked up his employer's cup, holding it out until Nick caught it between his scarred palms, then dropped into his own chair with a hopeless sigh. "Four weeks ago, such a thing would have been more than enough to soothe her. Unfortunately, Lady Monmercy's plot to destroy her maid, along with the duke of Norfolk's ongoing attempts to wed the Scots' queen and the threat of the northern barons to rise in rebellion and put Mary Stuart on Elizabeth's throne, leaves our queen like dry tinder, ready to ignite at the slightest spark."

Nick shrugged. "Aye, so I must be cautious in the sort of excuses I offer up for my delays. Jamie, everyone knows weddings take time to plan. Say I desire oranges for the feast and suddenly discover they'll take weeks longer to arrive than I expect? I'll do nothing rash, only stretch the process until these larger events you mention overtake us. Against their diversion, she'll forget all about me and this marriage."

"That would work if the only thing driving Sir Edward was a dislike of Catholics," Jamie replied, leaning forward in his chair to brace his elbows on his knees. "Unfortunately, he's watching his career at court disintegrate before his eyes. If he can find a way to save it by using you, he will."

Jamie went on, filling his voice with every ounce of sincerity he owned. "Do you see now why you cannot delay in marrying the lady? Although I believe every one of your servants loyal, who can say that enough coin might not sway one into revealing something untoward? Nick, imagine what Sir Edward could do with any of those letters you received from the earl of Northumberland, urging you to join him in his rebellion. What if the earl writes again? God save you, but Sir Edward will be rushing back to Elizabeth denouncing you as a conspirator the instant he catches sight of the messenger. Every moment that man resides at Graceton threatens all your efforts to rebuild your family's fortune."

Nick stared into his cup. Jamie knew him well enough

to see him work through the maze of possible events, reading his progress in nothing more than the flicker of his gaze. So, too, did Jamie know the instant Nick realized there was no escape from his marriage. It was the same moment the contentment drained from his face.

"I just didn't see it all," he muttered as he looked at his steward. "Tell me this. If I marry the lady, is it assured I'll get my title's restoration and Kit's marriage?"

Jamie nodded. "If Sir Edward can find no reason to complain, then the queen has no reason not to honor her bargain with you."

"Then I'll marry the lady." Nick's voice was harsh and low, sounding for all the world as if he'd spoken of his damnation, rather than agreeing to enter into a sacred state.

"What is it?" Jamie asked in concern.

Nick's head lifted. "You mean other than the fact you've told me I must marry a stranger and a heretic?"

Alarm bells rang in Jamie's head. Instead of the disappointment or anger any other man might have owned over such a turn, Nick's gaze was blank. His own eyes narrowed. "Tell me," he demanded. "What is it you haven't said?"

Nick might as well have been a brick wall.

A worried breath hissed from Jamie. If Nick wasn't willing to tell him, there was no way to wheedle it out of him. More importantly, Nick's silence meant he knew whatever he was hiding would distress his steward. The certainty of catastrophe settled heavily on Jamie's shoulders.

"I pray you know what you're doing," he warned as he gave way.

"You'll have to trust me, just as Cecily trusts me," Nick replied. "As to this wedding, the queen doesn't expect me to attend the ceremony, does she?"

"No doubt she does. It's customary for men to attend their own weddings," Jamie replied, trying for a lighter tone.

Although Nick was completely at ease with those few allowed to see his scarring, he hated meeting outsiders. Their inevitable reaction to his face, or even to the mask he wore to conceal his scars, left him depressed, often for weeks afterward. He hadn't traveled outside the house's walls during daylight hours since the day Cecily's mother had returned him here two decades ago, his health, such as it was, restored.

Nick shook his head. "I'll not do it. Stand proxy for me again."

Jamie cringed. That strange sense of connection to Lady Purfoy rose. If this was what came of his first round of vows spoken to Nick's wife, the second round would only make matters worse. He couldn't.

As Nick read the resistance in his steward's gaze, the fear in his own deepened. "I can't, Jamie," he almost pleaded, "not even for the queen. There must be some way around this."

Affection for Nick battled with his resistance. At last, Jamie sighed, his need to comfort Nick stronger than his reluctance to stand at an altar with Lady Purfoy once again. He gave way with a shrug.

"Whether it's you or me speaking for you, the marriage is just as legal. It's the consummation Elizabeth requires. She'd like nothing better than to have you produce an heir, thereby denying the family of Kit's betrothed any chance at owning your title. . . . Sir Edward has been commanded most strictly to see the consummation witnessed."

Worry flickered behind the relief in Nick's gaze. "I suppose I must," he said. "Now tell me how soon we can accomplish the wedding. A month hence? Or will so swift a ceremony be objectionable to Sir Edward?"

"A month! Wait until he tells you what the queen expects before you suggest anything," Jamie replied. "And once he's gone, we still have Lady Purfoy to guard against."

Nick's brows lifted again. "We're guarding against her?"

"We can't afford to be careless," Jamie advised, "not when we've so much to lose. I know Sir Edward has tried to recruit her to his cause. Although I believe she continues to resist him, I still intend to examine all the correspondence she sends or receives. No sense in letting her pass damaging information to someone outside the walls."

Consideration flickered through Nick's green gaze. "You're certain this is necessary? Kit speaks highly of the lady in his letter."

"So writes the man at whose feet lies more than a little fault for this unholy union," Jamie replied, his voice laden with scorn. "Best remember, it was your disrespectful brother, along with Lady Montmercy, who used your name in their filthy plot. It's also Kit who planted the notion of you wedding Lady Purfoy in the queen's brain."

"Enough, Jamie," Nick replied gently. "Kit sent an apology and explanation for the wrong he did and I've accepted it. If his words are enough for me, they'll have to satisfy you, as well."

Jamie wasn't the least bit happy about Nick closing the subject of Kit Hollier. He was even less happy to learn

Nick intended to once again forgive his obstinate younger brother. Kit deserved a scourging for promising to seduce an innocent in return for the repayment of his debts, rather than borrowing the coin he needed from his brother. Aye, but to pursue the subject when his employer had closed it was just as disrespectful as Kit was disobedient. He gave way with a heated breath and little grace.

At the sound, Nick lifted his chin to better ignore the frustration he no doubt saw shining in his steward's eyes. "Although I haven't much hope they'll comply, you'll instruct the household to accept this lady as their own. I fear all they can see is that she's a heretic. A day ago, I hadn't given much thought to their reaction; now their rejection will seem all the more sinister against Sir Edward's intent. Warn them I said that anyone who raises either hand or tongue in assault will immediately find themselves without a position."

"Mistress Miller as well?" Jamie asked, already knowing the answer to this. For reasons he couldn't fathom, Nick was inordinately fond of Graceton's old crone of a housekeeper.

Nick coughed out a laugh. "She wouldn't leave if I told her to go," he retorted. "If she's rude to the lady, offer my apologies to the lady on her behalf. Aye, tell Mistress Miller I want an even finer meal for tonight than what is now planned. That should keep her busy and out of the lady's sphere for most of the day. Also, tell Father Walter to keep to his chambers until Sir Edward departs." Father Walter, Nick's priest, occupied the lower floor of the ancient keep tower. That old construct's hall had been converted into a chapel for Nick's use.

Quiet settled between them for a moment, then Nick sighed. "I suppose I'll have to meet them."

"You will," Jamie replied with a nod of his head. "There's no escaping that."

"It'll have to be after the sun's setting." Nick needed the dimness to shield his fragile self-image. "See to it that the meal's late, so it doesn't seem that I'm putting them off. I don't think it'd be any good having them in there." He gestured nervously at his wreck of an office. "Can I use your sitting room?"

To bolster his friend's confidence, Jamie answered the question with a jibe. "And if I refuse? Insisting instead that you straighten that rat's nest in there?"

The smile returned to Nick's gaze. "Then I'm doomed never to meet my visitors. It'd take more than one day to clean that."

"God's own truth," Jamie replied with a laugh. "My sitting room is yours, your worship," he teased with a half-bow, then turned to leave through the hidden door.

"Jamie?"

It was the sudden fear in Nick's voice that brought Jamie back around to face his employer. "What is it, Nick?" he asked in concern.

Worry filled Nick's eyes. "Only that I need your vow," he replied, his voice low and intense. "Swear to me you'll not tell Cecily I've agreed to wed the lady. Let her continue to believe that the wedding plans are nothing but a ruse, as I originally intended. Her heart's a tender thing and she already worries overmuch about me."

The request stung right smartly. In all the years Jamie had been Nick's steward, not once had he shared their conversations outside this chamber, something Nick knew well enough. For his employer to ask him to vow silence now was tantamount to calling him a gossip.

Drawing himself up to his tallest, he offered Nick a stiff and formal bow. "You have my word, Squire Hollier." He tried to keep the emotion from his voice.

"Ach, what have I done," Nick cried at the realization of the insult he'd just given. He came to his feet to lay his hands on his steward's shoulders. "I beg your pardon, Jamie. I was only thinking of Cecily and her tears. I vow, this whole affair has me in such a whirl I cannot think at all.

His pride soothed, Jamie smiled. "God knows you're not alone in that," he replied. "I'm off, then, to tend to your *guests.*"

A new smile lit Nick's eyes. He pressed a bony finger to his nose. "Best you bathe first. They won't be guests for long, not the way you reek."

Laughing despite himself, Jamie gave his employer's shoulder a gentle cuff, then exited the chamber through the hidden door. Once that panel closed behind him, he leaned against it. As he stared into his familiar bedchamber, his spirits drifted down to the toes of his boots. Whatever scheme Nick had up his sleeve guaranteed this was going to be a hellacious wedding.

Chapter Eight

❦

"**Mama,** am I not riding well?" Lucy's piping voice floated back to the wagon on a gusty breeze. Belle looked up from the petticoat she was making for her child, a hand atop her hat to keep the wind from stealing it. Because the day had dawned clear and cloudless, they'd stripped the wagon of its canvas covering, which meant there was nothing to block her view save the arched ribs of the canopy's frame. Lucy was perched atop the forwardmost of the two horses pulling the wagon. Caught in the safe circle of Richard's arm, she leaned far out over her steed to look back at her mother.

"You are, my love," Belle called to her, answering the same question for at least the dozenth time in the last hour.

Lucy's face glowed with the praise. Or perhaps it was the sun. Despite Belle's warning, her daughter had removed her hat. With a wave, the child straightened, the sound of her happy chatter filling the air.

"Why didn't we think to let her ride with Richard days ago?" Peg asked, peering up at Belle from beneath her hat's broad brim as she took another stitch in her own project.

Next to Peg, Brigit laughed and closed her prayer book; she'd been reading to them as they plied their needles. "Would that we had." A brief grin touched her lips. "Sweet as the child is, she's a busy one. After weeks traveling to court, then another ten days trapped in this tiny wagon with her, I'm grateful for the respite."

Such honest sentiment catapulted Belle out of her worries, at least for the moment. For all Brigit's faults, she was truly fond of Lucy and Lucy of her. She laughed. "If we're all telling the truth here, then, I'm grateful as well."

As quickly as it had come, her amusement died. It was hard to think of anything happy when she knew within the hour she'd be meeting the monstrous man she must wed. Belle sighed. Even after ten days spent trying to accustom herself to it, she still wasn't ready to face her future.

Against all her commands that she shouldn't, Belle again scanned the landscape for some sign of her new home. Fields of wheat, burnished now that the harvest season was at hand, rolled out on one side of the road. Green and lush, a meadow stretched along the other. A bright stream, looking like a silver ribbon, snaked its way across that rich expanse. Ahead of them, the road descended into a wee tree-filled vale, only to rise again and circle a small hill.

As she traced the route as far as she could see, a mounted man appeared on the horizon. Dressed all in brown, he rode toward them briskly enough to make the road smoke behind him. Belle's heart lurched.

Never mind that Master Wyatt hadn't looked her way since that first night in the inn, all communication between them having been carried out by his servants. Early this morn, Graceton's steward had ridden ahead to warn the household of their new lady's arrival. Could it be he come to escort her to her new home?

Even as she tried to snatch back the thought, it found

fertile soil in her wayward heart. Craving need sprang to life, full-grown in an instant. Bravery, it whispered, would be so much easier if Master Wyatt were at her side.

Belle watched the approaching rider, trapped in breathless and sinful hope. The sun sparked golden on his hair. Her heart broke in disappointment. It was Sir Edward.

This, her mind scolded, was swift and just punishment for encouraging her sinful longings for a man who wasn't her husband. Dislike took hope's place. The young knight's attempts to win back her good opinion and ingratiate himself into her party were beyond irritating.

"Beware," she warned her servants in a low voice, "the pretty pest comes and off his schedule at that."

"My lady, you shouldn't speak so disrespectfully of Sir Edward," Brigit said in gentle reproof. "What if Mistress Lucy should hear and ape your manner?"

Fickle woman, Belle wanted to chide in return. Although Brigit was right to correct her, it wasn't for Lucy's sake that the governess spoke. Belle watched as Brigit set aside her prayer book, then straightened her hat and brushed the dust from her gown. Delicately craning her neck, the governess peered around Peg for a glimpse of the knight.

Belle's stomach turned. However improbable Richard might be as an object of Brigit's affections, he was a better man than the scheming, underhanded Sir Edward. Even if Brigit and the knight were of a class, the governess was a fool to set her heart upon one so unattainable. Ambition was the only thing powerful enough to overcome Sir Edward's pride and send him back, day after day, as he sought to win Belle's forgiveness.

But what right had she to judge? Was she not also

longing for a man she couldn't have? At least Brigit was an unmarried woman, free to hope wherever and as foolishly as she may.

Sir Edward met the wagon at the vale's bottom. As the knight brought his horse around so he could ride alongside them, Belle pushed her empty needle into the petticoat's fabric. She looked up in time to see him offer Brigit a quick smile. Pretty color bloomed on the governess's cheeks. He turned his gaze on Belle. Shadows of the panic she'd seen in Richmond's garden filled his eyes.

"My lady, you'll soon be at Graceton Castle." It was an insipid statement.

She retorted only with a lift of her brow.

His gaze flickered nervously. "Ah, aye, I thought it best we discuss your wedding ceremony before we arrive."

Irritation boiled into anger. There was nothing he wished to *discuss* with her.

"What is there to say?" she asked, lifting her wooden sewing box into her lap. She took out another length of thread to fill her needle, then began again to stitch at the half-made garment. "I will wed the squire and you'll watch."

"The ceremony, my lady," Sir Edward replied. "There can be no ceremony until we've dealt with the squire's chapel, which I suspect is filled with illegal Popish idolatry. It's the law that all such trash should be swept from all English sanctuaries and burnt."

Belle looked up so swiftly her hat nearly tumbled from her head. "Nay," she said.

Although she knew little of Papists or their rites, she was certain the burning of religious possessions wasn't likely to endear her to either her new husband or his folk. Elizabeth couldn't have commanded this. "I'd see the queen's writ commanding such a purge." It was a challenge, daring him to produce what Belle prayed didn't exist.

His brow creased in concern. "My lady, you surely don't mean to be wed among blasphemous emblems and idolatrous statuary?"

Belle's eyes narrowed. Her chin lifted. Whatever this new ploy was, it included attacking her husband's beliefs. Well, she wasn't going to give him an opportunity to use anyone's faith as a tool. "Since the queen sees fit to give me a Catholic husband, I cannot—nay, I will not—refuse him his beliefs."

"You cannot be serious," Sir Edward cried out.

His gaze shifted to Brigit. "Mistress Atwater, I see by your face that you, too, think your lady misguided. As a faithful woman, is there nothing you can do to show her the sin in her course?"

Brigit, who had already blanched at Belle's inference of conversion, grew paler still. With her hands clutched together in her lap, she gave a frantic shake of her head, then looked at the wagon's floorboards. Brigit was too shrewd to be used this way.

"I will add you all to my prayers," Sir Edward said tightly, then spurred his horse back in the direction he'd come.

"You cannot be serious, my lady," Peg cried, coughing in the dust his departure stirred. "You'd convert?"

"Oh, nay, my lady, you cannot," Brigit pleaded, ready now to do as Sir Edward suggested.

"Of course I won't," Belle returned, her voice sharp. "How can either of you believe me so capricious? I just don't think it's any of Sir Edward's business what I intend or how I practice my faith."

Richard's quiet laugh floated back to the wagon on the breeze. "Well done, my lady," he called to her as the wagon made its way around the hill. "Well done indeed. Now, I think we've arrived."

All the pleasure Belle felt at standing up to the knight drained away. Ahead of them on the road a stretch of gray stone wall lifted above the trees. Graceton Castle.

"Oh," Belle breathed as both Brigit and Peg shifted on their bench to look.

Caught in the river's bend, it was cloaked in ivy and topped by great stone blocks. At either end stood a rounded tower, their conical roofs rising above the rooftops, slate tiles glowing like pewter in the sun. Glass winked from the row of tiny square windows that marched across the wall just above the water's surface. Far larger and more graceful openings soared across the wall's second and third story.

The road led up to a massive gatehouse. Built of a slightly darker stone than the gray wall it pierced, two squat towers framed the arched opening of its gateway. Clinging to the outer wall at either side of the entrance were a goodly number of barns and outbuildings. One was the stable, for Sir Edward was dismounting before it, a groom holding the horse's reins as his manservant unbuckled the saddle packs. Tom, Master Wyatt's servant, stood not far away, as if waiting on the men.

"It's not a house," Peg said, her voice heavy with disappointment.

"Not a house?" Brigit exclaimed. "How can you say that, when there are windows and a roof." The sweep of her hand traced the line of that slate-covered peak barely visible above the wall's crenellation. "And chimneys." She pointed to the slender columns of brick that rose at regular intervals from the rooftop.

"I mean, it's not a house, but a castle remade into a house," Peg retorted, her expression sour as she glanced at Belle. "Do you remember Lord Montmercy's seat, my lady? Drafty and damp, it was. Dark and cramped, too. Faugh! I hoped for something more civilized."

Irritation washed through Belle. What right had Peg to complain? *She* didn't have to marry the owner of this place. "It will be what it is," she muttered.

"Nay, it will be what you make of it, my lady," Peg replied, "and here's the first change that calls for your hand."

The maid pointed to the gatehouse. They were near enough now to see that its forward section spanned the river. This made the opening so long it appeared more tunnel than doorway. A portcullis was raised high into the gateway's arch, so nothing of it was visible save for its rusting iron spikes.

"What sort of welcome can a body feel when the doorway looks a slavering maw waiting to devour the unwary?"

Brigit gave a tiny, fearful cry. Opening her prayer book, she began to read, her lips silently forming the words her eyes saw.

All of Belle's previous confidence evaporated. Her fingers clenched into the linen in her lap, her nails biting through the fabric until they dug into the solid, square outline of her sewing box beneath it. A raft of horrid little thoughts raced through her, one after the other and each worse than the last. What if her husband believed her a spy and never welcomed her? What if he took one look at her and knew she'd entertained sinful thoughts for his steward? What if he was so hideous she couldn't bear to bed him?

What if Squire Hollier, monstrous as he was, found her so ugly he spurned her? Even imagined, the humiliation of such an event made tears sting at Belle's eyes. A tiny whimper escaped her lips.

"Ach, my lady, you've gone all white." The wagon bench groaned as Peg shifted to sit next to her mistress. Her brown eyes were dark with concern. "Nay, now, you mustn't worry so, my little love," she crooned.

Murmuring gently, she removed her mistress's hat. Straightening Belle's coif, she smoothed a few stray hairs back within that cap's confines, just as she'd done when Belle had been younger than Lucy. "You'll see," she whispered, patting her mistress's hand, "it won't be as awful as you imagine."

Rather than comfort, her words made Belle feel hopeless, helpless and foolish. Reclaiming her hat from Peg, she settled it back upon her head so it hid her face, then sniffled as the wagon rumbled up to the gatehouse's mossy foot. "Oh, Peg, I'm such a coward."

"Nay, not cowardly, only sensible," the maid said, defending her lady from herself. "Who wouldn't fear being forced into a marriage as you have been?"

With the squeal of metalshod wheels and the steady ring of horseshoes on stone, the wagon entered the long gateway. Lucy hooted from her perch on the lead horse, then giggled at the sound of her rebounding voice. So taken with it was she that she began to chant, "We're here, we're here," just to listen to the words reverberate.

Such fearlessness in her child only made Belle feel worse. What sort of pride could Lucy have in a cowardly mother? As the wagon at last trundled out of the gatehouse and into the castle's yard, she straightened and lifted her chin. For her daughter's sake, she'd at least pretend bravery.

Peg turned on the bench to scan what lay within the walls, then loosed a happy gasp. "Oh, my lady, I was wrong," she crowed. "This is much nicer than I expected. Did I not tell you things were not as bad as they seemed? Look, Brigit," she demanded of the yet praying governess, "put away your book and look at this marvelous place."

Within its walls, Graceton Castle looked far more residence than fortress. Directly ahead of Belle, across the lush turf that carpeted the yard's wide expanse, was the building whose roof they'd seen. Built of a yellowish stone, four long, graceful windows cut into its face, while the grand, sheltered doorway at its far left end proclaimed it the hall.

What was surely the family's living quarters stretched from the hall's right. A wooden gallery clung to its second story, five fine oriel windows marking its exterior.

An ancient and crumbling ivy-clad keep stood on a mound at one side of the wide yard, its tiny, empty windows staring forlornly down upon the house that had replaced it. Roses tumbled over the low wall around its base, suggesting a private garden.

Richard whistled the horses into a leftward turn, giving Belle a good view of the kitchen buildings and brewery. The buildings were small and tidy, some made of stone and slate, others plaster and thatch. Nearly forty men and women dressed in maroon and gray stood in silence before these buildings. Their arms crossed and shoulders tensed, nary a smile touched a face as they eyed the newcomers.

Belle's fear, held in check by naught but a prayer and a ruse, burst forth anew. This wasn't a welcoming party, it was an army drawing its battle lines. They hated her even before they knew her.

Just when she was certain she'd embarrass herself and her daughter by bursting into tears, Master Wyatt stepped out of the hall's door. Her gaze clung to his familiar face and form as he strode toward the waiting mob. Gone was his traveling attire, replaced with breeches of black and a sleeveless brown doublet atop a white shirt. In keeping with a country lifestyle, he'd eschewed a ruff and left his collar open, revealing the strong column of his neck. Beneath his brown cap, his neatly combed hair gleamed a deep red as it framed his sun-browned face.

Offering Graceton's folk a smile and a nod, his face was relaxed, the tiny lift of his lips confident. Belle breathed again. If he wasn't worried, then she wouldn't be, either.

"Hello, hello, Master Wyatt," Lucy sang out, waving as she recognized him. "Welcome to my new home!"

Though a grin flashed across his lips, the crowd behind him wasn't as amused. Closing ranks, folk clotted and clutched together. A steely murmur rumbled from them. Master Wyatt shot a swift glance over his shoulder.

His frown told Belle that whatever it was they said hadn't been either friendly or welcoming. Again, her heart thundered in her ears. Beside her, Peg's eyes widened with the first inklings of fear. Brigit, who'd glanced up from her prayer book at Lucy's call, freed a quiet moan and turned her gaze back to its pages. No longer was her prayer silent. Instead, whispered pleas to the Almighty hissed steadily through her tight lips.

Richard pulled the wagon to a halt a few yards from the hall door. Master Wyatt stepped forward to catch the front horse's reins. All concern was gone from his face.

"Well now, if it isn't Mistress Lucretia Purfoy," he said to Belle's daughter, his voice raised to carry, his tone warm and kind. "I see you finally found yourself a mount."

Oblivious to the glares aimed in her direction, Lucy beamed down at him. "Aye," she chirped. "Do you see me riding?" She gleefully kicked her heels into the big horse's sides. The massive beast grunted at this assault.

He laughed, the sound deep and rich. "That I do, you little imp. But then, I never doubted you'd charm your way onto a horse's back."

Whether it was his words or his laughter, tension nigh on melted from the surly group. Men's arms were loosening, their fists opening. Women's faces had relaxed, with more than a few smiling at Lady Purfoy's daughter.

Belle looked back at Master Wyatt, only to find him watching her. His expression was noncommittal, but she read it in his gaze. He'd seen the hostility aimed at her and her party and had purposefully set out to diffuse it.

Deep within Belle, something new and subtle stirred. She wished there were some way to let him know how great his gift was. Instead, all she had to offer was her smile and even that came too late, for he'd already turned away.

A wave of his hand brought one man forward to take the lead horse's harness. Two footmen who had journeyed with them from Richmond followed to lift out the wagon's back gate. As they leaned it against the wheel, the elder of the two men glanced at her. A quick smile flashed across his lips. Although this was more an indication of recognition than welcome, Belle sighed. In that simple gesture lurked a promise. Given time, the other servants would come to accept her, just as he had.

Master Wyatt strode down the wagon's length to stand before the opening. Belle searched his face. There was nothing for her to read in his expression.

"Welcome to Graceton Castle, Lady Purfoy," he called out loudly enough that his voice rang against the enclosing walls.

Only then did it occur to Belle that she should say more than thank you in return. Pretty words congealed on her tongue only to melt away before she could string them into something both coherent and gracious. Scrambling desperately to say something, anything, she lurched to her feet, forgetting the sewing in her lap. Caught in the half-made petticoat, her needle box thudded hollowly against the wagon's bed. Without thought, Belle bent to snatch it up. Instead, the tangle of box and linen flew from her grasping fingers to strike Master Wyatt mid-chest, then drop to the sod at his feet. Mortified, she straightened, fingers pressed to her lips.

Master Wyatt glanced from the pile of fabric on the ground to her face. A frown touched his brow and was gone. In its place, the tiniest gleam of humor came to life in his blue eyes.

"Was that some sort of attack?" he whispered, his voice held so low that only she could hear him.

Instead of easing the situation, which was surely what he intended, a hysterical laugh filled Belle's throat. She tried to swallow it. Bad enough to be thought a clumsy fool; she wasn't going to guffaw like a madwoman. Despite her efforts, a mewling sound slipped past her restraining fingers.

Pity softened his expression. Reaching up, he caught her by the elbow and drew her a step closer to the wagon's end. "Just say you're glad to be here, my lady," he whispered.

His words worked like a key turning in a lock. Belle's tangled emotions eased. Air again filled her lungs. She looked down at him, something deeper than gratitude curling through her heart for him this time. Against that subtle sensation, the words she'd sought for and couldn't find a moment ago now sprang to her lips.

"Many thanks for your kind welcome, Master Wyatt. My thanks, as well, to all of you who took time to come and greet me," she said, proud that not a single quiver marred her voice. "I am very glad to be at Graceton Castle."

Peg was right. This wasn't going to be as horrid as she'd imagined, not as long as she had Master Wyatt as her protector.

Chapter Nine

❧

Jamie looked up at Nick's wife. Her hat was askew. Dust streaked her face and tired rings clung beneath her eyes. Wispy strands of hair escaped her braid to waft along the slim column of her neck. As she offered him a tremulous smile, gratitude nigh on pulsing from her, he thought he'd never seen a more beautiful woman.

The urge to pull her into his arms washed over him. His teeth clenched. What sort of nonsense was this? God save him, but only a moment ago Graceton's folk had been muttering about driving the lady's party back out the gate.

Catching Nick's wife by the waist, he lifted her from the wagon. A nod to Watt and John sent them leaping to help the remaining women to dismount. Jamie sighed, never so grateful to see men do as he commanded. He knew very well their peers wished them to refuse, to protest this marriage.

As Lady Purfoy's party and his men traded low-voiced small talk about the last leg of their journey, Jamie was surprised at the level of ease. Hope blossomed. Perhaps they would reach the wedding day with everyone's skin still attached.

"Mama!" Mistress Lucy came dashing toward them. Beneath the brim of her hat, her pretty face was reddened and Jamie guessed her head covering had been off more than on while she rode.

Lady Purfoy caught her daughter by the hand. "What are you to say?" she whispered.

"Oh." The child's brows pinched as if in concentration. Spreading her skirt wide, she curtsied. It was sloppily done, for she nearly toppled herself. When she was again steady, she raised her head to smile up at him.

"I am very glad to be at Graceton Castle, Master Wyatt." This obviously rehearsed speech was followed by a sweet shrug of her shoulders. "I forgot to say that earlier," she explained, then her smile widened. "Was I not riding well?"

Lord, but she was a cheeky thing. Aye, and with her face, a few more years would see men aplenty ready to tell her whatever she wished to hear. For today, he would happily fulfill her demand for a compliment.

"You were indeed," he replied.

As she squealed in pleasure, Lady Purfoy turned her child. "Run to Brigit, love," she murmured.

Truly, the lady's lack of formality was stunning. It was more than passing strange to hear a child's tutor referred to by her Christian name.

"Oh, aye!" Mistress Lucy cried, her eyes widening in new excitement. "She'll be waiting to know about my ride."

Tiny arms pumping, she dashed to the wagon's end. Her keeper was watching Watt and the lady's footman pull a heavy chest from the wagon's bed. As the governess caught the child's hand and leaned down to listen, the two men paused in their task. Their heads lifted as they looked out into the yard.

It was Sir Edward coming toward them, with Tom following miserably in his wake. The knight was enraged, or so said the way he strode across the yard. Jamie sighed. Really, he was too tired for this.

The knight stormed past the servants and came to a halt before Graceton's steward. Jamie caught the flicker of movement behind him as Lady Purfoy sidled a little nearer. Without thought, he shifted, placing his body between knight and lady, only to flinch inwardly at the meaning in that motion. Aye, but once done, he wasn't about to make a fool of himself by undoing it.

Sweeping his cap from his head, Jamie offered the bow due the knight's rank. "Welcome to Graceton Castle, Sir Edward." Despite his efforts, his tone was no friendlier than the greeting the lady had received from the castle folk.

"What sort of insult is this?" Sir Edward snarled in response. "You dare to quarter the queen's proxy in a gatehouse?"

"Pardon, Sir Edward, if my servant didn't explain," he replied, knowing full well Tom had, or had at least attempted it. "The gatehouse contains our best rooms. It was refitted for the squire's father, who was a scholarly man in need of privacy for his studies." It was an oblique way of saying Nick's sire had abandoned his wife and children for his books.

"Indeed, yon oriels," he pointed to the gatehouse's inner face where two fine bay windows let light and air into what had once been the castle's barracks, "are the most expensive windows in the castle. Of course," he continued, brows lifted, "if you prefer to stay within the house, we can accommodate you with a lesser suite."

Trapped, Sir Edward could but glare silently. Enjoyment

at this brief advantage emboldened Jamie to take a final jab.

"Moreover, in the gatehouse you can come and go as you please, or receive messengers in private, something I thought you might appreciate." It never hurt to let a spy know his cloak of secrecy had parted.

Sir Edward's eyes narrowed to vicious slits. "I require a bath."

"Already awaiting you there," Jamie replied briskly, "as is a warm meal."

"Inform the squire that I'll meet with him presently as regards this wedding."

Such arrogance hardened Jamie's jaw to iron. He forced himself to relax before he ground his own teeth to dust. "The squire cannot see you until this evening." There was nothing gracious in his refusal.

"He dares deny the queen's proxy?" Beneath the knight's outrage, threat hung heavy in every word. It was a patent reminder that if he disliked anything in the staging of this wedding, it would be the same as displeasing the queen herself.

"He denies nothing," Jamie replied evenly. "He sleeps. Given the fragile state of his health, all audiences must wait until he awakens this evening." The fact of Nick's health merely lent sincerity to what was otherwise a half-truth.

Sir Edward glared a moment longer, then turned on his heel. He collided with Lady Purfoy's footman, who was coming toward them with one end of his mistress's trunk in his arms. The knight stumbled to the side, caught his footing and stormed away; the footman reeled, feet sliding out from under him. Watt shouted as he lost his grip on the chest's other end. Lady Purfoy's footman collapsed. The chest hit the ground beside him with a weighty thud, bounced to the side, then slammed atop him.

With a quiet shriek, Lady Purfoy shot out from behind Jamie. Thinking she went to rescue her belongings, Jamie started after her to tend the servant. To his surprise, she was there before him.

"Richard," she cried, kneeling at her man's side.

In an instant, the other two women in her party were at her back, while her daughter completed the vignette, squatting at the footman's head to pat his face. Not one of them thought to set a hand to the trunk and free the man. Nay, all they could do was murmur like a flock of agitated doves.

"I'm not hurt, my lady," Richard said, shoving at the chest atop him.

As Jamie took one handle, Watt caught the other. Together, they lifted the trunk off the man and set it to one side. Jamie looked down at the fallen servant.

His hat under his lady's knee and his hair mussed, Richard returned Jamie's look with one of healthy and hale chagrin. It seemed he didn't much like the fuss being made over him. Being that sort of man himself, Jamie held out his hand. With a fleeting smile of thanks, the servant let his new steward pull him to his feet.

"You're certain you're well?" his mistress demanded, brushing at the clots of grass that clung to her servant's doublet.

"I am, my lady," Richard said, backing away from her, then bending to retrieve his cap. "I beg your pardon, I didn't see the knight. I hope your trunk isn't damaged."

She didn't spare a glance for the chest. "If it is, I daresay it can be mended," she replied with a smile. "Better it than you."

From the watching servants at the kitchen gate rose a new wave of whispering. Jamie glanced at the servants. They were watching their squire's new wife with new consideration. Even Will Prentiss's mouth was pursed in thought, Nick's cook being the most vehement Catholic among them, next to the housekeeper.

Jamie's hope for Nick's title's restoration doubled, as did the possibility the lady might survive past her wedding day. As for herself, Lady Purfoy appeared to have no idea of the miracle she'd just wrought. She watched Richard and Watt again pick up the trunk. Only when they'd carried it past her toward the hall door did she sigh as if finally assured her servant was uninjured.

When she rejoined Jamie, she stepped a shade closer than he had expected. Startled, he took a backward step. "My lady?"

A worried frown touched Lady Purfoy's smooth brow. She shot a nervous glance across the yard at the retreating knight. "I know you've no reason to trust me or my words, but I feel I must tell you. I've refused to aid Sir Edward in his plot against your squire," she whispered.

Jamie went breathless in surprise. What sort of ploy was this? She stared back, nothing but honesty shining in her clear gray eyes.

Artifice! Mimicry! his mind shouted. Instead, ten days of observation dared to suggest she was naught but the pawn Percy named her. That thought awakened his urge to protect her from a world bent on using her. He reached out as if to embrace her, only to freeze with his arm half-extended. What in God's holy hell was he doing?

Mistaking his motion for the customary offer of escort, Lady Purfoy put her hand into the crook of his elbow. Shuffling swiftly to make use of her error, Jamie rearranged himself into the appropriate stance. "If I could escort you to the hall, my lady?"

"Thank you, Master Wyatt," she said, peering up at him from beneath her hat brim. A sudden, shy smile flitted across her sultry lips. His heart stirred.

Not again. May God take his soul! A dull ache woke at the base of his brain. It had to be exhaustion doing this to him.

The desire to lock himself into his bedchamber rose until he'd never wanted anything more. What he needed was a few hours' peace, away from this woman, Sir Edward, Nick's plot to escape marriage, hostile servants and everything else that had gone wrong these past weeks. When he was rested, these strange reactions would cease.

There was a tug on his doublet's hem. Mistress Lucy stepped out in front of him. "May I have your arm, too?"

"You may have my hand," her mother replied for him, extending her free hand to her child.

Disappointment flashed through the lass's eyes, just deep enough to stir Jamie. He put out a hand. "I would be honored, Mistress Purfoy."

A glorious smile bloomed on the child's face. Before her mother had a chance to remind her, she offered him a far steadier bob this time. "Thank you, Master Wyatt," she said politely, then curled her tiny fingers into his palm.

Oddly, at the feel of her small hand in his the throbbing in his head eased. He smiled down at her. Despite her strange rearing, Lucy Purfoy was a well-behaved and like-able child.

Together, the three of them started toward the hall door, with the lady's servants following. After a few steps, the lass lifted her heels into a skip, needing the extra bounce to keep pace with the longer-legged adults. "I'm to meet my stepfather soon," she said between hops.

"You are?" Jamie asked in surprise. He'd no intention of introducing her to Nick.

"Aye, and I'll like him," she replied.

"You will?" he asked again, even more startled now.

"Aye." The child released his hand to race up the porch's three steps. The door at the top was ajar. Prying it open a stitch farther, she stepped into the opening, then turned to smile back at him. "I must like him, for he'll climb trees with me and teach me to ride his horse."

Jamie watched her disappear inside, then shot a sharp look at the lass's mother. "You promised her the squire would do these things?"

The lady gave an apologetic shake of her head, then released his arm to lift her skirts and start up the steps after her child. "Nay, I fear Sir William Purfoy did, daring to speak for an unknown man before he died. The worst of it is," she said as she went, "I don't know how to tell her the squire isn't well enough to do any of what her father promised."

The pounding in Jamie's head returned. Nick was easily charmed. If Nick were to hear of the child's expectations, he'd seek out someone to do for the child what he couldn't.

Jamie's jaw tightened as he watched Lady Purfoy step into the hall. Well, it wouldn't be him. He was Nicholas

Hollier's proxy only in his legal matters, not in the raising of his stepchild.

The need to escape grew far beyond merely retreating to his apartments. Unfortunately, his loyalty and his love for Nick had him trapped here. He'd simply have to come to terms with the fact that he'd lost the uncomplicated life he'd once enjoyed at Graceton.

Chapter Ten

❧❧

Feeling more confident than she had in days, Belle entered Graceton Castle's hall. Not only had Master Wyatt become her protector, there'd been no anger or questions over her warning about Sir Edward. That could only mean he'd decided she was no spy. Aye, things were looking better with each passing moment.

The door let her into a passageway, created between the hall's stone wall and a long wooden panel at her right. This was the hall's screen, meant to shield the greater room from door-drawn drafts. It was especially necessary here, where there was yet another door at the passage's end, no doubt giving access to the kitchen yard.

Belle stepped through the opening in the screen and caught her breath. Warm light flowed through the hall's tall windows, gilding everything it touched. The brick floor glowed a rusty red, while oak paneling gleamed golden. And the ceiling! Truss and hammer-beams did far more than keep the roof over their heads. Every inch of exposed wood was covered with carved tracery. Where the beams lifted away from the wall, wooden flowers nestled in their spread leaves. At the intersections of the rafters pendants of wood descended, the trefoils decorating those lantern-like projections looking for all the world like sprigs of clover. A ceiling vent as ornate as the rest opened above the hearthstone at the room's center.

As the steward came to a stop beside Belle, she glanced at him. "This chamber is truly amazing."

"If you say so," he replied with an impatient snort. "I fear all I can see is evidence of the last Lord Graceton's spendthrift ways. Every stone and piece of wood in the hall is imported. When the old lord tired of throwing away his coins in building, he finished the emptying of the family's treasury by housing hundreds of dispossessed monks and nuns. The result was near-penury for his children and grandchildren, and abeyance for their title."

Understanding blossomed in Belle. So, it was the offer to restore his title that Elizabeth was using to twist the squire into marrying her. Somehow, she doubted Squire Hollier was any happier about having his title restored through this marriage than his grandsire was to see it slip into disuse.

"Do you intend to stand at the door all day?" An old woman's quarrelsome words rang in the hall.

Belle's gaze shot across the chamber only to find the speaker standing like a sentinel at the hall's rear. Her back bent and a walking stick to brace her, the ancient woman had a nose that jutted out over the pucker of a nearly toothless mouth, while what little hair she had left beneath her coif made a minuscule knot at her nape. Like all the other servants, she was dressed in maroon and gray. The only difference was the white, high-necked partlet she wore atop her bodice.

A hiss of irritation escaped Master Wyatt. "That, my lady, is Mistress Miller, our housekeeper," he said in a low voice. "The only reason she remains our housekeeper at her age is because the squire refuses to force her out or put another woman in her place. She's got a vicious tongue. Although I've warned her to be civil, there's little chance she'll heed me. She never has before," he finished, speaking more to himself than her.

Belle looked at the old woman. The nasty set of Mistress Miller's jaw made it clear she had no intention of ceding the household's reins to a newcomer. Belle knew these next moments would be crucial to her future harmony. Without Mistress Miller's support, Belle might as well never issue a command; no servant would do as she asked.

"My lady?" Master Wyatt again offered his arm and led her across the room.

"Lady Purfoy, this is Mistress Miller, our housekeeper."

"I am pleased to make your acquaintance," Belle said, putting as much enthusiasm as she could manage in the statement, even adding a smile.

The old woman gave an indignant sniff. "Lady Purfoy," she replied, investing more than a little distaste in the two words.

"What an insolent creature!" Peg's irate whisper rang around them.

Belle's shoulders sagged. She hadn't thought about Peg provoking a confrontation. Not now, before she'd even bathed. What if the housekeeper refused to bring them warm water?

Mistress Miller turned a narrow-eyed gaze on the maid, then gave a dismissing jerk of her hairy chin and brought her attention back on her new lady. "Your belongings arrived," she growled. "We've already paid the teamsters, then sent those outsiders back where they belong. We'd no choice but to put your things in a storeroom whilst we awaited you." Her tone left no doubt of how extreme she considered this imposition.

Belle did her best to pacify the housekeeper. "I appreciate the care you've given my furnishings," she told the old woman, "and of course I shall repay the cost of my property's transport."

"You will not," Master Wyatt snapped.

Startled, Belle looked up at him. He was staring daggers at the housekeeper. Just as he'd warned, the old woman showed not a whit of respect as she glared boldly back at him.

"You, my lady, are the squire's betrothed wife." The way he lingered on the word was clearly for the housekeeper's benefit. "Squire Hollier will not demean himself or his station by asking his new wife to bear the cost of her dowry's movement into his household."

With an indignant sniff, the housekeeper turned away from her steward. "You there, Watt," she called out. "We go upstairs to choose the lady a chamber. Stir that puny, useless man," she said, meaning Richard, who stood near the hearth, "from his sloth and bring the lady's trunk above."

Anger flickered to life in Belle. What right had this old crone to speak so about her servant? But as she opened her mouth to chide, she caught back the words. The only servants she could take with her into the safety of her new chambers were her women. Richard would be left to fend for himself among Graceton's menservants. If Belle defended him now, it could go worse for him later.

"The sooner the lady chooses a chamber," the old woman grumbled, "the sooner we can clear her things out of our storerooms." The promise that she'd never allow this interloper to rule her hall glowed in the rheumy depths of her eyes. Then, turning her back on her better, she stumped away.

"She doesn't like you, Mama," Lucy said, frowning after the housekeeper. Confusion and surprise filled her expression, as if it were inconceivable that anyone would dislike her mother.

What little pride Belle owned came to sudden and outraged life. What sort of woman was she? Why, she was nigh on helping this ancient and frail hag humiliate her! Well, no more. If she ever wanted to be Graceton's lady in more than name, she'd better start acting like the position was hers.

Catching Lucy's hand, she followed the old woman into the chamber behind the hall. The room was small, its walls wainscoted with a pretty maple paneling. A thick rush mat covered the floor. Except for a long bench that stood before the fireplace in the far wall, it was empty. Indeed, it had the feel of a room that hadn't seen use in years. Still, Belle knew it for a solar, her parlor, a place where she could eat in private and entertain visitors.

In its corner was a set of stairs. Mistress Miller was already climbing them, taking each step with a tap of her cane and a groan. With Master Wyatt, Peg and Brigit at their heels, Belle and Lucy started up the steps. When they reached the gallery, Belle forgot all that was wrong to stare in pleasure. Oh, to be lady of such a place!

Sunlight flooded into the wide corridor through its five windows, laying the pattern of the panes against white plastered walls and dark wood floor. As tall as the ceiling, each window was nigh on deep enough to be a tiny chamber on its own. There was a seat in each oriel's bay, complete with a cushion. Two heavy chairs stood before one bay, as if to encourage a body to sit and enjoy the view.

Portraits hung along the inner wall, their frames gilded. There were so many they filled the gallery's length.

Belle's awe grew as she counted doorways. Seven private suites! Eight, if she added the gatehouse, and nine if another apartment hid behind the door in the curved stone wall at the gallery's end.

Mistress Miller had already started down the wide corridor, tapping rapidly past the first two doors. "This is where Master Kit stays when he's home and that's our lord's suite. You cannot have this one, either," she pointed to the next door, "as that's our steward's chamber."

That left only four chambers from which to choose. "Do any of them connect?" Belle asked as she trailed the woman, hoping for but a single door between her own chamber and Lucy's nursery.

The old woman pivoted on her stick to look back at her new lady. "Aye," she said, "but you cannot have those two. They're at the end of the gallery."

Irritation flowed into Belle. Spine stiff, she drew herself to her tallest, her jaw firm. "I don't care where they're located, it's the adjoining chambers I want." Her voice rang in the gallery, clear, firm and commanding.

"You don't," the housekeeper argued, "for 'tis there our ghost walks."

Peg gasped. Brigit gave a tiny moan. Belle's eyes flew wide. Oh, Lord! As if hostile servants and a husband who didn't want her weren't enough, there was a ghost as well? She drew Lucy closer.

"Truly, it isn't necessary that we have adjoining chambers, my lady." Brigit's voice trembled. "Perhaps the other two would be better?"

"Aye," Peg managed. "It's no imposition to move from suite to suite, not when one can enjoy such a fine gallery."

"There is no need to refuse those chambers," Master Wyatt snapped. "There's no ghost."

The old woman's chin jerked up as if in challenge. "You're an outsider here, Master James. You can't know."

James. Belle stared up into his face, all thought of spirits and hauntings departing. His given name was James. It suited him, unusual as it was, complementing his fine features and rare hair color.

"Say no more," Master Wyatt warned.

The old woman ignored him, her gaze slipping to her new lady as she spoke. "She's the spirit of one of Graceton's ladies, left barren because her lord husband refused her bed in favor of his common mistress. Wanting to reclaim her lord's affections, this lady did commit murder, ordering the slaying of the mistress and her lord's bastards. When her noble husband discovered what his lady had done, he carried her to the top of yon tower." The lift of her cane indicated the curved wall at the gallery's end. Only then did Belle recognize it as the castle's corner tower.

"There, he threw her off the wall to her death. Take those chambers and be warned," the housekeeper continued. "Never follow our White Lady. She'll lead you to the wall and bewitch you into leaping over it. Twice before she's done it, both of them women forced into unhappy wedlock just as she was." Her mouth twisted into a vindictive smile. "Just as you are."

"Enough!" Master James shouted, the word thundering around them.

At his roar, Lucy loosed a frightened cry and burrowed into Belle's skirt. No such fear plagued her mother. Indeed, as grateful as Belle was for Master James's protection, she didn't need it this time. The housekeeper should have ended her tale before she'd added that ridiculous codicil. Here was proof that all the woman had said before was nothing but an attempt to humiliate her new lady.

Graceton's steward chided the housekeeper. "I've endured your insolence and your bad temper for Squire Hollier's sake, but this goes beyond any toleration. In spinning this lie to frighten his wife, you denigrate not only the squire, but his family and his house."

"It's no lie," the old woman retorted, sounding almost hurt at the accusation. "Ask any of the servants and they'll tell you what I say is true."

His expression earnest, Master James looked at Belle. "My lady, I apologize on the squire's behalf. Mistress Miller's rudeness passes all bounds. I'll have you know my office is in yon tower. I've kept it there for all of the ten years I've been Graceton's steward, using that chamber both day and night. Not once in all that time have I seen anything remotely unnatural. Madame, if the adjoining chambers are the ones you want, I tell you you have nothing to fear in taking them."

Belle drew a relieved breath. His office would be next to her own chambers. Aye, he was right. As long as he was so close that her raised voice could bring him to her, there was nothing she need fear.

She looked at the housekeeper. "Those are the chambers I want and they're the chambers I'll have. See that my belongings are brought to me there. In two hours' time we'll want a meal. What we need now is warmed water, enough that each of us can have a fresh tub."

The housekeeper's eyes narrowed. Her chin jutted out. Although the bend of her head made a mockery of obedience, Belle fought her grin. It was Belle who'd won in this encounter, wringing compliance out of the old biddy.

"As you will, my lady, but it'll be only your own man serving you," the old woman said with a haughty lift of her gnarled brows. "None of our folk will go to that end of the gallery."

"They will, if I have to walk the distance with them every time," Master James snapped, turning as he spoke to fix his piercing gaze on the two footmen behind them.

Whilst they waited on a decision, they'd set the heavy chest upon the gallery floor. Richard stood at its back, as impassive and silent as ever. Beside him, the one named Watt was worrying his cap in his hands. He shifted uneasily from foot to foot as he glanced from the housekeeper to his steward. At last, he gave a halfhearted shrug.

"If none of the others will lift their sorry arms to aid the lady, it'll be me and John helping Richard here."

Mistress Miller's eyes widened at this betrayal. Her mouth began to move, as if she needed to chew up his words before they choked her. She turned and started back toward the stairs.

"Don't complain to me that you weren't warned, my lady," she threw over her shoulder as she went.

Belle watched her go, then glanced at her womenfolk. Brigit was frowning after the old woman, while Peg was in full glower. Crossing her arms over her bodice, the maid's brows rose. "What does that old hag think us, rustics to be driven off by a fanciful tale such as that? Of all the nerve! Lead on, my lady. Let's see what she meant to keep us from having. I've a suspicion those far chambers are finer than the other two."

Beside Belle, Master James laughed, the sound low and rich. "Wise words and God's own truth. My lady, shall I escort you to your chambers?" Once more, he extended his elbow toward her.

"Me, too," Lucy insisted, darting around her mother to stand beside the handsome man. "That is, if you please, Master Wyatt," she amended with a quick bend of her knee.

Master James smiled and extended a hand.

As Belle settled her hand into the crook of the steward's elbow, she leaned nearer to him. "Thank you for that," she breathed, so Lucy wouldn't overhear, then dared to ask for even more. "Master Wyatt, I mean no slur or complaint against my husband's household, but could you see that Richard's needs are met? I fear there may be a few here who would wish him ill-treated."

"Another truth," he returned, his voice as low as hers. "Aye, you have my word. No harm will come to him."

Belle smiled. With Master James at her side, she would make this place her home.

Chapter Eleven

❧

The sun had almost set before there was a tap at Belle's new chamber door. Seated in one of the three chairs that now filled the sitting room, she squeaked, her heart nearly shooting from her chest. She clutched Lucy's half-finished petticoat to her rose-colored doublet. May the Lord have mercy on her, it was time to meet her monstrous husband.

Because Peg was busy with her dinner, Brigit rose to answer the door. As the governess swept past a tall candelabrum, the flames danced. Her green skirts whispered across the chamber's wooden floor. The door cried quietly as it opened. Far brighter light than what their three candles offered flowed in to gild Brigit's pretty face.

She smiled. "Good evening, Tom," she said to Master James's servant.

"Mistress Atwater," he replied. "Lord Nicholas is ready to meet with your lady."

Belle's galloping heart slowed at this strange reference to the squire. Lord Nicholas? Why did Tom call him by the title he didn't yet own? It was enough to restore at least a little of her equilibrium. Folding away Lucy's petticoat, she came to her feet and straightened her gray and pink skirts atop her farthingale.

"Enjoy your meal, my lady," Peg said with a smile.

A touch of irritation shot through Belle, an echo of this morn's uncharitable emotions. *Enjoy your meal* when she was off to meet a monster, then sit in a hall filled with dozens of hostile servants? Catching up her gloves from her chair's back, she joined Brigit in the gallery.

With Tom's great branch of candles cutting a wide circle in the growing dimness, they started toward the squire's chamber. A moment later, Master James and Sir Edward appeared atop the stairs at the other end of the wide corridor. Like his servant, Master James also carried a branch of candles.

Belle watched him, liking the way the warm light traced his nose's fine line and marked the sharp arc of his brows. Beneath his brown cap, his hair glowed a burnished red. He'd not changed his dress for this evening's formal meal, only closed his shirt collar and tied a pair of brown sleeves into his doublet. It didn't matter that Sir Edward fair glowed beside him in his rich garments. To Belle's eyes, Master James was the better-looking man.

Both men offered Belle a bow. "My lady," Master James said as Belle gave him a quick bob.

Sir Edward straightened with a tense smile. "Good evening, my lady."

He received no response for his effort. It was an intentional slight. If Sir Edward retained any hope she'd ever forgive him his rudeness, he'd killed it the moment he'd walked away from the fallen Richard without a backward look.

With so many candles to light the gallery, Belle saw surprise play across the knight's face. She lifted her chin. If he were the sort of man who thought nothing of abusing those beneath him, he'd hardly understand another of his class despising him for it.

Although Brigit was no happier over the knight's behavior than Belle, her own social standing left her no choice but to be respectful. "Good evening, Sir Edward, Master Wyatt," she said as she curtsied to them both.

"Mistress Atwater," Master James said, "if you'll follow Tom, he'll lead you to the hall. Your lady, myself and Sir Edward will shortly join you."

As Brigit nodded and followed the servant, all Belle's fear and nervousness came rushing back. Why hadn't she realized she'd be facing her new husband alone? Beside her, Master James opened his chamber door.

Like a moth to a flame, Belle's gaze fixed on that doorway. The sitting room within was nearly full dark, with only a single candle upon the hearth's mantel. What sort of man sat in the darkness? Not a normal one, that much was certain.

Squinting, she peered into the chamber, trying to sort shadow from shape. A subtle gleam shone out from behind the candle, teased from the two silver cups that stood behind it. Aye, and behind them was a jug, its outline dark and solid. Two small chairs, actually nothing more than the same sort of cushioned, backed stools that Belle now had in her own sitting room, hunkered in the room's center. A single small table stood between them.

With a movement of his arm, Master James invited her to enter. Her heart set to leaping like a hare at the chase. He wanted her to go first? Nay, she couldn't, she just couldn't.

The steward's face softened, the corners of his mouth lifting in an encouraging smile. "Madame, pray enter," he said gently.

A sigh filled Belle at his words. Lord, but what a goose she was! She wasn't alone. Master James would be beside her through the whole interview.

Her heart bolstered, she shot him a grateful look and strode into the room. A third chair was positioned in the corner, a seat more massive than the others, with a tall back meant to protect the occupant from drafts. Belle tensed, more sensing than seeing the man who sat in its shadowy depths.

Master James and Sir Edward entered behind her, then the door closed. Heralded by the glow from his candles, Graceton's steward started across the room. As he came abreast of Belle, the light reached into the chair in the corner.

The man seated within it came to vibrant life. His attire was red, his stockings white, his shoes black. Belle's dread returned full force. There was nothing to see of his features or his hair. It was a black velvet mask, not unlike the sort executioners wore, that covered his head, reaching well below his chin. Two holes cut in the mask marked where his eyes should have been, while a slit cut across it for his mouth. Instantly, her mind began supplying all the possible disfigurements that might lie hidden beneath his disguise.

Master James set his branch of candles on the hearth near the cups. There was a glint behind the mask's eye slits. Belle breathed in relief. At least the squire did have eyes. She frowned a little, trying to peer past his velvet shield to discern his eye color.

Their gazes met. The squire's mask shifted on his face a little as his eyes narrowed. Belle flinched. Her gaze leapt to a spot above his head. May the Lord save her, but she'd been staring at the squire while he watched her do it!

Mortified by her rudeness, she dropped into a deep curtsy. "I am pleased to make your acquaintance, Squire Hollier," she managed, her voice trembling almost as badly as her knees.

"And I yours, Lady Purfoy."

It took Belle a moment to decipher his words. Not only was his pronunciation slurred, his voice was without inflection. Was this because of his disability, or had she insulted him?

Master James came to stand beside his employer's chair. "My lady, would you care to sit?" he offered.

"If the squire wills," she whispered, not wishing to do her new husband any further insult.

"I do indeed," the squire seconded.

Belle turned to the two chairs at the room's center. Arranged to face the corner, they sat just inside the circle of light thrown by the candles. The rustle of her skirts seemed overly loud in the silent room as she claimed the one farthest from her husband. As she settled onto its cushion, she glanced behind her for Sir Edward.

The knight still stood at the door. It was a moment before she realized he expected Squire Hollier to rise and offer the bow due him both as a knight and the queen's proxy. Aye, and it wasn't patience that bade him wait. With his chin lifted to an aggressive angle, affront nigh on wafted from him.

It was a childhood spent in a household of schemers and liars that came to Belle's rescue here. She was accustomed to being a mouse in the corner, adept at disappearing into insignificance after catching even the nuance of threat in a glance. It served her well, as long as the rancor wasn't aimed at her. Belle turned her gaze to the room's empty hearth and listened to the distant shouts and calls rising from the hall as the servants gathered for the meal.

Still no one spoke. She glanced at the squire. He watched the knight, or rather his masked face was aimed in that direction. If there was nothing to read in the subtle glint of the eyes behind his disguise, his gloved hands lay easily on the chair's arms. There was something in the way he held himself in the chair that spoke of innate confidence.

Pity woke in her. He was painfully thin. Plain she was, but at least she wasn't trapped in a weak body. A touch of outrage followed. Surely, Sir Edward didn't expect an invalid to rise and offer him this customary courtesy.

Long after the quiet had stretched into uncomfortable territory, the squire said, "Welcome to Graceton, Sir Edward. My pardon, but I fear I cannot rise and greet you as another might."

As she puzzled out his words, Master James sent his employer a sharp glance and shifted uneasily beside the chair. This teased curiosity out from beneath her nervousness; had Master James been expecting his employer to stand?

"Then you must not rise," Sir Edward said, his tone far more gracious than Belle had expected. The knight started across the room. Above the rustle of his expensive attire Belle caught the faint jingle of his gold-tipped ribbons. He halted near the empty chair to offer a brief bow.

"I'll bid you well met, Squire Hollier, and call us greeted. Now that the formalities have been addressed, shall we repair to the hall and discuss the upcoming ceremony over the meal?"

"Would that I could," the squire said with a subtle shake of his masked head. "Unfortunately, my disability makes it impossible for me to leave my chambers. If there's aught to discuss, we must do it here. Please, sit and take your ease whilst we speak." A faint air of amusement seemed to surround the squire.

Sir Edward sank into the empty chair. "As you will." His words were nearly a growl. It was quite the battle they fought between them, their weapons words instead of swords.

"Might I offer you drink?" the squire asked.

Even before the words were out of his mouth, Master James turned to the hearth. The steward filled the two waiting cups from the jug. Belle took hers and sipped. It was a good wine, not in the least thick or bitter.

Sir Edward shot her a sharp glance. "Do you lift your cup, my lady, without offering to Her Majesty's health?" he chided.

Choking, Belle nearly fumbled her cup in her haste to bring it from her mouth. Sir Edward raised his, then paused. "But what of you, Squire? Will you not also drink to Her Grace?" Again, that dangerous intensity filled his expression as he tested his host's loyalty.

Squire Hollier's shoulders rose in a helpless shrug. "Would that I could, but this," he lifted his gloved hand to point to his mask, "makes it impossible. Nonetheless, if you will drink for me, I'll supply the words. To our Gloriana. May she reign forever."

Belle glanced at Sir Edward, seeking some hint as to what she should next do. His face like unto a thundercloud, the knight raised his cup to his lips. In relief, Belle did the same, drinking deeply. As the wine hit her empty stomach, she discovered its smoothness hid a surprising potency.

"Now, as to this wedding," the squire said in blunt introduction of the subject she least wanted to discuss. "Has Her Majesty sent me any instructions?" he asked of Elizabeth's proxy.

Belle gulped another mouthful of wine. Heaven keep her. He would demand a Catholic service. What then? Would she be strong enough to play out the lie she'd told Sir Edward and bow her head in obedience to her husband and his religion?

Sir Edward looked at Belle. The resentment that burned in his gaze said he was no happier discussing this issue in her presence than she was to hear about it in his. He set his cup on the table between them.

"Her Grace understands you are an invalid and a man desirous of his privacy," the knight began, only to have his host interrupt.

"That is kind of her. Then she'd have no objection to my steward once more serving as my proxy for the wedding ceremony?"

Sir Edward's jaw tightened. Belle now knew him well enough to read his reactions and expressions. The resentment that filled his face said the queen had told her official witness the squire could use a proxy for the ceremony.

"It will serve," the knight said harshly. "However, Her Grace does insist on the union's immediate consummation. In this and as head of all families in our fair country, she takes up the role of your long-departed father, who would have commanded the same from you."

This won a nod from the squire. "I am content to do as

duty requires."

"As to the ceremony and celebration," the knight continued, "Her Grace doesn't ask that you invite outsiders, only that all is done in a manner that befits your station."

"Rightly so," the squire replied with a nod, his strange voice untouched with anger, when there'd been no mistaking the couched insult in Sir Edward's words. "Has she any expectations as to when the rite should take place?"

"Within two months," his opponent replied, sharpness creeping into his gaze as he watched the masked man.

Again, Squire Hollier nodded, but now his gloved fingers tightened on the chair's arms. "Acceptable. However, we now sit upon the brink of summer becoming autumn. I daresay my brother has told you that the coming of colder, wetter weather wreaks havoc with my health. Against the possibility of forthcoming illness, it would be best if we hurried the ceremony. As I see it, the only thing that holds us back is the calling of our banns."

He paused, his head moving as if he glanced from the knight to Belle. "If they are called first on Sunday next, a week from the morrow, then again a week hence as custom requires, we can celebrate our nuptials in a month. Since Lady Purfoy is an acknowledged widow and all the county knows why I've never wed, I doubt we need fret over anyone raising a protest."

Worry deepened until it gnawed at Belle's bones. May the Lord save her. In one month she was going to have to kneel before a Catholic priest and make a mockery of everything she believed. Lifting her cup to her lips, she swallowed another hasty mouthful of wine.

Beside her, Sir Edward blinked. "So soon?"

The squire's shoulders slumped. "Ah, I see Her Grace expects us to wait the full two months. Do you think it would be wrong of me to send her a message explaining my reasons for desiring a speedier ceremony?" Despite his disappointed posture, there was something about his words that suggested a smile.

Sir Edward started. "Nay, that won't be necessary." He held up a hand as if to stop a messenger from leaving the room. "A month is acceptable."

"As for the ceremony itself," his host went on, "I had in mind to use the one in Her Majesty's prayer book."

The silence that followed these words was so deep Belle could hear the hiss and snap of the candle flames as they ate up their wicks. She stared at her new husband in disbelief. Behind him, Master James's eyes were wide, his mouth ajar. For some reason, his surprise made her believe the offer genuine.

The squire wanted a Protestant ceremony! She wouldn't have to blaspheme. In her elation, Belle raised her cup and finished the contents all the way to the dregs.

Beside her, Sir Edward's ribbons rattled as he shifted forward in his chair. His face was slack as he stared at the masked man. "I beg your pardon?"

"I am content to use the English service to seal this union," the squire repeated more slowly this time, as if assuming the knight hadn't been able to decipher his words.

Sir Edward glanced from Graceton's steward to its master. His eyes narrowed as two small spots of color burned high upon his cheekbones. "I am certain Her Majesty will be overjoyed to hear of her subject's unexpected conversion."

Squire Hollier held up a gloved hand. "You mistake me. There has been no conversion. I am and will always be committed to the Catholic faith. However, it's to honor Her Grace that I choose to marry in the church her royal father founded."

As Belle again heard these miraculous words, they fair lifted her from her chair. She flew to kneel before her husband. "Oh, your worship," she cried, certain she was grinning from ear to ear. "How kind you are to offer this. I daren't speak for Her Majesty, but I am greatly honored by your sacrifice."

She was close enough to see his eyes beneath his mask. They were green. He studied her face for a moment, then glanced at his steward. When he again looked at her, there was new warmth in his gaze.

"Madame, it is my pleasure to offer it to you," he said. "Since you and I are content with these arrangements, all that remains is to make Her Majesty's proxy as easy as we.

All Belle's fear died. This was no monster; this was a man like any other, perhaps more decent than most, save that he had some reason to disguise his features.

Still floating in elation, she came to her feet, then turned. Sir Edward was glaring at her, his teeth clenched so hard that a muscle worked along his jaw. Those heated spots on his cheeks had spread until his face was flushed with blood.

Belle froze. Oh Lord, he was angry at her. But why? What reason could he have to object?

The knight's gaze slipped from her to the squire. "If Lady Purfoy is content, so am I," he said, his voice hard.

Belle sighed in relief and returned to her chair. "It's settled, then," she murmured to herself.

"Not quite," Sir Edward said, startling Belle, for she hadn't realized he'd overheard her. "Where will this ceremony take place?" he demanded of his host.

"The squire prefers to use the village church," Master James replied for his master.

"What? You'd not use your own chapel?" Scorn filled Sir Edward's voice.

Belle's eyes narrowed. She knew full well what the knight intended. He meant to trade upon the queen's authority to strip Squire Hollier's private chapel of whatever illegal Catholic items it might hold. She turned in her chair to look at the knight.

"I am astounded at you, Sir Edward. Squire Hollier has been naught but generous and honest with us this evening. I'm certain if there were a chapel we might use within the house, he would say as much."

The instant the words were out, she gasped, unable to believe how she'd said them. Pressing her fingers to her lips to keep anything else untoward from escaping, she glanced at the men in the room. If there was nothing to be discerned in Squire Hollier's mask, Master James was staring at her, his face alive with astonishment. Shame flickered in Sir Edward's eyes, followed by rage over the insult she'd done him in the presence of other men.

Belle folded her hands in her lap and bowed her head. This was what came of a woman who dared to meddle in the affairs of men. "I beg your pardon, Sir Edward," she whispered, neither expecting nor receiving a reply from him.

Across the room, Squire Hollier shifted in his chair. "I am flattered you should regard me so highly in so short a time, Lady Purfoy. Pray, Sir Edward, give the lady the forgiveness she craves, for I see she is much distressed at the trouble her words have caused."

Belle's head rose. Blinking back tears, she let a tremulous smile bend her lips. It was his protection the squire extended to her with these words. Squire Hollier was just as kind as his steward.

"But of course she has my pardon," Sir Edward managed to grind out.

"As for the village church," Squire Hollier went on, "it has served my ancestors for generations, ever since they moved out of the old keep. Tradition demands it serve for this wedding."

He leaned back in his chair, the picture of relaxation. "Now that we are all resolved, I will pass all responsibility for the arranging of this event to Master Wyatt. Should you have any other requirements, please inform him and he'll carry your messages to me. Please, go and enjoy your dinner."

Belle caught back a laugh. Not only was the squire dismissing the knight, a man his superior in rank, he was making it clear he had no intention of again meeting the queen's proxy face-to-face. Of course, he traded on the fact that once the wedding was done, he'd be the knight's better.

Against so bold a move, the hostility drained from Sir Edward's face, leaving a dazed expression in its place. "Dare I say I'm astonished at your flexibility. When I arrived this morn at Graceton I had no idea our business would be so easily completed."

The squire spread his hands wide. "For that you must thank Her Grace. Now that she's shown me I was wrong to think myself unfit to wed, I'm eager to rectify the situation."

Again, Squire Hollier's head moved as he glanced between Belle and the knight. "If you'll excuse me. I fear our meeting has left me overtired and longing for my bed."

A battle raged on Sir Edward's face. As little as he liked being dismissed, only a boor would persist against the squire's excuse. He came to his feet, his shoulders stiff, his back pike-straight. It was with obvious effort that he affected the customary bow.

"I bid you good evening, then, Squire Hollier. You can be assured that word of your cooperation will soon reach Her Grace's ears." This sounded more like a threat than reassurance.

As the knight turned to leave, Belle rose from her chair. To her surprise, her head swam a little. It seemed the wine had been much more potent than she'd thought.

"Stay a moment, Lady Purfoy," the squire bade her before she could move, then looked toward Master James. "Master Wyatt, would you fetch Tom for me as you escort Sir Edward to the hall?"

Surprise touched his steward's face. Belle stifled her giggle. Apparently, Master James wasn't accustomed to being sent on such menial errands. "As you will, your worship," the steward said with a stiff bow.

Taking the single candle from the hearth, Master James joined Sir Edward. As they stepped into the darkened gallery, the door shut behind them, leaving Belle alone with the man she'd feared as a monster only moments ago. Belle smiled at the masked man in his chair. It was truly miraculous that she could be so completely at ease in so short a time.

"Pray, sit," her new husband told her.

"As you will," she replied, dropping into Sir Edward's empty chair, content to use the nearer seat this time.

"Your journey to Graceton was without event?" It was a mundane question, meant to initiate conversation.

"It was." Once again, that giggle bubbled up in her, nearly escaping this time. She cleared it from her throat.

"I cannot tell you how glad I am to be out of that wagon. It's nearly a month we spent in it, traveling first to Richmond, then coming here. Indeed, by journey's end our traveling attire was so filthy, my maid says the skirts stood on their own when she took them down to the laundry."

Belle stifled a groan. Lord, but the wine was making her babble like a goose. She hoped the squire didn't notice, for fear he'd think her a sot.

Something like unto a chuckle rasped from Squire Hollier. "Is that so? Well, our laundresses are capable. Your garments will be returned as good as new. And how do you find your apartment'?"

Although a part of her knew this was but another customary question, all the joy she'd known upon entering her suite returned. "My apartment is magnificent, your worship. Can you believe it! There's a hearth in my bedchamber," she told him, forgetting that as master of the house, he was likely to know this already.

In her previous home, only Sir William's bedchamber had its own hearth.

"John and Watt found cots for my servants and chairs for the sitting room," she went on, yet adrift in thoughts of a warm chamber on a cold winter's morn. "There's even a small table, to be used when we wish to dine in our chamber. I must say, we were all terribly surprised by their kindness, especially after the welcome we received upon arrival," she finished with a laugh, only to catch back her amusement as she realized her error.

Would she never learn to be more circumspect? Belle bowed her head. "Pardon, your worship. I meant no ill toward your house or servants. Nor did I think to ask your permission to use the items your footmen found for me."

"No insult taken," the squire replied. "I know the servants were less than friendly in their greeting this morn. Take heart. Time will accustom them to you. As for your apartment, I expect you to be comfortable. If there is anything you need for your chambers Watt and John cannot find in my storerooms, pray speak to Master Wyatt about procuring it for you."

So long a speech seemed to strain him, for he paused to cough. The sound was deep, as if his lungs ached. Concern rushed through Belle, the emotion strong enough to again drive her across the room to kneel before him.

"You have told Sir Edward that you fear coming illness, your worship, but in that cough I hear that you already ail. I have a good hand with medicines and cures. It would please me well to tend you."

There was silence for a moment as he studied her through the slits in his mask, his green eyes filled with questions. Belle's heart gave a quirk. Here it was, the moment he decided if he would accept her only as his wife in name or make theirs a true marriage. Although a part of her trembled at the thought of his rejection, Belle sat back on her heels and let him stare as he would.

The lift of his brows made the mask shift slightly on his face. "You are kind to offer, but my present condition is the same as it's been for the past twenty years. I fear there's naught to be done for it that hasn't already been tried. As for tonics and tisanes, I have a healer who delights in forcing all manner of odd concoctions down my throat. I beg you to take no insult if I refuse. I fear I'm not willing to let another set of foul brews past my lips."

It was a rejection, but one so carefully done that she could only smile. There was no room in his life for her; theirs would be a marriage of policy rather than heart. Indeed, as private a man as he was, it wouldn't surprise her if she saw him no more after their wedding night.

Because he'd already given her far more than she'd ever expected, it was easy to honor his wishes. Belle nodded. "Know that the offer stands," she replied as she came to her feet, "should you change your mind."

"I shall take your words to heart," he replied, a smile coming to life in his eyes.

Again, he strove to be kind when he could have simply dismissed her. Belle's need to offer something in return expanded beyond the brewing of teas to the threat posed by Sir Edward. "Your worship, might I confide in you?"

Surprise widened his gaze. "But of course."

"As much as I regret speaking ill of the queen's proxy," Belle said, lacing her fingers before her as if in prayer, "I fear I must. Sir Edward has asked me to pry into your affairs on his behalf, something I've most vehemently refused him. Please, take heed. Where he's asked one and been denied, he may well seek another." Peace flowed over Belle as she fell silent. If what she offered wasn't the equal of all the gifts he'd given her this evening, at least it was something.

Another rasping cough wracked her new husband. "My

lady, I am indebted to you for the warning."

Behind Belle, the door groaned quietly as it opened. The squire glanced over her shoulder. "Ah, here is Master Wyatt and Tom," he said. "Go now, my lady, and make merry where I cannot."

Belle curtsied deeply. "Do you know, I think I shall," she said, straightening with a smile. "Good night, Squire Hollier."

It was with a girl's light step that she crossed the room to join Tom and Master James at the door.

Chapter Twelve

❧

As the lady crossed the room, Jamie leaned his head near to Tom. "Show her to the hall for me, will you?" he whispered. "I need five minutes alone here."

Knowing full well this wasn't what Graceton's master expected, Tom shot a questioning glance at his own master, then shrugged. "Aye, Master James."

His hand on the latch, Jamie waited until Lady Purfoy and Tom left the room, then shut the door behind them. It was only by the most stringent control that he managed not to slam it. When it was closed, he whirled on Nick.

"What in God's name do you think you're doing?" he demanded. "You were fair goading Sir Edward along every step in that discussion!" Never mind that Jamie himself had done the same to the man at court. If Sir Edward called him out, he could give a good account of himself. Not so Nick.

"Was I?" Nick asked in mock innocence as he removed his mask. Running his fingers through his hair to straighten it, he shot Jamie a glance along with what passed for a cheeky grin in him. "I hadn't noticed."

This only drove Jamie's worry higher. "And what in Satan's hell is this nonsense about a Protestant wedding? Not only is that heresy to you, your faith claims all such marriages are illegal."

Triumph filled Nick's gaze. "Why should my Protestant queen care about making this union legal to a pope she doesn't recognize? Nay, if Elizabeth wishes me to wed then it's only right we use this country's unique service. Besides, is this not the way to disarm most, if not all, of the traps yon knight might lay?"

Jamie glared at Nick. All it wrung from Nick was a pleased and rasping chuckle. Graceton's master rose from his chair, the strength in his legs miraculously restored.

"And what is this about being so feeble you cannot walk?" Jamie demanded.

"It suits my purpose to have the man think me an invalid," Nick replied, then shot his steward a chiding look. "You shouldn't be here. Get you to the hall, Jamie, and entertain my guests. I need time to think and pray. This evening's been very informative. There's much for me to share with my heavenly Father."

Frustration made Jamie's fists clench. "I went running like a footman for you once, but you'll not find me so easily dismissed when there's no one else about. I demand you tell me what it is you plan."

"Trust me," was all Nick said.

"How," Jamie pleaded, "when from what I've seen you're playing into the knight's hands?"

Rather than offer a word to soothe his steward, Nick walked to the table between the pair of chairs. Catching the cup Lady Purfoy had used between his hands, he tilted it until he could see into its bowl. A snort of laughter left him as he set it back onto the table, then he turned to look at his steward.

"You're wrong to worry over Lady Purfoy, you know.

She told me Sir Edward has tried to make her part of his plot and that she refused him, just as you suspected."

As he spoke of his betrothed wife, amused pleasure came to life in Nick's gaze. A dark emotion shot through Jamie. He didn't want Nick to think fondly of Lady Purfoy. This was just uncomfortable enough to set his teeth on edge. The lady was Nick's wife, not his.

The need to disguise his reaction, as much from himself as Nick, put harsh words on Jamie's lips. "Always so quick to trust. It wouldn't hurt you to be at least a little cautious."

Nick's head tilted to the side as if that angle might aid him in his study of his steward. "I've never before seen you ignore the obvious. Indeed, I didn't even know you were capable of it. What is it about this particular woman that should make you do this?"

With Nick's question, the sensation of holding Lady Purfoy close filled Jamie. Although nearly two weeks had passed, he could still feel the smooth skin of her brow against his jaw and the lift of her breast against his chest. He caught a deep breath, only to discover the air in his sitting room yet held traces of her perfume.

Desperate to destroy the memory, Jamie spewed the first words that came to lips. "It's her mother. We've no idea how much she learned at that noble bitch's knee. Lady Montmercy uses the pretense of innocence to conceal a nature that makes a viper look like a swaddling babe."

Astonishment widened Nick's gaze. "Jamie, this isn't like you. If you judged all folk by their relatives, I'd be my grandsire and you, your mother. All the proof I need of the lady's character lies in the way she came to my defense when Sir Edward sought access to Graceton's chapel."

It had been all the proof Jamie had needed, as well. Lady Purfoy was every bit the innocent she seemed. Panic worsened. If he couldn't stop Nick from this probing, in another moment his employer would realize his steward was trapped in a hopeless longing for his new wife. This time, he conjured up a bald-faced lie to be his shield.

"And I say that all we saw in her this evening was well-practiced mummery. I won't leave you vulnerable to her wiles." Jamie hid his grimace. It sounded ridiculous, even to his own ears.

Beneath his scarred flesh, Nick's jaw tightened. "Well then, if you're so certain she means to betray me, what say we make us a trap, baiting it with a piece of false information. You say you'll watch her correspondence. I wonder how long it'll take for our tidbit to find its way into her letters?"

"So be it," Jamie agreed without thinking. All he wanted was to escape.

Nick blinked in surprise. Irritation flared in Jamie as he recognized the message: Nick didn't want to go forward with this unnecessary and somewhat dishonorable plan. Aye, but neither did Nick wish to admit he'd been trying to pry into his steward's emotions.

Jamie's brows lowered in refusal. Not this time. Why should he forgive Nick for this, when his employer wouldn't even tell him what it was he planned in this marriage?

Since neither of them was willing to retreat, there was nowhere to go but forward. "Have you any suggestions as to the bait?" Graceton's master asked.

"Sir Edward looks for proof of your disloyalty, so let's give him something that's an obvious lie. I shall leave a note in my office stating that your cannon has been sent to Northumberland to aid in his rebellion."

"But I've sent my only cannon to Elizabeth," Nick replied swiftly. "The queen knows that."

"Exactly," Jamie retorted. "However, I doubt Sir Edward does. That way, if by some untoward chance I should miss this tidbit as the lady sends it on to court, it can do you no harm."

Nick's nod was brusque. "If that's settled, go and eat. Enjoy the evening as best you can, given that you're intent on abhorring the company. And speed Tom on his way back here. I want out of this." He plucked at his doublet.

Now that Jamie had a barricade in place, the need to show his friend that no harm was done woke. "Poor Tom," he said in an old and familiar complaint. "Serving two masters is more than any man should have to bear. You should get your own servant to tend to your needs."

Nick's smile returned. "Why, when I can use yours? Besides, Tom has no complaints, not when I'm filling his palm with silver for serving me where you and Cecily usually do. He's greedy enough for the coins, since they move his wedding day that much closer."

Shock hit Jamie like a blow. "Wedding day? Tom is to marry?"

Nick laughed until he coughed. Catching his breath, he came to lay a hand on his steward's shoulder. "You're a good man, Jamie, but you really must learn there's more to the world than what you let yourself see of it. Now, go. I truly do ache for my bed."

Chapter Thirteen

❦

Blinking herself into alertness, Belle drifted up out of her dreams, then grimaced. Peg's snores were nigh on rattling the wall between them. At last, the maid gave a great snort. Silence followed. With a quiet laugh, Belle rolled over and sighed. Lord, but it was heaven to be sleeping on her own mattress once again.

Because the night was so warm and the room stuffy, she'd not only opened her windows before retiring, she'd left the bed curtains tied to their posts. Now, waiting for sleep to retake her, she let her gaze roam over her new living quarters. The wall across from her was a rolling landscape of grays and blacks as shadows played across the design carved into the paneling. At its center was her precious hearth, its mouth a gentle black arch. The brass firedogs rising from its brick floor were but a muted gleam in the night. The white plastered mantel above it was painted a silvery gray by what moonlight filled the chamber.

Not a breath of air stirred. Uncomfortable, Belle kicked her coverlet all the way down to her feet, then removed her nightcap in the hopes of finding some relief. When that didn't help, she pulled her loosened hair over her shoulder to bare her nape.

Yawning, she let her thoughts drift back to this evening's

meal. The food had been rich, with at least three dishes in each course. As for the wine, she cringed with remembered shame over her behavior whilst meeting Squire Hollier. That experience had been embarrassment enough to make her sip at but a single cup for the rest of the night.

Since the dinner's intent was to display her to the residents of Graceton Castle, she'd sat at the hall's head. It wasn't an experience she wanted to repeat, nor would she need to, not until the wedding. From now on, her meals could be taken in the parlor's privacy.

Unlike other betrothal dinners, her husband hadn't been at her side to introduce her to the servants. Instead, Master James had once more acted as his employer's proxy. A sigh escaped Belle. It had been hard enough to think of herself as Squire Hollier's wife when Master James stood with her before Richmond's chaplain to recite his employer's vows. The task was even more difficult now that she knew she was to be wife in name only.

It was a shame Master James wasn't to be her husband. A tiny smile crept over her mouth. As near as she could calculate, he had all the qualities she required of a life companion.

Flickers of desire shot through her. She squashed them. Even if Squire Hollier didn't want her, their vows made her just as married to him as any cherished wife would be. Adultery was adultery, no matter how pretty the face you put upon it. Shifting on the mattress, she turned her attention to Brigit's behavior tonight.

Because Graceton Castle had neither chamberlain nor ushers, either position usually manned by gentlemen with whom Brigit might sit, there was nowhere appropriate for her except at the high table. With two men and two women at that table, it was only natural they'd be placed as couples. This left Brigit sharing a bench with Sir Edward.

At first, Belle hadn't been concerned. After all, the governess swore hatred for the knight because of how he'd treated Richard. Moreover, Sir Edward had been surly and curt at the evening's start. But as the night progressed, his mood seemed to soften. By the middle of the meal, he and Brigit were conversing. This progressed to the trading of witticisms and open laughter. By the meal's end, Brigit was obviously and deeply smitten.

Belle's heart twisted. Sir Edward was a very handsome man. Tonight proved that he could be as charming as he was good-looking. Then again, judging by Brigit's behavior this evening, Sir Edward might not be the one doing the seducing.

Ach, but what could Belle do save most sternly warn Brigit against the knight? Failure nipped at Belle. She simply didn't know what else to do with the girl. More and more, it was beginning to seem that she wasn't the sort of mistress a woman of Brigit's spirit needed.

A tendril of air whispered in through the windows. Overhead, the curtain rings, tiny ebony circles on an even darker pole, shifted with a gentle clack of wood against wood. Deep in the pit of her stomach, something pulled. The sensation was so odd, Belle put a hand to her midsection. As her stomach tension eased, yet another breath of air sighed into the room, this one cooler still.

Sitting up, Belle reached toward her knees to grab her coverlet. With the bed curtains open, she could see beyond the bed's end to the windows. She frowned. Until this moment, she hadn't realized air could look heavy, but that was how it appeared in the casement. As she watched, tendrils seemed to swirl and shift, congealing into a thick darkness.

Another puff of air hit Belle, this one so icy it raised gooseflesh on her arms. She caught a sharp breath. Well now, the weather was turning indeed.

As she slipped from her bed to close the windows, she caught the distant sound of weeping. Thinking it was Lucy, awake in the night and frightened at finding herself alone in a strange room, Belle turned toward the door, only to stop. It wasn't a child she heard, but a woman, sobbing as if her heart were broken. Wondering how any of the servants could be so distressed after such a pleasant evening, she turned back into her room and froze, her heart in her throat.

Misty white fingers of air swirled and drifted before the open windows. Rooted to the spot, Belle watched them coalesce into a woman's form. The sound of sobbing grew louder. A face appeared upon the apparition's shoulders. Where the squire's black mask had concealed all but his eyes, all of the ghostly woman's face was revealed except her eyes, which were naught but black spaces.

Belle's heart banged in her chest. She wanted to run, but not a single muscle moved. A scream filled her throat. With her jaw locked tight, all that escaped was a tiny, panicked squeal.

As if it heard, the spirit's head turned, scanning the room with its sightless eyes. Their gazes met, or would have met, if those sockets hadn't been empty. Mouth agape, Belle stared into those bottomless, blackened holes.

God save her, but this couldn't be happening! Paralysis shattered. Belle whirled. It was like running n a dream, her arms and legs moving as if through mud. It took an eternity to reach the door. Her fingers clawed at the wood as she sought the latch. At last it opened.

Gulping in air, she shot out of her bedchamber and across the sitting room. The outer door gave way with a quiet shriek. It was more sound than Belle could make. Gasping and shivering, she leapt out into the safety of the gallery.

❦

A door opened and closed. A chill gust of air followed, moving through Jamie's office with enough force to make the flames of his candles jig. He leaned back in his chair and stretched, watching the wild dance of shadows on the stone wall across from him. God be praised, Cecily had finally arrived.

His absence from Graceton had dimmed his memory of how miserable this chamber could be. The tower had its origins in a more violent time, when windows were never more than narrow slits. In the deepest of winter, Jamie cursed those tiny openings for being without glass, while for these few humid weeks of August, he cursed them for not being big enough to admit even a hint of the river's fresh breath.

More than ready to be done with his day, he came to his feet and straightened the papers on his desk. Most of this evening had been consumed in listing all the families to whom announcements of Nick's wedding would be sent. Although Nick was a recluse and his title in abeyance, the Holliers were not an insignificant family. Even if none of the notified would attend the ceremony, the gifts they'd send would both celebrate the event and renew their connection to Nick and his name.

As Jamie set the list aside, his gaze shifted to that idiotic note about the cannon. It taunted him for the fool he was. He should have just told Nick what he wanted to know. Unable to bear looking at proof of his own idiocy, he laid the sheaf of papers in his hand atop it.

Because this was home and there was no need for formality, he'd shed his doublet directly after the meal, leaving it hanging over the back of his chair. Now, as he reached for the discarded garment, he paused. It was a trick of the spiraling stairway that intensified the sounds made within it. If Cecily were climbing the steps, he should have heard every footfall, every scrape of hardened leather on stone. Not a sound emanated from the stairwell outside his office's open door.

He strode out onto the landing. Nothing disturbed the silence. If not Cecily, then who?

Suspicion prickled up his spine. He looked to the gallery door. Surely, Sir Edward wouldn't be so bold as to be prying on this, his first evening in the house.

Crossing the landing, he gently cracked the door. There was no illumination in the gallery, save for what moonlight streamed in through its windows. At the nearest oriel stood a shadowy woman dressed in white, her head bent as if in prayer. Born out of Mistress Miller's tale this morn, the possibility that he was at last seeing the ghost flickered through Jamie.

He rolled his eyes at such a thought. He was more exhausted than he thought if he was paying heed to her nonsense. More likely that this was one of the newcomers suffering from sleeplessness. Since the last thing he needed was for any of Lady Purfoy's party to see Cecily on her way to Nick's chamber, whoever it was would have to be shooed back to bed and right quickly.

Throwing open the door, he stepped out into the gallery. The woman whirled toward him with what sounded like a frightened gasp. Light from his office streamed past him to catch her in its muted glow. It found pale gold in the curling waves of hair that fell to her hips. It was Lady Purfoy.

Jamie caught his breath. The lady wore no bed robe atop her nightshirt. There was light enough to show him how that garment's thin fabric clung to her full breasts. His body tensed in the sudden longing to feel them in his hands.

"Oh," Nick's wife whispered in recognition.

Her single word brought Jamie's gaze back to her face, which by all rights it should never have left. Lady Purfoy's brow was creased, her eyes wide. Before he had a chance to ask her what she was doing in the gallery in the middle of the night, she launched herself at him. His breath huffed out as he caught her against his chest. Hands on her hips, he staggered back a step, struggling to hold them both upright. She latched her arms around his neck and buried her face into his shoulder.

The scent of her soap and roses filled his every breath. Her hair felt like silk where it tumbled over his arms. God help him, but all that lay between his flesh and hers was the fabric of two shirts. Her glorious breasts were touching his chest as she panted rapidly. The sensation was marvelous.

He swallowed. Even as his conscience warned that

he mustn't, his arms pressed her closer still. Her breasts flattened against his chest, and he could feel their every detail on his skin. Searing heat shot through him. His eyes closed.

Again, she shuddered against him. The movement was both heaven and hell rolled into one. Desire exploded to life, too huge to be denied. His head bent, his lips touching the curve of her neck.

Her skin was soft and sweet under his mouth. He raced a line of kisses down the length of her throat, then splayed a hand over the gentle roundness of her hip. With a careful nudge, he shifted her until her womanhood rested against his shaft.

As she felt the strength of his desire for her, she gave a quiet gasp. Her head lifted from his shoulder, her hands loosened at his nape. She began to straighten, her arms lowering as if to push him away.

Jamie frowned. Nay, he wouldn't allow it. She was his. Hadn't he spoken the words that made it so?

Closing his arms about her, he caught her lips with his, intent on destroying her resistance. The feel of her mouth beneath his was better than he'd imagined. Taunting himself, he plied her lips with tiny kisses, each press of flesh to flesh sending an exquisite wave of need rolling over him.

Her arms relaxed. Sighing against his mouth, her hands slid up to once more clasp behind his nape. As she yielded to him, his ache to own all of her grew until he was filled with it.

Jamie let his kiss deepen until his mouth slashed across hers. She melted into him, every inch of her touching him. All breath left him at the sensation and he lifted his mouth from hers to gasp in wonder.

With a sound of disappointment, she rose on her toes to catch his lips with hers. Lost in passion, Jamie slipped his hands between them to cup her breasts. She arched away from him, giving him room, her very motion begging him to continue. He obliged, fingers taunting and teasing her as he kissed her brow, her eyes, then touched his lips to her cheek.

And tasted the salt of her tears. Shock pierced his lust. She was crying.

Jamie froze. What in all hell was he doing? Forcing himself on Nick's wife, that much was obvious.

His hands opened. He straightened. As if not looking upon her would somehow shield him from the wrong he'd done, he turned his head to the side. With a tiny cry, she leaned against him, her arms tightening around him as she tried to draw him back to her.

Catching her hands in his, he stepped out of her embrace. "Nay, we mustn't," he breathed in mortification.

She jerked as if his words had struck her, and she stumbled back a step or two. There was light enough to show him the misery printed on her features. A quiet hiccough left her, then her face crumpled.

"God save me, what have I done?" she cried softly.

Her words were like a knife in Jamie's gullet. If ever he needed proof of her innocence, here it was. Where her lady mother would have used his lapse to bend him to her will, she meant to carry the weight of both their sins.

Whirling, she fled from him. Jamie watched her go. God forgive him, but he wanted his employer's wife as his own with every fiber of his being. And she wanted him.

There could be no doubt of that, not after their kiss.

Across the gallery, the lady darted back into her apartment. Her door closed with a quiet thud. Jamie stared at that solid panel, his heart aching. If Nick didn't want her, why shouldn't he have her?

His conscience coughed back to life. An honorable man didn't pine to commit adultery with his employer's wife, no matter what the circumstances. Neither did an honorable man allow another to go bearing the blame for what was his error.

The need to apologize for forcing his kiss on her filled him. Striding across the gallery, he lifted a hand to knock, then caught himself. The last thing they needed was her servants witnessing this. But if he entered without knocking, she might scream, thinking he meant to complete her ravishment.

With little hope he'd survive this night with a shred of honor left, he opened the door and followed Nick's wife into her chamber.

Chapter Fourteen

❦

Belle stumbled blindly into her sitting room, her knees trembling so badly she had to stop after a few steps. God save her, but in the aftereffects of that horrid encounter in her bedchamber, whatever it had been, she'd thrown herself at Master James like some common strumpet.

Her eyes closed. Instantly, her mind supplied the image of herself arching in the steward's arms, offering herself to him. She choked in embarrassment. Lord, but she might as well have begged him to touch her breasts! How could she have done something so bold?

How could she not, came the response, when his touch had been more pleasurable than anything she'd ever imagined? Sir William Purfoy's kiss had never made her blood sing in her veins. Nor had the feel of her previous husband's shaft against her body left her throbbing with need.

She hung her head. There was no doubting it. If Master James hadn't stopped her, she'd have committed adultery right on the floor of that lovely gallery. Belle's belief that she was a moral woman dissolved, leaving nothing but tatters in its place.

Behind her, the door opened. Startled, Belle whirled. There was light enough to show her it was Master James.

Oh, Lord, but he'd followed her, wanting more of what

they'd done in the gallery. She didn't know which was worse, the thought of repaying Squire Hollier's kindness with betrayal or that Master James now thought her no better than a whore.

Instinctively, she stepped back from him, only to collide with a floor candelabrum. As the pole tilted, its circular iron foot shifted. The grate of metal on wood was loud in the room's deep quiet.

With a quick step, Master James closed the distance between them. He reached for her. Propriety demanded she scream for Peg. Unfortunately, the rest of her body sighed at his nearness. Between the two, she made no sound.

Rather than embrace her, he caught the pole and steadied it. Then, lifting a finger to his lips, he bade her to silence. There was something in the way he moved that said he didn't intend to finish his seduction. Trapped between shame and desire, all she could do was bury her face in her hands. A tiny sob escaped before she bit her lip to stop it.

"Nay, I am not deserving of your tears," Master James breathed, "not after what I've done."

Stunned, she lifted her head from her hands. "What *you've* done?" she asked.

"Shhh." He touched a finger to her lips in warning. "Softly so. I'd not have your servants witness us as we are now."

The very idea of either Peg or Brigit seeing her with Master James in naught but her nightshirt left Belle too breathless to speak. She managed to nod her assent.

He loosed a relieved breath. "My lady, for whatever my word is worth to you now, I vow you've no need to fear me."

"I don't fear you," she replied just as quietly. Then the words she prayed might in some way mend her error tumbled from her mouth. "I know I've lost your respect. Such is as I deserve, given my actions this night. But I beg you on your honor, speak no word of this to Squire Hollier. He has been kind to me and I'd not repay that kindness by besmirching his name." Tears trembled in her voice.

"Nay, madame," Master James said softly as he took a step toward her. Although he didn't touch her, he bent his head over hers. A moment ago, his closeness had awakened her desire. Now, it was oddly comforting. "I'll not let you hold me blameless when there were two of us in yon gallery. We must share the guilt between us for what happened there."

Startled, Belle raised her head. Instantly, he shifted back until there was a decent distance between them. She studied his face in the moonlight.

"It was I who threw myself into your arms."

"And I who kissed you when you would have pushed me away," he said, bitter amusement staining his words. "Would that I had an excuse to offer, other than to say I was in the throes of some sort of temporary madness. Will you accept my vow that it won't happen again?"

Relief grew. If he wanted to share the blame, he wouldn't be telling Squire Hollier that his new wife was a whore. "I will indeed, Master James."

It wasn't until she heard him catch a swift breath that Belle realized she'd called him by his given name when he hadn't given her leave to do so. Feeling like a bumbling idiot, her cheeks burned with embarrassment.

"Pardon. I mean Master Wyatt. I wouldn't have behaved

so familiarly toward you, except that I was frightened, believing I'd seen the White Lady in my bedchamber."

A hysterical giggle rose in her throat. Not only had she seen the White Lady, but the spirit had seen her. She flinched. Oh, Lord, why had she told him this? She sounded like an ass.

"You cannot be serious," Master James said, his quiet tone disbelieving. "In your bedchamber, you say?" he asked, already striding toward that door.

With no idea how to explain what she'd seen, Belle could only follow him. Once in the doorway, she stared into the chamber she'd thought wondrous this morn. Moonbeams streamed in through the window, cutting through air that was as light and, well, airy as it was supposed to be. There was a welcome coolness to the night, not the bone-chilling cold she'd imagined with her dream-spirit's arrival.

Master James looked at her. "There's nothing here."

"So I see," she said in pained agreement. "I think I but dreamed I saw her." Perhaps her ghostly encounter was nothing but a nightmare, brought on by the strain of this wedding, three weeks of travel and a night of rich food and wine. If the housekeeper's tale had been a fabrication meant to frighten her, it had worked perfectly.

She looked up at him. His white shirt glowed in the moonlight, marking the broad line of his shoulders. He smiled. Traced by darkness, small crinkles appeared at the corners of his eyes.

"I regret the poor welcome you've had this day, my lady. Would that I could have made it better for you."

"It's kind of you to say so," Belle replied, "but then, you

have been kind to me from our very first meeting."

For a long, quiet moment, he studied her in the dimness, then shook his head. A low, bitter laugh left him. "Madame, I fear you have strange ideas about kindness. What say you? I'll accept your excuse and you'll take mine, each of us granting the other the forgiveness we crave. Henceforth, neither of us will ever again mention the incident."

Since there was nothing in all the world Belle wanted more, she nodded. Again, a slow smile touched his mouth. "With that settled, I shall bid you a good night," he said, turning toward the door.

Belle hurried ahead to open it for him. "Thank you again, Master Wyatt," she whispered.

He paused. "Until the morrow, then."

"Until the morrow," she breathed, and closed the panel behind him.

❧

As Lady Purfoy's door closed behind him, Jamie stared at the oriel before him. The sound of his name on her tongue yet resonated through him. Why should something so simple give him so much pleasure?

He turned toward his office and nearly jumped out of his skin. Cecily stood in the doorway between tower and gallery. Arms crossed, she watched him.

"Where have you been, Jamie?" she asked. "I was worried. It's not like you to leave candles burning in your office."

It was his desperate need to hide this night's misadvantage that brought the night's second lie leaping to his lips. "It was the child," he said, striding swiftly from the lady's door to the tower landing. His honor groaned as it suffered yet another puncture. Would that he could heal it by sleeping in the stables, but things had gone too far for so simple a solution.

"What child?" Cecily asked as he passed her to reenter his office.

"Lady Purfoy's daughter, Mistress Lucretia," he said. "She'd wandered out of her apartment. I had to wake the governess to see her tended." In case Cecily might be able to read the truth in his gaze, he busied himself with blowing out all the lamps and candles save one to light their way to his bedchamber.

"Nick said nothing about a child." There was a strange tone in Cecily's voice.

Turning, Jamie said, "I doubt he knows. I don't think I mentioned her to him."

Cecily stared at him, her brow creased, her fingers pressed to her lips. The strange emotion he'd seen on her face this morn again played across her features. Her hands dropped to her sides.

"You should have," she whispered. "You should have told him from the very start."

He shot her a confused frown. "Why? What difference does a child from the lady's previous marriage make?"

Cecily gave a shuddering sigh. "Nick should have an heir."

"Ah," Jamie breathed in understanding. It was proof of Lady Purfoy's fertility that was upsetting Cecily.

Between the time that Cecily and Nick had known each other as children and became lovers as adults, Nick's lady mother had seen Cecily wed to a man in a distant village. While heavy with her second child, an illness had taken Cecily's husband and first babe. Once they were buried, Cecily returned to her mother's home in Graceton's parkland almost dead herself. Despite all of Goody Elwyn's skill, she'd barely been able to save her daughter; the stillborn babe's coming had left Cecily barren.

Jamie opened his mouth, then caught back the words. It would have to be Nick who told his lover that he must not only go through with the wedding but consummate it before witnesses.

"He has his brother," he said instead.

Sorrow deepened in Cecily's eyes. "Aye, but Nick would be a good father. Indeed, a child of his own might even improve his health. It often does in a man. Why didn't I insist he wed this woman, instead of wishing to keep him for myself?" This last was an aching cry and a far more personal complaint than any Cecily had ever before voiced to him.

"Now, that's enough of that," Jamie said, stopping her before she could say more. He was already more intimate with Nick's lover than comfort would bear. He didn't need her confidences.

Herding her out of his office, he turned to close the door. "Why torture yourself with this sort of thinking? You know Nick. Once he's decided what he wants, he gets it. He always has." Only this time, Nick wouldn't get what he wanted. And as right as it was that Cecily should give him up to Lady Purfoy, her heart would still be broken.

He turned on the landing. It was the pain she didn't know she faced that made Jamie catch her hand. He smiled. "Enough fretting when Nick is waiting for you. Shall we?"

Cecily's answering smile was slow and small. "You're a good man, James Wyatt, tolerant and kind. I thank you for that."

Jamie only shook his head. For the second time this night, a woman had called him kind, when he knew well enough that all he was was expedient. "If you say so," he replied, and led her into the gallery.

Chapter Fifteen

❧

A door creaked open. The sound wormed its way through layers of sleep to penetrate Jamie's dream. "Hush."

A lusty image of Lady Purfoy faded as awareness grew.

"I'll be quiet." It was a child's piping whisper. "Is that my stepfather?"

"Nay, that's Jamie, our steward."

With Cecily's voice Jamie catapulted out of sleep. Eyes opening, he came bolt upright on the mattress, thrashing his way free of his tangled bedclothes. There, in the center of his room and gilded by the first hints of a rosy dawn, was a catastrophe in the making.

Cecily had Mistress Lucy by the hand as they crossed to the wall. The child had just arisen, or so said her rumpled nightshirt and the way her golden curls were matted about her lovely face. Her feet were bare, while the bridge of her wee nose was blistered.

"What are you doing?" he cried, even though he knew exactly what Cecily was doing.

Woman and child stopped to look at him. Regret dashed across Cecily's face, but Lady Purfoy's daughter graced him with a lovely smile. "Good morrow, Master Wyatt," she said prettily, even managing a bob. "I'm going to see my stepfather."

"Jamie, I'm so sorry. I didn't mean to wake you," Cecily said. "I found her in the gallery, asking after her stepfather. Since I didn't think you wanted me waking her dam or the lady's servants, I brought her here."

"She can't see Nick, not now," he cried, throwing back his bedclothes as he leapt to the floor. He was too late.

The latch in the hidden door clicked, the panel swinging into Jamie's bedchamber. Nick poked his head through the gap. "Cecily, have you come back for a kiss?" he called to his lover before he realized it wasn't just his steward and his paramour in the chamber.

Mistress Lucy caught one look of the stepfather she so craved and her eyes widened to great circles in her face. Whimpering, she retreated as far as Cecily's grip on her hand would allow. As he read the repulsion on the child's face, pain flickered through Nick's gaze. He started to withdraw into his chamber.

"You stay where you are, Nicholas Hollier." Cecily's command nigh on thundered in the bedchamber.

Jamie stared at her in shock. To the best of his knowledge, she'd never before spoken so boldly to the man who was for all intents and purposes her lord. Even more startling was that Nick did as he was bade despite his rank and discomfort. As if Nick could somehow turn the bulky robe he wore atop his shirt and breeches into a shield, he pulled its lapels until they stood upright about his face.

Crouching, Cecily brought herself to eye level with her rival's child. "This is your stepfather, Mistress Purfoy," she said, her voice low and calm as she stroked a soothing hand down the lass's arm.

"Cecily," Nick said, his fear of rejection roughening his

voice.

Tears threatened. "I want my mama," Lucy moaned, huge eyes fixed on Nick's ruined face.

Tom appeared in the sitting room doorway, hastily tucking his shirt into his breeches; his legs and feet were bare. "Did I hear you call for me, Master James?" he asked, his voice trailing away as he saw the odd group congregated in his master's bedchamber. He glanced across the tableau until his gaze caught on the child, then a fool's grin split his face.

"Why, Mistress Lucy. Come to meet your lord stepfather, have you? How did you find your first night's sleep at Graceton?" He spoke in that tone Jamie so despised, the one all folk seemed to use when they conversed with young children.

Wrenching her gaze from Nick, Mistress Lucy looked upon the servant. Against his friendly visage, fear ebbed from her face. "Good morrow, Tom," she said to him, even remembering to bob.

Yet crouching beside her, Cecily used the distraction to wrap an arm around the child and draw her close. "Come, lass, here is your stepfather."

Mistress Lucy cowered. Nick's jaw stiffened, his eyes narrowed. "Let her go, Cecily," he pleaded. "She doesn't wish to meet me."

With equal pain Cecily looked up at her lover. "But she does, Nick. Give her a chance to become accustomed to you. Please."

Graceton's master sighed. With his nod, Cecily's smile glowed.

Lifting the child in her arms, Cecily came to her feet.

Mistress Lucy yelped as she looked upon the disfigured an. Rearing back, she cried, "What does he have on his face?"

"Naught but scars, little one," Cecily crooned. "Talk to her, Nick," she begged, her voice low. "Tell her what happened to you."

Nick's breath exited in a harsh stream. "When I was but a lad, only a little bigger than you are now, I fell into a fire." He spoke slowly so his words were clear enough for the child to understand.

A battle raged on Lucy's face, the dream of an ideal stepfather warring against the cruel reality of Nick's scars. Curiosity won. Jamie recognized it in the way the child relaxed in Cecily's arms.

"You fell into a fire?" Lucy asked her stepfather, a frown creasing her perfect brow. "Brigit always tells me I must be cautious around a hearth and never let my skirts come near the flame. Did your governess not warn you to be careful?"

Glimmers of amusement took light in Nick's eyes. "I didn't have a governess to warn me. Even if I had, my brother and I were prideful lads and would have ignored her."

"You have a brother? I don't." The child's hand opened, her wee fingers stretching out to touch Nick's cheek. She traced across his brow, then descended one cheek. "Does it hurt?"

"Nay," Nick replied, letting out a shaky breath. "The burns healed long ago."

Lucy touched a fingertip to her own nose. "My mama healed my burn. It hurt yesterday, but not this morn."

A smile filled Nick's eyes. "You are fortunate to have so clever a mama."

The child wrinkled her nose at her stepfather. "It's odd,

the way you talk."

Cecily jiggled her a little, resettling the girl on her hip. "When the burns healed, they left the skin stiff about his mouth."

"Oh." Lucy's brow creased anew as she considered this.

"So, now that my face no longer frightens you, shall we see to the introductions? I am Squire Nicholas Hollier." Nick gave her an abbreviated bow. "And you are?"

Lucy looked at Cecily. "Please, I need to be down to do this rightly."

"Well then, down you go," Cecily said.

With her nightshirt held out from her sides, Lucy dropped into a curtsy so deep and unsteady it took a finger braced upon the floor to hold her upright. As she rose, she stood with her chin high. Jamie fought a smile. In this very formal stance, she was the picture of her infamous grandam.

"I am Mistress Lucretia Purfoy. It is my pleasure to meet you, your worship. And to be your stepdaughter." Courtly illusion crumbled in the next second as she loosed an elated giggle. "I didn't miss a word!"

Nick coughed out a laugh. "Well met, Mistress Lucretia," he replied, clearly pleased with his new kinswoman.

"Nay, you must say Lucy," the child instructed, even daring to point her index finger at her new stepfather. "My papa said you'd call me Lucy, just as he did."

"Lucy it is," Nick agreed.

"Pardon, your worship," Jamie said, his words owning a sharp edge, "but may I remind you that this is my bedchamber and I haven't yet had enough sleep to be civil."

Another laugh rasped from Nick as he shot a glance at

his steward. "You'll have to forgive our Jamie, Lucy. He's a bear in the morning." Then Graceton's master looked at Tom, who yet stood agape in the doorway.

"Will you fetch this lass and me something to break our fasts? Also, let her governess know I'll be keeping her charge for an hour or so, until we've had time to become better acquainted."

"As you will, Lord Nicholas," Tom said. The formal bend of his head belied the fact that his legs were bare.

Nick stretched out one of his ruined hands in invitation to Lucy. "Come then," he said. Lucy closed her fingers around his with no more hesitation than she'd shown in taking Jamie's hand the previous day. "There are scars on your hands, too," she told Nick as he drew her into his chamber through the door in Jamie's wall.

"I knew that," Nick replied with another laugh, then the panel clicked back into place, cutting off whatever else he might have said.

Jamie looked at Cecily. Tears glistened in her eyes. "She thinks Nick will climb trees with her, then teach her to ride his horse," she said, wiping at her cheeks.

"So I've been told," he said with the harsh cock of a brow. "Since we both know Nick won't be doing those things with her, who do you think he'll try to recruit to do it for him?" He slumped against his headboard once again. "He's been a happy recluse all these years. Why must he decide to change that now, when I not only have harvests to get in, but a wedding to plan?"

Amusement sparked golden in her strange eyes. "What, has Graceton no grooms capable of teaching a child to ride? Why, Master Wyatt," she drawled out his name, "if I didn't know you better, I'd think you almost eager to claim the child as your sole responsibility."

"What nonsense," he snapped back, even as her words pierced him. Cecily was right. He had been assuming he alone would be burdened with Lucy. Why?

She laughed. "Nick's right, you *are* a bear in the morning."

With that, she swept from the room, laughter in every twitch of her skirts. Confused and wondering why, Jamie forced himself to lay back upon the mattress. Despite that all hope of regaining sleep's blissful numbness was gone, he closed his eyes. It promised to be another hellacious day at Graceton Castle.

Chapter Sixteen

❧

Not ten minutes later, there was a tap at his open bed-chamber door. Jamie's teeth clenched. Sleep or no sleep, he wasn't ready to face anyone.

"Go away, Tom," he snarled, not needing to look to know who it was.

"My pardon, Master James," his man replied, "but you've a letter. It came by messenger with the dawn." That brought Jamie upright in a hurry. Still wearing naught but his shirt and breeches, Tom crossed the room to hand his master a fold of paper. Jamie flipped it over to read the imprint in the sealing wax.

It was Percy's. Both the timing of the letter and its lack of bulk said this wasn't his uncle's usual report on court doings. Concern woke. If Percy was sending a separate letter, something of great moment had happened at court.

"Sir Edward got his own missive by the same delivery," Tom said. "The note caused quite a stir in the gatehouse. The porter told me Sir Edward started shouting, then his manservant came running in naught but his nightshirt to demand ink and quill."

"Fetch my bed robe for me, will you?" Jamie asked as he rose.

With a nod, Tom padded across the room to retrieve

the garment from its wall peg. He helped Jamie shrug into it, then took a backward step. "If there's nothing else, Master James, I'll go dress now."

Jamie nodded. Tom echoed the movement, then turned for the door. Something twinged deep in Jamie. Where once the simple movement of his head seemed an expedient way to communicate with his servant, now it seemed somehow cold and unfriendly.

Before he could stop them, the words were out of his mouth. "I hear you intend to wed."

Tom whirled. Surprise lifted his brows. A slow grin, as if Jamie's interest somehow pleased him, split his face. "Aye, so I do, Master James. It's been many the year in the planning, with another year or so before I've finally enough saved to see my way to it."

Jamie cleared his throat. "Who is the fortunate woman?" His attempt at conversation sounded stilted, false.

Tom's smile grew. "Moll Wright, the harness maker's youngest. Her da's getting older and could use another hand in his shop, now that it seems her brother won't recover all his strength after an illness last year. Since my own sire was a tanner, I'm not without the skills needed to take his place," he said with a shrug. "But I won't join them until I've coin enough to buy my portion of the shop, free and clear." Pride dimmed into chagrin. "Not that I'm happy to leave you, Master James. You've been as good a master as any man could want. It's just that Moll won't have me if I remain in service."

Jamie's heart sank into a bed of irony. He'd been so self-absorbed, he had no idea Tom thought of leaving him. He forced a smile.

"If that's the case, then I feel fortunate to have kept you as long as I have. Tell your darling I said she's a lucky woman."

Across the room, Tom frowned. His eyes darkened in concern as he studied his master. "Thank you, Master James. Are you feeling well this morn?" he asked.

The question startled Jamie. "Well enough," he replied. "Why?"

"It's nothing," Tom replied.

Once his servant had exited the bedchamber, Jamie turned to the hidden panel. As was his wont, he entered without knocking. Nick and his stepdaughter were at the far side of the room. Lucy was peering from bedchamber to sitting room.

"It's a terrible mess in there," she was saying. "I think it needs a good cleaning."

Jamie's mouth quirked. "What a perceptive child she is," he called in announcement.

Nick shot his steward a narrow look from over his shoulder. "I don't hear her offering to clean it," he said.

In the doorway, Lucy turned with an excited jump. "May I?" she pleaded. "Brigit says I'll be a good wife. I'm already wondrous careful at tending my own things."

Sharp discomfort shot through Nick's gaze at the thought of a child sorting through his precious mess. Jamie smiled and crossed his arms, waiting to see how Nick would slither his way out of this. "Would you like to see the family of swans that nests beneath my window?" he asked his stepdaughter.

The distraction worked. Lucy dashed across the room.

"Where?" she squealed, clambering into the casement.

Rather than answer her, Nick sent his steward a questioning look. Jamie held up the fold of paper. "We've a note from Percy. It arrived only moments ago by royal messenger, along with a message for Sir Edward."

The significance of this wasn't lost on Graceton's master. "What does he write?" he demanded. Although Nick read well enough, he preferred Jamie to scan all correspondence first and sift the vital from the mundane.

Jamie broke the letter's seal. His gaze slipped over the words. "Percy says the queen is in high dudgeon. With tears and much begging for her mercy, the earl of Leicester has admitted to aiding Norfolk in his plot to marry the Scots queen.

"Huh," Jamie said, scanning the passage once again, seeking what Percy hadn't said in its lines. "Why should the duke of Norfolk form an alliance with Leicester, when none of the nobles have any liking for the queen's lover?"

Nick loosed a quiet laugh at that. "If I were to hazard a guess, it would be because the duke believed Leicester could use his influence with Elizabeth to make her accept the marriage. Read on," he commanded. "I'm waiting to hear if there's anything in what he writes that can somehow free me of "—he caught himself and glanced at the child in the window—"this ceremony."

Jamie did as he was bid, paraphrasing Percy's flowery style. It seemed the queen was waiting for the duke of Norfolk to confess that he courted Mary Stuart in defiance of her command, something Norfolk refused to do, even though few courtiers now dared even to be seen with him, for fear of royal rage.

"Good," Nick said. "This means Elizabeth's anger is firmly fixed in another direction, leaving Sir Edward beyond the scope of her vengeance."

"Hardly so," Jamie replied swiftly. "What Percy writes means matters are even worse for Sir Edward and for us. If the courtiers are shunning Norfolk, the most powerful man in our country, how do you wager they'll treat a simple knight like Sir Edward for his involvement in that same plot?"

Understanding flickered through Nick's gaze and all hope of escaping his marriage died. "Fearing he'll lose all connection and favor at court, Sir Edward will redouble his efforts to save himself," he breathed, "much to my detriment. What has Percy written there?" He pointed to the back of the message.

Startled, Jamie flipped the letter over. There were a few scrawled lines, no doubt added after the first message had been completed. He skimmed the words, then grimaced.

"The northern barons have left court, despite that Elizabeth bade them stay. Their excuse is that they cannot tolerate the crowding of her summer progress."

Despair darkened Nick's green eyes. He turned his head, staring past Lucy to the countryside that spread out beneath his window, as if he could see all the way to England's north country. "They mean to do it," he murmured. "With all hope of Norfolk's marriage to Mary Stuart dead, they go home to raise their shires in rebellion. There will be war, Jamie, civil war."

When Nick again looked at his steward, his gaze was haunted. It was the possibility that Northumberland would send another letter to Graceton, begging his fellow Catholic for aid, that worried him now. "What can I do to be rid of this knight?" he almost pleaded. "Can we stage this wedding any sooner?"

Jamie shook his head. "Not unless some news arrives that makes Sir Edward more frantic to return to court than to save his skin. As long as he believes his redemption lies here, he's not likely to rush his departure."

Panic gleamed in Nick's gaze. "Less than thirty days," he said. "Surely we can keep him at bay for that long. Send him hunting in my chase. Let him bring his hawks. Do whatever it takes to keep the knight away from here for as much of each day as is possible."

Jamie raised his hands in resignation. "I'll do my best."

A sharp rap on the apartment's door thundered in the silence. Startled, Nick turned. "Who can that be?"

"Only the lady or one of her servants," Jamie replied in newborn irritation. No one else would have bothered knocking on Nick's door. After ten years, Graceton's servants knew to channel all communication for their squire through Jamie, or Tom, should the steward be unavailable.

"I'll not have strangers in my quarters," Nick warned as he set a hand upon Lucy's shoulder. Jamie almost smiled. Apparently Nick no longer considered the child a stranger.

Jamie threaded his way through the sitting room. Whoever it was dared to tap again, this time with more strength. Irritation flared higher. Not even Lady Purfoy had the right to intrude upon her husband so.

He opened the door. Day's light tumbled in, the new day's heat enough to stir dust on the unswept floor. It was Mistress Atwater.

Dark rings, no doubt the result of last night's late meal,

clung beneath the governess's eyes. She wore but a single green skirt. No farthingale disturbed its line. Instead of her usual bodice, she wore a black doublet, no doubt because its front buttons let her dress without a maid's assistance.

As Jamie stepped into the gallery, the woman leaned to the side, trying to peer past him into Nick's quarters. Here was bold behavior indeed! Jamie closed the panel firmly behind him.

"Good morrow, Mistress Atwater," he said, letting his cold tone serve as a chide for her untoward curiosity.

"Good morrow, Master Steward," she replied with a quick bob. The flicker of her gaze took in his bed robe, his bristling beard and the hair that must be standing up on his head. "My pardon if I roused you."

"You didn't," he said, only now noticing the nervous wringing of her hands. It softened the steel in his voice. "Have no fear. Mistress Purfoy is safe within, visiting with her stepfather."

"Aye, so I'm told," she said.

Anger shot through him. If she knew, then she'd stepped far over the bounds in daring to knock upon the squire's door.

She drew a deep breath and squared her shoulders. "Master Wyatt, I mean no disrespect, but Mistress Lucy cannot stay with Squire Hollier this morn. 'Tis Sunday. It's the day we spend in prayer and quiet contemplation of our Lord. Perhaps she can visit with the squire another time?"

"Mistress Lucy will return to the nursery once she's broken her fast with the squire," Jamie said firmly. "From this day forward, please arrange the child's day so that she spends at least an hour in the squire's company. Early morning or evening would be best. If your lady finds fault with this, she may send her complaints to me."

Turning, Jamie reentered Nick's apartment.

Across the room, the window was now open. Nick sat in the casement with Lucy on his lap as they leaned out to peer down at the river. Jamie smiled, remembering a portrait of Nick, done before the accident. It revealed that Graceton's squire had once been as handsome a lad as Lucy was pretty. They could have been father and daughter.

"Well now, the swans are usually right there," Nick said as he straightened, carefully drawing the child back inside the opening. "I wonder where they've gotten to?"

Lucy smiled up into her stepfather's scarred face. "Maybe they're yet asleep," she said. Her tone was reassuring, as if she didn't want him to worry because he hadn't provided the promised entertainment. "It's still very early."

Something tugged in Jamie's heart. Nick really could use someone new with whom to pass his time. What if Cecily were right and affection for a child could make a man stronger in his health? The hope that Lucy's presence would buy Nick a little more time grew, then waged war against what the child's presence would surely cost him. At last, he sighed. Just as he'd always known he would, he gave way. Lucy had herself a stepfather's proxy.

Chapter Seventeen

❧

Standing at the center of the gatehouse's residence, Ned waited for his manservant to finish tying the last of the ribbons decorating his doublet. A full week had passed since they'd learned of Leicester's betrayal. All was lost and not just because the earl hadn't the courage to actually do as he claimed he could and convince Elizabeth to accept Norfolk's marriage plans.

"There," his man said, patting at the last perfect bow. Dick Backler paused to admire his work. Although twice Ned's age, he looked no more than a score and ten. The servant's attire was as carefully put together as the knight's; not a dark hair was out of place. "Once again, Sir Edward, you put these yokels to shame. By God, this is a backward place. I'll not regret putting it in our dust."

Hopelessness closed around Ned like a cloak. "You speak as if we had somewhere to go after we leave here. There won't be. At this very instant my name is being tossed about court like some tennis ball by those intent on ruining my repute. I'll be fortunate if my own brother looks me in the eye by the time they're finished, much less that Elizabeth ever smiles on me again."

A frown touched the man's forehead, then disappeared. Dick didn't tolerate creases of any sort. "None of that now,

Sir Edward. You know court. Things change from day to day, tides sweeping one faction out to bring in a new one. Stay steady in your course. It's not much you need to restore what you may or may not have lost. Remind yourself that however royal she might be, Her Majesty is still a *woman*." Dick filled the word with scorn. The servant despised all females.

"Easily said," Ned cried, panic again nibbling at his soul, "but it's hard to hold tight to hope. By God, I cannot even turn religion into an issue to exploit. Who could have known that so fervent a Catholic as Squire Hollier would suggest a Protestant ceremony? Or that so strict a Protestant as Lady Purfoy would be so flexible?"

"One wrong word," Dick insisted, his tone reassuring. "That's all you need to race back to court and voice your complaints, embellishing them as you may. It'll be up to the squire to explain himself."

"There's nothing here to use," Ned complained. "Hell take me, but the wedding plans grind steadily forward as if this were the happiest of matches, not a union forced down the throats of a hostile bride and groom."

Dick's gaze narrowed, just a little. "It'd be best for our futures if you stopped panicking."

Ned jerked at the reminder. Unlike that which bound other men to their servants, there was no loyalty in this relationship; Dick's only connection to him was in their shared desire to rise to the pinnacle of their respective classes. Two years ago, it had seemed a fair bargain. Dick's skill with fashion combined with Ned's native charm had resulted in him catching his queen's eye and reaping royal favor's benefits at a very young age. Now, that same ambition meant Dick would be the first man to abandon him if Ned were banished from Elizabeth's presence.

His servant strode to the oriel and threw open the window. The sounds of the castle's servantry gathered in the yard below flowed up into their chambers. "Ah, the lady is already in the yard," he called over his shoulder. "Just as you thought, she's brought Mistress Atwater with her."

Turning, he offered his master a small smile. "I can't imagine why you fret over failure when success lies within your grasp, even as we speak. You want to search the steward's office? Ask Mistress Atwater. That saucy bit would betray anyone and anything if you offered her a kiss."

Anger roared through Ned. How dare this *servant* speak so about Brigit! Surprise replaced anger. Lord save him, but when had he become fond of the governess?

With this discovery, everything became that much more complex. How was he supposed to use a woman he cared for, knowing that what he asked her to do would destroy her? Then again, what choice had he?

❧

Dressed in her everyday attire, a set of pale blue skirts beneath a darker blue bodice, with a gray cap upon her head, Belle sat just outside Graceton's garden. A canvas canopy had been raised to shade her, along with Peg and Brigit, from the day's uncertain sun. They were supposed to be making love knots, twists of ribbon that would decorate Belle's best attire on her wedding day. Not a length of ribbon had been tied these last minutes. Instead, they all watched Lucy.

Belle's precious child was wearing her brown traveling attire, renamed her riding habit, and was perched atop the smallest mare in Squire Hollier's stable. Her knuckles were white as she gripped the reins. A frown of fierce concentration creased her brow as she listened to her instructions.

Master James, dressed in the sleeveless brown doublet and black breeches that Belle now recognized as his daily attire, stood alongside Lucy's horse. Despite scudding clouds that made the day blink from dark to light, his hair gleamed a burnished bronze.

The fine crinkles around his eyes told her he was pleased by the effort Lucy was making. A tiny flame woke in a hidden corner of her heart. Belle sighed against it. She should have known it would be Graceton's steward who fulfilled her daughter's dearest dream.

That flame grew until it consumed her. May the Lord forgive her, but she couldn't help herself. She loved Master James for it, just as she loved him for not allowing her to take blame for their kiss. Just as she loved him for all the times he'd rescued her and shielded her from hurt.

Not that Squire Hollier hadn't been caring. Belle looked up at the gallery windows. The squire sat in the oriel nearest the hall, swathed in a thick robe, his face hidden beneath his mask. He'd come to watch her daughter's lesson. According to Watt and John, it was the first time in their memory that Graceton's master had been out of his chamber during daylight hours.

Although Belle was grateful for the way Squire Hollier had taken Lucy into his heart, no love stirred in her for him. Her gaze returned to Master James. His steward, on the other hand, did want her. She knew because he'd told her so both with words and his body on that night they'd kissed.

"Lead her out to the center of the yard, Old Will,"

Master James said.

Gray-haired, his back bent with his years, the groom led the plodding mare across the grass. Whistles and calls of encouragement rose from the kitchen wall. A goodly number of servants were gathered there, no doubt come to see their reclusive squire.

"Now, Mistress Lucy," Master James called, "make her walk."

Lucy's little heels struck the horse's sides. With a snort of complaint, the mare managed to lift her hooves into a slow walk. The lass squealed in exhilaration.

"Look at me! I'm riding by myself!" she shouted to all and sundry, then waved to her stepfather in the window. He raised a gloved hand in response.

Beside Belle, Brigit drew a sharp breath. "Lord, keep her safe in Your heart," she murmured.

Again, Belle hid her smile. Brigit didn't care much for horses. For herself, Belle hadn't forgotten the wondrous rush of freedom that came from pounding through the woods atop a massive beast. Indeed, it was only while riding that she ever felt truly strong and in control.

Lucy completed several circles. "I think you've mastered that direction," Master James told her. "Can you turn her and go the other way?"

Belle's hands closed around imaginary reins. Moving them as if she were guiding the horse, she willed Lucy to do the same. In the yard, the mare snorted and turned, now bearing toward them. With a laugh, Belle clapped her approval. "You've done it, love," she called.

Lucy beamed, then looked beyond her mother. "Watch me, Sir Edward!" she shouted.

Startled, Belle shifted on her stool and looked toward the gatehouse. Both the knight and his manservant stood there, watching the lesson. Today, Sir Edward wore a tawny doublet trimmed with ribbons, each tied in a meticulous bow.

The knight grinned, then lifted a hand in a friendly wave. "I see you, little one," he called back. "You're doing well indeed."

Belle straightened in surprise. She'd assumed the knight's dislike for her extended to her child. Perhaps she'd judged him too harshly. Indeed, Belle wondered if there might be more to the man than a single-minded determination to ruin her life.

"A little faster," Master James called.

"Oh, nay," Brigit cried softly, her fists clenched in her sewing project. "She shouldn't go faster, she's too small. What if she falls?" Turning on her stool, she looked at Belle. "Please, my lady, I cannot bear to watch. Might I walk in the garden until this is finished?"

Belle swallowed her laughter. "Aye, go," she said, then turned her gaze back to Lucy as her daughter kicked the old mare into a trot.

Not but ten revolutions later, Richard appeared beside Belle, a worrisome tension in his shoulders.

"What is it, Richard?" Belle asked.

"My lady, I beg your pardon for intruding," he said, then paused. His mouth opened and closed several times, as if in speech, but nothing passed his lips. Sadness shot through his gaze followed by a flash of some darker emotion, then he cleared his throat. "I thought I should tell you Sir Edward followed Mistress Atwater into the garden."

Hot color scorched his cheeks. "Lord help me, what am I doing?" he murmured to himself, then began to back away from her. "I beg your pardon, my lady. I've misspoken, when it's none of my concern."

"Stay, Richard," Belle commanded gently, even though he was right about it being none of his concern. Had it been any other man speaking to her about any other situation, she'd have roundly scolded him for his boldness. But this was Richard, the man who'd not only seen her safely to this place but bolstered her confidence every step of the way. It was a substantial debt she owed him.

"Thank you for your warning," she said, coming to her feet and putting a hand on Peg's shoulder. "Trust us. We'll see no harm comes to her."

"That's all I intended," he whispered, as if to assure himself of his motives. Whirling, he strode rapidly away, as if to put distance between himself and his breach of etiquette.

Belle watched him go. For Richard to overstep the bounds of propriety he so strictly observed, he must truly be aching over losing the woman he adored. For the first time since their arrival, she gave thanks the footman hadn't rank enough to dine with them in the parlor. It spared him from witnessing the many coy looks and circumspect smiles Brigit sent the knight.

Content to leave her precious child in Master James's hands, Belle waved Peg to her feet. Her maid shot her a worried look as they strode for the garden's gate.

"There's no doubting our Brigit's lost her heart to the knight," Peg said, "but surely she's not so far gone she'd let him have his way with her. Would she?" she finished uncertainly.

"Of course not." Belle put more assurance in her voice than she felt.

It would be all her fault if Brigit had given way. It seemed her warning to the governess about the knight hadn't been strong enough. A better mistress would know how to deliver her lessons so they had at least some impact.

They entered the garden. With tall walls to baffle sound, a deep stillness claimed this place, unbroken save for the distant gurgle of a fountain and the chirp of birds.

The tower loomed over them, its ancient stones wearing ivy like a leafy cloak. There was no sign of Brigit.

Belle glanced down the path that led strollers, maze-like, spiraling 'round and up the tower's mound to the keep's door. On the way, it passed planting beds and cut through hedges taller than any man. Not only did these thick banks of green offer walkers a bit of shade, there was a certain intimacy to be found in their dark recesses.

"Nay, I cannot." Brigit's voice rose from behind the nearest hedge. Belle's heart quirked. She looked at Peg.

Her hand pressed to her bodice, the maid met her lady's gaze.

Lifting her skirts, Belle started swiftly in the direction of the hedge, Peg following at her heels.

"Then do not," came Sir Edward's gentle reply, "and know I'll respect you all the more for refusing me."

Relief tore through Belle. It seemed the knight meant to act the gentleman with a woman he could have forced. Stepping quietly through the arched opening cut into that line of bushes, she stopped.

The pair stood face-to-face. Brigit's hands rested upon the knight's chest, Sir Edward's hands atop hers, as if to keep her fingers against him. All Belle had ever seen in his expression was arrogant zeal or frantic loathing. It was a warm affection that softened his handsome features now.

She opened her mouth to announce herself, then caught back the words. They were doing no wrong. Turning to leave unnoticed, she ran into Peg, who huffed to a halt with a loud scrape of gravel.

Brigit glanced toward the sound, then gasped. She sprang back from the knight as if singed, bright color staining her face, "My lady, we were only speaking," she cried out, not realizing her guilty reaction suggested that what she was doing and what she longed to do weren't quite synonymous.

In the hopes of finally driving home the message she'd tried so hard to convey, Belle cocked a chiding brow. "I saw what you were doing," she said, offering an accusation of nothing since she'd seen nothing.

Brigit blanched, then desperation filled her gaze. Belle's heart ached for her. Here was the price a woman paid for being both pretty and poor. It was a love match the governess hoped to make with the knight, something a plain woman in her situation would never dream possible.

"Perhaps it would be best if you returned to the house," Belle said, more gently this time.

Brigit's head bowed. "As you will, my lady," she said, and without so much as a fare-thee-well to her lover, she lifted her skirts and nearly ran toward the garden gate.

Belle looked at Peg. "Go with her, remembering it's comfort she needs just now," she warned, knowing from long experience how well the maid liked to lecture.

"Aye, my lady," Peg replied and hurried after the

governess.

It wasn't until her maid had disappeared that fear started through Belle. Well, here she was, right where she didn't wish to be: alone with Sir Edward. She turned to look at the knight.

His arms were crossed, his jaw tensed and his gaze hard. Anger and dislike nigh on wafted from him. The urge to run filled Belle. For Brigit's sake, she quelled it. It was Belle's duty to see to the health and happiness of her employees. To that end, there were things she and the knight must discuss.

"No wrong was done," he snarled.

Belle drew herself to her tallest, masking fear behind a calm expression. "I didn't think for a moment that it had been," she lied softly, wanting to repay his respect for Brigit with her own. "You have ever treated Brigit like the gentlewoman she is."

Surprise dashed through his gaze, then his eyes narrowed once more. "You say that, yet you send her away as if she was unworthy of your trust."

Belle gave a gentle shake of her head. "You mistake me. I send her away because of what lies in her heart for you. It's a place for you she's made there, Sir Edward."

Behind the shield of his cold demeanor pleasure flickered through his eyes.

"It's *marriage* she hopes you'll offer, despite her lack of dowry," Belle continued bluntly. "Has she misinterpreted your intentions?"

At his pained expression, Belle sighed. As much as he cared for Brigit, his ambition would never allow him to marry a woman without connections or wealth.

"I think it would be best if you saw her no more in private," she said.

"How dare you!" he nearly shouted. "Do you never tire of disparaging my character, my lady? I'm an honorable man, with no intention of misusing her. What wrong can there be in the two of us enjoying each other's company?"

"No wrong at all." She shrugged. "That is, if you don't plan to break her heart."

"I don't understand you," he snapped.

"Then I shall say it plain," she replied. "Sir Edward, she's not yet twenty. She still clings to the notion that love will out. Against that, I fear she'll forget all propriety and ask you to wed her." It was a lie; still, Belle felt justified in offering it.

"If you refuse her as it seems you must," she continued, "her pride will shatter. Since her pride is all she owns in the world, I pray you, do not take it from her."

It was his own caring for the governess that killed the resistance that flared briefly in his hazel eyes. In its passing the shadow of a decent man appeared in his gaze. Releasing a harsh breath, his arms opened, palms upturned.

"Not for the world would I hurt her," he said, his voice flat. "Were this year the last, I'd offer for her, her poverty be damned. I would," he repeated as if it were a vow, then his shoulders sagged. "But now . . . now I have nothing left to offer." His voice trailed away into an aching silence.

"Then you'll make no more attempts to see her in private," Belle said, to see him set firmly in the course he must take.

"It would be for the best," he agreed, his lips twisting into a facsimile of a smile. "Will you explain to her that we talked, you and I, and tell her what was said?" he asked.

"I will, giving you all the credit your behavior deserves," she said.

A bitter laugh left him. "You give me more credit than I think I'm due. I never thought I'd say this to you, my lady, but you have my heartfelt thanks." He turned and walked deeper into the garden.

Leaving him to his pain, she started toward the garden's exit, only to discover that Master James stood there. As he saw her appear through the hedge, worry eased from his face. Belle's heart leapt at this proof of his caring for her. She caught back the reaction. Would that there were someone to correct her, the way she must Brigit.

She came to a stop beside him. "Master Wyatt?"

His brows rose in question. "I beg your pardon, my lady, but Mistress Atwater ran from the garden, followed by Mistress Hythereve. Is something amiss?"

"Nothing that time won't heal," she replied, managing a smile. That was true enough.

"Ah," he said, instead of the questions he was too polite to ask.

Together, they returned to the yard. Everyone was gone, save for Lucy and the elderly groom. As Old Will led the mare toward the gatehouse, Lucy raced toward the hall door.

"The lesson is done, then?" Belle asked as she and Master James made their way far more slowly after Lucy.

"Aye." The steward nodded. "It was necessarily short after yesterday's exertion." On the previous day, Lucy had tried to teach her stepfather to dance. "The squire's lungs have had no strength since—" He fell into an abrupt silence.

Curiosity tingled in Belle. Lucy had told them the tale of Squire Hollier's tumble into the flames as a lad. It still startled Belle that so old an event seemed so current to all of Graceton's residents. Few of the servants would even speak about the incident, while those who did always referred to it as *the accident,* as if no other person in the world had ever experienced a life-shattering event.

"Your daughter's a quick study," Master James said in a brusque change of subject.

Still pondering Graceton's strange protectiveness of its squire, Belle offered an absent reply. "You're kind to say so."

The steward stopped. Belle halted too, looking up to see what was the matter. Wry amusement curved Master James's lips and glowed in his blue eyes.

"Once again, you call me kind, when it's not kindness I offer but the truth. Listen now and I shall tell you a fact," he teased. "Mistress Lucy will make a fine rider, if for no other reason than her determination to master the art."

That made Belle laugh. "Determined—now that's a good word for my sweetheart. However, I think there are other words that fit her better. Stubborn. Persistent, of a certainty. And utterly unbearable when she chooses to be."

Master James's smile widened, the warmth in his face meant only for her. Belle's heart filled. Lord save her, but she loved him. She caught her breath in wonder. How could it be that so exquisite a man might find her attractive?

"Why am I not surprised at your description?" he laughed as a footman approached and came to a halt beside him, offering a brief bow in Belle's direction. "Pardon, Master James," he said, holding out a fold of paper. "A passing merchant delivered this for the lady."

"For me?" Belle cried in excitement. It'd been a rare day indeed when she'd received a letter at the Purfoy manor, and she'd not written to one of her acquaintances since Sir William's death. Digging into her purse, Belle dropped a few pence into the footman's palm, then took the proffered letter. She turned it over in her hands. The wax that held it shut was smooth, untouched by a signet. Rather than being forwarded, it was actually addressed to her at Graceton Castle. Who knew she was here?

The mystery of it was too great to be borne. She broke the seal. The wax cracked, pieces showering onto the grass at her hems.

The paper unfolded with a crinkle. Her heart flew as she recognized the handwriting of her former governess, Mistress Alice Godwin. So dear had Alice been to Belle that she'd petitioned the woman to become Lucy's governess on the very day of her child's birth. Alice had refused, and rightly so. She was far too old to take on another student.

> *My dearest Belle, I hope this finds you happy and in good health*, read the greeting. *I have your new address from Sir William Cecil, our gracious Majesty's secretary. He has also confided the news to me of this marriage that Her Grace has seen fit to arrange for you. I hope you will accept my congratulations. My wish for you is as it has always been. May you find the happiness you dreamed of owning so long ago, along with the safe birth of many children.*

With the pleasantries addressed, the old woman's letter continued in blunt announcement.

I fear I have terrible news. Your lady mother has died.

Belle stared at the words, reading them again and again. Her heart felt like wood in her chest. She closed the letter.

"My lady?" Master James asked.

Incapable of responding, Belle started abruptly toward the hall door. What sort of Christian was she? Her mother was dead and she didn't feel a thing.

Chapter Eighteen

❧

Now that wedding announcements were at last all written and delivered, Jamie set aside his evening hours to catch up on all the harvest reports, petitions for justice and requests for extensions on payment of rents and fees that had gone wanting in the interim. But now, instead of setting pen to paper and working, he stared down at the correspondence and didn't see a word. How could he when he was stuck like an ox driving a millstone, all his thoughts traveling around and around in the same rut?

What grave message had the lady's letter contained that could drive all the life from her face?

Leaning back in his chair, he released a breath sharp enough to make the candles on his desk flicker. He rubbed at his tired eyes. Cecily had crept into Nick's bed a half hour ago. He might as well retire, since God knew he wasn't accomplishing anything here.

Reaching out, he snuffed all but one candle. The night's gentle darkness closed about him, sighing into the chamber's corners and curling sleepily about the legs of his chair. Still, Jamie sat and stared blindly out into the dimness.

Why hadn't he thought to warn Graceton's men not to approach him with messages unless he was private? Now, instead of shielding Nick from potential harm, all he'd done was prove to himself he wasn't much of a spy.

Jamie's gaze shifted to the top of his desk. It was still there, hiding beneath the sprawl of papers, bait for a trap that would never spring. He pulled the note out from beneath his stack of correspondence, then smoothed it beneath his hands. Why keep it, when he knew no one was coming for it?

Even as the urge to tear the thing in twain rose, he killed it. Nay, this damned letter had its value, if nothing else than as a reminder of how great an idiot he could be. Screwing it into a ball, he set it back on his desk.

At that same instant, the door leading to the gallery creaked quietly as it opened. Given the late hour, Jamie was certain it was Tom, coming to remind his master to go to bed.

But the footsteps marked the walker's path up the tower stairs. Jamie frowned. The only thing in that direction was the door leading out onto the castle's wall. Who in their right mind wandered along a shelf of stone set nearly four stories above the ground in the middle of the night?

Taking up his candle, he crossed the chamber to open his door. Chill air, thick with the scent of moldering damp, rushed into his office. The flame died. Both office and stairwell plunged into an instant blackness.

Jamie loosed an irritated breath. Whoever it was had left the door open at the tower's top. Setting aside the useless taper, he stepped out onto the landing and reached blindly for the tower wall. With the cool curve of its stones beneath his fingers, he started upward, seeking out each step with a careful foot.

At the top of the stairs night's silvery light spilled in.

Gone were the clouds that had plagued the day, whisked away by the sun's setting. Yet an hour from its zenith, the moon was but a slender crescent as it drifted like some celestial boat in a river of stars.

The narrow wall stretched out before him, spanning the distance from this tower to the next. Merlons studded the wall's forward edge, the great square blocks of stone looking like giant teeth. With nothing in the gaps between them, the careless could, and had, easily stepped through to die in the river below. At the wall's back was the hall's roof, rising a dozen feet above it to its peak. Shingles made from thin slices of slate gleamed like ebony, while the slender chimneys jutting up out of it looked like so many silver needles.

She stood halfway down the wall's length. Her garment clung to her slim shape, the night's tepid breeze lifting its silk hem. Moonlight turned her golden hair to silver.

Lady Purfoy.

The sudden warmth in his heart warned Jamie he should turn and leave, right this instant. There was no trusting himself with her, not anymore. But as he took a backward step, she sighed and leaned her head against the stone before her in a pose fraught with pain. The need to comfort filled him.

Before he knew what he was about, he went to her. She looked up at the sound of his footsteps and gasped. Even though there was no escape for her in any direction, she took a quick backward step.

"I was just preparing to leave my office when I heard someone climb the steps," he said, hoping a friendly grin would put her at ease. "I came after you to warn you. My lady, Mistress Miller spoke the truth when she said two women have fallen to their deaths from this wall, although I doubt her White Lady was the cause of it. It's dangerous up here in the day, what with slick stones and the possibility of gusty winds. It's doubly so in the dark."

Even in the dimness he could see her shoulders relax, as if concern for her safety somehow made this chance meeting more acceptable. "I suppose you're right," she agreed, "but I was desperate for a breath of air. It seems none of the river's freshness reaches as far as my window."

"Perhaps you simply spent too much of the day within your apartment's walls. You didn't come to dinner this evening," he said, daring to encourage her into a conversation.

"Aye, we decided to dine in our chambers tonight," was all she said as she once more turned to look out over the darkened landscape.

Jamie came to stand beside her. The castle had a fine prospect of the long valley that spread out beneath it. From here, he could see the glimmer of the river's surface as it made its way around darkened orchards and past the gentle fields of grain that had yet to see the scythe. The square tower of the village church thrust up into the night sky, its form a solid black against the salting of stars in the sky behind it.

"I fear it was a short meal Sir Edward and I shared, what with you, Mistress Atwater and Mistress Lucy all absent."

Her laugh was short and filled with irony. She sent him a swift, sidelong glance. "I can imagine it was. I've noticed the two of you have little liking for each other."

Then she sighed. "Mistress Atwater and I are going to abandon the dinner table until after the wedding."

His heart dropped. Taking a meal with Lady Purfoy had become the highlight of his day. It was the way she listened to him. No matter how mundane the issue, she made it seem vital and new.

"But why?" The question leapt from his lips.

Rather than snub him for his impertinence, her eyes glistened in the night as she studied him. There was a moment's hesitation, then she shook her head. "I fear the reason is a private matter."

"Pardon, my lady," he said swiftly, trying to reclaim his forgotten manners. "I only hope it isn't anything I've done that should make you avoid our table."

"Oh, nay," she cried, reaching out as if to lay a hand on his arm, only to catch back the gesture before she touched him. "It's not you, you've been naught but—"

"Kind?" he interrupted, supplying the word he knew she intended. Despite his disappointment over her news, he smiled.

This time when she laughed, there was only pleasure in it. The sweet sound filled him, feeding the dangerous softness that resided in his heart for her. It was a warning, an alarm telling him it was time for them to part. Aye, but no matter what his head knew, his feet might as well have been nailed to the stones beneath them. Save for chance and impersonal meetings in the gallery or hall, this was the last opportunity he'd have to speak with her until the wedding. Suddenly, thirteen days seemed like an eternity.

"What was our heavenly Father thinking when He created bats, I wonder?" she asked, as one of those creatures swooped near enough to them to be seen. "Why do you think He gave some mice wings and not the others?"

Something stirred deep within Jamie. She was telling him she didn't want this meeting to end any more than he did.

"Ours nest in the top floor of the old keep tower," he replied, gratefully following where she led.

"Do they?"

When she said no more, a companionable quiet settled between them. Jamie found he was content to stand beside her and enjoy her presence. After a few moments, the skin at the back of his neck began to prickle. Someone was watching them.

He glanced toward the tower door. There was no one there. When he brought his gaze back on Lady Purfoy, she'd leaned her cheek against the merlon.

"What does our Lord think of me, I wonder?" Her tone was distant and sad.

"Nothing but good," he replied in utter certainty.

"I doubt that," she said with a tiny, aching laugh, then turned her head to look up at him. Pain marred her gentle features.

Again, the need to comfort tore through him. "What's this? Whatever it is, it cannot be so bad as that," he said, attempting to soothe with words since propriety didn't allow more.

"So you would say," she replied, lifting her head. Tears glimmered in her eyes. She blinked them away, then drew a bracing breath. "My lady mother has died and, God help me, I cannot find an iota of grief within me for her passing."

She cringed, as if shocked by what she'd said. "Pardon. I didn't mean to speak so frankly. I don't know why it is that I always behave so familiarly toward you."

Where she saw a lapse of manners, he found a compliment. The warmth within him grew. "I see no wrong in sharing your heart's burden with a friend," he told her.

The moon's light was bright enough to show him the astonishment that filled her face. "You'd call yourself my friend?" It was a breathless question.

He hadn't really thought about it when he'd said it. "As our husband's steward, what else would I be?" This was almost a challenge.

New joy took light in her eyes. "There aren't many who've ever named themselves my friend."

Jamie recognized a certain depth of loneliness, similar to what had always lived within him. The urge to kiss her woke. Startled, he took a step back, hoping a little more physical distance might ease it. It was only as he moved that it occurred to him she'd just told him what lay in her letter.

"It was the notice of your lady mother's death that came this afternoon?"

"Aye." Her voice was small.

For all the queen's shouting about removing heads from necks, it was hard to believe Elizabeth might actually have wreaked that punishment on Lady Montmercy. Ach, but if the queen had given way to execution, what did that mean for Nick? He dared to probe further.

"It's been less than two months since I last saw your lady mother. She seemed hale enough at our last meeting, although she was somewhat upset." *Hysterical* would have been the better word.

"Apparently she became ill shortly after her confinement to the Tower," Lady Purfoy replied, not seeming to notice she was being interrogated. "Her caregiver said she passed into a strange state, neither speaking nor moving of her own volition. She ate, but only if a spoon was pressed between her lips. Given that, it's a wonder she clung to life as long as she did."

The lady loosed a choked sound as she stared out into the distance. "A dozen times I've read those words," she told the sky, "each time waiting to feel something—pity, or at least compassion for another soul who'd fallen afoul of our Lord and paid the price. There's nothing in me," she cried, then caught her breath.

"At least I didn't dance for joy at the news." This last was a personal aside not meant for his ears, spoken on a bitter breath.

"You would never be so cruel." The words left his mouth before he could stop them.

Lady Purfoy looked at him, a sad smile touching her lips. "I doubt our Lord would agree. He knows how I've failed to obey His commandment and honor my mother." She struggled for a moment, as if words filled her, but she wasn't certain she should free them.

Then the pain deepened in her expression. "If only someone would tell me how I'm to honor a woman who wasted no opportunity to tell me how ugly I am and how deeply my birth shamed her."

Her words stole Jamie's breath. Ancient as they were, memories of his mother returned with all the freshness and clarity of yesterday's events. At his father's insistence, he'd spent one day a week with his dam. More times than not, she'd ended the encounter by screaming she wished he'd never been born. Despite the caring his nurse and his tutor showered on him, such hatred directed at so small a boy had been shattering.

It was the pain of his mother's rejection, and the unfairness of his father's attempt to teach one of God's command-ments by exposing his son to her hatred, that made anger explode in him. The emotion was so huge his hands shook with it. Craving the privacy of his office where he could knot it safely back into his heart, he started to turn away.

Tears glistened to life in the lady's eyes. Jamie froze. He read it in the crease of her brow and the worried pinch of her lips. If he left her now, she'd blame herself and her hon-est speech for it, no matter what explanation he might offer. To her, it would be but one more rejection in a lifetime of rejections.

Anger melted into the need to heal the wrongs done to them both. The silk of her bed robe was soft beneath his palms as his hands closed about her upper arms. He pulled her into his embrace. She gasped as she came to rest against him, but there was no tension in the hands she braced against his chest. Lifting her head, she looked up into his face. Her bed robe fell open to bare the slender length of her throat to the night. Her skin glowed like alabaster in the starlight.

"She had no right to say such things to you," he told her, his voice sounding like a growl to his own ears. "Between the two of you, I think you by far the more valuable soul. Indeed, the sweetness and caring of your nature put many a vain beauty to shame. My lady, it isn't you who should honor your mother for giving you life, but she who should have been honored because she bore you. Your birth was her life's crowning achievement."

The lady's lips quivered. "I think I'm not worthy of your high opinion."

"And I think you are wrong," he replied, forgetting

all caution to lift a hand and stroke his fingers along the smooth curve of her cheek. "I cannot imagine your lady mother ever naming you ugly. However well-made the world accorded her features, I think you by far the prettier and no man can convince me otherwise. So I have believed from the moment I first saw you."

She closed her eyes as she lost her battle with tears. Twin droplets slid out from beneath her eyelashes to trail down her cheeks. Catching her face in his hands, he used his thumbs to brush them away. With a shuddering sigh, he leaned her cheek against one of his palms, then opened her eyes to look at him.

"You are so—"

"Nay," he interrupted with a harsh laugh. "I'll not have you say it. I am not kind. I'm forthright, stubborn and prideful to a fault. Some have even dared to name me thick as a brick. All those I accept, but not kind, never kind."

A smile trembled to life on her mouth. "Then I shall cherish your good opinion of me all the more," she whispered. "In all my life, no one has ever preferred me over my mother."

There was a subtle softening in her expression. That warmth in his heart lifted into a new heat, bringing with it the need to touch his lips to hers. He almost did it. He would have done it, but this woman was special above any other he'd ever met. To give way to passion and commit adultery would dishonor what he felt for her. Releasing her, he took a backward step.

"I think it's time we returned," he said softly.

"I think you are right," she replied, just as softly.

The sadness had departed from her face. In its place

was a new emotion. Jamie caught his breath. Although she was promised to Nick, it was Graceton's steward she loved. However wrong it might be, Jamie's heart sang.

Turning, he led the way to the tower door. As he stepped through the opening, he met with a wall of chill air. Jamie released a surprised breath. He hadn't realized the air in the stairwell was so much cooler than the night.

"Have a care," he said, speaking over his shoulder to her.

When they were again in the gallery, he stopped with her before her apartment door. She dared to step close and lay her hand against his arm. "My thanks. You've rescued me once again, Master James," she said.

Just as it had the first time, his name on her lips sent pleasure shooting through him.

"Oh, my pardon," she said. "I hadn't meant to call you by your Christian name."

A quiet, ironic breath left him at this. "Why should you not, when everyone within these walls does?"

"I don't know," she said, sounding truly bemused at herself. "I suppose I wasn't certain it was appropriate. What sort of name is James?"

"Scots," he replied. "I'm named for my maternal kinsmen, who hail from that country. But my family has always called me Jamie." He started in surprise. So much for avoiding intimacy.

"Jamie." She said it as if she were trying it on her tongue. "It has a foreign sound, but I like it."

Then she grimaced. "Oh, Lord. I just realized that once the squire's title is restored, everyone here will be calling me by my given name, awful as it is."

He kept his laugh quiet. "Awful? What's so awful about Arabella?"

"Nothing," she said with a quiet snort, "were I a striking beauty. Since I'm not, I'd have been far better off with simple Mary or plain Jane. I think I wasn't but three when I insisted my nurse and Peg address me as Belle."

Belle. He studied her face, then smiled. "You're right. Belle suits you."

A brilliant smile dashed across her face. Jamie's need to feel her in his arms stirred anew. He took a single, backward step. As if his movement had been a signal, she reached for the door's latch.

"Good night, then," she said, her reluctance to part from him in every syllable.

"Good night, my lady," he said.

They stayed where they stood. A current of heat flowed between them, slowly growing in intensity. She drew a deep breath, her breasts lifting beneath the silk of her robe. Jamie's pulse quickened. Lord, but if there was so much pleasure to be had in just standing near her, what would he find in her bed? It was definitely time to leave.

Raising a hand, he once more brushed her cheek. "Go," he breathed, "please."

The moon had sailed far enough across its nightly sea to send its light streaming through the oriel behind him. In the silvery glow he saw the hesitation in her face. "It's wrong. I know it is," she whispered.

"What is?" he asked.

"Words, conversation. That's all we'll ever have to share between us." It was an acknowledgment of her love for him and his for her.

"Aye," he agreed. Although he'd already accepted this particular truth, to hear it spoken woke a desperate ache in him. Why shouldn't he have her, his heart complained. Nick didn't want her. Jamie countered its protest with the reminder that, in sharing this evening with him, Belle was trusting him never to use her admission of affection to his advantage. Her respect was more important than his need.

The worried pleat between her brows eased as if she'd come to some decision. "If words are all we have, then I cannot bear to be without the sound of your voice. Good night, Master James. I will see you on the morrow at the dinner table." With that, she ducked inside and shut the door.

Joy shot through him. She wasn't going to deny him her presence. Turning, he started down the gallery. He was utterly and completely in love with Nick's wife.

Chapter Nineteen

❧

Dressed in his courtly best, Jamie stood in the center of his bedchamber. The weather had turned early this year. Outside his window, the wind lifted into a raging howl, spattering a few of heaven's tears against the panes. How well it reflected what lay in his heart.

His gaze slipped to his bed. With only hours until the speaking of the vows, Mistress Miller's maids were stripping the bed curtains to give them a good thrashing. So, too, were the linens being changed. In the room's far corner lay a pile of flower garlands, thick with asters and marigolds. All this preparation so Nick could lie with the woman Jamie loved.

Until this very moment, the thought of the bedding hadn't seemed real. Now, Jamie's stomach took a sick twist. Belle was his. He didn't want anyone, even Nick, to touch her.

Suddenly, Jamie understood how Cecily could so completely ignore this marriage. Nick had finally confessed to his paramour, saying that the wedding was unavoidable, and still Cecily continued to act as if nothing were amiss. Why, this morn she'd been cool and calm as she left Graceton, while Jamie devoured his heart. Why couldn't he be as clever at overlooking what he didn't wish to see?

"Master James?" Tom came to a halt beside him.

Jamie tore his gaze from the maid plumping pillows to look at his servant. The promise of a problem filled Tom's face. Good. He needed as many distractions as he could find, anything to keep him from thinking about what would happen this evening.

The servant held out a letter. Jamie snatched it. It bore Percy's seal. His heart fell. Although news from court was certain to divert, it wouldn't last long enough. There was nothing he could do about the actions of the high and mighty.

"It came a few moments ago by royal messenger," Tom said. "Sir Edward also received a packet. Peter says it has the queen's seal on it."

Worry didn't flicker even in Jamie. The packet could only contain Elizabeth's token. Of course the queen would deliver her gift to her proxy, who would make a more formal presentation at the celebration.

"Is there anything else?" he asked hopefully. "Have you heard how it goes in the kitchen?"

A month hadn't given the household enough time to prepare. As of last night all that the cook had finished were the hundreds of small sweet cakes needed for distribution after the ceremony. Jamie knew the kitchen staff had worked throughout the night preparing the two gigantic meals that would be served this day. The first was simple enough, being the roast beef and mutton intended for the villagers; the second, the Graceton's folk, consisted of far more complex dishes.

After the meal was finished, Nick would sleep with Jamie's woman. Jamie nearly gagged. If tearing his heart out of his chest would make this stop, he'd do it.

"I don't know," Tom replied, perplexed to be asked about the kitchen.

Jamie rubbed a hand over his throbbing brow. As if it weren't bad enough he was driving himself mad, now he meant to take his servant with him. "Pardon, Tom. I'm only nervous."

Sympathy warmed his servant's gaze. "That'd be natural, wouldn't it?" he offered in an attempt at comfort. "Not only do you plan all, but you must also play the part of the bridegroom."

Fresh agony shot through Jamie. He sent Tom a weak smile. "Aren't you glad I'm not the groom? Think how much worse I'd be if I were."

Amusement lit Tom's face. "It was you who said it, Master James, not I," he said as a maid, her arms filled with linens, collided with him. As he staggered back, she called, "Pardon," and rushed out the door.

"Go see what's what in the kitchen, Tom. I'll be in the squire's chamber." He was hoping for a catastrophe, God help him, anything that would put this event off another day. Jamie opened the hidden panel and stepped into his employer's chamber. Yet dressed in his bed robe and nightshirt, Graceton's squire was pacing before his windows. With his head bowed and a bony finger pressed to his scarred lips, his steps were brisk, even frantic. He gave no sign he knew his steward had entered.

Jamie closed the door. A blessed quiet, free of all bustle and chatter, claimed the chamber. Nick halted, his eyes closed.

"What do you want?" he whispered harshly.

"We've another note from Percy," Jamie replied, frowning at such strange behavior, only to decide it wasn't any stranger than his own. What a pair they made. Jamie would act the part of the bridegroom wishing he weren't acting, while Nick was the bridegroom and simply wished he weren't.

"What does it say?" Graceton's master still didn't look up.

Jamie opened Percy's note and scanned his uncle's spidery scrawl, then his heart simply stopped beating. "Christ Almighty."

Nick's head snapped up. "What is it?" he asked, leaving his windows to stand next to Jamie.

"Percy says that Norfolk has left court without Elizabeth's permission. This has terrified Her Majesty, who fears he intends to raise the country against her. She's removed the Scots queen from the earl of Shrewsbury's custody, closed the ports and has alerted the militia. Worse, fearing she'll soon face her mother's fate, she's rushed for the safety of Windsor Castle's thick walls."

Eyes wide, Nick's brows rose to the limit of their mobility. "Who can blame her for her fear," he said. "We all know Norfolk has more armament and can bring more men onto the field in the next month than she's been able to raise all summer."

Hope sparked in his gaze. "Tell me what this means to our knightly guest," he demanded. "If all Englishmen must choose between Norfolk and Elizabeth, which way does he run?"

"Run?" Jamie said with a harsh laugh. "This leaves Sir Edward nowhere to go. Indeed, all he is now is a grain between two millstones. I'll wager he throws his lot in with Elizabeth. Sir Edward's face is pretty enough to make him think he might win her forgiveness, even if she never forgets."

The hope in Nick's gaze died. "Which means we'll find no quarter in his direction."

There was a tap at the panel, then Tom stepped within, holding yet another fold of paper in his hand. "Pardon, Lord Nicholas. Master James, it seems there was a letter for his lordship in the packet Sir Edward received."

Once he'd handed the paper to Jamie, he backed out of the chamber and closed the panel behind him. Jamie showed Nick the letter. It was sealed with the royal signet.

"Wondrous," Nick sneered. "Felicitations over this happy event from the woman who forces me into it. Read it to me so I can say I heard it," he commanded almost harshly, "then go write her back, offering our joyous thanks for all the bliss her meddling brought into our lives."

The fog of Jamie's jealousy lifted, at least a little. He bit back a smile. The queen deserved her thanks without any of the sarcasm Nick intended. Jamie was grateful for her meddling. Although he and Belle dared share no touch, being in her company this past month had made him the happiest he'd ever been.

"So what does it say?" Nick asked.

Rather than a personal note written by Elizabeth's own hand, Cecil had scribed it for her. Elizabeth had at least signed it, conveying her magnificence by filling the entire bottom of the sheet with her name. Jamie skipped the effusive and flowery greeting to reach the letter's body, then flinched.

"What?" Nick asked, his voice deepening in new worry.

Jamie cleared his throat. "She says:

> 'We have considered your request to release your brother, Master Christopher Hollier, to attend your wedding. We find it inconvenient to be without his service at the moment. Again, We would remind you of your duty to your family line. News of your wife's fecund state will be most joyously received by us. Know that if your efforts in that direction be lacking, We will consider it disobedience against royal command.'"

The queen's words drove Nick across the room. He collided with his bed, then dropped to sit upon the mattress. "Mary, Mother of God, have mercy on my soul," he prayed quietly, then looked up at his steward. "She makes it sound as if it would be treason to refuse to bed Lady Purfoy."

Jamie nodded. That was exactly what it sounded like to him.

The fear and worry in Nick's gaze deepened. "Where did I err, Jamie?" he pleaded. "All I wanted was a marriage for Kit. In return, I wouldn't abdicate my title in favor of Kit." That Nick would refuse his title and leave this earth with no heir to follow him truly affronted Elizabeth's sense of order. "Why should she strike out at me so?"

"You mistake her," Jamie said. "She's not striking out, she's demanding proof of your loyalty. If you bed the Protestant wife she saw fit to give you, she'll construe it as a sign you don't mean to rise with Norfolk and the other Catholic barons. Refuse, and it follows you're a rebel. Given the circumstances, you can hardly blame her for pulling in every favor and debt she's owed."

Nick stared at Jamie. The color drained from his face. "This message, it came through Sir Edward." It was a flat statement.

"Aye," Jamie agreed, a little puzzled.

"Then Elizabeth's told him to demand the consummation," he muttered.

A breath of confusion left Jamie. "But of course she has. Nick, this should come as no surprise to you. I told you from the first the queen would like nothing better than for you to sire a child and carry forward your bloodline."

Nick stared up at him, his gaze tormented, his shoulders hunched. "Help me, Jamie. I'm trapped and I can't think of any way out."

Understanding dawned. Despite all he'd been told and all he'd seen, Nick yet clung to the belief he could escape taking a wife he didn't want. The irony of it deepened until Jamie wanted to laugh.

What a pair they were. Together and each to their own purpose, they'd blinded themselves, seeing only what they wished to see. Now, what they'd tried to avoid rose up to box their ears.

Before Jamie could speak, there was another tap on the panel and Tom threw open the door. This time, there was a frantic look on his face.

"Pardon again," he called, "but there's a row in the hall. The village musicians want to take refuge from the wind and Mistress Miller won't let them in."

Jamie's heart leapt. Now, here was a problem he could handle. He managed a rueful look and a shrug toward Nick, then whirled and strode from the room.

Chapter Twenty

B<small>ELLE SAT IN HER APARTMENT'S ANTECHAMBER,</small> once again dressed in her pink and gray attire. Ribbon love knots were tacked to the surface of her sleeves and skirt. She plucked at one. It was a fairly ridiculous affection, given that this marriage was hardly a love match.

Marriage. The word rang in her. Today, she would wed Squire Hollier, a man who, however kindly, had made it clear he didn't want her.

But only a fool would ignore the obvious. Squire Hollier wasn't a strong man. If, as he indicated, he didn't intend to make her his wife in the true sense of the word, she had nothing to fear from childbirth's perils. Given that, it was likely she'd outlive him.

"It's heavy, Mama," Lucy cried as she entered the sitting room from Belle's bedchamber. Her daughter was once again dressed in her best blue garments with her pearled cap upon her head. The velvet bag she carried drooped over her hands.

"We should expect nothing less of a gift from a soon-to-be peer," Peg told the child, her voice alive with pride. Belle's maid wore scarlet and yellow; her better garments had come to Graceton with her lady's furniture.

Brigit trailed silently behind them, again dressed in her

green. Save for the functional brown traveling attire Belle had given her, these were the only garments she owned. Her arms were crossed, her pretty face marred with a sullen look. So it had been since that day in the garden: Brigit standoffish during the day, while her nights were spent in tears. That dream of a love match would take its own sweet time to die.

"Open it," Lucy demanded in excitement as she dropped the sack into Belle's lap.

"Aye, my lady. Let us all see what he sends you," Peg urged.

"As you will," Belle agreed and opened the drawstrings. What tumbled into her lap were two smaller bags. She laughed. "Oh, Lord! What if this is naught but one of those tricks, where the containers become smaller and smaller?"

Instead, the smaller of the two bags yielded a great, square brooch of ancient style. A sprig of holly was carved on its face in the same shape used on the squire's family crest. Emeralds served for leaves, while a small cluster of rubies represented its berries. However fine the pin, it was an impersonal gift, meant for any woman as long as she was one of the long line of women who wed Hollier men. Still, Belle held it up so the others could see.

"Very pretty," Lucy said in approval, "but mine is nicer." She touched her own brooch. The squire had given it to her yesterday. Within a golden oval, filigree twisted and turned. A pearl pendant dangled from its bottom.

"That's no way to speak, Mistress Lucy," Brigit said in sharp chide. Although she'd been short with them all these last weeks, she'd been especially so toward Lucy. "Beg your lady mother's pardon."

Resentment woke in Lucy's gaze. Her lower lip set to trembling. She looked to her mother for rescue. Belle couldn't give her daughter what she wanted, not when Brigit was right to chasten.

"Sweetling, a polite woman makes no comparisons, only offers compliments of another's gifts," she said, hoping a soft voice would balance the sting of the governess's harshness.

Lucy bowed her head as Belle opened the second bag. This time, a strand of pearls spilled out her lap, its gleaming brightness saying no woman before her had ever won it. She caught its loops in her fingers. Nay, it wasn't all pearls. Every fifth bead was a pink stone. Instead of a clasp of gold, it was silver that held it closed.

As it did with each passing day, Belle's love for Graceton's steward grew. A week ago, Jamie had asked her what she intended to wear to the ceremony. Now, she saw he'd used that information to have the piece made for her. Though this gift came in the squire's name, it was another man's caring she saw in it.

To hide the sudden rush of joy she was certain stained her skin, Belle donned the strand and came to her feet. It was long enough to reach to her waist.

"Oh, they're lovely, my lady," Peg said in awe. "As befits a noblewoman of your stature, of course," she completed.

"They are better than my pin," Lucy said, trying to rectify her earlier error as she caught her mother's hand in hers.

A quiet wail woke from Brigit. "I cannot bear it," she cried, backing slowly toward the door that adjoined the two apartments. "I'll not do it, my lady. I'll not pretend joy at your marriage, when you've stolen mine from me."

"Mistress Atwater!" Peg's voice thundered in the chamber. "You overstep yourself."

"Nay, Peg," Belle said, holding out a hand to stop her maid. "It's about time she lanced what festers in her. Mayhap once she's purged it she'll regain her good humor."

Belle looked at the governess. "I took nothing from you, Brigit, because there was nothing for me to take. Sir Edward told me he couldn't ask you to wed him."

"You lie!" Brigit's childish shout echoed around them. Tears filled her dark eyes, then trickled down her cheeks. "You're cruel. Each night you keep me so far from him at the table that we cannot share so much as a single word, lest we shout it."

"Brigit, love," Belle said with a shake of her head, "if I intended to keep you from Sir Edward, I'd command you to dine in your chambers. Moreover, there's nothing I can do to keep the knight from speaking to you, should he wish to do so. That he doesn't can only mean he chooses not to engage you in private conversation."

As she heard the truth, Brigit's face twisted in pain. "I don't believe you! You've said something to turn him from me because you're angry over being forced into wedding the squire. Because you're not happy, you can't bear for anyone else to be either. You want to ruin my life! Well, I won't let you. I know what I need to do to win him back. I'll have him, do you hear?"

Sobbing, she turned and ran through the adjoining door to the nursery. As it slammed after her, Lucy whimpered and leaned into Belle's skirts. Belle pulled her daughter close, feeling the weight of her own sin settle upon her shoulders. A good mistress would have found a way to stop

Brigit's infatuation the moment it began. Because she wasn't clever enough to know how to do that, her wee family had lost the peace and happiness they'd once enjoyed.

"Huh, what sort of gratitude is this for the home and employ you've given her?" Peg's voice was harsh, her arms tightly crossed over her bodice. "This is your reward for your leniency, my lady. I'd have had her over my knee months ago."

"But you're not me," Belle replied. "And you know very well she doesn't mean what she says. Give her time. Once the wedding is over and Sir Edward leaves, she'll come to her senses. I hope," she finished with a sigh, then looked at the closed nursery door. "Perhaps she shouldn't attend the ceremony?"

Peg gave a huff. "Perhaps?"

This teased a breath of a laugh from Belle. "As you will. We'll leave her here."

There was a tap on the door. Peg swept across the room to answer it. It was Tom.

"It's time," he said. "Sir Edward awaits your lady in the hall to lead her to the church."

❧

By rights it should have been two unmarried men who led Belle to her wedding, but there were only two unwed men of rank at Graceton, Sir Edward and Jamie. Since Jamie had to serve as the squire's proxy, that left only the knight to do the deed; there were no appropriate married men to lead her home. Against such a dearth, the wedding party made do with but one tradition: music to make Belle's way to the church merry.

Unfortunately, simple ownership of an instrument was no guarantee of talent, at least not in this village. It was raucous bleats and piercing squeals that followed Belle and Sir Edward as they exited the castle through the postern gate and crossed the footbridge. The cacophony echoed against Graceton's tall wall as they made their way down the river's edge toward the church.

A laughing Lucy let the wind blow her ahead of them, her hands pressing her cloak hood to her ears to stop the noise. Not allowed such a remedy, Belle gritted her teeth and glanced up at Sir Edward. Despite the concealment of his cloak, she found the same pain Brigit knew etched on his handsome features. Against it, she doubted he even heard the noise.

As they neared the village's church, Belle shook her head. What had once been a tidy little church beneath its square Norman tower had been expanded, with no attempt to ease the transition from ancient walls built of raw flint nodules, some halved to reveal their dark hearts, to smooth blocks of gray stone. Just as with the ornate hall, this had been another selfish expenditure, for the enlargement was to make room for the last Lord Graceton's tomb.

Belle stepped inside the door. His final resting place filled the church's rear. Pillars of marble rose from its four corners to support a stone canopy, the lord lying in effigy atop the crypt's lid, his peaceful repose eternal. The squire's grandsire had been a brawny man with a big nose, full beard and a pinched brow. Kneeling around the base of his tomb in poses of eternal adoration and devotion were statues representing the wife and children who'd gone to their heavenly reward before him.

Sawing out a happy tune, the musicians crowded into the doorway behind her and Sir Edward. As Peg and Lucy escaped up the aisle to claim their places near the church's altar, Belle stripped off her cloak. Sir Edward took it from her, sacrilegiously draping the garment over the head of one of the old Lord Graceton's children, then offered her his arm.

With an off-key lilt echoing into the rafters above them, Belle let him lead her up the aisle, past the many tables heavily laden with food. Everyone from castle and village gathered here this day, their number easily reaching four hundred. Perhaps it was the prospect of a rich meal and a day of celebration that drew them, but there was a smile on almost every face.

Fearing her reaction, Belle had kept her gaze away from the altar as long as she could bear. Now, as she came to a halt before it, she let her gaze shift to Jamie. Her heart melted. Oh, but he cut a fine figure in those golden-brown garments of his. His doublet displayed the broad line of his shoulder, while his ruff clung to his strong jaw-line. Beneath his brown stockings and golden garters, his legs were well-made indeed.

The corners of his mouth lifted into a small smile as he studied her in return, admiring her, just as she'd admired him. Their gazes met. That hunger she'd come to know so well these past weeks appeared in his blue eyes. It was for her, only for her, that this happened. Longing twisted in Belle. Here in his presence, all she could do was wish it were him she married this day.

At last, the musicians lowered their instruments and slipped away into the congregation. In the ensuing quiet, those who came to witness coughed and shuffled. Sir Edward released her arm. Belle sent him a thankful glance. With a nod, he stepped aside, taking his place as witness, just as the queen had commanded of him.

Stepping close to the man she loved, Belle looked up into his face, praying he could see her affection for him in her eyes. He did. A sudden current of warmth flowed between them.

Tall and lank, Father William, Graceton village's chaplain, had a cowlick at the back of his head that sent a strand of graying hair skyward. His surplice needed a good darning where the moths had gotten to it and his ruff, a good dose of starch.

He glanced from the bride to the groom's proxy, then cleared his throat. "Dearly beloved, we are gathered here in the sight of God and in the face of this company to join together Squire Nicholas Hollier, through his proxy Master James Wyatt, and Lady Arabella Purfoy in holy matrimony," he intoned.

A faithful woman would have listened to the words. Indeed, a faithful woman would have put herself to contemplating the meaning of the rite as she prepared to enter marriage's holy estate. Belle tried, she truly did, but she kept losing herself to the heavenly sensation of standing so near to Jamie.

"If there is any man among you who can show just cause why this couple should not be lawfully joined together, let him now speak, or else hereafter forever hold his peace." The minister's voice boomed as he offered the challenge.

Belle started. She hadn't realized they'd gotten so far into the ceremony. Not expecting an objector from among these humble folk, Belle didn't recognize the sudden hush of the watchers. Then whispers hissed among the congregation. Beside her, Jamie drew a swift, sharp breath. Turning, Belle looked to see what was happening.

Standing at the back of the church was a woman. Beneath a heavy brown cloak, she wore a red bodice and brown skirt. A simple kerchief covered her dark hair. Misery pinched her thin face as she stared up the aisle.

Wondering who she was, Belle glanced at Jamie. Pity darkened his gaze. It said he not only knew her, he cared about her.

The same couldn't be said for those who watched. Their whispers had grown into a deep and threatening muttering. Men pushed their womenfolk behind them, while mothers hid their children. Near Belle a pregnant woman gasped and turned her face to the side, her hand clutched protectively to the bulge of her belly. Across the congregation, many a hand rose, fingers crossed to ward off evil.

"Cecily Elwyn." The chaplain's voice echoed up into the rafters overhead, his tone uncertain. "Have you anything to say against this wedding?"

In the doorway, the woman gave a quiet cry. Whirling, she ran from the church. Jamie took a step as if he meant to follow her, then caught himself. There was a new tension in his shoulders, as if it took all his will to force himself to once more face the minister.

As Belle turned with him, she leaned her head close. "Who is she?" she whispered.

Jamie bent far enough to put his mouth near her ear. "A local woman unfairly judged to be a witch."

"Then, as there is no objection," the chaplain bellowed

out as if in defiance of the interruption, "this wedding pro-
ceeds. Master Wyatt, if you will take the lady's hand."

Pain tore through Belle. In the next moments, Jamie
would speak the words that made her another man's wife.
Tears stung at her throat. Lord save her, but this was wrong.
She couldn't marry one man when it was another she
loved.

Jamie took her hand. Belle gave way to depression. It
was too late. But then, it'd been too late the day she'd collided with him in Richmond's garden. It was to hide her tears
that she stared at their joined hands.

"Now, repeat after me: 'I, Squire Nicholas Hollier,' " the
minister instructed.

"—take thee to be my lawfully wedded wife," Jamie
repeated.

As he spoke, Jamie's finger traced a circle in the cup of
her gloved palm. The subtle caress startled Belle out of her
misery and she lifted her gaze to his face. His heart was in
his eyes. She caught her breath. He wanted her to accept
this vow as his own, even though he spoke the words in the
name of another man.

"At bed and at board," he continued, "for fairer and
fouler, for better, for worse, in sickness and in health, to love
and to cherish, till death us do depart according to God's
ordinance; and thereto I plight thee my troth." It was his
promise to her. For as long as she lived at Graceton Castle,
he would see she wanted for none of a husband's care, save
in one thing.

When Belle finished her vows, Jamie breathed deeply,
the corners of his mouth lifting as joy filled his gaze. Only
then did Belle realize she'd forgotten to name the squire

as her husband. Jamie was interpreting her fumble as her promise to be his wife. For the first time in her life Belle was grateful for her clumsiness. Even though fate denied them the chance to be man and wife in the way of most couples, she would cherish this moment as the most joyous in her life. This man, this handsome, caring man, loved and wanted her.

"Have you the ring, Master Wyatt?" the chaplain asked.

And so the ceremony continued; the donning of the ring followed Belle's introduction as the squire's new wife. Then the minister launched into an uninspired and blessedly short sermon on how Belle should achieve marital bliss with her new husband. Much to her surprise, scorn filled her at the churchman's instructions. Although Squire Hollier had been kind to her and especially Lucy, he'd made it clear that first night he wanted no wife. All this advice aside, the best way Belle could serve her new husband was to make no attempt to serve him at all.

With the sermon's ending, it was time for the sharing of the cup. The chaplain started back to the tables in the nave. Jamie offered Belle his arm. When she'd tucked her hand into the crook of his elbow, he pulled his arm close to his side, forcing her to step nearer to him. It was the sort of game courting couples played, one in which Belle had never before participated. Now, she stifled a giggle and clung close to him, even daring to lean a little on his arm.

They stopped at the forward table beside the churchman. At its center was the mazer. Carved of maple, the big wooden cup was filled with dark, sweet wine. A sprig of rosemary trailed over its lip.

Lifting his hands, the chaplain administered the blessing. "Bless, O Lord, this bread and drink, this cup, even as Thou blessed the five loaves—"

As his benediction droned on, Jamie leaned over until his mouth was nearly pressed to Belle's ear. She shivered at his closeness. His breath was like a caress when he spoke. "What do you think these folk expect of our kiss, me being the squire's proxy and all?"

It was sinful. It was wrong. Belle didn't care. She couldn't wait to feel his lips on hers.

"Decorum?" she whispered in return, knowing it wasn't the answer either of them wanted to hear.

"Pity," he breathed, then straightened.

Raising the cup to his lips, the chaplain took his sip, then handed it to Jamie. He sipped and handed it to Belle. Their fingers touched. Fire flashed through her veins. Against that heat, it was more than a dainty taste she took to steady herself.

As she passed the cup to Sir Edward, anticipation pulsed in her. Jamie was receiving the chaplain's kiss of blessing. All the breath left Belle's lungs. In the next instant, her husband's proxy would pass that kiss to her.

Jamie turned. He placed his hands upon her shoulders. His warmth penetrated the fabric of her bodice, through skin and sinew until it filled her. Her knees trembled as she raised her face to him. His head lowered. She closed her eyes. His lips were warm and soft on hers. He tasted of the wine. She breathed in, filling her lungs with his scent as she reveled in the feel of his mouth on her.

And then it was over. As he drew away, she wanted to cry out, to catch him back by wrapping her arms about his neck, as she'd done that night in the gallery. She knew, because it had happened once before, that her kiss could leave him gasping in need.

Only she couldn't put her arms around his neck. It was a sin. She was married to another man.

Pain worse than any she'd ever known tore through Belle. Her eyes filled against it. Bowing her head, she stared at the ridiculous ribbons that covered her skirts, promises of love for a man who would never love her. She wanted to tear every one of them off and run screaming back to her chambers.

However accidentally, she'd given her vow to Jamie, and taken his unspoken one from him. He was her husband and the need to be with her husband before God and all the world was going to eat her alive.

Chapter Twenty-One

꧁꧂

A gust of wind hit the top of Graceton's hall's roof. It blasted past Cecily, where she stood between two merlons. Down it went into the valley below to scour Nick's lands, ripping drying leaves from their branches. Against the darkening sky, the tossing trees seemed to reach out after those bits of foliage like mothers pleading for the return of their stolen children.

Or wives, their husbands.

Tears stung at Cecily's eyes. Heaven's rage spent, its breath died. In its wake the sounds of raucous laughter and merry music drifted up from the hall along with the smoke from its fire.

She shouldn't have trusted Nick to outwit his queen. Even as she thought this, she caught it back. This wasn't Nick's fault. If she wanted to blame anyone, it would have to be herself for daring to hope love might win, when she'd known it couldn't.

She'd been warned. Her mother had told her, all those years ago, that unlike the poor and landless, Nick would never control his own destiny. No matter how he might thrash and fight his fate, wanting and willing it to be otherwise, he would marry a woman of his own class.

Today, her mother's words proved true.

"Oh, Nick," she cried to the valley below her, "how could you?" For the past four hours she'd stood here, seeking a strength she didn't have. Now, as the sun set and the time grew short, her heart still resisted.

Tears started afresh. The weather had turned early this year, even earlier than last autumn. Another gust roared over the peak of the roof, the pitch of this blast higher than the last. Its breath was frigid indeed. As it struck her, she was shoved forward into the gap between the stones. Of a sudden, her feet were sliding out from beneath her.

As the sheer drop opened up in front of her, Cecily cried out in terror. She snatched at the merlon beside her, fingers digging into solid stone. Heart pounding, she caught her footing and righted herself. It was all the warning she needed.

Knees yet trembling, she made her careful way to the tower door. Once she'd slammed it against the elements, she leaned her back against that solid panel, panting in relief. The stairwell was dim, while the promise of winter left the air within it icy. The wind whistled past the tower's narrow windows. Save for that, her rasping breaths were the only sound.

As calm returned, Cecily dared to laugh at herself. Why hadn't she simply let loose and fallen? It would have been a much easier and far less painful solution to her problem. Her lips took a harsh twist. What a coward she was becoming! She'd known her path wouldn't be easy the first time she'd come to Nick's bed. Ten years after the fact was no time to be bemoaning that choice. It was finally time to do what she'd always known she must.

⌘

As his position demanded, Ned danced in the ring beside the new lady Hollier, a smile plastered on his face. Aye, but behind it, he was weeping.

Norfolk had left the court. Now, in the queen's panic over what her duke meant next to do, Elizabeth's questions would fly. And someone desperate to save his own neck would name Sir Edward Mallory a traitor.

'Round and 'round Ned's thoughts went, just as he and the dancers circled the hearth. It always came back to the same. His career at court was finished. So be it. The price for saving himself had always been too high.

Once more, as he turned with the dance, Ned caught a glimpse of the screens that guarded the hall's door. Dick stood there.

He blinked. The servant held Ned's cloak in his hands as if he expected his master to be leaving. There was a startling eagerness in the man's expression.

It was puzzle enough to make Ned step out of the ring, offering the new Lady Hollier an abrupt apology. Snaking through the crowd of shouting, laughing servants, he came to a stop before the man. "What is it?" he demanded.

"Salvation," Dick replied, his eyes fairly glittering with excitement. "Bid these yokels farewell. In an hour we can be on our way to Windsor to rejoin the court once more. God be praised."

Ned's eyes narrowed. It might have been living under the certainty of doom for so long, but he was deadly sick of this man's sneering at anything that wasn't of Elizabeth's court.

"Be plain," he snapped. "What's happened that makes you think I can leave before the squire's made his lady a wife in more than name?"

The sparkle in Dick's eyes took on a vicious quality. "It's that forward bitch. Even now, she sits in yon gatehouse, warming her toes before your fire. No matter the fate her lady threatened, it wasn't enough to stem her desire for you."

Ned's jaw tensed. Dick didn't know, mainly because Ned had neglected to tell him, that it wasn't Lady Hollier who stood between him and Brigit. It'd been agony to sit at the dinner table each night and see the hurt his silence was doing her.

His servant's mouth lifted into a savage smile. "It seems she's brought you a present, straight from the steward's office."

Dismay circled in on Ned. He closed his eyes. "Nay, Brigit," he breathed to himself.

Why had she chosen to search Master Wyatt's office now, just after he'd decided his future at court was dead? It was the worst sort of irony.

"Go to her," Dick urged, when his employer made him no audible reply. "I'll give the steward your excuses, staying here until you return so you'll have the privacy you need."

"Aye," he said at last, offering his servant a brusque nod as he took his cloak from the man. "Say to Master Wyatt that I'll be gone no longer than a half hour."

"So I shall," the servant said, his smile smug and his bow mocking.

Ned bit back the urge to scream at the man to cease. Whatever else happened, it was time for him and this servant to part ways. Turning, he made his way to the hall's door and into whatever it was his future held.

❧

His back to the open parlor door, Jamie sat at the high table and watched Sir Edward's hasty departure. The tenseness that had plagued Jamie all day deepened. The fact that there had been no warning of an incoming messenger from the men he'd stationed at the crossroads didn't mean there was no message. Was this more bad news from court? If so, for whom, Sir Edward or Nick?

The knight's servant was coming toward the table. Somehow, Jamie didn't think he meant to answer any questions.

The prissy little man offered a bow that would have put Leicester himself to shame. "Pardon, Master Wyatt," he said as he straightened. "There's a matter that needs my master's attention. He begs your indulgence and says he'll be gone no longer than a half hour."

Swallowing his bitter laugh, Jamie gave a brusque nod to acknowledge the message. There'd never been any doubt over the length of the knight's absence. The appointed time for the bedding was in less than an hour. Since Sir Edward had made it clear he didn't believe Nick would consummate the marriage, there was little possibility the knight would miss the moment he'd come to witness.

As the man retreated to a darkened corner of the hall, Jamie's gaze was drawn back to the dancers. Belle was among them, her feet flashing. A flicker of pleasure awoke beneath all the other emotions trying to drown Jamie. With Sir Edward gone, he could watch her for the next half an hour without worrying what the queen's proxy might see in his gaze.

One of the cook's assistants darted from the surrounding crowd and leapt toward Belle. It was the ribbons tacked onto her skirts he was after, even though tradition said it wasn't yet time for their taking.

Belle saw him coming and gave a half-turn of her body, the movement denying him his prize. The audience groaned in disappointment as he came away empty-handed. Watt made the next attempt. As the footman sprang back, he gave a shout of triumph and held his arm high. A bit of ribbon was caught between his fingers. Belle threw back her head and laughed.

The merry sound melted Jamie's heart. She was uncomplicated and honest. If he wanted to know what she thought, he asked. She didn't dissemble or tailor her words into what he wanted to hear. As complex as his life had been these past months, it was easy to long for and adore such simplicity.

Somewhere behind him there was a loud crash. It echoed down the stairs and through the parlor. Frowning, he turned on his bench to look into the empty chamber.

All that answered him was silence. Jamie released a breath.

Just as he shifted on the bench to face the hall, again there was another distant explosion. Jamie froze. For all the world it sounded like a chair being thrown into the gallery. There was a clang of metal, then the crystalline tinkle of breaking glass.

Jamie leapt to his feet. What in God's holy hell was going on? He heard Nick's cough. It was a deep and wrenching sound, one that boded no good for Graceton's master.

Snatching up the high table's branch of candles, Jamie flew through the parlor, then took the stairs to the gallery two at a time. He came to a skidding halt before the shattered remains of a table and the chair from Nick's office. Broken ink pots spouted wee black lakes across the wooden floor. Leather bindings bent, expensive tomes were soaking up the oily remains of clay lamps. The wind whistled in through a broken pane in the oriel, its breath strong enough to roll a bent metal candlestick through shards of glass.

Nick coughed again from inside his office. This time, the rasping bark continued without pause. Terror shot up Jamie's spine. It wasn't often these spasms took Nick, but when they did he could go so long without breath that he fell unconscious. Worse, the bouts were always followed by illness.

Not tonight! Nick couldn't fall ill, not when his life depended on the next hours. Sliding and stumbling through the mess, Jamie pushed his way into his employer's apartment.

The carnage was worse here. No desk, table or lamp remained whole. Head bent, Nick stood beside the remains of the second table, his arms wrapped around himself in helpless embrace as he fought to breathe.

What with so much spilled oil and the possibility of fire, Jamie snuffed his candles before he tossed aside the branch. Then, striding over the litter, he swept the thin man up into his arms. Jesus save him! Nick had lost enough weight that he felt no heavier than Belle.

Stepping carefully, Jamie carried Graceton's master into what had once been a fine bedchamber. Now, a crippled chair lay on its side, soaked in spilled wine. There was naught left of the bed curtains, save rags, while the linens lay half on, half off the mattress. A thick dark puddle lay before the hearthstone, the fire's light gleaming on its liquid surface. Against the pungent stink of the mixture Cecily had made Nick a few weeks ago, tears stung at Jamie's eyes.

Jamie sat Nick on the mattress, his back against the bed's head. Still trapped in the spasm, Nick arched, his body fighting to free his lungs. Kneeling on the mattress over him, Jamie tore open Nick's expensive doublet, then his shirt. As he'd done too often before, he rubbed at his employer's thin chest, trying to force Nick's lungs to relax.

Minutes passed like years. Still, the straining coughs continued. At last, Nick gasped and began to gulp in air like a drowning man.

Relief filled Jamie. He sat back on his heels and watched as Nick sagged against the wall, his head lolling to the side in exhaustion. Quiet settled over the room, unbroken save for the fire's gentle hiss.

At last, Nick's head lifted. His eyes were closed, his face yet ashen from his attack. "Leave me, Jamie," he said. His voice was ragged from the damage the spate had done to his throat.

"Nay," Jamie replied gently. Nothing mattered, not that Nick had brought the attack on himself by destroying his furnishings or that Jamie had no clue why Nick would want to ruin his possessions. "You could have another attack."

"I don't want you here," came Nick's hoarse response.

A touch of anger flared. Nick had no right to send his steward running like some servant. "If you don't want me, then I'll send Tom up here to watch over you. You can't be alone."

At the word *alone* Nick's eyes flickered open. Even in the bed's dimness, Jamie could see the pain that filled them. "I *am* alone," he whispered. "She's left me."

Jamie sighed, anger dissolving into understanding. Cecily had been here. Her need to protect Nick had brought her here, to make certain he did his duty as she knew he must.

"It will but be a temporary parting," Jamie replied. "Once life here settles into a routine, she'll be back."

"She won't!" This pained shout cost Nick another, blessedly shorter round of coughing.

When he caught his breath, he reached out to curl a desperate hand into the front of Jamie's doublet. Despite all the pain Nick's ailments had cost him over the years, Jamie had never seen him give way to tears. Now, they gleamed in his eyes.

"Jamie," he pleaded, an agonizing, rasping grate. "I cannot live without her. She's my wife."

"What?" So great was Jamie's shock, it came out a bare breath.

"My wife," Nick repeated hopelessly.

Jamie shoved back from Nick. Emotions tumbled through him. There was anger, at how Nick had used him. This swiftly became disgust, aimed at himself for not realizing this was what Nick had been hiding from him. Fear followed, against what this attempt to outmaneuver the queen would cost his employer.

Lastly, there was selfish relief. If Nick was married to Cecily, then he wasn't married to Belle. There could be no bedding.

But if there was no bedding, Elizabeth would drag Nick to Windsor. Rage tore through Jamie, strong enough to drive him off the bed. Stumbling back into the remains of the chair, he glared down at his employer. What sort of choice was this? Either he aided Nick in making Belle into a whore, or he stood aside and watched the queen kill his dearest friend.

"May God damn your soul to hell!" he roared.

Nick only stared at him, his gaze dull. "He already has."

"Well, do not look to me for rescue," Jamie shouted, venting weeks of tension in the words. "This is one mess you've made all on your own. I won't be the one to sweep up the slop."

"I'm not asking you to," Nick said, then slid down onto the mattress.

Jamie stared at his employer. It wasn't like Nick not to tease him into compliance.

Nick's gaze was deadly dull. "I love her, Jamie, and she, me. Despite that she's going to annul me so I can get children on the wife Elizabeth sent." He paused to cough, then looked up at his steward. "If this is the price I must pay to regain my title, I'd rather die. Kit can restore it once I'm gone." With that, he turned his back to the room.

Anger drained from Jamie. "Nay," he said.

Reaching into the bed, he forced Nick onto his back. His employer gazed up at him, a terrifying blankness filling his eyes. New panic soared through Jamie. Nick meant it.

"Coward," Jamie goaded. "Will you dishonor Cecily's sacrifice by refusing to live?"

"Poor Jamie," Nick breathed, the flicker of a sad smile appearing and disappearing in one swift instant. "Rescuing me has become a habit for you. Not this time."

Jamie shook his head in refusal.

That blankness in Nick's gaze had eaten up his soul. He closed his eyes.

Pain tore through Jamie. It was death's mask he saw hovering over his friend's face. He wasn't going to lose Nick, not this way. Aye, but how was he to prevent it, when Nick refused to bed Belle?

Panic rose, only to explode into relief. What a fool he was! He was worrying about putting Nick in Belle's bed, when that wasn't what needed to happen. Nay, all that he need do was convince Sir Edward that the consummation Elizabeth expected had occurred. That he could do, but only if he had an ally.

❧

Belle stood at the center of the parlor, her back to its closed door. As she stared up at Jamie, she bit her lip in confusion. He couldn't have said what she thought she'd heard.

"But . . . how can I not be married to the squire? Didn't you stand as his proxy today and speak his vows?"

She watched as he closed his eyes, then drew a deep breath as if to calm himself. "Pardon, my lady. I fear I've made a mess of the explanation and started at the wrong end. You cannot be married to the squire, because he married another in secret."

"Ah," Belle breathed. The face of the woman at the church today rose in her inner vision. She sighed, understanding that poor creature's misery. "The woman at the church."

Jamie nodded. "Cecily Elwyn."

Belle turned her gaze away. So, the squire toyed with her. She waited for rejection's searing pain to fill her. Instead, there was nothing.

This was so unexpected Belle probed her heart, seeking some explanation for it. She found it in the congregation's vicious reaction to the woman. Not only was the squire's true wife as plain as she, but they'd suffered a similar scorn and spurning in their lives. A strange sense of connection woke in Belle. Coupled with the fact that she didn't want to be married to the squire, it was hard to feel anything but relief.

"Here is the heart of the matter," Jamie went on hastily. "In only a little while Sir Edward will return to demand the bedding. Rather than dishonor his marriage vows or misuse you, the squire is content to let Elizabeth wreak her vengeance on him, even though this guarantees his death."

Sometime in the last moments, Jamie had lost his cap. Now he ran his fingers through his hair. "You've seen him, my lady," he went on. "The squire's not a well man. He'll never survive a journey to court." Pain flashed through his eyes and he shot a distracted glance up the stairs. "God damn him, he's up there willing himself to death as we speak," he said in what was more a comment to himself than to her.

"Why would he do that?" Belle asked.

This brought Jamie's attention back to her. His attempt at a smile was but the gritting of his teeth. "It's complicated. But Mistress Elwyn has asked her husband for an annulment."

He paused, the harried look in his eyes softening into compassion. "You see, she cannot give him children. You can."

Belle loosed an awed breath. Her esteem of both the squire and the woman he'd chosen over her rose. Cecily would give up her noble husband so he might have an heir, and the squire would rather die than lose the one he adored.

"This he does, when he could have used me and satisfied his queen with no one the wiser to his ploy," she said in wonder.

The squire had held success in his hands. No one, not even Jamie, had known he was wed. If anyone had, the news would have been spilled at church today, when his secret wife appeared. The hatred the villagers had aimed at the woman guaranteed that.

Jamie reached out to catch her gloved hands, his fingers lacing with hers. "Do you trust me, Belle?" he asked, daring to step over the barrier of custom to use her name.

"Aye," she answered without hesitation.

"Then help me concoct a ruse," he nearly begged. "Help me convince Sir Edward he has seen you and the squire to your marriage bed and witnessed the union's completion."

"You mean to take his place," she breathed, a strange tangle of desire, fear and joy filling her. Then she shook her head. "It won't work."

Relief that she didn't refuse him out of hand made him smile. "I'll be masked and robed, as is the squire's custom."

"That's all fine and good where your face is concerned, but it's all of us that will be exposed," Belle told him. By tradition the bridal couple stood fully disrobed before their witnesses, to guarantee there were no hidden flaws that threatened the marriage's vitality. "The squire is a frail man,

while you"—she let her gaze run from his head to his feet—
"are tall and strong."

With those words, she thought of seeing Jamie
unclothed. There was nothing more she wanted to do in all
the world than feel his skin against hers. With a gasp, she
snatched her hands from his and took a backward step, her
fingers pressed to her burning cheeks.

"Lord save me, what am I thinking?" she whispered,
although she knew exactly what she was considering.
Now that adultery was no longer a threat, its name was
fornication.

"Nay, you mistake me, my lady," he said with a shake of
his head. "It's a ruse I plan, nothing more. On my honor
and my oath, I intend that we should occupy the bed for an
hour, rustling about long enough to satisfy Sir Edward."

Of his honor Belle had no doubt. But then, it wasn't
him she mistrusted. Belle didn't think she could lie next to
him and not touch him. Aye, and if she touched him once,
she'd want to touch him again. Before long she'd be skip-
ping happily down the road to sin. Not that it would be
sin for long. After all, if she wasn't married to the squire,
she was technically free to wed Jamie. Belle sighed. It was
a shame they couldn't wed between now and the bedding,
then there'd be no question of right or wrong.

With that, the memory of today's ceremony filled her,
bringing with it the recall of silent vows. Belle caught a surprised breath. But they *were* married!

True, their banns had not been called, and the sharing
of their vows had been private, but the courts had adjudged
folks wedded because of a single sentence spoken in some
field with but one other person there to witness. Here, the
sharing had been done before God's own altar and in the

presence of His anointed minister with at least four hundred folk to watch.

Belle's eyes flew wide. Lord save her, but she hadn't spoken the squire's name in her vow! Given that, could there be any doubt that Jamie was her husband? After all, it had been at him she'd looked when she'd spoken.

Joy filled her. Certainty grew. They were married, wedded good and true.

In that case, there was no need of a pretense. Sir Edward would have his consummation, just not of the union he expected. Belle looked up at Jamie, ready to share her new understanding with him.

Worry creased his brow as he watched her. "Time is very short, my lady, with much that must be prepared if this ploy is to succeed. A nod to say you'll aid me is all I need."

Belle set aside the announcement of her discovery. It could wait. After all, they had all night.

"Aye," she said. "Do as you must to rescue your squire, knowing I will be your ally in it."

Relief and happiness mingled in his gaze. He lifted her hand to press his lips to her knuckles, giving Belle reason to regret her gloves.

"You have my undying thanks, my lady," he said as he released her, then nigh on raced to the parlor door. "Tom," he bellowed almost before it was full open, then disappeared into the crowd.

Belle was content to exit the parlor at a slower pace. Desire grew, turning her lips upward against its pressure in her heart. Anticipation added its spice, giving that longing a richness she'd never dreamed possible. In less than an hour she would share a bed with the husband she adored.

Chapter Twenty-Two

❧

With the wind howling at his back, Ned climbed the stairs that led to the gatehouse's second-story residence. It roared past him as he opened the door, filling the foreward-most of the apartment's two chambers. The windows rattled in their frames and sudden flames leapt from the coals on the hearth.

Ned shut the door, then leaned his back against it. The only sounds were the hiss and spit of the fire and the wind's muted moan. He looked toward the single stool set before the dying fire. It was empty. If Brigit wasn't here, there was only one other place she could be.

Lady Hollier's warning, that the governess might ask him to wed with her, echoed in his mind. Ned looked toward the bedchamber door. Now, a different sort of offer came to mind. His eyes closed.

The image of Brigit on that first night in the inn's courtyard filled his inner vision. Then, her expression had been innocent as she looked up at him. That woman wouldn't have dreamed of waiting for a man in his bedchamber.

Guilt cut into him. He'd done this to her. Trapped in his ambition, he'd touched something sweet and left it befouled.

It took great effort for Ned to lift his feet and travel from outer to inner door. He tried to tell himself that all Brigit wanted was the fire's heat. It was a lie, or so said the quiet desperation he'd seen in Brigit's face these past weeks. There was flattery to be found in the thought that she should love him so dearly. Aye, but the softness he held in his heart for her made it impossible for him to accept her offer. He, of all people, didn't deserve her sacrifice, not when his intent had been to use her.

Ned stopped in the bedchamber doorway. Here, a far friendlier blaze danced upon the hearth, tossing its merry light against finely plastered and paneled walls. Indeed, there was illumination enough to fill the depths of the tall-backed chair that sat before the fireplace. Unfortunately, Brigit wasn't where he expected to find her. Instead, it was only her cloak that lay in the seat, thrown carelessly over its arms.

With a sinking heart, Ned looked toward the bed. It was ornate, its curtains a deep, rich red. Brigit sat at its center, her back braced against the headboard. Although her bodice and skirts were yet intact, she'd loosened her shirt until it spilled from her shoulders to bare her chest from chin to bodice top. Firelight gleamed against the white swell of her breasts and found a hint of red in the ebony depths of her unbound hair.

Of a sudden, he couldn't bear that she was making this offer. It demeaned both them and what they felt for each other. "Nay, Brigit," he breathed, incapable of louder speech.

Although she couldn't possibly have heard his words, a nervous smile flickered across her lips. She touched the mattress beside her in invitation. "Come sit by me, Ned," she called.

Her words were a husky plea, promising a pleasure about which she knew nothing. No career, no ambition, nothing was worth what this was costing him. Ned shook his head.

"Nay, Brigit, I won't," he told her, his voice colder than he had intended. "Close your shirt, lass, and bind up your hair."

She gasped. Raw color flooded her face. Hunching her shoulders, she pulled her shirt closed and knotted its strings. Then, looking as chastened as her charge might if caught in a misdeed, she slipped from the bed and dashed to the chair. A quiet sob left her as she concealed her hair beneath her cloak.

Ned's heart ached. He should never have come here tonight. Now, what Lady Hollier had warned against had come to pass. Brigit's pride was shattered.

Turning, the governess took a hesitant step toward him. "I did as you said and searched the steward's office." Her voice was tiny and shamed. "I found this."

She stretched out her hand toward him. A single sheet of paper dangled from her fingers. It wore more creases on its face than did Graceton's elderly housekeeper.

"It says that Squire Hollier has sent his cannon to the earl of Northumberland to support him in his rebellion."

Ned eyed her in surprise. Aye, there was shame in her voice, but it'd been put there by his refusal. Where was her worry or fear, either of which should have plagued a woman in the process of betraying her new employer? Instead, what he heard in her voice was something akin to Dick's smugness.

When he didn't reach for the sheet, Brigit took another step toward him to force the paper into his hand. "Here," she said.

Even as he told himself not to do it, Ned's hand opened. His fingers curled about the sheet's corner. Brigit sighed, as if relieved to have the thing out of her grasp.

"Aye, take it," she said, a tiny smile touching her lips. "Now, return to our queen and show her that her squire is nothing but a Catholic traitor. I hope it's enough to restore your good name with Her Grace."

"Why are you doing this?" Ned asked. Nay, it was no question, but a plea. "Don't you realize that in aiding me you betray the squire?"

"What care I for the judgment of a Catholic?" she retorted, her tone bold as she gave a toss of her head. There was just enough nervousness in the gesture to reveal her supposed courage as the bravado it was. "If exposing Squire Hollier means I can remove Mistress Lucy from his influence, I say the sooner you do it, the better for my charge."

This startled Ned. Somehow, because Lady Hollier didn't seem at all concerned over her daughter's involvement with the squire, he'd expected the same moderation from her servants. "Brigit, I care for you," he said softly. "I don't want you to lose your home because you dared to help me."

Her pretty face hardened. "Home? I have no home. I think you mistake me for something other than the servant I am. But if it's my position you mean, then you need have no worries over that. If you were to turn this moment and walk to the hall with that," she pointed to the note in his hand, "telling Lady Hollier what I've done, I wager she'll merely demand I admit to my sin. She hasn't the spine to do more," she finished with a casual shrug.

Until this moment, Ned hadn't realized he was so conservative a man. Brigit's disrespect for the woman who'd taken her in and given her a livelihood offended him. Again, his heart sank.

This was all his fault. He had been the serpent in Lady Hollier's garden. In putting his temptation in Brigit's path, he'd betrayed the lady and led her innocent servant to this ugly moment.

"Ned," Brigit continued, her voice softening as she dared to come another step closer. She placed her hands upon his chest and looked up into his face. "I don't want to remain with Lady Hollier. Why should she get two husbands and me be denied even one? Nay, I'd hoped doing this for you might show you the sort of helpmate I could be for you at court. We could go far together, you and I."

It was a breathy promise. As she made it, her hands slid up his doublet to the lace at his nape. Her eyes darkened, her lips parted in invitation.

Had it been desire for him Ned found in her eyes, he might have given way and kissed her. Ah, but what filled her face was the reflection of his own ambition. His stomach turned. He caught her by the shoulders and pushed her back from him.

"You're using me," he shouted in accusation.

Outrage flared in Brigit's gaze. "And why not?" she threw back. "It's naught but what you were doing to me when you begged me to get your precious piece of evidence. Now, I've done what you asked. You should be willing to do something in return. Marry me."

Ned's eyes narrowed. Anger ate up all his guilt. "I won't."

He wadded the paper in his hand and threw it at her. It flew past her to land at the foot of the chair. "Have it back," he snarled. "I don't want it. I don't want any of it." His voice rose, until he was nigh on screaming. "I don't want the queen's favor or the constant scheming or the ever-present fawning. I'm done with it all!"

As his rejection of courtly life thundered in the chamber around them, Brigit's eyes widened. Tears glistened n their depths. Her mouth quivered downward and her pretense of bold worldliness dissolved. All that was left behind was a frightened, but still defiant, child.

It was her defiance that made Ned turn on her, intent on giving this babe the lesson she so dearly deserved. It was the kindest thing he could do to her at this point.

"And I don't want you," he told her, making his voice cold and hard. "Get thee gone from me, little girl, taking your ploys and wiles with you. Ponder this. What if I'd used you this night as you planned and planted a bastard in your womb? Do you think your lady would yet keep you, offering naught but a lecture to chide you then?"

Brigit choked on her sob. She whirled, her cloak flying out behind her as she raced for the bedchamber door. A quiet wail escaped her before she'd reached the outer door.

Ned listened, waiting for the slam as she departed before he dropped to sit in the chair. In time, the hurt he'd done her would ease. Perhaps, after an even longer time, she might come to think kindly on him for doing it.

Minutes ticked away as he stared at the fire, watching the flames as they leapt and played upon their stage. Like a mouse emboldened by the night, the room's quiet crept out of its corners to enfold him in its embrace. There was something comforting in the silence.

After who knew how long, his gaze slipped to the crumpled paper. The fire's light gave it an ivory cast. The temptation to pick it up and smooth it out woke. So, too, did the desire to throw the thing in the fire and be done with it and all else that remained of his courtly life.

Between the two, a battle raged, each trying to claim ownership of his heart. Aye, but as they warred, they tore that organ to shreds. Ned felt it die. A new coldness seeped through him. Only then did he realize he was late for his return to the hall.

It was the thought of Dick finding this note that made Ned snatch up the wad of paper. He smoothed it out, then folded it and tucked it into the breast of his doublet. Whatever else, the note was his to reveal or not as he chose. Only when he was certain it was secure did he leave his bedchamber.

❧

Jamie drummed his fingers against the tabletop. It was so loud in the hall, he couldn't hear the sound they made. His jaw clenched. This wasn't going to work, although not for any of the reasons he'd expected it to fail. Nay, it wasn't going to work because Sir Edward was late for the bedding. Everything hinged on his being eager to do as the queen commanded and witness the marriage's consummation.

Jamie snatched up his cup and drained it to its dregs. When a maid appeared, the lift of her pitcher an offer to refill it, he nodded. Would that the wine could give him a little of the serenity that Belle possessed.

The woman who should have been Nick's wife sat on the next bench, Lucy cradled in her lap. Tired circles clung beneath the child's eyes as she rested her head against her mother's breast. Jamie almost smiled. The lass was doing her best to remain awake for the bedding, but he feared she was losing the battle.

Hovering behind Belle, her face awash in impatience, was that coarse maid of hers. As she caught Graceton's steward's eye, the servant had the impertinence to speak. "I vow, Master James, this is the strangest place. Doesn't anything happen here as it should? Where is that knight?"

"There," Belle said softly, lifting her chin a little to indicate the far side of the hall.

Jamie looked toward the opening in the screens. Sir Edward was threading his way into the crowded room.

Jamie forced himself to calm. For this moment, he needed to think no further than convincing the knight to dispense with the bedding's customary disrobing.

Sir Edward stopped before the high table. "My pardon for being away so long, Master Wyatt. Can we finish this? I need to make an early departure on the morrow."

Jamie stared at him. It was the first time the knight had ever spoken to him without a note of challenge in his tone. Worry strained at Jamie's control. The last thing he needed tonight was another surprise.

"But of course," he replied. "However, before we proceed with the bedding, the squire has some conditions."

"Now?" The word exploded from the knight, his usual animosity restored.

"Now," Jamie repeated. He dared to smile. "Of course, if

you feel any of them inappropriate, the squire will happily submit his requests to either Her Majesty or the archbishop for clarification on their legality."

At the possibility of his departure being delayed, Sir Edward released a steaming breath. "Spew them, then. I'll hear you out, making no guarantees of agreement."

Jamie's brusque nod hid his heart's leaping. They were halfway over the first hurdle. He laid out the first condition.

"The squire will come to the lady's bed masked, gloved and robed. Since neither his frailty nor his disfigurement is at issue in this marriage, he sees no reason to expose them. Only within the confines and privacy of the bed curtains will he disrobe."

Sir Edward scowled at this, it being completely counter to the tradition of a bedding. Still, it was public knowledge that Nick was anything but vigorous or whole. At court, Jamie had more than once tried to use his employer's frailty as a means to free Nick from the proposed union. This robbed Elizabeth's witness of any right to complain about the supposed bridegroom now wanting to keep those infirmities disguised.

"And?" the knight asked, the word serving as tacit agreement to the first condition.

One step achieved! Hope soared. Jamie fought to keep from grinning.

"And myself, my servant and a footman will remain in the sitting room with you. We come not only as witnesses, but to minister to the squire, should the exertion be more than he can tolerate." Given that Sir Edward expected the squire to provide his own witnesses, it wasn't so much the plot's second step as a screen behind which Jamie could hide.

"And?" the knight replied without hesitation.

"And that's all he asks," Jamie said, his shrug casual.

The knight blinked as if so simple a list surprised him. "I can see no reason to object to these. What of you, my lady?"

Amazement whirled in Jamie, then worry again strained at its bonds. This had been too easy. He turned to look at Belle as she answered the knight.

"I have no objection," she said softly, meeting his gaze as she spoke.

Jamie caught his breath. Her face glowed, her love for him softening her features as it brought warm lights to life in her eyes.

Behind him, Belle's maid bellowed, "It's time! It's time for the bedding!"

Eyes wide, Jamie whirled on the maid, wanting to throttle her. Not only wasn't it her announcement to make, she was making it too soon! Belle couldn't leave yet.

From the hall, a bevy of chambermaids rushed forward to crowd around their lady, hissing and giggling about the bedding like the geese they were. Whistles and catcalls echoed up into the rafters, lusty acknowledgment of what was to come. The musicians mustered, grabbing up their instruments, ready to pave the way to the bridal chamber with as much noise as possible. Desperate to stall, Jamie shot a frantic look toward the screens at the hall's end.

A miracle strode in, wearing the guise of Belle's footman, Jamie's second ally in this plot. The man's hat was gone, his hair stood on end. There was a tear in the front of his doublet. As their gazes met, the corners of the footman's mouth lifted ever so slightly.

"Lady Hollier, isn't that your servant?" Jamie called in a clumsy ploy to draw Belle back into the hall.

Startled, Belle turned in the parlor's doorway. "Richard!" she cried out when she saw the man, then rushed back into the hall, bringing the women with her.

"Oh, Master James," she cried, catching Jamie by the arm. "Something's amiss. Here comes my footman, looking all undone."

Jamie nearly laughed. He'd counted on her affection for her man to wring an honest reaction from her and she hadn't disappointed. Now, even the musicians fell silent as a path opened to allow Richard to proceed to the high table.

"Pardon this interruption, Master James, Sir Edward," the footman said with a bow. "I've been down in the village, and a brawl's started. I think it'll need someone with a firm voice to end it."

His news provoked a happy growl from the male half of Graceton's servants. As Jamie hoped, they were just drunk enough to think a good tussle was a fine way to finish the night. There was a moment's pleasure in Jamie over the trouble he was making for the village's bailiff. Robert Northfield was a vicious bitch's son and one of Cecily's most vocal detractors.

"My thanks for your warning, Richard," he replied. "But surely Master Northfield can see it ended without too much blood being shed."

Richard gave a rueful shake of his head. His expression was convincingly earnest as he glanced from Jamie to the knight. "Pardon, Master Steward, but if you're counting on your bailiff, your trust's misplaced. Master Northfield is at the center of it all and for that I must take the blame. Being an outsider, I had no way of knowing I erred when I mentioned a family, the Bywards I think they are, was talking of buying up the miller's fields."

That was all it took. The feud between the Northfields and the Bywards was legendary, extending generations back into Graceton's history. Eager to join a familiar fray, Graceton's menfolk ran for the door. Their woman followed, some to throw punches for their chosen side, others intending to pick up the pieces.

Jamie set his fists on his hips and sent his best frown after them. "May God take them all, now we're truly in for it," he growled in contrived frustration, then shot a glance at the knight. "Pardon, Sir Edward, but if what Richard here says is true and the bailiff's in this, it could rage out of all control. I must go into the village. Would that I could tell you how long I'll be before I manage to quell it."

"No more delays," the knight snapped, his eyes narrowing.

"You misunderstand me," Jamie said, holding up his hands to protest an innocence he didn't own. "The squire places high value on his village and his folk. As much as he might like me as his witness this night, I know he'll not object to my absence, given the circumstances. Please, let the bedding go forward without me."

Giving the knight no chance to object, he whirled and stormed across the hall for its door, Richard at his heels. Jamie could hardly believe he'd come this far. Once they were in the darkened yard, the wind tearing at them, the footman came to walk alongside his new steward.

"My thanks," Jamie told him, heading not toward the postern gate and the village, but to the tower door Cecily used to enter the gallery.

The man sent him a smiling sidelong look. "My pardon for the delay. It took a while to reach the bailiff, busy as he was trading kisses with another man's wife."

They stopped at the tower's foot. Jamie laid his hand on the man's narrow shoulder. "Now, go back to the village and seek out the minister. Coward that he is, you'll need to prod him into the role of peacemaker. Just keep telling him how much Graceton's squire depends on him to preserve the village. Should anyone ask after me, you know I'm about the village lanes because you came to the village with me."

"As you will, Master James," the man said with another smile and a nod.

As Richard strode off toward the postern gate, Jamie opened the door to the tower and climbed the stairs. He cracked the door to the gallery, then peered around its edge down the corridor's length. Bathed in the golden glow of candles, Belle and the few maids who'd remained to see her into what should have been her marriage bed were entering his apartment. Looking neither right nor left, Sir Edward followed at their heels. When all were inside, Watt shot a glance toward the gallery's end, then stepped in after them. He shut the door behind him with more force than was necessary, so Jamie would be certain to hear it close.

Wishing he had a cloak to catch around him, Jamie waited a moment, then slipped into the corridor. Down its length he crept, passing his own apartment door to enter Nick's. A single candle burned on the mantelpiece. It was light enough to show him that Watt, John and Tom had done no more than clear a pathway in the destruction. They'd wait until Sir Edward was gone before doing more. It wouldn't do to have the knight ask difficult questions about broken furniture.

He opened the bedchamber door. Just as he'd instructed for both this room and his own, the flames on the hearth had been allowed to die down to coals. The dimmer it was, the better his chance of success. He glanced at Nick's bed.

Gone were the remains of the bed curtains, leaving the thing looking barren indeed. A new coverlet lay upon the empty mattress. Instead of Tom, it was John who leaned against the frame. The footman was staring into the fire as he awaited his steward's arrival. Fearing to speak, in case his voice could be heard in the next room, Jamie crossed the chamber and came to a halt near the man. John started, but thankfully made no sound, then came to assist his steward in disrobing.

"Where's Tom?" Jamie whispered, when the man was close enough.

"With Lord Nicholas in Master Kit's chamber," the man replied, his voice just as low. At Jamie's command, Nick had been moved into the neighboring apartment for this night. It wouldn't do for Sir Edward to hear coughing coming from more than one man.

"Why? Did the squire fight you taking him from his chamber?" Jamie hissed.

John shook his head. "Him? Nay, he slept through it without waking. Tom stays because the lord's breathing isn't easy and he's more familiar with what needs doing."

Worry filled Jamie. Surely it wasn't possible for a man to will himself to death in one night. He calmed his fears with the vow to go to Cecily on the morrow and convince her to return.

Stripping off his doublet, Jamie stepped out of his breeches and shed his stockings. His shirt went next, then John reached into the bed and retrieved Nick's bulky robe. He handed it to Jamie, then caught up his steward's garments and carried them from the chamber. One rusty gleam from Jamie's clothing and all was lost.

Jamie shrugged into the robe, thankful for the fact that he and Nick were of a height. Donning Nick's gloves, he caught up the mask. With nothing to do but wait for Watt's knock, Jamie turned the thing in his hands. Save for its fine fabric, it didn't look much different from what executioners wore.

A chill shot up his spine. This was an omen, a promise of where this ruse would lead him if Sir Edward uncovered the ploy. His stomach twisted, his nerves stretching to their breaking point. Ach, this wouldn't do at all. If he didn't get hold of himself, he was certain to do something idiotic when that door opened.

As John returned to the room, he caught the man by the sleeve. "Is there wine?" he croaked.

John nodded, then stepped to the hearth for the cup and jug Jamie hadn't noticed there. "Tom thought you might need it," he whispered as he handed the filled cup to his steward.

Jamie drained the first cup without tasting it. By the time the second cup was gone, a pleasant warmth had taken the place of the knots in his stomach. Watt's knock sounded on the hidden panel. It was time.

Drawing a bracing breath, Jamie pulled Nick's mask

over his head. His world closed down to only what he could see from its narrow eye slits. It was a strange and cloying sensation, leaving him more than grateful for John's arm as they moved to stand before the hidden panel.

When the door opened, Watt immediately stepped inside to take Jamie's other arm. Jamie let himself sag between them, then shuffled like some oldster into his own bedchamber. It was a good thing Nick had told the knight he couldn't walk unaided. A single long step tonight could be all their undoing, showing Sir Edward strong, healthy legs where they should be bird-thin.

His bedchamber was cooler than Nick's, but not as dim. Carefully turning his head, Jamie scanned the witnesses. The chambermaids had backed into the doorway. In their faces fear mingled with their perverse desire to see their scarred and invisible master. Peg stood at their fore, the now sleeping Lucy draped in her arms.

Sir Edward stood near the hearth, the grimness Jamie had seen earlier once more affecting the man's fine features. It might have been the narrow focus of the mask that did it, but Jamie now saw that the sharp-edged interest the bastard had shown throughout the whole of the wedding's planning was gone.

Worry shot through him. Why should Sir Edward no longer care what happened with this wedding? He forced the thought from his brain. Now was not the time for that question, not when he needed to concentrate on how to get past the bed curtains and reveal as little skin as possible.

His head shifted until he found his bed. Belle stood near its foot. Her hair was loose around her, falling in gentle waves to her hips, its color gleaming like spun gold in the fire's low glow. She'd traded her summer bed robe for a thick woolen affair the color of ripe plums with embroidery trailing down its front. The garment parted near her knees to reveal smooth calves and slender ankles. In the low light, her bare skin looked like fine marble.

Desire stirred in Jamie. He fought it back. A ruse, he reminded himself, this was nothing but a ruse.

He and the footmen halted at the bed's head. Rather than wait for the announcement, Belle simply released her hold on her robe. The garment slipped from the gentle slope of her shoulders to pile into soft folds around her feet.

All the breath left Jamie's lungs. He forgot about queens and knights. Her legs were slender, her arms graceful. Outlined by seductive shadows, her full breasts gleamed in the room's low light. Lucy's bearing had left no mark on the gentle curve of her belly, while it was the promise of pleasure he saw in the roundness of her hips and the golden curls that cloaked her womanhood.

His shaft filled. Only then did Jamie realize this plot was the worst mistake of his life. It was all fine and well to love Belle when he thought the satisfaction of his desire impossible. It was quite another to face the potential of that satisfaction and know that touching her without the speaking of vows was disrespectful, not to mention dangerous. But God save him, how was he supposed to lie beside the woman he loved and not touch her?

Chapter Twenty-Three

✧

As Belle let her robe fall, a wondrous, whispery warmth filled her. The need to touch Jamie within the close confines of yon bed grew until she had to bite the inside of her cheek to keep from smiling. It wouldn't do to have Sir Edward think her so eager to join a scarred and—gauging by Jamie's portrayal of him—incompetent man.

"I find no flaw," her husband said. His voice was hoarse and flat, a fine mimicry of the scarred man's manner.

Since there was nothing for Belle to view and accept, she did not speak. Instead, she nodded at Watt. The servant pulled back the bed curtains, then, between them, he and John lifted the supposed invalid and wrestled him as far back into the bed as possible. With all concealed behind their turned backs and the drape of the curtains, they set to disrobing her husband.

Not even a glimpse of skin escaped. Belle's heart sighed in disappointment, even as her head accepted the necessity of secrecy. She would have liked to have looked upon Jamie.

Watt straightened, holding the discarded garments in his hands. John stepped aside, letting the bed curtains close a little. It was time.

Trying not to grin like a madwoman or race across the

room like a child, Belle ducked into the draperies. Jamie was clutched to the far wall, his back to the room. She slid between the bedclothes as John dropped the curtain's edge.

Darkness claimed the interior of the bed. Belle turned on her side, her front to her husband's back, and savored the way his body's heat reached out across the space between them. She smiled as his scent filled her lungs. What need had she of light?

"Good night, my lady," Peg called, the maids adding their own faint farewells amid the dim tap of their shoes and rustle of their skirts marking their departure. The apartment door closed. From the sitting room came a gentle creak of wood as Sir Edward settled into the chair; Watt and John would stand.

Reaching out, Belle laid her hand on the bulge of her husband's shoulder. His skin was smooth beneath her fingers. As she traced a line down the strong length of his arm, her heart lifted to a new beat. Oh, it was heaven to touch him and know she had every right to it!

With a shudder, he rolled onto his back. Putting the pillow beneath his head, he looked at her. His face was a pale oval in the dark, a bare gleam to mark his eyes.

"What are you doing?" His voice was but a shocked whisper.

Belle stifled her giggle. She'd been so busy with thoughts of touching him this past hour that she'd forgotten he didn't yet realize they were wed.

"Why, nothing at all," she teased, as she reached out to comb her fingers through his hair. It was thick and silky.

"Do not."

When he jerked his head to the side, her hand dropped to his cheekbone. Belle was content to trace its line to his jaw, enjoying the way his skin took on a new texture where his beard began. A wondrous shiver shot through her as all disappointment over not having a chance to view him evaporated. Becoming acquainted with his body this way was just as nice.

As she found the curl of his lips, his mouth moved beneath her fingertips, as if to kiss them. Still Belle's hand descended. Stroking her fingers over his chin, she followed his throat to his chest. As she smoothed her hand over its swell and fall, the sensation of the springy hair that coated him there tantalized her palm.

"Stop." The command shuddered from him, making it sound more like a plea that she continue.

Smiling at this, Belle set her fingers in the cunning dip at the center of his chest and traced that hollow downward to discover his belly was trim. A shiver wracked her. Down went her hand, until she found proof of his desire for her.

He gasped. His hand closed around her wrist. There was no strength in his grasp as she traced a fingertip down the length of his shaft. That warmth in Belle grew hotter still, until her woman's core felt swollen with it.

"God save me," he breathed, then shifted onto his side and thrust back from her. So sharp was his movement that the ropes supporting the mattress squealed. "I vowed. A pretense," he said, his whisper hoarse with his wanting her.

"So you did," Belle whispered in return, smiling into the dark as she closed the gap between them. The ropes squealed in the quiet room.

With his back to the wall, there was no escape for him.

Hip-to-hip they lay, her breasts pressed to his chest, his shaft resting against the curls covering her womanhood. He groaned quietly, then put a hand on her shoulder.

Belle's smile widened. If he meant to push her away he'd have to do better than this weak-wristed touch.

Resting a hand against his chest, Belle touched her mouth to his throat. As he'd done to her that night in the gallery, she laid tiny kisses along the length of his neck. His breath sighed from him. Beneath her palm she could feel his heart lift to a new beat.

Her lips reached his jaw, then she touched her mouth to his. He sighed against her lips. His hand slid from her shoulder to her nape, his fingers threading into her hair. The movement of his mouth beneath hers was gentle. Ah, but it was the passion he'd shown her that night in the gallery Belle craved.

As he'd taught her that night, she let her kiss deepen until her mouth slashed against his, so he'd know how much she wanted him. A quiet sound rumbled deep in his chest. Then his body tautened against hers, and his kiss deepened, offering her glorious proof of how much he wanted her in return.

As he realized what he was doing, Jamie gasped and tore his mouth from hers. God help him, but he hadn't expected her to try and drive him mad with desire. Or that she'd prove such a wanton, despite that their encounter in the gallery had more than hinted at her passionate nature.

Capturing her taunting hands in his, he pressed her back into the mattress, wringing a loud cry of protest from the bed. With his thigh to pin her in place, Jamie braced himself on his elbows and lifted himself far enough above her to look into her face.

Her eyes were half-closed, her lips swollen from his kiss. A strand of hair trailed across her cheek. She drew a breath and her breasts shifted against his chest. He shuddered. Where their bodies touched, small fires took light under his skin. Fortified by the wine, his need for her set to leaping. Even as it tore great chunks from his control, he knew he had to tell her nay. They had no choice.

"We can't do this," he told her softly. Then, just in case Sir Edward was listening more closely than he should, Jamie forced a cough.

Belle waited until he quieted. "Of course we can," she told him. "You are my husband."

Jamie frowned. Was she daft? "I am not," he whispered.

"You are," she insisted.

Beneath his thigh, she lifted her hips, just a little. However small the movement, it was provocative enough to make him bite back a groan.

"You say I can't be married to the squire," she whispered. He wasn't quite certain how she did it, but of a sudden one of her hands was free. She lifted it, tracing the length of his nose, then rested a fingertip on his lips. He couldn't help himself, he kissed it.

"Well then, if I'm not married to him, I must be married to you. Was there not a minister? Did you not give me your private vow? As for me, I never spoke the squire's name in the giving of my vow." The earnestness in her voice said she was utterly convinced what she told him was the truth.

Logic insisted it wasn't that easy. Even if she wasn't married to Nick, the complications ran so deep it would take a court decision to confirm it. Still, she was right. They had traded their own vows. Nick was married to another.

Jamie's thoughts whirled as he sought some sort of rebuttal to this. God help him, but between the wine and her touch, it was impossible to think. Nay, but he didn't want to refuse her. This was the woman, his soul whispered, who was his wife. She would bear his children, adoring and respecting them the same way she did Lucy. It was her uncomplicated world he craved, for in her honesty he would find the same happiness Nick knew with Cecily.

With Nick's name came the reminder of the bedding's purpose. Jamie banked his desire. Outside this chamber a man listened, expecting to hear an invalid's paltry thrusts and gut-wrenching coughs. That wasn't the sort of lovemaking he craved to share with his wife.

Trying to set himself firmly into the course he knew he must take, Jamie shifted across Belle and with a sigh, she leaned against him. The need to enclose her in his embrace and hold her forever next to his heart filled him. Then she lifted her head and touched her lips to his ear. Desire shot through Jamie, blinding in its intensity.

Her mouth was on his jawline. Although he swore he wouldn't do it, his head turned. His lips found hers. Their kiss was achingly soft.

His eyes closed as he breathed in her scent and tasted her with his tongue. He smoothed a hand up the length of her slender arm. Her skin was like silk against his fingers. The heel of his palm found the roundness of her breast. Even as he told himself he mustn't, his fingers moved. He cupped the fullness of her breast. She gasped against his mouth.

Across the room, the bedchamber door shut with a definitive thud. Jamie's eyes flew wide, his mouth lifting from Belle's as he stared into the darkness. It was the agreed-upon signal to follow Sir Edward's departure from the sitting room.

Panic shot through him. Why would Sir Edward have left so soon? Where was the man's insistence on seeing the bedding fully witnessed?

"Please," Belle breathed, the touch of her fingers against his cheek bringing his face back to hers. "You are my husband. I am your wife. Love me, husband," she pleaded.

That this sweet and wondrous woman should crave his love was more than Jamie could resist. With a quiet growl, he caught her in his arms. Then, with all the passion she'd wakened in him, he took her mouth with his and pulled her down beneath him onto the mattress.

Belle gave a joyous cry as she and her husband dropped upon the mattress. Although she opened her legs in invitation, he didn't enter her. Instead, he slid lower until his mouth came to rest against her breast.

Startled, because this was something she'd never before experienced, she froze, but not for long. The feel of his tongue on that sensitive flesh turned mere heat into a throbbing pulse. A sound she didn't recognize as her own left her throat. Praying he'd never cease, she combed her fingers through his hair. When he suckled like a babe, need became a wild thing in her. Her hips lifted of their own accord.

The motion teased a groan from him. Straightening atop her, he came to once more claim her mouth with his. Belle cradled him atop her hips, her legs parting until the tip of his shaft touched her nether lips. Still, he didn't give her what she craved.

Releasing her mouth, he rose above her on his elbows,

then caught her face in his hands as he looked down at her. "Love me, wife." It was a hoarse command.

Belle laughed. "I do," she replied and lifted her hips to take him within her.

They gasped as one as he entered her. Then he lowered himself to lie full atop her. As his lips toyed with hers, his hand slipped between them to find her breast. What he did sent a ripple of such passion through her that Belle arched against it.

With the movement came a strange pressure. Caught in its grip, Belle's need to move again grew. Her husband seemed to sense this, for he began to move in slow and gentle thrusts. A quiet moan left her. She felt more than heard his laugh.

"Shhh," he warned against her lips. "You're supposed to be bedding an invalid barely capable of walking. Try not to enjoy this too much."

With a grin, she caught him by the hips and lifted, forcing his shaft deep into her. Air rasped from him in what was almost a groan. She took his mouth with hers, plying him with taunting kisses. Pleasure's pressure grew, and again she rose beneath him.

"Stop," he pleaded, nigh on shaking against what she did.

"Why?" she asked, astounded by the command.

He groaned. His mouth slashed across hers. Passion's ripple became a wave, driven by his movement within her, each thrust carrying her ever higher. His breathing grew ragged, his rhythm quickened.

All at once, Belle exploded into a joy so great she was certain her heart would burst with it. Arching beneath her husband, she let his seed fill her. And when he came to rest atop her, tears pricked her eyes. Their silent and spoken vows were now a true marriage.

Tearing his mouth from hers, he kissed her cheek, her brow, the tip of her nose. "Lord, how I love you," he whispered with such astonishment that Belle laughed.

She touched his mouth with hers. Against the ebb of need, the new emotion shuddering through her was soft and infinitely sweet. So this was what it felt like to love a man. No wonder some women gave way to their emotions and let loose their hold on virtue. She gave thanks that she was already married to him, else Belle suspected she'd be a hopeless sinner.

"And I you," she told him, "my husband."

Chapter Twenty-Four

❧❦❧

The bed dipped as someone sat on its edge. A rush of cold air made Belle shiver, then burrow deeper into the warm bedclothes. Even with her eyes closed, she knew it was Jamie. There was no mistaking his touch as he tucked wayward strands of hair behind her ear.

"Belle, wake up. I need you." Eyes yet closed, she smiled at the word *need*. Hope kindled for another bout of love-making. Rolling onto her back, she reached for him. Rather than bare skin, it was the fabric of his shirt she felt beneath her fingers.

Disappointment was like a bucket of ice water. When had he left their bed? She sat up, bedclothes clutched to her chest against the room's chill.

A new fire leapt and danced on the hearth. Despite its best efforts it wasn't making much of a dent in either the cold or midnight's shadows. However, it did offer light enough to show her that Jamie wore not only his shirt, but his everyday doublet and breeches as well.

The worry that marked his face woke an answering concern in Belle. "What is it?" she asked, lifting a hand to touch his face.

At first, he leaned his cheek into her palm, then jerked away from her caress as if it pained him. "It's Nick."

Belle frowned at his rejection of her touch. "He has worsened?"

"Aye. I've done all I know to do. Now he's fevered and struggles for breath," Jamie said with a tired nod. "Will you help?"

It was guilt she read in his reaction, as plainly as if it were written there. A stake of fear pierced her heart. Perhaps this entire wedding *had* been nothing but an elaborate mummery meant to satisfy the queen. But Jamie wasn't so heartless. Now that he and the squire had achieved their goal, he was suffering over how he'd used her.

Not wanting to believe this could be true, Belle again reached out to touch his face. This time, he caught her hand before her fingers met his skin. "Nay, do not," he muttered.

Humiliation circled in on her like an eagle on carrion. She was a greater fool than Brigit. At least the governess had given only her heart to the man who wished to use her, not her body.

"Tell me," she demanded, the anger in her voice echoing in the quiet chamber.

He looked at her, startled. Even then, he couldn't keep his gaze on hers. His eyes shifted to the side. "Tell you what?"

Belle's lip curled. Did he think he could fool her, the daughter of Lady Elisabetta Montmercy, with so poorly wrought a mask of innocence? Nay, he'd have to do better than that.

"Why can I not touch you?" she demanded again, determined to wrench the truth from him.

For a long moment, the only sounds in the room were the screech of the wind along the castle's wall and the crackle of the fire. "Because I cannot bear what I have done to you," he said at last.

Tears leapt to Belle's eyes at this confirmation. Nay! She wouldn't let his words of love be falsehoods. How could they be, when she'd felt their truth in the melding of their bodies?

He turned to look at her. Misery touched his handsome features. "Belle, I'm being torn in two. Nick's not just my employer, he's my friend. Because of that, I owed him my protection. That's what I gave him this night. But in the doing of it, I endangered you. You," he reached out to trace a fingertip down the curve of her cheek, "who are sweet and good and loving. You, who deserve my protection as much as Nick."

It didn't matter to Belle's heart that he was confessing to abuse. His words made her long to be in his arms. "Why do you say you endangered me?" There was a catch in her voice.

"We aren't married," he said, his voice low. "We can't be, no matter what sort of private vows we shared yesterday." His head bowed. "Dear God, as if it weren't already complex enough with Nick being married to two women at once. What if you come with child?" This was a bare whisper. "If I don't claim the babe as my own, then I'll have made my child Nick's heir and stolen another man's inheritance from him. But if I do, he'll be my bastard and, you who has done no wrong, will be adjudged a whore."

His words sent relief rushing through Belle. Her love for him rose up in all its fullness. So wondrous was the sensation that it was hard to imagine anything they'd done between them being a sin.

Easing across the mattress, she knelt at his side and lay her arm across his shoulders. "I think you overrate my fertility," she told him. "I was four years wed to William Purfoy before his seed took and I was brought to bed with Lucy."

The man she loved raised his head to look at her. The guilt was gone from his gaze. To her astonishment, it was disappointment that replaced it.

"I never thought I would want children," he said, then caught her chin in his hand and touched his lips to hers. It was a brief kiss, and when it was done, he came to his feet.

"This must be the last time we touch. It will also be the last time that I can tell you of my love for you." The pain returned to his face. "My duty belongs to Nick."

Now that she'd held him in her arms and made him one with her, Belle needed more than patience to sustain her as they made their way into the future. "What if this were not your duty and I was not the woman your employer must appear to have wed?"

It was hope that brightened his face. "Then, my lady, I would kneel before you and tell you that, although I am a poor man without house or lands to offer, my heart is yours. I would beg you to be my wife."

As he gave her what she so needed, Belle smiled. "And if I were free, I would gladly agree to take you as my husband, endowing you with all my worldly goods, such as they are. Now, if we are to be proper once again, you must fetch my robe. I will tend your Nick, who may or may not be my husband."

Chapter Twenty-Five

It was like watching a man drown. Belle would fight Nicholas Hollier's lung infection into remission. The squire would own a few hours' respite, only to sink again beneath the heated waves of another fever. So it had been for the past seven days.

Belle filled a cup with a newly brewed potion, this one sweeter than the last, then paused to wipe at the stray, damp hairs curling along her brow. Despite that the weather outside was unusually cold, it was warm in here. Nay, it was hot, what with toweling jammed against every gap in the windows and doors and the fire at full blaze. Against the heat, Belle wore naught but a single skirt atop one petticoat. The sleeves had been stripped from her bodice. Jamie, who slept in a chair in the room's corner, wore only his shirt and breeches.

Head spinning in exhaustion, she crossed from the hearth to the bed. There was no one save Peg to spell her. Brigit had no skill in the art of physick. Belle would have considered training the young woman, except that the governess had been positively morose since Sir Edward's departure from Graceton. At least the nightly tears had stopped.

There were maids aplenty to wipe up the slop and change the linens, but Jamie didn't feel any of them capable of treating his Nick. Nor would the village healers do, at least not according to Graceton's steward. And Cecily Elwyn refused to come despite Jamie's repeated pleas.

As Belle leaned into the bed, she grimaced. So many times had she made this movement in the past week a knot had formed in the small of her back that simply wouldn't ease. Catching Squire Hollier's chin in her hand, she turned his head toward her. Yet trapped in the fever's hold, he offered only a mutter of complaint.

She paid no heed to his scarring as she dipped her spoon into the potion. These past days had made her well acquainted with his disfigurement. She now knew those rigid swirls of skin were far more sensitive than she'd ever dreamed possible. If the water she toweled onto his face was too cool or too warm, his teeth would clench, making it even harder to spoon her potions down his throat.

She might have squeezed his cheeks to force open his mouth, but the squire's skin was too stiff for that All Belle could do was press her spoon to his lips and try to force the thick liquid past his teeth. He groaned and turned his head to the side. Once again, the stuff that might cure him dribbled from his lips to puddle in the ridges that marked his face and stain the bed linens near his head.

Belle straightened with a jerk. The spoon clattered back into the cup. Thick liquid sloshed over its rim onto her hand. She rubbed it off on her skirt, then kneaded angrily at the ache in her back. How was she ever to win out over this infection if she couldn't get anything down his throat?

For the first time, she gave way to her frustration and anger. "Cease, you," she scolded, certain the fevered man as beyond hearing anything she said, "or I'll walk out of here and let you have your wish to die!"

To her surprise, her patient's head turned on the pillow toward her. His eyes opened. She could see him struggle to focus.

"Cecily?" he rasped out.

That startled Belle, then hope rose. She might be able to use the instant to her advantage.

"Aye," she lied. "Now be a good lad and take this for me."

Filling the spoon again, she pressed it to his lips. Like a dutiful child, he slurped the potion into his mouth. Then he turned his head to the side and spat it out.

"Faugh, Cecily. You know how I hate the taste of that stuff!"

Jamie stirred in his chair, stretching himself awake.

Belle controlled her frustration and once more filled the spoon. "You'll take it, even if you gag on it," she told her patient and again pressed the spoon to his lips.

Squire Hollier reached up to grab her wrist. The rugged scarring that covered his palm caught on the fabric of her shirt. Blinking, fighting for focus, he stared at her.

"Cecily never forces that stuff on me. Who are you?" he demanded, every inch a nobleman in that instant.

Before she could answer, panic flashed through his gaze. He tried to shift across the bed away from her. "Where's Jamie? Where's my mask? Go away."

That he could be worried about her seeing his face whilst he lay dying was irony indeed. Setting aside her potion, Belle caught him by the shoulders to press him back into the mattress, then settled to sit at his side. With gentle fingers, she combed at the damp bits of hair that clung to his brow. Slowly, the tension left his muscles.

"Belle?" Jamie's voice rose from the chair. "Is he awake?"

"A little," she called to him without looking up.

Jamie rose so swiftly his chair screeched against the floor. As he came to stand behind her at the bed's side, he glanced at her. For an instant, there was a subtle softening to his features and his love for her shone in his face.

Too soon, grief and concern for his employer took its place. Worry flared in Belle. What would happen when the squire died, as he surely would? Would grief prevent Jamie from offering her marriage openly because she should have been his friend's widow? Each time he looked so at her, it grew.

"How is he?" Jamie asked.

"No better," she replied softly.

As if he were listening to their voices, the squire stirred. There was a new pace to his breathing. Belle grimaced at the way the air rattled in his lungs. She didn't know what it was that kept Nicholas Hollier clinging to life, but cling he did.

The squire's gaze shifted to Jamie. "Where's Cecily?" he asked.

Jamie shook his head. "She won't come, Nick, even though it eats her alive to refuse." His voice was deep with sadness. "She says you are no longer hers to care for."

Belle heartily wished the woman would change her mind. Any sort of aid in tending this patient would be welcome indeed.

The squire's eyes closed. For a moment, Belle thought he'd drifted back to his fevered dreams, then his eyes opened again. This time, he turned his gaze toward Belle. It was pain of the heart, not of the body, that filled his eyes.

"She'll come if you ask it of her. Please," he whispered, "I need her."

Belle's breath left her in a slow stream of air. It was his life the squire had just placed in her hands.

There really wasn't any choice in the matter. She nodded. "Aye, I'll go to her for you."

Gratitude darkened his gaze. "Thank you," he said simply. The tension began to ebb from his body. There was a new peace in the way he sprawled upon the mattress. Belle's heart clenched. He didn't want his wife here to save him. Nay, it was a farewell he needed to say to the woman he loved.

Nick looked to his steward. "Jamie, it's time my brother came home," he murmured.

Jamie caught his breath at the request. The grief on his face deepened.

When his steward made no reply, Graceton's master stirred again, blinking as he fought to remain conscious. "Say you'll call him for me," he whispered.

"Aye, Nick," Jamie replied, his agreement falling reluctantly from his lips.

Content that what he requested would be done, Nick let himself drift back into his heated sleep. Belle looked at Jamie. He'd leaned his brow against the bedpost. His eyes were closed.

"Damn me," he whispered. "This is all my fault. If only I'd realized how determined you were not to marry save for your heart's sake."

He thrust back from the bed. Anger turned his mouth to a harsh line. "Aye, I'll send for your brother, but you'll not be shed of life so easily."

It was a commanding look he sent at Belle. "Go fetch that maid of yours to care for him, then meet me in the stables. Once Cecily is here, he'll improve. He always does." Whirling, he snatched up his doublet from where he'd dropped it and strode for the door.

Belle stayed where she sat as she watched him go. No matter what he wished, there was no cure for what ailed the squire. Aye, and however gifted this Cecily Elwyn was, the woman was no miracle worker. Despite what Jamie might want to believe, it was only a matter of time before the Lord took this soul home. That much Belle had heard the first time she'd listened to the squire cough more than a month ago. At best, all the squire's two wives could do for him was to make him easier as he met his end.

Chapter Twenty-Six

❧❧

A shrieking, frigid wind tore through the treetops, sending showers of drying leaves down upon Belle as she followed Jamie along the path. He'd set a swift pace. At first, Belle wanted to shout that all the haste in the world wouldn't alter matters. Instead, the day's cold, seeming all the sharper after the excessive warmth of the squire's chamber, ate up all desire to complain. Belle huddled deeper into her fur-lined cloak, then shivered as another gust of wind spattered icy rain against her stockinged calves. She didn't own a riding habit and Graceton didn't own a sidesaddle. Although she didn't mind riding in her everyday wear, not with her attire already so filthy that a little horse sweat wasn't going to make them any worse, her skirts weren't wide enough to cover her legs while she sat astride. All she wanted now was to be out of this weather, even if meant arriving at Mistress Elwyn's cottage sooner than she wished.

Her stomach took a nervous jump. God save her, but this whole meeting was awkward. Nay, awkward was what it would have been if the healer were a doxy of whom the squire was fond. Instead, Mistress Elwyn was the woman the squire so adored that he'd defied a queen to have her to wife.

They were well into Graceton's parkland before Jamie

drew his mount to a halt at the edge of a forest glade. Belle rode up beside him and stopped. The clearing was covered with careful plots, barren now that the herbs had been harvested.

Belle's eyes widened in astonishment as her gaze fell upon the building at the glade's center. To call such a place a cottage was to put on airs. It looked more haystack than house, what with grayed and aged thatching extending from the roof's peak to only inches from the ground. In charming incongruity, a new and neatly painted dark green door stood in an oblong opening trimmed out of the thatch. A pair of shutters marked its only window. Except for them, and the distillery meant for the brewing of potions at its back, the hovel gave the impression of being more an elf or animal den than a home.

"This is where she lives?" she asked Jamie in disbelief.

"Aye, yon dwelling and this land is all hers," came his almost harsh response. "Sir Robert Hollier gave full title to her mother and all her descendants in payment for bringing Nick back to life after his tumble into the fire."

Belle shook her head. For herself, she couldn't imagine bringing any injured child of hers to such a place, save that she wished that child to die.

When they'd dismounted, Jamie came to catch her mount by the bridle. "We'll leave the horses here," he said, his tone brusque, as if he meant to break down yon door, then wrench the inhabitant from her house's walls.

Belle shook her head. "It would be better if you waited here," she told him. "As often as you've been here, she'll think you've only brought me to plead your case for you. Where she might close the door on the two of us, it could be she'll listen if it's only me."

As she spoke, Belle lifted a hand to touch his cheek. To her pleasure and surprise, Jamie leaned his cheek into her gloved palm. Even shadowed by his cloak's hood, she saw his gaze soften with the affection he yet held in his heart for her. She sighed against it. If only she knew how to ensure that caring would be there always.

"You're a good woman," Jamie murmured, catching her hand in his to lace their fingers. "There aren't many of your ilk who'd even consider doing what you do this day, especially not after the way Nick's misused you."

Belle's only response was a quirk of her brows. She didn't want to be a good woman, she wanted to be proclaimed to the world for what she was: Jamie's wife. With a wry smile, she pulled her hand from his. "I hope I won't be long."

Leaving him to stand between the two horses for warmth and shelter from the wind, she turned and crossed the plots. With a brisk tap on the door she announced her arrival. One shutter creaked slightly as it opened for the occupant to peer out to see who called. Not even the wind was loud enough to mask the woman's gasp as she recognized who it was upon her doorstep. The sound of the bar lifting followed, then the door opened, its leather hinges groaning.

Cecily Elwyn looked much the same as she had at the church. Her skirt was brown, her bodice red. A white head scarf covered her dark hair. Where only misery had touched her thin face a week ago, it was a far deeper pain that now etched itself upon her visage. After Brigit's ordeal, Belle recognized the mark of nightly tears in the dark shadows that clung beneath the woman's eyes.

As their gazes met, Belle caught her breath. No wonder the villagers accorded Cecily Elwyn a witch. The woman's irises were a true yellow color, their depths flecked with pale green.

"Lady Hollier," Mistress Elwyn said as she dropped a wee curtsy.

Perhaps it was the exhaustion, but this struck Belle as funny, or at least ironic. A nervous laugh escaped her as she bobbed in return. "Nay, I think I am only Lady Purfoy. It's you who are Lady Hollier."

"Oh, nay." Fear darted through the healer's eyes. Chewing her lip, Cecily began to back into her home. The movement was worried enough to make Belle regret her attempt at humor.

"Pardon, it was a poor jest and I meant nothing by it. I fear I'm so tired just now that I cannot think." She stepped inside as she spoke.

It was the squire's love Belle saw reflected in the wild construct's single room, as if he'd set about making his wife's home as comfortable as possible once he found he couldn't budge her from her forest den. The interior walls gleamed with a fresh coat of whitewash. A plain bed, big enough for two, took up most of the single chamber's one end. Thick blankets and furs covered its mattress.

There was a hovel's usual open hearthstone at the chamber's forward end. A single stool stood near it. Hanging over the flames from a metal tripod was an iron pot, the smell of stewing chicken wafting from it. With no chimney, smoke drifted upward, puddling against the underside of the thatch as gray fingers probed its thickness for the roof's smoke hole.

What little space remained spoke of healing. The wall behind the hearthstone was rife with great bunches of drying herbs and roots. More hung from the roof's narrow crossbeams. Shelves lined the chamber's back wall. Filling them as neatly here as in any apothecary's shop were small jugs, jars, bladders, leather pouches and wee barrels. A small table held two mortars ready for use, as well as an array of iron pots and bowls. All the equipment showed signs of use, meaning that however many villagers despised her a good number availed themselves of her skills.

"Why are you here," Nick's wife demanded.

So blunt a question deserved an equally blunt answer. "I've come to ask you to return to Graceton."

Despite her hard look, Cecily's voice trembled as she said, "Nay, I cannot. You should be his rightful wife now. Perhaps the steward hasn't told you. I've requested an annulment. Although it may be a year or more before it's granted, no one need ever know Nick and I were wed."

Belle nodded. "He's said as much."

"I can't go back." There was a pained intensity to Cecily's voice as she placed her fist against her bodice as if to ease an ache. "For ten years, my lady, he was mine. To be near him now, knowing I must spurn his every fond look and touch, is more than I can bear."

Belle sighed, all too well understanding this particular sort of torment. It was no different for her with Jamie. The sense of connection only made what she had to say harder still. "You must come back, Cecily," she said softly, daring to use the woman's given name. "It's time."

The woman beside her drew a sharp breath as she recognized the message in those words. Tears started to her eyes. She blinked them away, then shook her head. "Nay," she breathed in denial.

"Aye," Belle said gently, laying her hand upon the woman's shoulder. "Nick needs you, Cecily, just as I need your skill to help make him comfortable as he passes."

Cecily jerked, then backed across the chamber until she collided with the table. The pots rattled.

Belle followed, then took the healer's hand. Cecily's work-hardened fingers clenched around Belle's, as if all that kept her standing was the gentlewoman's touch.

"You must have known months ago he faced this," Belle said, her voice soothing and low.

The color drained from Cecily's face as her single nod confirmed Belle's comment. Even so, a tear slipped from the corner of Cecily's eye to trail down her cheek. Her mouth pinched as she tried to hold back a sob.

Belle laid an arm about the woman's shoulders. "Cecily, what I hear in your husband's lungs says to me that you've had him far longer than our heavenly Father originally intended. Come to him now, content to let him go. Take with you my assurance that as I give him over into your care, it's with no expectation that you hide your love."

A keening sound escaped the healer. Her hands flew to her face as she buried her cry into her palms. "I'm not ready to let him go," she mourned into her hands.

"Are we ever ready?" Belle asked, stroking a hand down her sister-wife's back. "Come now. Find your cloak and we'll be on our way."

Rubbing the tears off her cheeks, determination came to life in Cecily's gaze. "What am I doing, grieving for him already? Where there is life, there is hope. A moment, my lady, while I gather the things I'll need for him. It's fever and the filling of his lungs that plague him now?"

"Aye," Belle replied, then dared a tiny smile. "I was hoping you'd have something to offer him. God knows, he'll take nothing I make for him."

Cecily laid a coarsely woven sack upon the table and began pulling items off the shelves on her wall. "Take no insult from his refusal, my lady. He'll accept only half of what I brew for him, and that only because I've given way to tears as I begged him to it."

"I've noticed he's not at all an easy patient," Belle said, making herself useful by dousing the flames on the cottage's hearthstone with water from a bucket, than laying the pottery cover atop it.

Cecily paused to shoot a wet and wary look over her shoulder at the woman who should have been her lady. "Why are you doing this, when I have stolen your husband from you?"

Wiping her ashy hands on her skirt, Belle smiled. "How can you steal from me what I never wanted? Besides, I've thought much about you since the wedding day. You and I, we are much alike, I think."

Cecily's brow creased in surprise. "We are? How so?"

"We are similar in appearance, being no great beauties, either of us," Belle said, then realized how odd the comment sounded. "Pardon, I hope you don't mind me saying so."

Nick's wife only laughed. "I've never had any pretension to beauty, knowing what I am. How else are we alike?"

Grateful that she'd offered no insult, Belle continued. "We've both been scorned by those around us. And we both love a man it seems we're bound to lose."

"Ah," Cecily said with a swift smile as she turned back to gathering items off her wall. "But if you're not married to Nick, why do you worry over losing this man you love?"

"I fear his love for me won't endure past the squire's death," Belle replied before she realized what her words revealed.

"What?" Cecily whirled to look at her. Intelligence gleamed in the woman's strange eyes as she added the sum and found its total. "It's Jamie you love," she breathed in astonishment.

Belle grimaced. This was what came of exhaustion. She lost all control and spewed whatever thought happened to be preying upon her at the time. "We've done nothing improper," she said, only to realize that this wasn't precisely true, not if Jamie were right about them not being married.

Drawing the string on her sack, Cecily smiled, her grin broad enough that it made her face glow. "Of course not. Jamie's not one for impropriety." Her amusement faded and she sent Belle a rueful look. "You're wise to fear Master Wyatt's reaction. For far too long he's lived only for Nick's need for him."

Tears rose to fill Belle's throat as she heard confirmation of what she'd seen on Jamie's face. "So it seems," she murmured.

"You're right," Cecily said, coming to stand beside her. "We *are* much alike. I'll offer you my sympathy, guessing at the sorts of burdens you've borne . . . and I'll share with you my joy at finding a kindred soul." She dropped into a deep curtsy. "Thank you for coming to me this day. You've done me more kindness than I deserve."

This was enough to steady Belle's teetering emotions.

A wry smile touched her lips. "Enough of that," she said as Cecily rose. "If you're ready, it's time we returned."

Cecily's nod was brief and filled with confidence. "I am ready, my lady."

Chapter Twenty-Seven

❧❧

On the return to Graceton, Cecily sat behind Belle in the saddle, the heat of an additional body making the day's cold far more tolerable. As they reached the stables, two lads darted out to take the horses. The lad who came toward Belle started as he saw the woman seated behind her, his face whitening. He crossed his fingers and began to back away from the horse.

Belle frowned at him. Now that she knew Cecily, his reaction seemed all the more unfair. No matter how strange the woman's eyes were, a few moments' conversation with her would convince anyone she was no witch.

"Come hold your lady's horse, you fool," Jamie barked at the lad as he dismounted.

The fear of losing his position was greater than the lad's fear of Cecily. He crept close to Belle's horse and caught its bridle. Still, he turned his back so he didn't have to look upon the woman he believed to be a witch.

Cecily dropped her sack, then slid to the ground. Belle followed in a flurry of skirt and petticoat. Shoulders hunched against the wind, Jamie strode for the gate. Cecily picked up her sack and followed. Belle kept pace, linking her arm with the healer's as they walked. "What reason have they for thinking you evil?" she asked, the wind brisk enough to rip the words from her lips.

"It was my mother," Cecily replied, leaning her head near Belle's so the gentlewoman could hear her. "Her need for solitude drove her as far away from the village as she could go and still survive."

Amusement flashed through the woman's strange eyes. "Our home, my home, was once a hunting hut for one of Graceton's lords, abandoned long before Nick's grandsire took his title. My mother believed no man cared that she'd claimed the place when in truth Graceton's huntsmen avoided it and her. They feared her and her companions."

At Belle's questioning look, Cecily smiled. "My mother healed injured forest creatures, keeping most of them as pets. They were dearer to her than I ever was."

Belle shot the woman a startled look. "She kept wild creatures?"

"She not only kept them," Cecily said, "she spoke to them. There were more than a few in the village who called them her familiars. All that kept her from the hangman's noose was her uncanny ability to cure those most horribly injured, folk like Nick." There was a catch in her voice as she spoke his name.

They entered the castle's gate and the battering of the wind abated for the moment. In this respite, both women paused to catch their breaths. Jamie was already in the inner yard.

"Well, that explains why they might accuse your mother of witchcraft," Belle said. After the wind's roar, her comment rang like a shout in the gateway's quiet. "What did you do to win that accusation?"

"You mean beyond the color of my eyes?" Cecily shifted her sack from one shoulder to the other, then smiled, the lift of her lips bitter. "It's the man who sired me on my mother," she said, starting for the gate's opposite end.

"What an odd way to speak of your father," Belle said, hurrying to keep pace.

"It might be, if I knew who he was," Cecily replied. "All I know is that he took my mother by force when he made me."

"Nay!" Belle cried, the word echoing about them.

"Aye," Cecily said. "When the villagers learned my mother was with child, they sent the bailiff to wring my father's identity from her, in the hopes of forcing a marriage and relieving them of spending community funds to support a bastard. As if my mother would ever have taken their coins," she added in a quiet and bitter aside.

"To this day I don't know if she meant to conceal the man's identity, or if his misuse left her more addled than she'd been before my begetting. What she told the bailiff was that my sire had evaporated with the morning's mist. Then I was born with these eyes." The lift of her hand indicated her yellow irises, then Cecily shrugged. "After that, there weren't many who didn't think me the devil's spawn."

"That would be enough," Belle agreed with a nod, a little more unnerved by the tale than she wished to reveal. "What of the minister? Hasn't he ever offered to question you, in order to prove or disprove what is suspected?"

"Him?" Cecily asked, her tone bitter. "He hasn't the spine to stand against the bailiff and his family. Nor does he like the fact that Nick pays my fine for not attending his church."

They paused at the opposite end of the gateway. Ahead

of them, Jamie was bulling his way across the yard, his head lowered against the wind. As Belle watched him, a wholly new concern spiked in her. She glanced at Cecily.

"About Master Wyatt. I didn't mean to offer the confidence I did." She followed this with a nervous shrug.

Again, Cecily laughed. "If you're asking me to keep your secret, who am I to spill it, married in secret as I am?"

Smiling, Belle gave the woman's arm a grateful pat. "Well then, my sister-wife, brace yourself. We're back into the wind."

Locking their arms, they lowered their heads and drove out into the yard. The air battered at them. By the time they reached the hall, they were gasping in exertion and shivering with the cold. Belle swept through the doorway, throwing back her cloak hood as she went. It was dark enough in the passage that she nearly ran into Jamie before she saw him waiting in the shadows.

"My lady," Jamie said, his voice strained and cautious, "it might be better if we entered by the tower door."

"Why?" Belle replied in astonishment. "I'm not going back out into that, not when I'm so close to the warmth of my own fire. Come, Cecily," she said, turning to once more catch the healer's arm. Belle dragged the woman past Jamie to enter the hall through the screen's opening.

It was the dinner hour and servants filled the many tables, their heads bent over their trenchers as they ate, their conversation muted. However invisible Graceton's master might be, his illness had thrown a pall over those who served him. At the nearest table, scullery lads looked up, their eyes wide as they recognized Cecily. One crossed his fingers. Beneath Belle's hand on her arm she felt Cecily's flinch.

Anger woke at their reaction. Somehow, in less than an hour, Cecily had joined those few Belle accorded as her family. She wasn't going to let blind ignorance hurt someone dear to her.

She looked at Jamie. "Is this why you suggested the tower door?"

Shooting Cecily an apologetic look, he nodded. "Aye. Wrong as they are, it's still what they believe."

Eyes narrowed, Belle drew herself to her tallest. "Am I not lady of this hall?" she demanded, even though she was certain her true title was Mistress Wyatt. "I'll bring whomever I please into my own home."

Jamie's expression lightened with admiration. "So you shall," he said.

Belle laid a protective arm across the woman's back. "Come, Cecily," she said, forcing Nick's reluctant wife deeper into the room.

With each step they took, more folk turned to watch. The repetition of the healer's name became a harsh murmur, a warning being called forward, table by table. If some stared boldly at the one they named witch, others turned their heads so as not to see her. Still others lifted crossed fingers to ward off the devil's eye.

At the room's highest table, Mistress Miller came to her feet. With her gnarled fingers braced upon the table's top to steady her, the housekeeper shot her usual challenging look at Belle before turning a vicious glare onto Cecily. "What is this?" the old woman called out, her voice echoing about the quiet room.

"What it is, is none of your business, Mistress Miller,"

Jamie called back, his voice hard with command.

The crone gave the steward her customary dismissive sniff. "You'll not bring that creature into my hall. Out with you," she commanded, waving at Cecily as if she could sweep the woman from the hall with the movement of her fingers.

An instant and complete silence claimed the watching servants. Every soul in the room looked to their steward to see how he'd react to such blatant insubordination.

They were looking at the wrong person. Belle's anger soared into full-blown rage as she recognized the gauntlet the old woman had just thrown. Now that Graceton's squire ailed, the hag meant to claim the hall as her sole domain. Releasing Cecily, Belle strode to the high table and stopped before the old woman, her fists braced on her hips.

"You'll not have," she called, her voice ringing up into Graceton's ornate rafters. "How dare you speak so to your lady?"

The crone eyed the gentlewoman before her, then gave another, quieter sniff, as if Belle wasn't worthy of her best scorn. "Lady you might be, but you're an outsider here. You know nothing of this woman. It's her who's made Lord Nicholas ill, doing it because he dared refuse to wed her, taking you in her stead. She's poisoned him."

If the old woman had believed what she'd said, Belle might have forgiven her. Instead, what glowed in the biddy's eyes was the certainty that her invented accusation would swing the servants into supporting her grab for ownership of the hall. It was past time for someone to stop this vicious upstart's tyranny.

"That's a lie," she retorted.

She returned her gaze to the housekeeper. "I have had enough of you. Not only are you a liar, but you're insufferably rude. I'll have no servant under my roof who dares to argue with me. Your employment here is ended."

Outrage filled Mistress Miller's gaze. "You're mistaken if you think you can oust me so easily."

"Spew another word and you'll rue this moment for what remains of your life," Belle warned, her voice raised so all could hear. Save for the crackle of the fire, her words were the only sound within these walls. "Have you any kin in the village?"

Behind the old women's sneer, shock started through her eyes. With a haughty lift of her chin, the housekeeper refused her lady the requested information.

"She has grandchildren." This came from Graceton's cook, whose rank was high enough that he shared this table with the housekeeper. It was a quavering cry and wild-eyed look the old woman sent the cook.

"Good," Belle said with a relieved nod. This made everything much easier. She wouldn't have thrown an ancient from her home with no place to seek shelter from the winter.

Turning, Graceton's lady faced those she now ruled. Cecily was watching her, fear for her lady, not for herself, filling her gaze. Aye, but approval glowed in Jamie's blue eyes. He gave her the barest of nods to encourage her in what she did.

"You there, Watt and John," she called to the two men. "Will you help Mistress Miller remove her belongings to her kinsman's house in the village?"

"Aye, my lady," Watt said as he made a fine show of leaping to his feet. "That we will."

"Nay," the housekeeper cried out, panic now filling her voice. "You've no right to do this to me. My tenure here is guaranteed by the old lord's will."

"What you say is true," Jamie called out. "However, Lord Graceton's will also set aside an endowment for you, to be given to you on the day you choose to leave the household. As it seems you've made that choice this day, you'll leave here with coin enough to see you comfortably settled. Those who give Graceton their care are cared for by Graceton."

He meant this last to soothe any dissension that might rise from the housekeeper's public dismissal. It served its purpose. There was no hostility in the folks' faces or their voices as they conferred with their neighbors over this turn of events.

Content, Belle returned to Cecily. "Come, Mistress Elwyn," she called out for all to hear as she caught the healer's arm. "Come, help me tend my husband with all the skill I know you own."

With Jamie at their heels, they strode into the parlor. The dining table filled the small room's center. That it was set for the meal meant Lucy hadn't yet eaten.

Belle paused and Cecily released her lady's arm. "I'll go see to Nick," she said, swiftly crossing to the stairs.

"My maid's with him now," Belle called after her. "Will you tell her to send my daughter down for the meal?"

"Aye." Cecily's agreement floated down from the gallery.

The door to Nick's apartment opened and closed before Belle turned to face Jamie. A smile played at the corners of his mouth. "Thank you," he murmured.

"For what?" she asked in surprise.

"Why, for bringing Cecily to Graceton when I couldn't, for protecting a woman you barely know and, most of all, for ridding the hall of that crone. I can't believe you've done it. She's behaved as if she were the lady here since her youth, when she was old Lord Graceton's mistress."

"She wasn't!" Belle cried in surprise, even though she didn't doubt him. No wonder the old woman had thought of this house as her own.

"She was," Jamie replied with a laugh. "But that's no less astonishing than you. I had no idea you were so commanding."

Pleased that she'd surprised him, Belle lifted her chin in fine mimicry of her lady mother's arrogance. "Best you remember that. There's only so much I can bear before I get angry," she said.

"I shall take the warning to heart, my lady," he said.

The need to prolong this moment ached in Belle. "Since you're thinking so kindly on me just now, would you consider sharing the day's meal with me and mine?"

"I'd be delighted," Jamie replied with a smile, but it was the desire to do more than share a table with her she read in his eyes. Before she knew what she was about, she'd lifted her face to him in a different sort of invitation. His head lowered, just a little, as he accepted. In the gallery above them a door flew open and Lucy's voice rang out. Belle leapt back from Jamie in disappointment. Their moment of privacy was done.

In Nick's apartment, the sound of his breathing filled the room. Still, Cecily waited until the lady's maid left the room before she leapt toward his bed. Nick was drowning with every breath.

Her sack clattered as it hit the floor as tears stung at Cecily's eyes. Lady Hollier was right. It was death he faced.

Denial again tore through her. She wasn't ready to let him go. Reaching into the bed, she smoothed the hair back off his brow, then stroked her fingers down Nick's scarred cheek, past his jaw to his neck. His pulse was thready and weak. "Oh, Nick," she cried softly. "What have I done?"

Between her touch and her voice, his eyes opened. He struggled to focus. "Cecily?" It was a breathless sigh.

Her tears came faster. She tried to smile. "Aye, my love. I'm here."

"She brought you," he gasped out, relief and wonder tangling in his gaze. Then love for her pushed all other emotions from his eyes. It was just as true and deep as it had been before the moment she'd returned the ring he'd given her. There was no coin she could offer or deed she could ever do to repay Lady Hollier for this moment.

"Oh, Nick. I'm so sorry. I should never have left you," she breathed, combing her fingers through his hair.

He tried to lift his hand to touch her face, but his arm failed him and his hand fell back onto the mattress. "Closer," he begged. "I need you close to me."

Even as her head told her she must hurry to mix cures and concoct potions, her heart made her loosen her cloak, then slip onto the mattress beside him. As she caught her arm around him and laid her head upon his shoulder, Nick sighed. The tension drained from him. His hand came to rest at her waist.

So great was his heat that it nigh on scorched her through her clothing. Was he so far gone that she couldn't bring him back? Cecily closed her lips on a sob, not wanting Nick to hear her crying over him. It was her strength he needed now. Although she managed to stop it, he still knew.

"Don't cry," he soothed, his hand stroking up her side.

His words shattered her control. Another sob wracked Cecily. She clutched him closer. "I shouldn't have gone," she moaned. "Look what I've done to you."

Turning his head, Nick braced his forehead on hers. "Nay, no tears, not over that," he said, his words broken and breathless, his eyes closing with the effort it took for him to speak. "All I care is that you're back. You are my heart and soul, Cecily. I need you."

It was a long speech for a man fighting to breathe. Too long. With his next breath, he drifted peacefully back into his fevered dreams.

Cecily touched her mouth to his rugged cheek, to the corner of his jaw, then to the place where his throat met his shoulder. "Nay, it's you who are my heart and soul," she told the sleeping man.

Easing off the bed, she reached for her sack. This was no mere skirmish she and Lady Hollier were fighting. Nay, if she was to keep Nick with her, it would be all-out war she waged.

Chapter Twenty-Eight

❦

The promise of a gale carried Ned across Windsor's wide upper yard to the fountain at its center. If this autumn's weather was any indication, the coming winter was going to be colder than even the last one. As he took shelter from the frigid wind against the upper courtyard's water source, he scanned the household's lodgings.

Here at Windsor, the courtiers lived in a long building that claimed the inner face of the castle's south and east walls; as tall as the wall, each individual apartment had its own doorway and upper-story window. Last night's rain had left puddles on the lodging's lead roof and marked its white stone face with gray stains. The windows stared back at Ned, seeming naught but disapproving pewter eyes and no less intimidating than the great round keep tower that thrust up from its mound to his right.

Or perhaps it was only a reflection of his present state of mind. It was over. All he needed to do was meet with Elizabeth's newest knight. Unfortunately, Kit Hollier was avoiding him, which was why Ned found himself freezing in the middle of Windsor's miserable courtyard this morn. Those who knew said Graceton's heir had been called home to his ailing brother's bedside. Ned meant to intercept him before he left.

It wasn't but a few moments later that a becloaked Kit came striding out of his residence, two men at his back. All three were dressed for traveling in the cold, wearing leather jerkins atop thick woolen doublets, and boots gartered to their thighs beneath heavy cloaks. Stepping forward, Ned placed himself directly in his former friend's path.

For a moment it seemed the taller man might push past him, then, at the last instant, Kit halted. Framed in his cloak hood, Kit's face was thin. A narrow sandy-brown beard encircled his wide mouth. It was wariness that filled the man's green eyes as he offered Ned a cold nod.

Ned swallowed. It was his just desserts for setting out to abuse a friend's brother to save himself. He extended a hand. "My congratulations on your knighting, Kit."

There was an instant's hesitation before his former friend clasped his hand. "My thanks for that," Kit said, "but you know as well as I it signifies nothing, save that I am my brother's heir. Now that he is Lord Graceton, I must be Sir Christopher. Ned, I fear I cannot tarry. It took Richard here," he lifted a gloved hand to give a jerk of his thumb toward a man Ned recognized as Lady Arabella's servant, "three days to reach Windsor from Graceton. The roads were so bad he lamed his horse."

"So, it's true, your brother ails," Ned said quietly. "I'd hoped the news was wrong. From what little I saw of him, Lord Graceton seemed a good man."

The reserve thawed from Kit's face. In the man's slow smile Ned saw the possibility of restoring what his ambition had nearly ruined. It was a warmer nod Kit offered this time. "I'll tell him you said as much when next I see him."

"Please do," Ned replied, then slid his hand into his doublet to finger the fold of paper. Even as he willed himself to pull it from its resting spot, shame kept his hand where it was.

Seeking to buy time to build his nerve, he said, "I'm leaving Windsor today as well, on my way to Berwick to help the earl of Sussex prepare for war."

Kit's brows rose. "Are you? Well then, I wish you well indeed. If it comes to battle, I expect I'll see you there. It seems it'll be me who leads Graceton's men north." As he fell silent, he shifted impatiently, his gaze darting toward the walls that lined Windsor's inner gateway.

It was now or never. Ned gave himself no time to think as he pulled the note from his doublet and nigh on thrust it into Kit's hand. "Would you return this to Master Wyatt for me?" The words came out in a heated rush.

"What is it?" Kit asked. Then, because it wasn't sealed, he flipped it open. As he scanned the words, a sharp laugh left him. "Where'd you get this bit of nonsense? Graceton only has one cannon and it was given into Elizabeth's custody months ago."

Bitter amusement bubbled up in Ned. Of course. Graceton's steward was too crafty a man to leave such incriminating evidence simply lying upon his desk for governesses to find.

"Take it to him, nonetheless," he said, his voice sounding flat in his own ears. "I expect it'll have some meaning to him." It meant something to Ned that he had held it in his hand and never used it. Who would have known two months ago that convincing Master Wyatt that Edward Mallory still held tight to his honor could be so important to him?

"As you will," Kit said with a shrug, then undid the button on his jerkin to slip the paper inside it. This time, it was he who extended his hand for Ned to clasp.

"Good journey to you, Ned, and I look forward to meeting with you in the north country."

Gratitude came and went in Ned as he caught his friend's hand. "To you as well, Kit. Until we next meet," he said, forcing a smile, then whirled. It was with a businesslike stride that he crossed the yard, even though he had nowhere in particular to go.

❧

In the weeks of Nick's illness, Jamie had converted Nick's sitting room into a chamber to suit all purposes. During the day, while Belle tended Nick, Jamie used it as his office. Once night fell and Cecily took Belle's place with Nick, the sitting room became a dining chamber for Graceton's gentlefolk. When the meal was done, it became their parlor, where they spent their idle evening hours.

A routine of sorts had developed as the days passed. After dining, Belle, her maid and Lucy's governess retreated to their chairs, set at one side of the sitting room's small hearth. Most often, they sewed. On some evenings, as tonight, Mistress Atwater read to herself from her prayer book.

With the women thus occupied, Jamie found himself once more serving as a stepfather's proxy, entertaining Lucy. Some evenings they played simple card games. On others, he worked at teaching her the more complicated board games. This evening he meant to introduce her to music, something that had been lacking from their nightly gatherings.

As he took his now accustomed spot on the bench across the hearth's width from the women, Lucy came to sit beside him. He reached into his doublet and pulled out a whistle. "What's that?" the child asked.

Rather than answer her, Jamie lifted the slender tube to his lips. It was a tune from his boyhood he teased out of that reed, a sweet song about a love-struck pair who had to surmount great obstacles before they could wed. Not until he had blown the last note did he realize how the song he'd chosen reflected his situation with Belle.

He glanced at Lucy's mother. This evening, she wore no head covering beyond her blue snood. Where the netting didn't conceal it, the firelight made her hair gleam like spun gold. As their gazes met, new color touched her cheeks. Deep within her clear gray eyes, where only he could see it, he found she'd heard and deciphered the message his heart had unwittingly sent her.

A dull ache set to throbbing in Jamie. It was his desire to turn his back on his responsibility and claim Belle as his own. Guilt followed, just as it always did, the sensation sharp and deep. Wanting Belle as his wife seemed tantamount to wishing Nick dead, or at least that was how it felt, even though every improvement Nick made overjoyed him. And so it went, his emotions at war with themselves, each and every time he caught himself feeling anything about either Nick or Belle.

As if Belle had read his thoughts in his eyes, concern replaced the affection in her gaze. "That was very pretty," she said, her voice a little sad as she looked back at her project. "I didn't know you were a musician, Master James."

"I'm not," Jamie said, turning his gaze to the whistle in his hands. "At least, not much of one."

"May I try?" Lucy asked, leaning her head against his arm as she looked up at him.

Firelight burnished the child's fair skin and made her deep blue eyes seem almost violet. There was something sweet indeed about the way she clung to him. He smiled at her and handed her the whistle.

"Not only can you try it, but the whistle is yours. Someone said you've no ear for music and I don't want to believe it's true. I want you to prove this person wrong."

Lucy gasped and sent a glare across the room toward her governess. "Brigit!"

Mistress Atwater lifted her gaze from her book. Something had drained all the life from the pretty woman, stealing the color from her skin and putting dark rings beneath her eyes. Even the thick braid that trailed from beneath her coif to rest against her breast seemed to have lost its ebony sheen. Although the governess meant to look at Lucy, her gaze flickered toward Jamie instead. Not for the first time in these past weeks, he caught guilt's flash in her dark eyes. As she realized he was watching her in return, she gave a tiny start, then dropped her attention back onto her book.

"I only said you couldn't carry a tune," she said, speaking to its pages rather than her charge. From either side of her, Belle and her maid shared a worried glance, then looked back to their respective projects.

Wondering what it was that played out among them, Jamie helped Lucy set her fingers onto the whistle's tube. "Now, put your lips to the tip and blow gently."

Lucy gave a great puff. The whistle's shrill squeal made all three women groan. Jamie laughed.

"Gently, lass, gently," he coached her again.

Lucy looked up at him. Sincerity filled her gaze. "I *was* blowing gently."

"Then you must blow soft as a whisper," he replied as the sitting room's door opened.

Jamie frowned. All of those allowed to enter without knocking were already within the room. Lucy scrambled around on the bench, rising onto her knees to look over the seat's back at whoever came. Jamie turned as well.

Kit Hollier stood in the doorway. Mud stained Kit's boots. So waterlogged was his cloak that his jerkin beneath was also soaked. He scanned the altered sitting room.

"Where is everything, Jamie? What are all of you doing in here?" Panic and pain darkened his green eyes. "Oh, God! Tell me I'm not too late."

Against so honest a show of grief, none of the irritation that usually plagued Jamie in Kit's presence woke. It was good to see proof that, no matter how irreverent or disobedient Christopher Hollier might be, it was true affection he carried in his heart for his brother. There were some families, Jamie's included, where a healthy and hale second son could be a very real threat to an invalid or ailing heir.

"Nay, you're not too late, Kit," Jamie replied. "Indeed, Nick does far better this week than last."

Kit closed his eyes. "God be praised," he said, his head bowed. When his eyes opened again, his gaze fell on Lucy. Surprise darted across his face, then he smiled. "Lord, child," he said, "but you look like your lady grandam."

Lucy, her whistle still held tight in her hand, shot Jamie

a quick look. "Is it him?"

"It is," Jamie replied, the lass's intensity teasing a smile from him. For the past week, she'd been practicing her introduction to her new step-uncle.

"Should I do it now?" she asked him.

Touched that she was seeking his guidance, rather than her mother's, Jamie nodded. "If you will."

Flashing him a quick grin, Lucy slipped from the bench, then came to stand in the center of the room. It was a deep curtsy she offered Kit, managing the honor this time without the bracing finger she'd needed when she'd introduced herself to Nick. As she rose, she lifted her chin to its proudest angle.

"I am Mistress Lucretia Purfoy," she said, speaking clearly and slowly as she'd practiced. "I am pleased to meet you . . . um—" Here, she faltered, Her brow creased.

Kit leapt to the pretty child's rescue. "It's pleased I am to make your acquaintance, Mistress Lucretia. I am your step-uncle, Sir Christopher Hollier."

"Sir Christopher!" Jamie cried. "Does that mean Nick's title is restored?"

"It does," Kit replied, a small smile touching his lips. "You now serve Graceton's lord, Jamie."

Surprise, relief and gratitude tangled in Jamie. Their ruse had worked. Sir Edward had found no further tool to use against Nick. Unbidden, the reminder of the wrong he'd done Belle that night woke and all pleasure in the achievement died. Once again, Jamie's love for her set to warring with his affection for Nick. If ever he'd needed proof that no man could serve more than one master, here it was.

At the other side of the hearth, Belle rose from her

chair. The honor she gave Kit was far less elaborate than her child's. There was a twinge of jealousy in Jamie as he watched her smile at Nick's brother. He'd discovered he was a miserly man, wanting all her smiles for himself.

"Sir Christopher, since it seems the squire is now Lord Graceton, I suppose that makes me Lady Arabella." Jamie recognized her reluctance to admit she was truly married to Nick in this convoluted introduction.

A quick grimace touched Kit's lips. Stepping into the room, he took his sister-in-law's hand and offered her a courtier's flowery bow. "My lady, I must beg your pardon. I fear I'm the reason you found yourself forced into marriage with my brother."

As Kit spoke, he shot a sidelong look at Jamie. In that glance was another apology, this one aimed at Graceton's steward. It was Jamie's forgiveness he begged for saddling Graceton's steward and its household with this woman. Jamie didn't know if he should laugh or weep over this.

"You'll get no pardon from me," Belle laughed, "for I have no regrets over what's happened."

Jamie knew he shouldn't, but he couldn't help himself. He looked at Belle. In that brief instant their gazes met, it was their mutual joy over her coming to Graceton that they shared. He forced his gaze back onto Kit.

"Kit, Nick's sleeping just now, but it's not unusual for him to waken later in the evening. Since there's no need for haste, why not shed those sodden things, then come take your ease with us? If you haven't eaten, I'll call for a meal. We could use new fodder for our conversations."

Not only did Jamie want to hear the details of the restoration ceremony, but he craved news of Norfolk and

the northern earls. All Percy's last note had said was that
Norfolk had fled London for his home. Now, the whole
country sat on pins and needles, waiting for the duke to call
his retainers to rise in rebellion.

Nick's brother rubbed a tired hand over his mud-splat-
tered face, then glanced down at himself. His grin was
crooked. "I'm in a state, aren't I? We stopped only to feed
and water the horses today so we could arrive by this evening. Aye, give me half an hour or so and I'll happily share
my news."

Turning, he started out the door, then caught himself. "Oh, I almost forgot. Sit Edward Mallory sent you
something."

Jamie's brows rose in alarm. Across the room, the governess straightened with a jerk. Her eyes widened as her face
blanched. So strange was her reaction that Jamie shot Belle
a questioning look. Both she and her maid were watching
the governess.

"Aye, it's the strangest thing," Kit was saying as he
stripped off his gloves and unbuttoned his jerkin. From
inside it, he drew forth a single fold of paper.

Jamie stared at it, knowing what it was even before Kit
handed it to him. His gaze shifted to Mistress Atwater. She
also recognized it, or so said the sudden glisten of tears in
her eyes.

From her stance at the room's center, Belle glanced from
the governess to Jamie. Although she recognized the guilt
in her servant, she didn't know its source.

Taking the sheet from Kit, Jamie turned it in his hands.
So many times had the paper been wadded and straightened that it now owned a cloth-like softness. The journey

to and from Graceton left its edges frayed.

"What do you make of it?" Kit asked. "When I read it, I thought it looked like your hand, but it's utter nonsense as Elizabeth has Graceton's only cannon. Still, Sir Edward seems to think you'll find some meaning in it."

Unfolding the note, Jamie looked at the words he'd written, bait for a trap that should never have sprung. Sir Edward was right. There were meanings to be found in the note's return. One was that as much as Sir Edward wanted to use others to save himself, he was too honorable a man to do what he had plotted. The second was that there was a traitor in their midst. Wondering if Sir Edward intended his message to serve as a warning, Jamie lifted his gaze from the note to look at the governess. Guilt nigh on writhed in the woman's face. Here at last was an explanation for what had been plaguing her these past weeks.

"Do you know, with Nick's illness I hadn't even noticed it was missing," he said lightly. "Aye, but gone it was, all the way to Windsor with Sir Edward." With a subtle glance at Mistress Atwater he added, "All that leaves me wondering is who took it from the corner of my desk and gave it to the knight?"

Chapter Twenty-Nine

❧

Belle's heart ached as she understood what Jamie was saying. With a sad, slow breath, she turned to look at Lucy's governess. "Oh, Brigit," she said in dark disappointment.

The tears filling the lass's dark eyes spilled down onto her cheeks. Her lips trembled. "I—I . . ." she mumbled, sounding wholly guilt-stricken.

"Lying will only make matters worse," Belle warned softly. "Say it plain. You took the note from Master James's desk, didn't you?"

The young woman's mouth twisted. She nodded. There was nothing but misery in the motion.

Belle's ache deepened. This was all her fault. She'd known how badly Brigit wanted to escape her fate. So, too, had she known what drove Sir Edward. Why hadn't she realized when she'd seen them in the garden just where those two ambitions might lead if they merged? Now, between her blindness and her leniency, Brigit was ruined.

"Oh, lass, how I wish you hadn't," Belle said, her voice quavering as she battled her own tears. "Many things I can forgive, but not so deep a betrayal of my trust as this. I think it would be best for us both if you returned to your father's house."

Fear, born of the sort of punishment that would likely greet her there, filled Brigit's gaze. Leaping to her feet, she dropped her book and hurtled past Nick's brother out of the room, no doubt on her way to cry her eyes out in her chamber.

"Should I stop her?" Sir Christopher asked, his face alive with confusion as he half-turned to follow the woman.

"Nay," Belle said with a sigh, "but thank you."

Nick's brother gave her an uncertain smile. With a quick nod he left the sitting room.

"Would you prefer that I go to her, my lady?" Peg asked. Despite all her bluster, Peg was as fond of Brigit as she was of Belle.

"Nay. I think this is mine to do," Belle replied, pointing to the taper Brigit had been using to read. "Just hand me yon candle to light my way."

As Peg brought her the candle, Lucy caught her mother by the hand. Worry filled her daughter's eyes. "Why is Brigit crying? What did she do? I want to go with you."

Judging by Brigit's past behavior, Belle fully expected the governess to lash out at her. It wasn't something Belle wanted her child to hear, all the more so because Lucy liked Brigit. She wanted her daughter's memories of the woman to remain kind.

"Nay, sweetheart, you must stay here," Belle said.

"But I want to go with you!" Lucy repeated, tears filling her eyes as her voice took on a shrill edge.

"What is this?" Jamie said, coming to his feet to claim the child's free hand. "Will you abandon me, mistress? My, but you're a fickle one, you are. Why, you've barely tried the whistle I brought you."

As Belle shot him a thankful smile and received a

322 · Denise Domning

friendly lift of his brows in return, Lucy glanced from her mother to her proxy stepfather. A battle raged on her pretty face. It was her growing adoration for Graceton's steward that won. She released her mother's hand. "I'll stay with you, Master James," she said, running to retrieve the whistle as she spoke.

He smiled at her. "That's my lass."

Belle strode out into the gallery, leaving Nick's apartment door ajar behind her. A full-fledged gale drove rain against the oriels. Against it, the night was inky. Belle's single candle cut but a tiny circle in the wide corridor's darkness as she made her way toward the nursery.

The farther she got from the hall, the colder the gallery became until she swore she could see her breath cloud before her. Shivering, she stopped before the nursery door. The faint sound of a woman sobbing met her ears. Belle sighed and steeled herself to face Brigit, then opened the door.

It was warmer in Lucy's sitting room than in the gallery, even though the room's fire had died. Wanting to warn Brigit she was coming, Belle pulled the door shut with a bang. The weeping ceased.

The door to Brigit's room, the smaller of the apartment's two bedchambers, was open. There wasn't much in the tiny and windowless room save a cot and Brigit's small chest. Belle frowned. The governess wasn't sprawled upon her bed.

She turned toward Lucy's chamber. Given that it had a fire, perhaps Brigit was there. "Brigit?" she called as she reached the door.

Some servant had recently fed the fire in Lucy's chamber,

for hearty flames leapt and danced in the hearth. But Brigit wasn't sitting upon the stool near the hearth or lying upon Lucy's bed.

Belle turned to look across the sitting room to the nursery's open door. This was strange indeed. She could have sworn she'd heard the woman weeping. She retreated to the gallery and turned to retrace her steps. It was hard to imagine Brigit running to the house's common area, but there was simply nowhere else for her to be.

As she passed Nick's apartment, Belle caught the sound of Jamie's voice. He was explaining to her daughter how people sometimes did things they shouldn't, then paid a price for their mistakes. Any other time such proof of Jamie's caring would have pleased Belle. Tonight, it only added to her worry.

Sighing, Belle made her way down the stairs and into the parlor. Lucy would grieve over losing Brigit, who would be gone before week's end. So, too, would her daughter grieve over Nick's earthly departure. Ah! If only children could be protected from life's pain.

As Belle opened the parlor door, a gust of icy air blew past her with force enough to snuff her candle. That the hall screens weren't enough to baffle this night's wind was proof of the gale's strength. Those few who lingered in the hall were gathered near the blazing hearth. Although there were no women among them, she found Richard in their midst, yet wearing his traveling attire. As if he sensed her presence, he lifted his head.

"My lady?" he called.

Carrying her dead candle, Belle closed the distance from parlor door to fire. To a man, the servants rose to offer her their respect. So it had been since Mistress Miller's departure. Tonight, Belle barely noticed.

"Did Mistress Atwater pass through the hall a moment ago?" she asked her footman.

Even in the firelight, she could see Richard's face tighten in concern. "Nay, no one has come this way at all, not since I arrived."

Only then did it occur to Belle that the sobbing she'd heard might have come from the tower stairwell. She whirled to stare back the way she'd come. The candle holder clattered as it hit the hall floor. She pressed a hand to her mouth.

Forgetting all convention, Richard came to stand beside her. "What's happened?" he demanded.

Belle turned and grabbed him by the arm. "Oh, Richard," she cried, "I think Brigit might have gone out on the wall!"

Terror for the woman he adored dashed through Richard's eyes. Ripping free of Belle's hold, he raced across the hall. Belle caught up her skirts and followed at a dead run.

She took the parlor stairs two at a time. Richard was already across the gallery when she reached the top. The sound of a running man had brought Jamie to the door of Nick's apartment.

"I need you," Belle cried, grabbing his arm as if to pull him out into the gallery.

With a brisk nod he stepped out of the door; Lucy shot through the opening behind him. "I'm coming, too," she said, catching her mother's free hand.

Releasing Jamie, Belle dragged her daughter back into

the sitting room. Peg was on her feet, her chin lifted as she tried to see what went forward in the gallery. Belle shoved Lucy across the room toward the maid.

"Hold her." So great was her fear that Belle's words came out as a cold, hard command.

Surprise blossomed on Peg's face. Lucy's face crumpled. "I don't want to stay here, Mama," she began to whine.

"Take her now!" Belle shouted, her words echoing around the chamber.

Lucy froze, her mouth quivering and her eyes wide. Cecily appeared in Nick's bedchamber doorway, her face alive with alarm. Peg nigh on leapt upon Lucy. "I've got her," the maid said, catching the child by the arms. "Go!"

Turning back to the doorway, Belle once again caught Jamie by the arm. They started down the gallery at a jog. "What is it?" he asked.

"Brigit's out on the wall," she replied in terse explanation.

"Oh, Lord," he sighed, then stopped, catching her by the shoulders to force her to halt as well. "Belle, stay here. I'll see to her."

"Nay!" Belle said in sharp refusal. "Brigit is mine to care for."

Even in the gallery's darkness she could see the argument form on his face. She had no time for this. Ripping free of his hold, she ran toward the gallery's end.

"Belle," Jamie called after her, but she was already in the tower.

With two doors open, the wind moaned its way down the spiral of the stairway. Belle barely felt the cold as she scaled the steps. About halfway to the top, she again caught the sound of a woman sobbing as if her heart were broken. It sounded so close that hope spiked in Belle. Could Richard have already coaxed Brigit back into the house? A few feet from the tower door, the weeping ceased abruptly.

"Brigit," Richard called, his voice raised to a shout. "Come back. Come away from the edge."

Belle gave a terrified cry and tore up the final steps to halt in the doorway leading to the wall walk. Richard stood a few feet in front of her, bracing himself against a stone merlon. As Jamie came up behind her, Belle leaned out to peer down the wall's length for Brigit, then gasped.

The governess was so far out on the wall that she was standing above Nick's chamber, clinging to another merlon. Her coif was gone. The wind ripped long streamers of hair from her plait. They writhed and curled up toward the thick layer of charcoal clouds seething only a little way above their heads. Grayed by the night, her green skirts billowed. Aye, but it wouldn't be long before the drumming rain weighed them down with moisture.

"Come, Brigit. Come to me," Richard called. For an instant, the wind ebbed. He strode from one merlon to the next. "There's nothing you've done that's so bad you should come out here on a night like this."

Forgetting caution for a moment, Brigit straightened and whirled toward him. "How would you know?" she shouted, then the next gust caught her.

She staggered to the side, her feet sliding on the wet wall walk as she fought for balance. A frightened moan left Belle's lips as the image of Brigit tumbling over the wall's edge tore her heart in twain. God save her, but she couldn't let this girl fall to her death. She didn't breathe until Brigit caught the merlon and was safe again.

Richard advanced farther. "Lady Hollier is frightened to death for you. Now, come back inside the house."

"She isn't frightened for me," Brigit shrieked. "She doesn't care what happens to me!"

Belle gave a pained squeak. "You're wrong, Brigit," she called. "I do care."

Jamie caught her arm, then pressed a finger to his lips as if to warn her to silence. "Richard," he called to the footman, motioning the servant back to them.

The force of the wind was such that it took Richard several minutes to battle his way back to them. "Aye, Master Steward?" he asked as he ducked into the relative shelter of the tower's upper landing.

"You should go back downstairs," Jamie said, his tone as commonplace as if he were suggesting a walk in the garden. "I'll stay here to watch over her."

Belle frowned at him in confusion.

"You heard her," Jamie said calmly. "There's no shame in her voice, only anger. I think she's trying to use your fear for her to change your mind about sending her away. I'm wagering that once you and Richard are gone and there's only me to talk to, she'll come off the wall."

What he said conflicted with every need boiling in her heart. "Nay." She shook her head. "She's still my responsibility. I can't leave, not while she's on this wall."

Richard shot a fearful glance over his shoulder at the woman he loved. "How can we leave her?" he whispered.

Brigit chose that moment to lift her head from the merlon. "I beg you, my lady," she sobbed, "don't send me home."

The genuine fear and pain in the lass's voice shot through Belle. With a gasp, she pushed at Richard so she could see the governess. The wind rose into another gust, this one strong enough to flatten Brigit against her block of stone.

When it ceased, the young woman stayed where she half-lay, clutching the merlon. The sound of her sobs rose above the wind. "Help me, my lady. I'm so afraid," Brigit cried, sounding for all the world like Lucy.

Belle's heart broke. It no longer mattered what Brigit had done. "I'm coming, sweetheart," she cried, leaping past Richard and out into the raging night.

"Belle!" Jamie roared from the doorway behind her.

Belle paid him no heed as she trotted along the wall's top. Icy rain pelted her, stinging her skin as it soaked her shirt. With naught but slick stones beneath her feet and the wind in her skirts, she more slid than strode. She was half-way across the wall before the next gust hit.

Reaching for the nearest merlon, Belle clung, fighting for balance against the battering wind. The force of the blast pulled at the combs holding her snood in place. In the next moment, the netting tore free, then sailed out over the wall's edge, her hair streaming out after it.

"Oh, my lady, I'm so afraid," the governess cried out again, spurring Belle's need to reach her. She dashed past two merlons and nearly reached the third when the next gust caught her.

The wind picked up her skirts. Her feet slid. Suddenly, Belle could see the river below the wall, boiling and swollen with rain. Heart pounding, she threw herself forward, her fingers digging into the chilly stone. Panting in terror, she pulled herself to safety.

"God take you, Belle," Jamie raged from four merlons back where the wind was holding him captive. "You stop this instant!"

Belle barely heard him as she looked ahead. The governess was now only two merlons away. "I'm coming, Brigit," she called, more to steady her own heart than to reassure the lass.

"You should leave me, after what I've done," Brigit cried without lifting her head from the stone. "Oh, my lady, I'm so ashamed."

Here was proof that Jamie was wrong. It wasn't anger, but shame that filled Brigit. Aye, and where there was shame, there was regret. With regret came the possibility of redemption.

Belle tried to lift her feet and nearly toppled over. Her brush with death left her knees too weak to support her.

"Come to me, sweetheart," Belle called instead. "Come now, while the wind is low."

Brigit only shook her head. "If I come off the wall, you'll send me home," she sniffled.

Strong arms closed about Belle's waist as Jamie yanked her back against him. "I don't care what she does, but you're coming off this damn wall right now." His voice was hard and angry in her ear.

"Nay," Belle cried, clinging to the merlon with all her might. "I can't go back without her."

"I don't want to go home," Brigit sobbed, her voice rising with each word until she was nigh on howling with the wind. "Oh, please, my lady. Please, I promise I'll never again err."

It was more than enough contrition for Belle. "Of

course you can stay, Brigit. Just come off the wall with us."

"Thank you, my lady. You'll not regret it, this I vow."

As the governess stepped into the space between the merlons, a blast of air came screaming over the hall's roof, its shriek so high it sounded almost human. It pummeled Jamie and Belle, shoving them against the stone at their side. Brigit screamed, arms flailing as she tried to reach the stone in front of her. Her hair snaked out over the wall's edge. Her now heavy skirts followed.

Even as Belle stretched out her arms, trying to span a distance three times their length, Brigit lost her balance. "Nay!" Belle shouted. From the tower's door, Richard echoed her denial.

They were too late. Brigit was gone.

"Nay," Belle breathed as she sagged against Jamie.

Jamie tightened his hold on her, then leaned over the merlon. There was no sign of the governess on either of the river's banks. If, by some miracle, she'd survived the fall, that meant she was now tumbling in the water's raging current. Certainly unconscious and dressed in heavy clothing, there was no chance she'd survive.

He turned to look toward Belle's footman at the tower's door, but the man was gone, no doubt to the river's edge.

Only when Jamie had guided a trembling Belle back to the shelter of the tower did he let himself believe they were safe. His relief was deep enough to make his own knees weaken. He leaned back against the tower wall, Belle caught close in the circle of his arms.

A ragged breath tore from him. He'd nearly lost her tonight. God save him, but he had no idea how precious Belle had become until he'd seen her teetering on the wall's edge. In that moment, he'd discovered his life wasn't worth living without her in it.

Belle's hand curled into his doublet. Jamie looked down at her.

There wasn't an inch of either of them that wasn't soaked through. Her hair was like a web, the long wet strands tangling around them as if to bind them, one to another. She lifted her face to look at him. Misery pinched her features.

"Oh, Jamie," she whispered, "I killed her."

That Belle should feel the least bit of responsibility for the fate that tantrumming chit brought on herself went straight to his heart. He caught her face in his hands. "Nay, love, you didn't. She was playing a game and she fell."

The feel of her chilled skin against his palms brought with it the need to comfort her. Lowering his head, he touched his mouth to hers. Her lips clung hungrily to his. Jamie tasted the salt of her tears.

After a moment, he released her mouth. "God help me," he breathed, his lips brushing hers as he spoke. "I thought I'd die when I saw you sliding toward the edge."

Once again, he caught her mouth with his. This time, there was far more passion than comfort in his kiss. Footsteps rang on the stairs. They leapt apart.

"My lady?" her maid called out as she climbed. "What's happening? Richard raced by a few moments ago and without a single word. Where's Brigit?"

Frustration grew in Jamie. Until he could claim Belle as his own, their every touch would be adjudged sinful.

Belle's tears were flowing again. She looked up at him. "What if the river carries her too far and you don't find her?" It was a plea.

Even though the maid was rounding the last turn of the stairs, Jamie dared to lift a hand and touch her cheek. "Even if it carries her all the way to the sea, I'll find her for you. I'll not leave her out there alone, on that you have my word."

There was a quiet gasp from Belle's servant as she caught sight of the caress. Jamie let his hand fall to his side. Then, pushing past the servant, he went to do as he had vowed.

Chapter Thirty

❧❧❧

Dawn two days after they laid Brigit to rest in the village churchyard found Jamie sitting on the stool next to Nick's bed. Nick's breath was coming in short, rattling gasps. Yesterday afternoon, his fever had spiked anew. Overnight, the heat became so great that Father Walter had come.

It was against the possibility that Nick wouldn't survive the night that the Catholic priest had administered his patron's final rite. Then they'd waited. Now Kit slept on the sitting room floor just outside the bedchamber door. The priest had gone to take his rest in Cecily's makeshift chamber, while the healer lay curled on Nick's bed between her love and the wall.

Only Jamie and Belle were still up and about. Belle stood at the bed's end. Her face was marked with exhaustion as she wrung out another cloth to lay upon Nick's brow.

In the window across the room the pink of dawn lightened into the gold of a fully risen sun. Jamie's hope brightened with it. No matter how weak Nick's body might have become, his will was stronger. If Nick decided to live, then live he would.

Even as Jamie told himself this, a part of him argued that less air seemed to fill Nick's lungs with each breath.

Indeed, his friend's body had grown quiet; he lay with

the stillness of a man already dead. Panic flicked in Jamie.

As if he felt his steward's reaction, Nick's eyes opened. They gleamed with the life that seemed missing from the rest of him. There was a touch of sardonic amusement in their expression, as if Nick found it odd to be in this state somewhere between life and death.

Jamie's nerves tightened until he thought he'd scream. It was acceptance of death he saw in Nick's gaze. Reaching out, he caught Nick's hand, then willed him into the next breath.

Belle laid her hand upon his shoulder. "He needs to rest. You should go," she said. Her face softened with sadness. Aye, but she'd worn the same expression since they'd laid Brigit to her final rest.

"I'm not leaving," he replied.

Graceton's lord coughed, the sound liquid with what was drowning him. "Damage—from—gale?" he asked his steward, his voice breathless, his words so low Jamie could barely hear them.

Belle leaned into the bed to lay her cloth upon Nick's forehead. "He's asking you for a report on the damage the storm did," she said.

Anger rose. He glared at the woman he loved. Did she think he, who had lived ten years with Nick, needed a translation from a woman who'd dwelt here not quite two months?

Nick's hand moved in Jamie's, catching his attention. He turned his gaze back to his employer. There was no mistaking the command in Nick's gaze. In irritation, Jamie gave way. If Nick wanted the local reports, he could share them, having heard them all yesterday.

"The bailiff says a number of cottage roofs were damaged, but only Goody White's hovel was toppled. It was fortunate that most of the grain was already in the barn in preparation for flailing, so little of that was lost. I've not yet heard from your other manors." Graceton held two small manors, actually no more than small working farms with naught but hamlets around them. "The foresters say quite a few trees were felled in the parkland."

Nick's eyes narrowed. "Go." His voice was naught but a raspy thread. "See—damage."

Pain tore through Jamie. His dearest friend was sending him away when Nick had never needed him more. "Nay!"

Gentle laughter started through Nick's gaze then died as if he hadn't the strength left to entertain the emotion. "What sort—of steward—?" His voice devolved into panting.

"I won't go," he warned Nick, but his words came too late. Nick's eyes had closed. With a sigh, Graceton's lord slipped into something that wasn't quite unconsciousness or sleep.

So quickly did Jamie come to his feet that he overbalanced the stool. It crashed to the floor. On the bed, Cecily murmured and eased closer to her love.

"Damn you," Jamie cried to the unconscious man, "you're sending me away so you can escape while I'm gone!"

Belle caught him by the sleeve. "Hush, Jamie," she chided gently. "He's only resting."

With her touch, the need to feel her in his arms overcame him. It didn't matter that the bedchamber door was open. It didn't matter that Kit might waken and walk in at any moment, or that a servant might enter. Jamie pulled the woman he loved close to him and bent his head into her shoulder.

"Nay, he's not resting," he grieved. "God save me, Belle. He's leaving me."

Her arms encircled his waist. She touched her lips to his jaw. "Aye, my love. He is."

It was quiet confirmation of what Jamie most dearly didn't wish to hear. His heart clenched. "If he's dying, then why does he send me away?"

Leaning back in his embrace, Belle waited until he straightened, then looked up into his face. "Because he knows how much you want him to stay. He's trying to make it easier for you to let him go."

Jamie turned, Belle yet caught in his arms, and looked at the man on the bed. All that remained of his friend was a wasted and frail shell of flesh. Disgust at himself rose in Jamie. What sort of man was he that he selfishly demanded Nick keep living, when that state had become torment? Then, as if it had been lurking fully formed in some hidden place within him, acceptance woke. As it claimed his heart, all he could hear was the sound of Nick's labored breathing.

Nay, he could not sit here and watch his dearest friend slip away from him. With that thought came the urgent need to do something, anything, to take his mind off what was happening. Again, Jamie studied Nick, this time feeling nothing but the love he carried in his heart for his employer.

How well they knew each other. In Nick's command to survey the storm damage, Graceton's lord was anticipating and accepting his steward's need for action as Jamie came to terms with his passing. Jamie's heart tightened. Of a sudden, his eyes burned.

Belle reached up to brush her fingers against his cheek. Catching her hand in his, he pressed a kiss to her fingertips.

"God help me, but I'll miss him terribly when he's gone," he breathed into the cup of her palm.

Tension drained from her with a sigh. "I know," she whispered.

Releasing her hand to wrap his arm around her waist again, he tried to smile at her. Her mouth quirked in response. The love she knew for him filled her gaze.

It was a brief kiss they shared, made all the sweeter by its shortness. When he released her, she looked up at him, tears in her eyes.

He touched her cheek. "I am riding out. Before I go I'll tell Tom how to find me. Send him for me when it's time."

The ghost of a smile touched her lips. "That I shall," she said softly.

❧

With his jerkin atop his doublet and his cloak over his shoulders against the day's persistent drizzle, Jamie rode away from Graceton's stables. He followed the river's edge toward the village. His intent was to give a cursory inspection to the damaged houses before joining the foresters in their chores.

As he neared the church, he caught the steady tap of a hammer coming from its roof. It was the chaplain's lay servant who clung to the slick slate tiles, pounding those loosened by the wind back into place. Beneath his perch, a ladder leaned against the church wall. At its foot was the chaplain.

Without a churchman's robe over his doublet and breeches, Father William looked even lankier than usual. As he saw Jamie, he raised a hand in greeting. "Good morrow, Master Steward. How does our lord this morn?"

The question only stirred Jamie's already aching emotions. "As well as can be expected, given his ailments," he said, his tone brusque. God save him, he hoped he'd not have to spew the lie too many times this day.

Another hour found him with Graceton's foresters. With axe and saw, they worked to turn the fallen trees into firewood to feed the castle's many fireplaces. As they moved from woodfall to woodfall, Jamie took care to mark their progress so Tom could find them if need be.

It was well past midday when they finally broke for their meal, that being nothing more than bread and cheese, with a flagon of ale to wash it down. Huddled deep into their sodden cloaks, they retreated to what little shelter they could find beneath barren branches. Standing a little apart from the others, Jamie leaned back against a tree's trunk as he ate, listening to the commoners talk among themselves. Hope rose. If Tom hadn't come yet, it could be that Nick had rallied.

It was the man farthest from Jamie who lifted his head first. The other woodsmen followed suit, all of them staring in the same direction through the trees. It took Jamie another moment before he caught the sound of pounding hooves.

His heart dropped. Even before Tom brought his horse to a churning halt in the soft sod, Jamie had tossed aside his meal and was striding for his mount. The misery that filled Tom's face needed no words to explain it.

It was time.

❧

It was at a full gallop that Jamie rode past Graceton's stables and into its gateway. In that tunnel-like opening, the clash of the horse's iron shoes upon the stones rang around him like an alarm bell. Across the yard he drove his mount, their path marked by the great clods of earth its shoes tore from the rain-soaked sod. Shivering and sidling, the horse cried out in complaint as Jamie yanked the poor creature to a halt at the hall's door.

Leaving the horse to the grooms who came racing after him, Jamie threw himself from the saddle. In the door he raced, then through the opening in the screens. The whole of the household was in the hall. Caught in small groups, they stood or sat, their heads bowed, their voices hushed. Some of the women were sobbing.

Jamie ran across the room, praying he wasn't too late. Through the parlor he went, then up the stairs to the gallery. The door to Nick's apartment was open. Lucy clung to the door's frame, a lost and lonely look upon her face.

As he passed her, she leapt to catch his hand. "Now, I'm to have no stepfather," she cried, her voice tiny in fear.

Jamie swept the child up in his arms. Heedless of his wet clothing, she wrapped her arms about his neck and rested her head upon his shoulder. As he carried her across the sitting room, he touched his lips to her cheek.

"You'll still have me, lass," he murmured, striding into Nick's bedchamber.

In the room, old Father Walter knelt at Nick's bed's end. His beads were slipping through his fingers as his lips moved in silent prayer, paving a path for his lord into heaven. Belle stood not far from him. The sadness on her face had deepened until tears clung to her lashes. Kit knelt near the center of his brother's bed, his forehead pressed to the mattress's edge, his shoulders heaving as he grieved in silence for Nick. Cecily sat on the bed, braced against the headboard. Nick was cradled in her lap, his head braced upon her shoulder, his face tilted upward toward the woman he loved. His eyes were closed.

Gone were the tears and panic that had filled Cecily's face yesterday. In its place there was only the love she bore for her noble husband. She was rocking gently, crooning as she moved. It was a lullaby, meant to soothe a child into sleep, that she sang.

Carrying Lucy in his arms, Jamie stopped beside Belle. She took her daughter from him. "He's been waiting for you, I think," she whispered. "Go. Bid him farewell."

The aching in Jamie's heart grew until he was certain that organ meant to shatter. Shedding his sodden cloak as he went, he stopped beside Kit. When he'd stripped off his filthy gloves, he caught Nick's hand.

Words tangled in him. There was so much he wanted to say, but none of it seemed worth saying at the moment. As he sought to straighten his thoughts, he moved his fingers against Nick's palm, tracing the rigid scars that marked it. His eyes stung. At last, he simply bent his head to press his lips to Nick's knuckles.

"I shall miss you, my friend," he breathed against the man's already cooling skin. "Good journey to you. May you find the joy and freedom you deserve in your God's presence."

Although Jamie was certain Nick must be beyond reach of his words, the man's fingers moved a little. Grateful that he'd been heard, Jamie gently set his lord's hand back into his lap. Cecily gave a quiet gasp.

Nick's eyes were open. He was studying the woman he'd chosen as his wife, his eyes a brilliant green. In his lap, Nick's hand shifted. His arm strained as if he sought to lift it.

Reaching out, Jamie caught Nick's hand, then placed its back against Cecily's cheek. Gratitude flickered in his friend's gaze, then his eyes closed.

It was with a quiet, peaceful sigh that Nick departed, the sound bearing Cecily's name.

Cecily's arms tightened as she drew her husband closer to her breast. Then, keening, she bent her head over Nick's and rocked him as she wept.

Chapter Thirty-One

❦

Jamie sat at his desk aching as he stared at ten years' worth of shared planning and goals, ten years' worth of achievements as he and Nick rebuilt Graceton's wealth, piled upon it. Yesterday, they'd laid Nick to rest near the old keep tower as he'd requested.

All of Graceton's servants had attended the service, as had most of the villagers. Only Cecily had been absent. Although Belle argued that of all people Cecily deserved to attend, Nick's wife had adamantly refused, then returned to her woodland home. Jamie knew why. After so many years of hiding their relationship, Cecily couldn't bear to make a public show of her grief. Instead, she'd retreated to her hovel, where she could mourn Nick just as she loved him, in secret.

At the tap on the door, Jamie stirred himself from his thoughts. "Come," he called.

He expected Kit. Although Graceton's new lord would wait until Cecily was collected enough to read the will, there were details of the estate to discuss, especially now that Jamie had announced he wouldn't remain on as steward. Too long had he been Nick's protector, that position too often turning him into Kit's detractor.

Instead, it was Belle, dressed in the same black garments

she'd worn when he first met her. Warmth flickered in the cold embers of his heart at the reminder, its heat a promise that what lay so heavily upon him now would someday give way to happiness.

"We're dining now. Will you join us?" she asked, stepping into his office.

"Is it so late as that?" he asked.

"Later," she said with a quick lift of her brows. "We're all off our schedules just now. The sun's nearly set."

Jamie sighed. The thought of eating in the dining room where he'd be expected to converse was more than his grief allowed. "I'm really not hungry," he started.

Belle took a few steps toward his desk. "Please, come," she said quietly, sadly. "It's only a meal, a bit of food. You needn't speak if you don't wish."

Behind her the gallery door slammed shut. She gave a yelp and whirled. Startled, Jamie came to his feet and looked past her toward the door. "What was that?"

"I don't know," she said, taking a backward step.

On the landing, the air began to thicken. As impossible as it seemed, he swore he could see tendrils twisting and writhing in the dimness. A gust of air rushed into the room, ice cold and strong enough to snuff all the candles in the chamber. From somewhere came the faint sound of a woman sobbing.

Belle squeaked and backed swiftly away from the door, until she collided with the front edge of his desk. "Nay," she cried. "This can't be happening again."

The weeping grew louder, seeming to radiate out of the tower's wall. The chill in the room worsened, until Jamie's breath clouded before him. "What is this?" he demanded in confusion, coming out from behind the desk to stand next to Belle.

Before him in the doorway the writhing air congealed, then took on an unnatural, glowing whiteness. Whimpering, Belle whirled and threw herself against him. As he embraced her, she buried her face into the front of his doublet. "She has no eyes," she cried into the folds of fabric.

Caught somewhere between fear and disbelief, Jamie could but watch in horrid fascination as a woman's body appeared in the doorway, her form draped in ghostly clothing. Hair appeared to hang in long strands about her shoulders, then her head formed. There was a mouth, a nose, ears.

Jesus save him, Belle was right! Where there should have been eyes, there was naught but two gaping, blackened holes. His heart leapt up to lodge in his throat, all the while pounding out a frantic denial of what stood before him.

The sound of sobbing was now so loud Jamie's ears ached against it. Belle cried out and cupped her hands to her ears. The spirit's head began to move, as if the specter were scanning his office, seeking something.

Or, someone. Stunned, senses reeling, Jamie found himself staring deep into the fathomless wells of Mistress Miller's White Lady. Fear tore through him. What if the housekeeper was right and the specter meant to bewitch them into leaping off the wall? However grief stricken he was over Nick, he wasn't ready to join his friend in death. Ah, but escape meant walking through the creature to reach the gallery.

Heart pounding at the thought, Jamie pulled Belle closer to him and started toward the door. Belle moaned a little when she realized what he meant to do, but kept her head buried against his chest and shuffled along beside him. Its empty gaze still fixed on him, the specter held its position until they were within arm's reach of it. Then, as if it had seen them coming and meant to let them pass, it drifted back onto the landing.

Jamie's stomach twisted at this proof of its awareness. Was it biding its time before entrancing them? Ducking his head over Belle's, he closed his eyes and stepped out of his office. Unnatural and bone-chilling cold enfolded him.

He took a step, then opened an eye to gauge where they were. His shoulder was passing through the ghostly woman's chin. Her empty eye sockets were but inches from his face. Jamie recoiled from the eerie contact, stumbling to the side and carrying Belle with him as he went. By the time they caught their footing, they were standing on the upward stair's lowest step. Below them on the landing, the White Lady drifted to block the gallery door, her empty eyes yet watching him.

Anger came to life beneath Jamie's terror and his arms tightened around Belle. The ghost was trying to drive them onto the wall top! He wasn't going to let this awful creature kill them, not when he was so close to happiness.

"You vile bitch," he called to the specter, his voice hoarse. "We're not going up these stairs."

❧

Belle heard Jamie's voice, but her terror was so deep she could make no sense of his words. Hoping that he was saying the ghost was gone, she lifted her head. Just as had happened all those nights ago, she once more found herself staring into the White Lady's orb-less eyes.

Even as Belle yelped and turned her head back into Jamie's doublet, images flashed through her mind. She saw a man and a woman, laughing, loving. Children, then blood and tiny bodies sinking beneath the river's surface. There were blocks of stones being laid as a wall was built and the light disappearing, little by little. At last, there was only the woman, bound and grieving, trapped in a fearsome, lonely and unending darkness.

Belle blinked in horrified astonishment. The specter was telling her a tale! Behind terror, curiosity woke and she again dared to lift her head from Jamie's shoulder.

As she did, the sound of weeping rose until it thundered in the tower's stairwell. There was now a note of panic behind the sound of the tears. Belle frowned, knowing the ghost meant something in the sound, but utterly confounded over how to decipher what the message was.

On the landing the specter spread her arms wide and lunged at them. Belle screamed and once more cowered into Jamie's arms. Jamie cursed and caught her closer still. "Begone, you foul creature," he shouted.

New images flooded Belle's mind. Now, it was as if she stood on the wall top looking down into Graceton's valley, only where the village should have been there was a small city instead. Tall houses crowded one against the other, narrow streets dashing and darting through them. A thick wall enclosed it all. Only the church's tower was the same. The image settled on the church. Set directly before the sanctuary door was a scaffold, the sort used to dispense justice to murderers. Or, witches.

Belle's blood ran cold. She jerked her head up out of the protection of Jamie's chest. This time it was the living woman who sought out the dead woman's gaze. Like a candle's halo, panic shimmered from every misty line of the specter's cloudy body.

Belle couldn't have explained why she knew, but with every fiber of her body she knew what the ghost was trying to tell her. With a shout, she thrust out of Jamie's embrace and wrenched around on the step. Snatching up her skirts, she flew up the steps, praying with every step that the White Lady was wrong.

※

Belle's push sent Jamie staggering back on the step. He crashed against the tower's curving wall, his breath nearly driven from him. Belle turned and dashed up the stairs.

"Nay, Belle," he shouted, lunging after her and missing. "Don't give way to her spell!"

As he started after her, sound roared from the walls around him. Faster than he could ever have imagined, the specter streamed past him to block the stairway. Jamie threw himself at the creature's unearthly body. It was like slamming against a block of ice. Bellowing in pain and surprise, he stumbled back down the steps to the landing.

At the top of the stairs, the tower door opened. May God take him! Why hadn't he put a lock upon it after Brigit's death? Rage exploded in Jamie.

"You can't have her," he raged, once more leaping up the stairs toward the ghost.

The specter dissolved, gone in the blink of an eye. Panic shattered Jamie's rage. The White Lady was following Belle so she could push his wife over the wall's edge! He raced up the stairs.

"Nay, Belle," he shouted. "Don't leave me. I'm coming."

"Jamie!" She turned his name into a bloodcurdling scream.

Jamie swore he flew up the remaining steps. On the wall, Belle stood before the first merlon. There was no sign of the ghost. He snatched her into his arms nigh on trembling in relief only to have her fight free of his embrace.

"Look," she shouted, pointing down into the village. In the churchyard a bonfire burned, just bright enough to turn those folk gathered around it into naught but dark forms. By their number, Jamie guessed most of the village was there. Raised before the church door was a makeshift scaffold, naught but a few planks of wood laid atop upturned barrels beneath the spreading arms of a tree. The noose already dangled from the thick branch. It was the red of Cecily's bodice that identified her as the crumpled form lying upon the scaffolding's surface.

What an idiot he was! He should have known how those who hated Cecily would use Nick's death to their advantage. Why had he allowed Cecily to go home, unprotected and alone?

Rage at himself evolved into a cold, hard hatred. By God, he'd see every last ignorant man among them dead for what they'd done, even if he had to kill them all himself. Grabbing Belle's hand, he whirled and started for the stairs, already shouting for Kit and Graceton's men.

Chapter Thirty-Two

❧

From the corner of what had once been Nick's bed, Peg gave a sigh of relief. "Thank heavens, she sleeps at last."

Belle nodded. It had taken them nearly an hour to cajole Cecily into drinking a little of the potion that had so eased her husband's pain. Now, Belle leaned into the bed to pull the blankets up over the healer's shoulders.

"Poor thing," she said softly. "How dare the villagers burn her home, then try to hang her!"

Peg gave a snort. "Who can account for what folk will do when they're afraid? I say it's a good thing that you and Master James saw her from the wall top. I hope the new Lord Graceton keeps his word and deals most harshly with that Northfield family for destroying her property. Aye, and he should flog that old biddy, Mistress Miller, for inciting the crowd against poor Cecily! I swear she only did so because you protected her!"

Belle laughed. "No need for flogging, I think. Lord Graceton has wounded Mistress Miller far worse than any blow could by refusing her plea to be reinstated as housekeeper here."

Silence woke between them for a moment as they both watched Cecily stir in her sleep, then Peg shot her mistress a sharp glance. "You wouldn't be ready to tell me what you were doing with Master James out on that wall, would you?" So it had been since Peg witnessed Belle and Jamie in the stairwell after Brigit's fall.

"It's none of your business," Belle replied with a lift of her chin. So she would have said even if she'd been out on that wall by herself. She doubted anything could induce her to speak about their ghostly encounter.

Turning, Belle led the way into the sitting room. Much to her surprise, Jamie stood at the hearth, his back to the bedchamber door as he studied the flames. He wore no cap and the fire's light made his hair gleam a deep red brown. So, too, had he stripped the sleeves from his black doublet. The white of his shirt sleeves seemed brilliant in the room's dimness.

He was waiting for her. Hope woke in Belle's heart, then faltered. Was he here to say he'd changed his mind about his affection for her, or would he be asking the question she so needed to hear? Whatever it was he meant to say, one thing was certain. Belle didn't want Peg overhearing it.

It was a quick, dismissing glance she shot her maid. The woman's eyes, already narrowed, tightened even more until they were naught but slits. She glanced from the steward to her lady. Her arms crossed, her toe tapped.

A laugh bubbled up in Belle. What would Peg think if she knew she was weeks too late with this? Belle swallowed her amusement and again sent her maid a look of dismissal.

Peg's brows rose, then she gave a great huff, the sound loud enough to make Jamie turn, and stormed from the sitting room. She left the door open wide behind her. It was a warning that she meant to linger to see if Belle would dare to close it.

Jamie offered Belle a small smile. "How is Cecily?" It was a quiet question.

"Only bruised," she replied. "We've given her a potion to help her rest."

"Good," he said with a nod. "I suspect she hasn't slept much these past weeks."

Again, his mouth quirked upward. "What a night, eh? That creature was so, well, unbelievable."

It wasn't a discussion of Graceton's White Lady that Belle wanted to share with him just now. Two months ago, she'd never have dared it. Now, she strode to stand before Jamie and looked boldly up into his face.

"Why were you waiting here for me?" However confident the question, she waited breathlessly for his answer.

His eyes warmed. The corners of his mouth lifted. "To ask you a question," he replied.

"What question?" Belle's voice trembled even as her heart leapt in excitement.

"Not yet," he said, a teasing gleam coming to life in his gaze.

He reached out to tug at her headdress's tie. Belle tried to stop him, but was too late. The headdress clattered onto the floor behind her.

"What are you doing?" she cried, turning to retrieve it, only to have Jamie catch her hand and pull her back around toward him.

"Leave it," he said, studying her face with a smile. "I didn't like you in it the first time I saw you wear it. I find I like it even less now."

Amusement bubbled up in Belle. What sort of game was this? Did he think he could speak like a husband without first having secured that position?

"By what right do you criticize my clothing?" she demanded, fighting a smile.

Laughter flashed in his gaze. "By no right at all save my own judgment," he retorted, still withholding what she so needed to hear.

As he spoke, he slid his hand beneath her plait at her nape. Shivering, Belle leaned forward to brace her hands on his chest. As desire rose, her need to hear *the question* dimmed.

He tugged on the string to her ruff, then removed that bit of pleated lace from atop her shirt collar and dropped it. Belle watched it slide down the folds of her skirt to lay upon the floor at her hem, then looked back at Jamie. "What are you doing?"

New heat filled his gaze. With a touch of his finger to her lip, he bade her to silence. The brief brush of skin against skin was as much a caress as a warning.

His hand dropped to her shirt collar. It opened. With his fingertip he traced the edges of her shirt against her newly bared skin. Belle caught her breath. Sliding her hands up his chest, she laced her fingers behind his nape, then lifted her face in invitation. He lowered his mouth to press his lips to one corner of her mouth, then the other.

"I warn you, I'm a solitary sort of man, given to moods and melancholy," he breathed against her lips.

"I know that," she whispered in reply, her heart soaring with his words. Now certain of what he intended, she let him remove the tie at her plait's end, then loosen her hair until it hung free around her.

"Ask me," she whispered as he combed his fingers

through those strands. When she heard him say the words aloud, their marriage would be complete, even if he insisted on a second ceremony.

"What is this?" he complained, kissing his way across her cheek to the corner of her jaw. "Here I am trying to do this properly and you're rushing me."

He kissed the corner of her jaw, then touched his lips to her ear. "After all, you're now a widow." He lowered his mouth to the curve of her throat. Belle's eyes closed as she tilted her head to the side, giving him leave to do more of this sort of thing. "Why rush, when you've two months of mourning ahead of you?"

"Two months," she cried in protest, even as she stood still, not wanting his caresses to ever stop. "Nay, I'll not wait so long. If you're right that Cecily and I shared a husband between us, doesn't that make me but half a widow, with only a month's seclusion ahead of me?"

He laughed quietly against her throat. "Hardly proper," he murmured as he kissed his way downward toward her shoulder.

"Please," she whispered, begging him to both speak and continue kissing her.

He touched his lips into the hollow at the base of her throat. The next caress was placed at the upper edge of her bodice, in the valley between her breasts. Belle gasped. Her fingers threaded through his hair. Lost in pleasure, she closed her eyes and arched into his caress.

He groaned, his arms coming around her waist to pull her against him. Lifting his head, he caught her mouth with his. It was the memory of the pleasure they'd made on her wedding night that filled their kiss.

After a moment, Jamie tore his mouth from hers and gave a shaken laugh. His eyes had lightened to the color of the sky. "You're right," he agreed. "Two months is too long."

With that, Belle's need to hear the question grew until she thought she might die if he didn't speak it in the next instant. "Say it," she demanded.

He grinned. "Wed with me, Belle." Lowering his head, he touched his mouth to hers.

Belle gave a joyous cry and tightened her arms around his neck. Their mouths met again and she filled her kiss with happiness. Jamie's hand slid up her back to cup her head in his palm, and he returned her joy with passion. The heat they shared was a promise that their next bedding would be far better than the first.

"Jamie?!" came the new Lord Graceton's shocked call from the sitting room's doorway.

Cursing Kit Hollier, and himself for not closing the door, Jamie released Belle. She sprang back from him as if she thought there was some way to hide what they'd been doing. It was a useless ploy. Her ruff was off, her shirt open, her hair free and uncovered. Her sultry lips looked all the more alluring swollen from his kiss.

Holding two folds of paper in his hand, Kit stared at them, his eyes wide. "Egad," he said, his voice low and astonished. "Nick told me the night Mistress Atwater died, but I didn't believe him."

Jamie frowned at that. "What did Nick say?" he demanded.

Kit's astonishment transformed into amusement. "It seems Cecily mentioned that you and his wife were in love.

I said he had to be wrong." He grinned. "Lord, but I was certain you'd never give your heart to any woman, Jamie. But then, she"—Kit gestured with the papers he held toward Belle—"wasn't truly his wife, was she?"

Flickers of concern shot through Jamie. He glanced at Belle. She had pulled her hair over her shoulder and was rapidly replaiting it. Worry, relief, confusion all showed in her eyes as she met his gaze. There were traces of embarrassment yet burning on her cheeks.

Soon, Jamie wanted to tell her. Soon, we'll be married and we'll never again have to care that someone witnesses our affection. He looked back at Kit.

"Since it seems you know Nick married Cecily, you must also know that Cecily had begun annulment procedures. I think it would take a court to decide which marriage took precedence."

Kit only waved away his words. "I neither care nor need to explore the details of what Nick did. I just wanted to show you this. With Cecily here and safe, we'll read Nick's will upon the morrow. It was my brother's desire that this be read at the same time. I thought it a cruel request when he had me write these, given your years of faithful service to him. Now I see he knew you even better than I thought."

Jamie's confusion grew "What are you talking about?"

"These codicils to his will." Kit gave him the papers he held. "Read the top one first as that's the order Nick intended, then the second."

Opening the uppermost paper, Jamie glanced at the date on the sheet. Written in Kit's hand, just as he'd said, it had been scribed the day prior to Nick's passing. Scanning the customary legal verbiage, he jumped down to the meat of the message.

Once he'd read it, a strange ache took hold in his heart. He flipped it over to read the second sheet. When he was finished, he wasn't certain whether to be angry at Nick, or to laugh until he cried. Here in his hand was Nick's last attempt at manipulating his steward.

"Belle," he said quietly, calling the woman he meant to make his wife to his side. "You should hear this, as it concerns you almost more than it does me."

Belle shot him a worried look, then came to stand beside him. Jamie dared to put an arm around her and pull her nearer to him. Although she gasped and glanced at Kit, she didn't try to free herself from his embrace.

Jamie read:

> " *'If after my passing, my steward, James Wyatt, agrees to wed with my widow, Lady Arabella Hollier, and they together agree to take into their household Mistress Cecily Elwyn, protecting her as if she were like unto their own family, Lady Arabella is to have as her dower property my manor of Meynell. This she will keep for her life's span, including all rights, fees and incomes the manor generates. In addition, Master Wyatt will have for his life's span the income generated by the mill in Blacklea and the right to sell all wool that Blacklea's home farm produces. Along with that, he is to have twenty-five pounds to invest as he knows well how to do. It is my hope the amount will grow into a sum sufficient to serve as a dowry for Mistress Lucretia Purfoy should our queen fail* *

to provide the inheritance she promised.'"

Belle looked at him in surprise. Shuffling the papers, Jamie said, "Now the second one.

> *'If my steward, Master James Wyatt, refuses to wed with the woman the world believes to be my widow, the details of my marriage to Cecily Hollier née Elwyn are to be made public, including the notation in Father Walter Tolliver's Bible as a testimony to the legitimacy of our union. As my acknowledged widow, Cecily Hollier will keep for her life's span all rights, fee and income from Meynell Manor. I give to Lady Arabella Purfoy only my deepest regrets for having so misused her and wish her well in pressing our queen for the dowry her majesty promised for Lady Purfoy's sweet child, Lucretia. As for my steward, Master James Wyatt, I give to him the desk he's used during all his years of faithful service to me, in the hopes he'll use it wisely in the future.'*"

It wasn't even subtle. Jamie stared at the paper again. Should he refuse Belle, Nick would leave Cecily wealthy enough, but bereft of the family and protection she so needed just now. So, too, was the revelation of his bigamous marriage meant to make Belle a laughingstock. And, insult to injury, if Jamie refused to do as Nick willed, Lucy would be left impoverished, for now that Nick was dead the queen had no reason to aid Lucy, and Elizabeth never wasted her time where there was no advantage.

Warmth and gratitude filled Jamie's heart. Nick had wanted those he loved to have what they most needed after

358 • Denise Domning

his passing, only, being Nick, he couldn't just give it. "He had to do it," he said with a laugh. "He couldn't bear to leave me without giving me a final tweak." That Nick's attempt came an instant later than necessary only made it all the more precious.

Jamie held up the second paper. "May I?" he asked Graceton's lord, his brows lifted in question.

Relief and understanding filled Kit's gaze. "As you will."

Screwing the note into a wad, Jamie tossed it into the fireplace. The flames were on it in an instant, browning and curling the edges, then gobbling it up to leave naught but ash.

"This, my lord," Jamie said, handing the remaining sheet back to Kit, "is the only codicil to your lord brother's will."

Then Jamie's arm tightened around Belle. He pulled the woman he loved closer to him. "Now, you may congratulate me. Just before you entered a moment ago, I'd asked this wondrous, glorious woman to be my wife."

Meet Award-Winning Author
Denise Domning
www.denisedomning.com

✣

Hailed by critics as a "first class writer on her way to the top," Denise Domning's first book ever, *Winter's Heat,* a medieval romance, sold to the second publisher who read it, then went on to win the *Romantic Times* coveted national award for Best First Historical Romance of 1994. Writing as Denise Domning she went on to do four more medieval novels following the FitzHenry family, two novellas (one of which the editor referred to as the "best non-Western Western" she'd ever read), and two books set in the time of Queen Elizabeth I.

Writing as Denise Hampton for Avon Books she returned to the thirteenth century and followed a group of friends through the court of King John, then dabbled briefly in the Regency Era with *Almost Perfect* before taking a break from writing.

For the past few years Denise let her left brain run rampant working as a web designer, putting all her creative efforts into remodeling her home and generally enjoying life with her husband and three cats. She's toying with some ideas for books that take her from pre-history to the modern family.

Love to read?
Read what you love . . .
with QuestMark Romances!

QuestMark proudly presents:

Blue Rain
by Tess Farraday

For the Love of Grace
by Ginna Gray

Lady In White
by Denise Domning

Out of the Blue
by Kasey Michaels

Rose of the Mists
by Laura Parker

The Angel Knight
by Susan King